Tree of Angels

Penny Sumner

ORION

First published in Great Britain in 2004
by Orion Publishing Group Ltd

Excerpt from 'Marriage and Love' in *Anarchism
and other Essays* by Emma Goldman (New York,
Mother Earth Publishing Association, 1910). Used
by permission of Betty Ballantine.

Excerpt from 'Mad Blake' by William Rose
Benét in the *Second Book of Modern Verse*, edited
by Jessie Rittenhouse (Boston and New York,
Houghton Mifflin, 1919). Used by permission
of James Benét.

A version of Chapter One appeared as a short
story, 'The Betrothal Cake', in *Stand* magazine, Spring 1998.

A CIP catalogue record for this book
is available from the British Library.

ISBN 0 75286 126 3

Typeset by Deltatype Ltd, Birkenhead, Merseyside

Printed in Great Britain by Clays Ltd, St Ives plc

The Orion Publishing Group Ltd
Orion House
5 Upper Saint Martin's Lane
London WC2H 9EA

For my son, Benet Plowden

Blake saw a treeful of angels at Peckham Rye,
And his hands could lay hold on the tiger's terrible heart.
Blake knew how deep is Hell, and Heaven how high,
And could build the universe from one tiny part.

From 'Mad Blake', William Rose Benét

Prologue:
1918

Shortly after ten o'clock on the morning of Friday, 20 December 1918, an angel hovered over Sydney Harbour.

There had been numerous sightings of angels in recent years: over the Battle of Mons and at Ypres and Loos. At Mons the beating of massive wings drove back the German advance, saving the British Second Corps from certain annihilation. After this, however, the heavenly visitors adopted a gentler shape, comforting the dying and wounded, and even appearing on the British side of the Channel so that a young woman at Piccadilly Circus, looking up and glimpsing a celestial wing tip reflected in a first-floor window of Swan and Edgar, would fall down in a faint, knowing a loved one had made the supreme sacrifice on the battlefield. But other manifestations brought happier news and, where British mothers once had visions of Red Cross nurses who appeared at the end of the bed to reassure them that a missing son would be found safe, now the figures began to assume haloes.

The Southern Hemisphere, on the other hand, could not boast of any such visitations and a certain disgruntlement at this neglect might explain the relish with which The Brisbane Courier *and The* Melbourne Age *traced the sightings of angels over Europe's battlefields back to a fictional short story which had appeared in the* London Evening News. *From thereon the appearance of angels was put down to rumour and – as one stern editorial in the Brisbane paper announced – mass hysteria.*

Against this historical background, an angel over Sydney might have caused as much embarrassment as wonder. But, as it was, the moment would go unacknowledged for out of the hundreds of potential witnesses gathered at the harbour, not one looked up. Those on board the approaching Marathon *had been yearning for a glimpse of this shoreline for many a long week, while those on the shore were shielding their eyes from the glare reflected off the water.*

It is true the seasoned stare of the Sydney Morning Herald *journalist did not stay solely with the ship, for he knew his article – to be entitled 'Home for Christmas' and destined to be sandwiched between 'The League of Nations: Where it Affects Australia' and 'Bolshevik Menace: Lithuania Requests Help' – would rely as much on details gleaned from the dock. The* Marathon's *arrival was of especial interest as it was one of the first vessels to include a sizeable number of civilian passengers since the end of the war, and the* Herald's *representative had already noted how a scattering of relieved applause ran through the crowd when a port official nailed up the notice confirming the ship to be free of influenza and not subject to quarantine regulations. Close to where he was standing two banners were in place and he recorded that the first, in blue, simply read* WELCOME HOME HEROES ALL *while the second, in red, stated that* SYDNEY THEATRE-GOERS WELCOME MISS ANTONIA ROCHE, *Miss Roche being a rising actress, fresh from London, who was to star as principal boy in* Peter Pan *at Her Majesty's. The journalist had spoken to one of the admiring theatre-goers and had also gleaned, from remarks overheard, that there were high expectations for the reception that Their Excellencies the Governor-General and Lady Helen Munro Ferguson were to host for the returning soldiers the following evening. He chatted briefly with some of those in his immediate vicinity, including a Mrs Horsefield, who was here with other members of the Anglican Church Ladies' League to welcome a young, Cambridge-educated vicar, destined for an affluent Sydney parish.*

All conversation ceased, however, as the tug boat began the business of manoeuvring the Marathon *into position and a robust male voice shouted from the back of the crowd, 'An Australian Christmas!' thus launching a spontaneous choir of voices, young and old, male and female, into a thunderous rendition of 'The First Noel'. It was an unexpected and surprisingly moving moment, causing our journalist to stop scribbling in his notebook in order to wipe a drop of moisture*

4

surreptitiously from an eye with his sleeve. As he performed this small act he was faintly aware of something large and winged overhead – a pelican no doubt. Under normal circumstances he would have greatly enjoyed watching a pelican fly magnificently across the most famous harbour in the world but on this occasion camaraderie and the Christmas spirit won out and, raising his voice with the others, he returned his gaze to the ship.

And so it was that there would be no report of that morning's miraculous appearance in the next day's newspapers, the angel simply fading away until it was nothing but a tawny fleck of cloud, floating across an otherwise clear antipodean sky.

Book One

1910–1918

Before I rose from my bed, I understood that I was now to proceed through the world *as an angel*, under the immediate guidance of the Lord, to proclaim the tidings of his second coming. With that came an uncertain impression that I was to do this in an extraordinary way, and by singing – and this idea haunted me throughout my changes of insanity.

John T. Perceval, *A Narrative of the Treatment Received by a Gentleman, During a State of Mental Derangement* (1840)

One

Russia, 1910

The kitchen smelled of rosemary and lime.

Every evening the pine table was scrubbed lightly with salt, which was left overnight and then wiped away with a damp cloth in the morning. Nina sat under the table. She was eleven years old and frightened of the pictures on the cards: the woman with the mad dog, the hanged man. She was wearing new shoes and next to them could see a hairpin and a cherrystone, stuck in a crack between the cedar floorboards. She could also see the new leather slippers her sister Katya was wearing, and Darya Fyodorovna's best boots. Darya was the housekeeper and her boots, which were not new but old, reeked of charcoal and beeswax.

All morning the kitchen had been nothing but bustle in preparation for Katya's betrothal party, for from today she would be formally betrothed and in the spring of next year there would be a wedding. The household had been up since dawn but there was a lull now and Katya had prevailed upon Darya to do a reading of the cards. There had been whispers and laughter but then Katya's voice was loud overhead, 'What about Nina? I'm to marry and have children and will go on a long journey across the sea to the other side of the world. But what about her?'

'A journey, yes, but not as long as yours. No, I see a long life for your sister, with more than one husband,' here the house-keeper spat into the fire, 'and many houses.' The spit hissed like it was alive.

Next to the table there was a cupboard and under the cupboard Nina could see a tray where Cook hid the knives in case robbers or Jews broke into the house at night. If she could reach the tray, she told herself, she would take hold of the

9

biggest knife there, the one with the red handle and a blade wide as a sword, and plunge it into Darya Fyodorovna's heart. Not because it was Katya who was to go on a long journey, nor because of what the cards had predicted about husbands – at eleven years of age the number of husbands is neither here nor there – but because of the last bit about houses. For Nina had always lived on her family's estate and knew she would never want to live anywhere else.

'And children?' Katya continued. 'How many children will Nina . . .'

But at that moment Nina scrambled out from beneath the table. 'I don't believe it about the houses,' she glared, 'and am going to tell Mamma!' Because although the cards and ouija boards and table rapping were all the rage in the fashionable circles of Moscow and Petersburg – even, it was rumoured, in the royal court itself – Mamma did not approve. However, at that moment the men came to the door to begin carrying the chairs out on to the lawn, after which they would come back for the betrothal cake.

There was a clapping game: 'The bride in the carriage, the bride on the stairs, the bride in the church with a crown in her hair!' Looking at the cake on the walnut sideboard, Nina couldn't help but hum this to herself. The cake had taken two days to make and more than a dozen eggs had gone into it, the yolks mixed separately from the whites, which were beaten until they turned to sugar snow. And then the fruit was stirred in, raisins, plums, candied peel, all soaked in brandy. Now that it was finished however, the strongest smell was of marzipan. For the cake wasn't all cake, it was only cake in the middle covered by marzipan an inch deep and decorated with a pattern of almonds and sugared cherries. The final touch was the pink ribbon around the base, ordered from the spring Maples catalogue and sent all the way from London. The ribbon had come in the same parcel as the dyed chiffon for Mamma and Katya's dresses and the lengths of blue and white cotton for Nina's sailor suit. She would have liked a chiffon dress too but Mamma said she'd have to wait until she was seventeen, as old as Katya. Which meant there were six years to go.

Near where the ribbon was tied into a bow were two sugared

cherries that looked like eyes, with a pair of almond eyes nearby. The cherry eyes were those of the man Katya was to marry, Dmitri Borisovich, who in life also had a cherry nose, while the almond eyes were Katya's. The Dimitri eyes looked straight ahead into the room but the Katya eyes were looking sideways, through the dining room wall and past the fruit trees in the orchard, all the way to the end of the valley. It was a way of looking she'd had since the morning Papa informed the household that his eldest daughter was to be betrothed. Darya and Cook had immediately begun measuring out crystallised fruit, steeping raisins. The smell of hot brandy had sent Nina to sleep and she remembered waking to the clunk of the metal weights on the scales and Darya talking in a low voice.

'So don't think you can avoid a loaf in your oven that way, Ekaterina, because that's how the peasant women do it.' Her laugh was harsh. 'That is why Father Sergii makes them stand at the back of the church. So now you know. Pigs! They can't even keep in their shit.'

Katya had stood up, very slowly, and slapped the older woman across the face. Then she started looking beyond people, beyond, Nina sometimes thought, Russia itself.

The brightly coloured flowers growing in pots along the veranda were wilting already, it was so hot, and the head gardener's wife was watering them from barrels, the grass glistening diamonds in her wake. To Nina's left the lawn at the front of the house sloped down past the vegetable gardens and the conservatory, behind which was the orchard, planted with apple, pear and cherry trees. At the top end of the orchard, at the back of the house, was High Field, and at the bottom of the orchard, where the lawn also ended, was Low Field, which eventually fell away steeply to a stream. On the other side of the stream, beyond the willows and the beehives, the fields proper began.

'Get on, you!' the gardener shouted amiably at the boys raking the gravel drive. Later in the morning the carriages would begin to arrive, having turned right at the crossroads off the road which led to the town three miles away. The estate's house had been designed by Papa's grandfather, a brilliant but eccentric man who had it built all on one level because his mother had fallen down a flight of stairs as a child and afterwards walked with a limp. During his lifetime the occupants of any carriage approaching the crossroads could tell if the master wasn't in a mood to welcome guests because there would be no flag flying from the flagpole at the end of the front veranda. The flagpole had been taken down long ago but along the back veranda there was still a mural which had been painted by one of the farm's serfs, a talented artist. The mural was very faded now, invisible in places but still beautiful: an exotic garden with a palm tree – just like the one in the conservatory, although no one knew which had come first, the painting or the real tree – and strange birds and flowers.

At the far side of the front lawn, at the end of the drive, tables had been set under the lilac trees. The larger tables were already covered with lace cloths while, across a smaller one, Cook was tenderly stroking a plain white cloth into place, the woman beside her holding aloft the muslin shawl that would keep away the wasps. Nina had to flatten herself against the shutters as two of the men lurched the cake out of the front door, down the veranda steps and across the damp grass. 'Ai!' Cook shrieked, skirt and apron flapping as they stumbled. But the cake was safe, was being lowered on to the table, and Cook's attention was already elsewhere as she scolded a red-faced girl that if any of the Dresden plates were broken someone would be sent home with a sore head. Above the cake, the shawl was tossed into a blue sky and descended like a veil.

There were seven tables altogether. One for the cake, two for the children, their governesses and *nyanyas*, and four tables pushed together for the rest of the guests. Nina was old enough to sit with the adults although not old enough for wine, even though Papa had let her sip champagne at the breaking of St Pyotr's Fast. He'd lifted her against his broad chest and held the glass to her mouth and both he and Mamma had laughed. Nina had laughed too, the bubbles in her nose. But when she asked if she might have a little wine today Mamma had shaken her head, and when she pulled at Mamma's pearl ring and reminded her about the champagne, Mamma simply smiled and said that was different.

Before breakfast this morning the men had brought buckets of ice from the ice cave. There were two buckets at the end of each table and, on the ice, lettuce leaves held sturgeon eggs, fresh-water crayfish and smoked salmon. There were, of course, special knives and forks for the fish, but at the far end of the table the elderly Countess Grekova was now steadily eating her salmon with a soupspoon. Mamma was particularly fond of the Countess who, she said, had been very generous as a young woman and was known for the *salons* she used to hold for writers and artists. Watching the Countess today, Nina couldn't help wondering whether someone shouldn't scold her for the spoon, and for her yellow teeth. But then she heard Aunt Elena confide to her neighbour that the old lady had stopped caring what the world thought a long time ago, so scolding would probably do no good.

At the other end of the table the conversation had turned to the Dowager Empress, who'd travelled to England for the funeral of Edward VII, standing beside her sister at the coffin. It was said she would spend the summer in England. It was also said that the new king, George V, was so like the Emperor in appearance that they looked more like brothers than cousins. And then the funeral and the royal cousins were forgotten as Darya clapped her hands and the girls ran to replace the fish plates with platters of crumbed veal and mushrooms, lamb cutlets covered in raisin sauce, roast goose with apple, and duck glazed with orange and lime.

Nina was greedy though never fat – Mamma would not have allowed that – and her mouth watered at the lamb cutlets although she finally chose goose because of the skin. With the goose she had roast potatoes, baby carrots dribbled with honey, and red cabbage fried with flakes of almonds. In the centre of the table stood the *tvorog* cheese in the shape of a pyramid, and next to it fragrant pancakes rose from a bed of mint. Nina didn't like the bitter cheese, but she did like pancakes, indeed she liked pancakes even more than goose, so after eating most of the food on her plate she slipped the remains under the table to where Cuckoo, the Countess's bad-tempered dachshund, was waiting.

'Why, yes,' Mamma nodded across the table at Father Sergii, who had mushroom in his beard, 'yes, I expect our next crop of apples to be superb. And you shall have some of them.'

Nina forgave the old man the mushroom for he was in love with Mamma. 'Your mother,' Papa would announce, 'could have married a Grand Duke.' At night, when Nina was getting ready for bed, Darya would tell her folktales – about the witch, Baba Yaga, whose hut could run through the forest on legs, or a wise girl who answered an emperor's riddle. But sometimes instead of these stories she would describe the dresses Mamma used to wear to the Mariinsky Theatre, and how she'd been known throughout Petersburg for the pearls she wore in her waist-length, blue-black hair. By the time she was seventeen years old she had already received two excellent offers of marriage. 'But your mother', Darya lowered her voice, frowning slightly, 'was an only child, her parents' pride and joy, and they agreed she should marry for love.' Andrei Karsavin had recently graduated from the School of Jurisprudence and a month after they met Mamma agreed to marry him and live on his estate.

A wasp circled sleepily in the steam of the samovar and Nina watched it. Suddenly Papa thumped the table, making everyone jump. 'What you don't understand about modern farming,' he thumped again, 'and what you *must* understand is this . . .'

Before he could go on, their neighbour, Sergei Rudolfoveich, turned to Mamma. 'I believe our Andrei's agrarian passions to be of a religious tenor,' he wagged his finger playfully, 'and if you are not careful, Irina, he will leave you one day to become a *skhimnik.*'

'Andryusha,' she exclaimed in mock horror, 'a hermit?' causing all who heard her, including Papa, to laugh.

Father Sergii coughed at that moment and Nina wondered what he would make of this joke, but his eyes, which were surprisingly clear and as blue as the sky overhead, showed he hadn't been listening. 'And pears?' his voice faintly querulous.

'Pears, Father?' Mamma stopped laughing and tenderly touched the back of his hand.

'My wife's pears. They have also been a disappointment.'

The bride in her carriage, the bride on the stairs. 'To the bride.' The man in uniform seated next to Katya raised his glass but Katya replied quietly, 'I am not a bride today, Ivan Vasilyevich, and will not be one for a year yet.'

The crowns held over the heads of a bride and bridegroom were to remind them that even though they might anticipate riches on earth they must not forget Christ's suffering on the cross. Darya had explained this in the kitchen this morning and when Nina asked why a bride's dress must be white, when pink or lemon was prettier, Darya had said this was because white is the colour for a princess and on the day of their wedding every woman is a princess and every man a prince.

Nina couldn't imagine Dmitri Borisovich looking like a prince but Ivan Vasilyevich looked like one from a picture book, with his neat moustache and his medals. The gardener had burst into the kitchen one morning last week to say that Ivan was back on his parents' estate after three years and it was rumoured he was leaving the army. Today Nina longed to see the curved sword everyone knew the young officer had won from a Turkish general, but he didn't seem to have brought it with him and she couldn't ask him about it because his attention was fixed solely on Katya. Ivan Vasilyevich hadn't seen Katya for a very long time and, when he had arrived, he'd taken her by both hands and declared she'd changed so much he could barely believe she could be little Ekaterina Andreyevna at all. Dmitri Borisovich had slapped him on the shoulder, laughing that Ivan was right, and that Katya had grown up to be the most beautiful woman in the region.

'Strawberries,' it was the Countess, 'strawberries are good but raspberries are better.' The old lady, still wielding the soup-spoon, had dribbled raspberry spit on her blouse, making Nina wonder whether she ever really had had a *salon* and why it was that old people didn't have *nyanyas* to keep them clean. There were also pastries for dessert, but Nina preferred raspberries too and filled a bowl full of them, with ice cream, cream and sugar. She also took a chocolate wafer but when she bit into it the centre oozed peppermint, and she had to spit it into a corner of her napkin before slipping the rest of the wafer down the side of the chair – where Cuckoo nipped her sharply on the thumb.

'Ah!' she cried, then, 'No!' because her gold charm bracelet with the basket of flowers and the cat and the harp had slipped from her wrist. 'No, Cuckoo!' The stupid animal might eat it, might even choke and die there under the table and how would they get it back then? 'Please!' But no one was listening. The servants were busy collecting trays from the veranda and she wasn't supposed to feed Cuckoo anyway.

'Please!' She stood up and reached across the table to where Dmitri Borisovich, beaded with sweat, was drinking vodka and swaying his head in time with the gramophone. 'My bracelet . . . Cuckoo!' At first he blinked like a puzzled bear, but then nodded, reached for a fistful of chocolate biscuits and disappeared under the table. A moment later the tablecloth rose next to Nina's chair and Cuckoo raced out, chasing the biscuits.

'That', Dmitri whispered solemnly, 'will keep Cuckoo occupied.'

'And the bracelet?' Nina asked, joining him on the damp grass.

He shook his head. 'Where exactly did you drop it?'

In the greenish light under the table his face was a large cheese and Nina couldn't help but giggle.

'Where?' he whispered again. However, something hard was digging into her right knee.

'Here,' careful not to bump her head or brush against Aunt Elena's crocodile shoes. 'Here,' she hissed triumphantly, 'I've found it.'

But instead of looking at the bracelet Dmitri Borisovich stared past her. Cricking her neck round Nina was surprised to see a hand, emerging from the sleeve of a uniform, moving blindly under the tablecloth. Then another, smaller, hand came down to guide it and between them the two hands pulled Katya's lemon skirt up over Katya's white-stockinged knees.

Nina was curious about what might happen next but her companion was no longer watching, his forehead on the ground. 'Please tell me, Nina Andreyevna,' he whispered hoarsely, 'please tell me that I am shamefully drunk.'

As she looked at the grown man wedged under the table, Nina understood he must be. 'Yes, Dmitri Borisovich,' she agreed. 'I'm afraid you are very drunk indeed.'

Papa and the older men had retired to the study for cognac and cigars, while the younger men were carrying hunting rifles and bottles of plum brandy to Low Field.

'Why do they need rifles?' Nina pulled at Darya's sleeve. 'Is it in case of wolves?' Dmitri Borisovich was surely in no condition to face anything so dangerous.

'Wolves? No, by St Nikolai, the young gentlemen haven't gone to shoot at anything that I know of, more fools they.' Darya snorted and slapped her skirts. 'The coffee. Where are those wretched girls with the coffee?'

After going to the privy at the end of the veranda, Nina went into the drawing room, where the table was covered with plates of pistachios, *langues de chat*, dock leaves with aniseed and sugared hazel nuts. Only the Countess seemed to be eating, however, the rest of the ladies either fanning themselves or pinning their hair. Nina slipped a pistachio into her mouth, along with a hazelnut, but then Mamma caught sight of her and beckoned with a glass. 'Ninochka. Take this to Katya, please, in her room.'

In the hall the marsala flooded hot across her tongue and up into her nose until she coughed nut and sugar. Katya didn't answer when she scratched on her door, so she went to her room to read for a while. She hadn't liked *Great Expectations* at first but she was enjoying it very much now she'd got to Miss Havisham, ghostly in her wedding dress. 'I do hope you'll enjoy this,' Miss Brenchley had said. 'I'll look forward to discussing it with you on my return.' Miss Brenchley was their governess and Mamma had given her permission to go home for two months because her father had died and she hadn't seen England in five years.

Nina read to the end of the chapter and then remembered the wine. This time she pushed Katya's door open; the room was dim and cool, the shutters closed, and Katya was sitting in front of the dressing-table mirror.

'Close the door behind you,' she said. And then, 'Well, this is a sorry mess, isn't it, Nina?'

Nina didn't have to think of an answer, however, because at that moment a shot rang out, then another. 'They're shooting at nothing,' she informed her sister.

'Nothing but the sky.' Katya stood up. 'Come, we must go down there.'

'Katya!'

'Nina, I need you to help me. It's time I told Dmitri I cannot marry him.'

And Nina suddenly understood that Katya had started looking beyond the valley because she'd changed her mind about marrying Dmitri Borisovich. Or maybe she'd never wanted to marry him in the first place.

'But why, Katya?'

Her sister gave a weary smile. 'I don't know, Nina, I don't know.' She sighed, pulling at the ribbon on the front of her dress. 'Do you remember last summer, when we crept out of the house at night and lay on the grass to watch the stars?'

'And the next morning Darya wondered why I had twigs in my hair . . .'

'I thought I understood things last summer. Things like love. But then everything got confused. I can't explain why, Nina, it just did.'

Nina would have liked to ask how it was possible to get confused over something as simple as love, for surely you knew if you loved someone or not? But Katya put her fingers to her lips and led the way along the hall and down the veranda steps. The children were playing skittles in the shade of the lilacs and behind them the cake sat on its table, a fat bride in a veil. Cook and Darya would be angry, Nina thought when she saw it, because of all their work. But no doubt it would get eaten anyway.

Skirting the conservatory they followed the path to the gate, which the young men had carelessly left open. The grass in Low Field was damp and Nina could see that Katya's new slippers and her lemon dress would be ruined, but Katya didn't seem to care, her fine lace shawl dragging behind as Nina hurried to keep up.

'Katya!'

A shot, followed by men shouting, and Katya started to run, calling, 'No! Oh no!' her shawl falling to the ground. By the time Nina had stopped to pick it up, and brush off the grass, the lemon dress was no longer in sight.

Two

Katya married Ivan and not Dmitri. The wedding had taken
place a month after the betrothal party and was a quiet, family
affair, the newly-weds leaving immediately afterwards for Nice,
where Ivan was to join his uncle's business.

That was over eighteen months ago and this morning Nina
remembered her sister's final warning about what it meant to be
a woman. 'Blood is something you'll have to get used to,' Katya
had said, 'for your turn will come.' In summer it was a pleasure
to walk with outstretched arms between the clean sheets
billowing and cracking on the lines like sails; but hidden in the
middle there was always a row of stained rags, like the flags of a
deserted ship, the *Marie Celeste*. Those belonging to the servants
were torn pieces of old cloth. Mamma's were stitched squares of
cotton which, when dry, were sprinkled with lavender water and
discreetly folded away in the bottom drawer of the big
wardrobe.

It had been a shock when Katya told her what the rags were
for, even though she knew the farm dogs bled. Everyone knew,
for when the bitches were on heat they were kept on the roof of a
shed, tied up so they wouldn't jump down to the yowling dogs
below. Nothing like that happened to women of course,
although the rags on the line were shameful enough and meant
that for a time each month a woman was considered unclean: if
Cook's time fell during Holy Week one of the other women had
to cook the Easter cakes. Katya had said that one year all the
women in the house were bleeding together and a woman from
the village had come to do the baking.

However, the blood on the snow this morning wasn't human

blood; Cook was cleaning some trout. 'A murderer!' she said, a fish jumping in her hand like it was still alive.

Darya had met Sergei Rudolfoveich's steward on her way back from the market and was full of news about an escaped murderer. 'The boy ran into the yard, white with fear and yelling at the top of his voice that the man was hiding in one of the outhouses. The master gave chase on his horse and stabbed the wretch through the heart with his hunting knife.'

'Ah!' Cook emptied the steaming bucket of bloody water and fish heads over the rails to the chickens waiting below.

Nina clutched the collar of her navy wool coat and imagined it was Papa, and not Sergei Rudolfoveich, who was the hero of the story. She'd heard the story twice already this morning but would have been happy to hear it again; Miss Brenchley, however, couldn't always follow the servants' Russian and wasn't easily side-tracked from her duties, even by a murderer. 'Come,' Nina felt herself being nudged in the direction of the steps, 'we'll have a few minutes' walk in the garden before lunch.'

Mamma's maternal grandmother had been half English and half French. Her father, responsible for the English half, had been a merchant and had brought his daughter with him on a trip to Russia, where she had met and married a wealthy merchant in Moscow. She had taught her daughters both the languages she had been brought up with, and they in turn passed these languages on to the next generation. Nowadays it was the fashion for children to be brought up speaking English in particular, and Nina had spoken it since she was a baby, first with Mamma and Papa and then with a series of English governesses (Miss Brenchley was the fourth if you didn't count Miss Roberts, who stayed for only three days and left in tears). Nina was better at English than French and Mamma said this showed that she took after her great-great-grandfather.

The word Nina was searching for at this moment, however, was one she'd come across in one of the French novels Katya had left for her to read – although she couldn't explain this to Miss Brenchley because the Englishwoman didn't approve of French novels and certainly wouldn't think them suitable for a twelve-year-old girl. There were many things the English didn't approve of – Mamma said it was their national temperament – and for this reason Nina had to be constantly careful so as not to offend her governess. It could become very tiring.

'Nina?'

The word found its own way into her mind. '*Suicider*,' she said, the syllables floating upward in the cold air.

Nina was well aware that it was a peculiarity of Miss Brenchley's face that it didn't look pretty until she frowned. 'If that woman ever does marry,' Cook sometimes said, 'her husband will have to keep her in a bad temper in order to stay in a good one himself.' But Miss Brenchley was already twenty-five so Nina thought it most unlikely she would marry, even though she could look as pretty as she did now, frowning and pulling at the opera glasses which she used to watch birds.

'*Se suicider*,' the Englishwoman corrected, tugging at the leather strap. 'To commit suicide.'

'Yes. I know a story about a young man who – so his mother said – "committed"?'

'Correct.'

'Who committed suicide. His mother said this was because Mamma's aunt, my Great-Aunt Adelaida, was too friendly.'

'Whatever do you mean, Nina?'

Looking sideways, Nina saw the frown deepen to such an extent that Miss Brenchley looked almost beautiful. 'Great-Aunt Adelaida was Mamma's mother's sister, the youngest of the family. On her eighteenth birthday she agreed to marry a young man she'd known since she was a child and whose family had a magnificent estate, near Schlusselburg . . .'

'Which isn't far from Petersburg, is it?' Miss Brenchley's passions in life were ornithology and geography, in that order.

Nina had no idea, but if she confessed as much Miss Brenchley might be encouraged to take her back inside the house to study a map. 'I think it is,' she lied. 'Anyway, a few weeks after her birthday, Adelaida and her family and friends went for a picnic at a famous waterfall. After the picnic the gentlemen climbed up the hill to see the waterfall from the top and the ladies went for a walk in the forest. Suddenly there was a terrible shout and Adelaida and her friends ran to the bottom of the waterfall and found the body of her fiancé.'

'How dreadful.' The governess stared at the stable roof but didn't raise the glasses. 'He must have slipped, the wet rocks . . .'

'His brothers and sisters had all died as babies and his mother, who was a widow, never recovered from her grief. She said that Adelaida was responsible, that she'd been talking so much with one of the other young men that her son had had a jealous rage and jumped.' As she said this Nina somehow sensed it was the sort of thing Miss Brenchley might not like her to say so she added quickly, 'But Mamma says that isn't true and that it was because he'd had too much plum brandy to drink.' She knew, however, that Mamma didn't really believe this.

'Oh.' The way Miss Brenchley said this made it clear that young men in England didn't drink plum brandy. Maybe they drank sherry instead. Miss Brenchley kept bottles of sherry at the back of her wardrobe.

When Mamma told the story about Great-Aunt Adelaida she always nodded her head sadly; but she did so with a little smile so you couldn't help but smile too, even though it was very sad for the young fiancé and for his mother. Nina once asked Mamma how long ago it had happened and Mamma said fifty years and that, as her own parents, and Adelaida, were dead, it was possible they were the only people who ever thought about the young man now. Mamma had told Nina the young man's name but she'd forgotten it. She would have liked to run into the house to ask Mamma what it was, but Mamma was very tired these days because she was going to have a baby (it would be a boy, Nina was sure), and Dr Sikorski had said it was important she have lots of rest.

'Mad he was,' Darya's blue-grey eyes narrowed as she cut Nina a slice of cherry cake, 'and foaming at the mouth. Just last week he killed an innocent bank clerk, a man with a wife and two young children. Who knows how many others might have been murdered in their beds if Sergei Rudolfoveich hadn't risked his life to go after him?'

At one end of the kitchen table a maid sobbed she'd be too frightened to walk to the bathhouse tonight. Nina took her cake to the other end and went back to rereading Katya's latest letter. The two-month-old twins, Marina and Sofia, were over the croup but Katya remained exhausted by motherhood and the behaviour of her French servants who were always threatening to leave. 'The French,' Cook had snorted, 'eat disgusting food and are Catholics. You must tell your sister not to trust any of them.' Despite all this, however, Katya still liked Nice very much and had made many friends among the large Russian community, most of them also with young babies.

Reading this, Nina wondered if her sister's new friends knew that on the afternoon of the betrothal party Dmitri Borisovich had challenged Ivan to a duel. The duel hadn't taken place, which was a lucky thing for Dmitri because Ivan was an expert shot. Katya had stood in Low Field in her lemon dress, pleading with Dmitri to take back his challenge and before breakfast the next day Papa had gone to visit both young men. He returned home and shouted at Katya in his study for a very long time. Afterwards Katya had run to her bedroom and sobbed and sobbed till she could hardly breathe and Mamma had had to send the maids running for wet flannels. A month later Katya and Ivan were married.

It was this that had been on Nina's mind before lunch when she told Miss Brenchley about Great-Aunt Adelaida and her unfortunate fiancé. She remembered hearing Mamma say to Darya, 'Only think, what if Dmitri had killed himself, like that poor young man did over Aunt Adelaida?' Which was how Nina knew Mamma didn't really think it was an accident at all. Perhaps she would go to Mamma now and ask her.

Whenever Mamma told the story of how she came to Papa's estate, twenty years ago, she would say that first of all she fell in love with a young law graduate, and then she fell in love with – of all things – the morning room.

Nina always protested at this because their house was the most beautiful she'd ever seen, with its curtains of honeysuckle and wisteria and the woodwork carved as fine as lace. So surely Mamma must have fallen in love with the house when the carriage approached it beneath the lilac trees? But no, her mother would laugh and shake her head – they didn't arrive until late, it was already dark, and the servants and peasants from the village had been holding lamps as they waited to offer her wooden platters with the traditional welcome of bread and salt. It wasn't until after breakfast the next morning that she actually saw her new home.

But she loved it then? Of course! However, the morning room had taken a special place in her heart and her first project as a young wife had been to decorate it. Darya supervised the sewing of the turquoise curtains, and rolls of flocked burgundy paper were sent from Paris, along with a black and red carpet stitched in Tabriz and a lacquered Chinese screen. Papa had ordered the stately Royal typewriter as a surprise from the Maples catalogue. The furniture was sent away for new upholstery to match the curtains, and Aunt Elena, Papa's sister, had brought boxes of ferns from her greenhouse.

Now Nina could see the finished lunch tray on the brass table in the hall. 'Mamma?' She turned the handle and pushed open the morning room door. She wanted to ask her mother about the name of Adelaida's fiancé, and whether her younger cousins, Mira and Tatyana, might come again soon so they could go skating on the frozen stream as they had before Christmas. Aunt Elana had arrived with them in a sleigh decorated with ribbons and bells and the gardener had said that for their next visit he'd construct a toboggan run.

'Mamma, the young man who drank too much plum brandy and fell down the waterfall, I can't . . .' But Mamma was asleep on the sofa, a pillow under her head and her blue silk kimono covering her feet. She must, the doctor said, have as much rest as possible, staying in bed until close on lunchtime and taking only a short stroll in the afternoon. Usually she would be awake now but at breakfast Papa had mentioned that today Mamma was particularly tired. The only sounds in the room were her rhythmical breathing and the ticking of the ormolu clock.

Nina let her eyes adjust to the dim light. Mamma didn't usually like the curtains in the morning room to be closed during the day and kept them tied back with heavy tassels. Despite this the turquoise fabric had faded to the palest of blues, like a late summer sky, and the frayed edges had been repaired with green satin. It was still a lovely room, however, always smelling of flowers. Nina tiptoed across the carpet to the corner of the room that held the black iron safe and the bookshelves. The maidenhair fern on top of the safe hung down over both sides and she gently ran her fingertips through the fronds before stooping to the lowest bookshelf in the corner, where Katya's old novels were kept. Mamma shifted on the sofa, murmuring something, and Nina froze until her breathing fell back into sleep. While this happened she changed her mind about looking for a book: firstly because she didn't want to wake her mother, and secondly because if she went back to her room she would have to pass Miss Brenchley, who might enquire about her reading material. At this moment the governess was absorbed in her bird books, trying to decide which type of swallow built the nests on the stable roof. Darya, on the other hand, had gone outside to check on how the vegetables had been stored, and Nina decided to join her.

'Saa!' The housekeeper shooed the bad-tempered rooster which had followed Nina through the barn door. 'There's nothing here for you!' She threw a piece of ice in the bird's direction but although it glared it didn't move. Darya's nose and cheeks were red from bending to tease potatoes from the sacks. 'Wretched bird. One of these days I'll have him as soup. Those girls aren't much better, leaving the sacks open. I told them to put them in the cellar but they're too lazy to do anything.'

A potato rolled across the ground and Nina stopped it with her boot. 'Darya?'

'Yes?'

'Will Miss Brenchley ever get married?'

'No.'

'Because she's too old now?'

'Because not all women desire a husband, Nina Andreyevna.'

Darya had married when she was young but her husband had died six months later, after forgetting to boil the drinking water during a cholera epidemic. Darya sometimes talked about him to the women in the kitchen but always ended by saying, 'To tell the truth, I barely missed him, for I soon discovered that nothing ever came to the boil with that man!' The women always laughed loudly, slapping their thighs. Nina wondered why a woman as practical as Darya Fyodorovna had married a man who wasn't even capable of boiling a kettle.

The housekeeper led the way along the path beside the smokehouse and Nina followed behind, skipping across the icy stones. *If I step on a crack the bear will take me!* Skipping and skipping again. *Boy, girl, boy, girl, BOY!* Everyone knew Papa wanted a boy to take over the running of the estate, and the gardener's wife had predicted a boy months ago, spinning an egg threaded on a piece of hair from Mamma's tortoiseshell hairbrush. If it had been the gardener's wife here now, Nina would have enjoyed talking about the baby, but for some reason Darya frowned on any such gossip.

As Darya lifted the latch on the gate, a voice came from the veranda. 'Darya!' Mamma called softly. 'Nina! After you've collected the eggs I'll meet you both in the conservatory.'

The conservatory had been built at the same time as the house and for many years it was one of the biggest in all Russia. Over the years it had become smaller as the panes broke under hail, or from branches flung down in a storm, so that it was now one-quarter greenhouse and three-quarters empty framework. However, the boiler in the corner continued to work and there were still four glass walls and a roof high enough for the palm tree that had been brought as a seed all the way from Africa.

In spring and summer Mamma and Papa sometimes took coffee on a folding table there. This afternoon Mamma wasn't sitting at the table but stood at a raised flowerbed, holding her heavy fur coat across her belly with one hand while in the other she turned something over and over. '*Smotri!*' she called out, her long black hair hanging loose so that she not only sounded, but looked, like an excited girl. 'Look, Nina!' The shell was pink and flat against the palm of her hand. 'Impossible', Mamma murmured, 'that a shell should be here.'

But this wasn't the first shell that had been found in the conservatory; nor was it impossible, because Papa's mother had often taken her children to Biarritz, where her own parents had seen Napoleon III and his Spanish empress, Eugenie, walking along the sands. On their return home Papa and Aunt Elena used to hide driftwood and shells in their suitcases and these forbidden relics eventually found their way into parts of the garden. Mamma seemed to have forgotten this and was holding the shell as if its dirt-caked presence were truly a miracle.

'A shell,' Nina nodded meaningfully at Darya, 'Mamma has found one.' The housekeeper put down her basket and tenderly stroked the shell and Mamma's hand at the same time, saying that maybe the shell had come all the way from Africa with the palm tree, or that long ago a bird had flown inland from the sea and dropped it. As they talked, Nina picked up a piece of palm frond and trailed it along the brick floor, imagining a large white bird flying over jungles and sea and mountain tops. Then she remembered she'd meant to ask Mamma about the young man. 'Mamma, the . . .'

At that moment Mamma gave a single, sharp cry and collapsed forward into Darya's arms. The older woman staggered back, knocking over the basket and sending eggs and potatoes rolling across the ground. 'Your father!' she shouted at Nina. 'Run to the house and tell them to send immediately for your father, and the doctor. I need the men here quickly!'

Papa held Mamma's hand as the men carried her on a trestle bed over the snow. 'I am sorry, Andrei,' she kept saying in a tired voice, 'I am so sorry.' Nina began to cry, even though she told herself she was being silly and that everything would be all right: the baby was just a little early, that was all.

No, what made her cry was Mamma saying she was sorry like that, looking only at Papa, and the blood spoiling her dress, and the goodness of the men acting as if they couldn't see. Nina's knees went weak when she first saw the blood, there seemed to be so much of it, but then she remembered it was normal, like the rags. There was always blood when there was a baby. She'd watched kittens and calves being born and seen the mothers lick their newborn clean with their tongues.

After Mamma had been carried into the bedroom Nina spent the rest of the afternoon with Miss Brenchley, who took down *The Illustrated History of Great Britain* and showed her the familiar pictures of the Tower of London and Big Ben and described in detail the Changing of the Guard and afternoon tea at Fortnum and Mason's. Thinking about tea now made Nina feel hungry, even though Cook had remembered to tell one of the maids to bring her some supper. She decided she would like some cake and went along to the kitchen to ask for some, but the maid, Bella, who was simple in the head, was crying and wiping snot on her sleeve. Cook, who was watching pans of water on the stove, looked up as Nina came in and said they were busy and that she should return to her room. She didn't offer her anything more to eat.

Back in her room Nina sat on the bed and said a prayer and then attempted to read *Middlemarch*; she was unable to concentrate, however, reading the same sentence over and over. It might be better if she had one of Katya's novels but she didn't want to go down the hall to the morning room because it would mean passing her parents' bedroom.

'Nina,' Miss Brenchley was standing in the doorway, 'it's very late and you really must try to sleep.'

But she was too excited about the thought of the new baby – her little brother. They hadn't even chosen a name for him yet. 'I don't think I can. Will the baby come soon?'

Miss Brenchley stepped closer and Nina could see that her face at this moment wasn't pretty at all: her skin was blotchy and her eyes red. 'Nina, I've offered to do anything I can to help. You must help too, by staying here. Do you promise me you'll do that?'

Luckily she thought quickly enough to cross her fingers under the book. 'Yes.'

'Good. Now I must go, in case I'm needed.' Unexpectedly she leaned down to kiss Nina on the forehead. 'God bless you, child. Pray for your Mamma.'

No, she couldn't go down the hall to the morning room without being seen, but if she tiptoed she could get there along the veranda. A few minutes after the governess had left, she opened her door and crept through the drawing room and out the French doors.

Father Sergii said there was a star for every saint in heaven and that not all saints are recognised while they are here on earth. Tonight the sky was so full of saints it didn't seem possible there could be different names for them all. There was a full moon as well, and in its light the snow sparkled sharp as crystal.

'Get down!' From around the corner of the house the doctor's man snarled at a yapping dog. She pulled her coat closer and listened: there wouldn't be a fire in the morning room but she'd brought matches in her pocket in order to light a candle. She'd choose a book and then say a prayer for Mamma and the baby in the icon corner.

'Damn you!' The dog yelped.

It wasn't as cold as she'd expected, and from outside the barn door there came the glow of cigarettes and the sound of men's voices. She stood still for a moment, considering whether she might go back inside and put on her outdoor boots so she could walk across the gleaming snow to the conservatory. Sometimes she and Katya had crept out to the conservatory at night, pretending they were on a beach in Africa, with fireflies darting through the palm trees and the sound of the sea. Nina had never seen the sea but now Katya saw it every day in Nice.

'No!'

At first she thought it was the doctor's man again, but the shout had come from inside the house. There was a crashing sound, like breaking glass, followed by heavy footsteps, and she was alarmed to see a figure stagger down the steps at the far end of the veranda. Her thoughts flew to the murderer.

'No!'

It was Papa, in his shirtsleeves with no coat.

'Papa!' she called, running along the veranda because he was ill, falling down on the snow then getting up again. 'Papa!'

There were voices all around and lamps. 'Yus!' Darya was shouting at the gardener. 'Stop him!'

Dr Sikorski pushed past and called down to the men. 'Hold your master, whatever he says, and do not let him go! On my orders.'

They were grabbing at him. 'How dare you touch Papa!' Nina heard herself cry. 'How dare you!' She threw herself towards the steps, but someone held her hard by the shoulders, and although she kicked and screamed on the veranda, while her father cursed and fought below, neither of them managed to break free.

Three

Mamma wept at her own funeral. Nina swayed when she saw her mother's marble face wet with tears, but Aunt Elena gripped her elbow. 'It's the ice, Nina. The ice is melting, that's all.'

Behind them Countess Grekova grappled with a miracle. 'The tears of a saint!' Her hands clawed the air. 'Holy Mother of God, we are blessed!' One of her daughters appeared with a kerchief and smelling salts and bundled her away.

The funeral took place five weeks after Mamma's death. In winter such delays were common, for many of the roads were impassable except by sledge and the ground too frozen to dig a grave. As it was, Papa wouldn't have been well enough to attend if it had been any earlier: Dr Sikorski had ordered he be watched constantly, and for the first fortnight he was never left alone, even when he used the privy. When the men proved too frightened to sit with him at night, Darya took her bedroll from the sewing room and stretched out on the floor of the guestroom where Papa now slept. The window was nailed shut and she locked the door, putting the key under her pillow. 'Isn't she afraid?' Nina heard the gardener's wife ask Cook, her eyes wide with excitement. 'The master could strangle her and then kill himself.'

Cook didn't reply.

The morning after Mamma died the house had been heavy with the smell of blood, like tarnished silver, and through the shutters Nina had seen the men carry the mattress from her parents' room to Low Field to be burnt. Then the carpenter had begun to build the coffin. He worked on the veranda at the High Field end of the house, leaning against the work-horse in his leather apron and shaving long curls of wood that drifted, gentle as feathers, to lie on the snow. When the coffin was finished Nina stood and watched as the man lovingly oiled it so that the grain glowed like honey. And then the coffin was carried into the house so Mamma could be placed inside.

Later Aunt Elena had waited with her and Darya as the coffin was carefully carried down the steps – the narrow end going first – into the stone cellar. A crucifix was put on top, dried thistles and juniper scattered all around, and it was packed in ice, the men solemnly passing along the buckets. Please may this not be happening, Nina kept repeating in her head, please may it not be true. Part of her had accepted that Mamma was in the coffin: she was dead and would never be coming back. But another part couldn't accept it, for it wasn't possible that Mamma, with her beautiful laugh and dancing hands, could be gone for ever. Aunt Elena was saying something about how much the men had cared for Mamma and then Nina heard her say, 'Your parents loved each other very much, Nina. But you must always remember that love can create a sort of madness.'

Nina didn't understand what she meant.

After the funeral it must have been felt that Papa was out of danger because Aunt Elena returned to town to look after her own family and Darya went back to sleeping in the sewing room. And so the house returned to what seemed like normality – but which Nina gradually understood could never be normality, for Mamma had been their anchor and without her they were adrift. Everyone knew Papa roared at the men and that in the fields his rages were feared, but Mamma had turned his temper into a family joke. 'Your father takes his temper off with his boots,' she would laugh. 'It's a black dog that stays outside the house.' With Mamma gone the black dog bounded in, flinging itself against objects and, increasingly, the servants. To begin with he wasn't unkind to Nina, although he wasn't kind either. She felt numb, dazed with grief, but he never spoke to her about it: in fact he barely spoke to her at all. As the weeks turned into months, she began to grow afraid of him.

Gradually the servants started to leave. Miss Brenchley went first, in early spring, after Papa flew into a fury when she spilt oil at the dinner table. 'I pity you with all my heart,' she said to Nina, 'but I cannot stay.' A month later she accepted a position with an American family in Persia. Her new employer promised views across the Persian Gulf, a servant of her own, and, if she wanted it, an Arabian horse. But it was really the thought of the bird life that had convinced her. Her eyes were bright. 'Falconry! Just think, Nina, for Persians it's the sport of kings.' Nina didn't feel anything as she watched her pack. There would be no more lessons, no more reading together. What did any of that matter when Mamma was dead?

By the middle of the summer four housemaids and three of the kitchen staff had found employment in town. Papa didn't instruct Darya to replace them. Nina suspected that Cook would have gone too but for the fact that her husband, a big, silent man, and their two equally silent sons worked on the farm. So where the summers had once been filled with company – carriages coming down the gravel drive, Mamma and her friends strolling on the lawn in their pretty hats and dresses, the *moujik* bringing village gossip to the kitchen door – now there were few visitors and Nina and the servants often found themselves speaking in whispers. Instead of laughter it was the wind that flowed from room to room, and at night Bella was to be heard sobbing herself to sleep under the stairs. One night Nina went to ask her what was wrong and the girl said she was frightened of the mistress's ghost rattling the doors.

As autumn set in, it was usual for the timbers of the house to be oiled and the gaps that opened under the windows to be plugged with horsehair mixed with clay. But Papa no longer appeared to notice the cold: the men weren't ordered to prepare the clay and at night the rooms could be bitter.

Eventually Darya complained.

Papa was outside the kitchen door, stamping into his galoshes. 'The cold is nothing but the icy breath of God, Darya.'

'The devil's farts,' she retorted.

Nina froze, sure that Papa's hand would strike, the way that only the week before it had struck a cowherd who let a cow develop an ulcerated udder. But instead, he nodded calmly. 'Those too,' he said, 'those too.' That afternoon he sent the men to work on the house.

With Miss Brenchley gone, Nina spent her time reading, working her way mechanically through the shelves in the morning room. Darya never left her alone for long, however, insisting she put her book aside and come out into the garden for some fresh air. 'Your father,' she would explain as they watched the chickens being fed, the cows being milked, 'is torturing himself with the thought that it was his desire for a son that killed your mamma. He loved her so much, and now that love has turned to . . .' She hesitated. Miss Brenchley had been more forthright. 'I fear for your father's mind,' she said simply on the morning of her departure. 'I urge you, Nina, to write to your sister immediately, asking that she sends for you to live with her in Nice.'

Maybe Papa *was* mad, but although she wrote to Katya once a week Nina didn't say anything about this to her sister. Katya had been desperate about Mamma's death and it would be wrong to upset her further. Besides, Katya now had a third daughter, Irina, and in a couple of her letters had confided that Ivan's business wasn't doing as well as he'd hoped. Sometimes Nina offered the letters to Papa but he never took them, and when she warily read extracts aloud he didn't appear to be listening. In her letters to Katya she pretended to be replying on his behalf, passing on kitchen gossip about the farm: the number of calves that had been born, how many pounds of butter had been churned. When she told Katya about the servants leaving she implied it was because, with only Papa and herself to look after, there wasn't enough for them to do.

She did sometimes go to stay with Aunt Elena's family in town but these visits weren't a success. Her cousins, Mira and Tatyana, had lessons with their governess, went to parties, had friends to visit: their life was no longer hers and she felt pitied and was anxious to return home. 'Andryusha,' she once heard Aunt Elena plead, 'send Nina to live with us. She's only thirteen and shouldn't be left without a governess or tutor.' But Papa firmly said no and, hearing this, Nina's spirits lifted a little. Although she wasn't happy with her current life, she was cheered that Papa didn't want her to go, hoping this meant he needed her. She could see her aunt was angry, her knuckles white in her lap, but Elena didn't argue any further. She continued to visit and always brought something for Nina: some new hair ribbons, a seed pearl and coral brooch for her birthday (which Papa no longer remembered), some new but sombre clothes. The clothes were very necessary because when Nina looked in the mirror now she could see she was taller than Katya, as tall as Mamma had been. But she didn't need any outfits for social events as Papa no longer invited guests: there were no dinner parties or luncheons and at some stage, though she hadn't really noticed, they had stopped attending church as well. Father Sergii, like Dr Sikorski, was no longer welcome, and when the elderly priest turned up to bless the beehives Papa angrily ordered him away. If a neighbour's carriage trundled up the drive they were rarely invited to alight. Many months after the funeral Countess Grekova had arrived in a troika pulled by three horses, Cuckoo growling on her knees. The old lady didn't seem to remember that Mamma had died and Darya had had to tell the driver to take her back to her house in town. Sergei Rudolfoveich still came to talk with Papa but he often left looking worried. One day, after he had inspected a new tractor which had been packed in crates and sent all the way from Germany, Nina heard him mutter to his steward, 'Dear Heaven, a small fortune! And for what? If it breaks down there's no one to repair it.'

Everything changed, however, with the arrival of Dr Vilensky. It was the spring of 1913, over a year since Mamma's death, and a few weeks after Nina's fourteenth birthday. Nina was in the kitchen when she heard a carriage clatter up to the house. Papa had surprised her by announcing the night before that a guest was coming to stay. As she went down the veranda steps now she saw that the man alighting from the carriage was tall – Papa was six foot but the new arrival was even taller – and that her father had taken him by the shoulders, greeting him as if they were brothers. What struck Nina most, however, was the way the doctor was dressed. His suit was very modern and elegant and, as she remembered to make a small curtsey, she noticed that he was wearing the most elaborate waistcoat she'd ever seen. For a moment she almost laughed, thinking of the rabbit in *Alice in Wonderland*.

Looking at the waistcoat again as they had afternoon tea, she thought the blue silk material, with its intricate pattern of leaves, seemed familiar and realised she must have seen it in one of

Mamma's English journals. 'Dr Vilensky,' she stood up in her eagerness, 'your waistcoat is so beautiful. It's from Liberty's, isn't it? In London?'

The doctor had already said a few words to her, of course, but now he looked at her as if they hadn't been introduced at all. Although his blue eyes were sharp his voice sounded dazed, as if he had no idea what she meant. 'I don't really know,' he said. 'Perhaps . . .'

Papa was also staring, not as if he'd never seen his daughter before but certainly as if he hadn't seen her for some time. 'Nina,' he gave a small frown, 'you should go and finish your lessons.' Could it really be possible he didn't know she no longer did any lessons? She didn't say anything but quietly left the room.

For dinner Darya had the table set with the Dresden plates, the best silver and crystal wineglasses for Papa and Dr Vilensky. There was soup and roast chicken and mutton in a raisin and apple sauce, followed by a caramel pudding. Papa was almost like his old self: asking the doctor questions about clinics in London, New York and Vienna, slapping the edge of the table for emphasis. It appeared he and the doctor had been corresponding for months and their conversation was all about how far behind other countries Russia was in the state of its medicine and hospitals. Dr Vilensky had spent a year working at a big hospital in London (she was correct about his waistcoat!), and he stabbed the air with his fork as he described how the walls of the wards were whitewashed, windows opened for cross-ventilation, the menus checked for their dietary provision. Nina didn't find the subject of this conversation of much interest but it was infinitely preferable to a silent supper with Papa, so she was pleased the doctor had brought two large trunks and was apparently intending to stay for some time.

There could be no doubt that at first Dr Vilensky brought a certain calm to the house. He and Papa spent hours talking in the study, or walking together across the fields, and in the evenings he gave Papa some white powder on a piece of paper. After only a fortnight or so Papa, while not back to his old self, was less extreme in his moods and the effect was noticeable to everyone.

In the mornings and after lunch, while Papa was busy with the farm, Dr Vilensky sat in the study, reading or writing letters. One evening the doctor saw Nina with a book and politely asked what she was reading.

'*Great Expectations*,' she replied, adding quickly, in case he thought she hadn't read it before, 'Miss Brenchley, my governess, said it was the sort of novel you can read twice.'

He shook his head. 'I've never read it.'

'It's very good.'

Dr Vilensky had lived in London so no doubt he'd read lots of, other English books. 'I realise others do find enjoyment in novels,' he said, 'but all my time is spent on medicine; I have none left for such distractions.'

Nina was surprised, then, to find their guest sitting on a stool near the High Field fence a few mornings later, a sketchbook in his lap and a pen in his hand. It was a warm morning. He'd removed his jacket and seemed to be drawing the house. The drawing lessons Miss Brenchley had given Nina had been remarkably unsuccessful, although Katya had produced some very respectable water-colours and evidently had some talent. Maybe Dr Vilensky was talented too. Nina watched him for some time before finally gathering her courage and walking over to him.

'Hello, Dr Vilensky. I wonder if I might see your drawing?'

He looked at her again with those blue eyes, not unkindly, but as if she were a puzzle he found difficult to solve. 'I'm sorry to disappoint you,' he said, 'but I'm not drawing.' He showed her the sketchbook and she could see what he meant straight away: the doctor had indeed made a recognisable outline of the house but there was no delicacy in his depiction, no shading and still less detail. The veranda was there in shape, but without any of its beauty.

'I see,' she said politely, although all she did see was that Dr Vilensky was no artist and that his morning would have been more fruitfully spent reading a book.

An hour or so later she looked out of the kitchen door to see him directing the gardener and one of the stable boys as they hammered pegs into the ground and tied lengths of string between them. What was happening? She wandered through to the dining room, where Darya was inspecting the silver. 'Dr Vilensky,' she said. 'Do you know what he's doing?'

The housekeeper breathed heavily on to the side of an engraved teapot. 'He is measuring the house.'

'But why?'

Darya looked up and Nina was struck by how much older she'd become over the past year, her eyes as wrinkled as a grandmother's. 'Andrei Andreyevich should tell you more,' she said slowly. 'You're no longer a child and he should tell you his plans. It is wrong of him not to.'

Darya was unhappy about the maids leaving and about Miss Brenchley not being replaced, everyone knew it. But you knew these things because of the way she stomped from a room, slapped her palms against her heavy forearms: Nina had never heard her criticise Papa aloud before. She felt very strange.

'What are his plans, Darya Fyodorovna?'

The silver teapot was placed next to the milk jug. 'A hospital,' she said quietly. 'Your father blames your mother's death on Russian medicine. He wanted to modernise the hospital in town but the doctors there refused to listen to him, so he's planning to try his ideas here. He's going to turn this house into a hospital.'

But the house couldn't become a hospital: it was where they lived, it was their home. Dr Vilensky would no doubt realise that as soon as he made his measurements; he would see it wasn't possible.

The nurses, Mrs Kulmana and Leila – or Miss Chizhova as she was introduced at first – arrived one afternoon in a small carriage, followed by a wagon piled high with tin trunks and wooden crates. Almost a month had passed since Dr Vilensky had made his sketch and in that time a surprising amount of work had been done. The lawn where the tables had been set up for Katya's ill-fated party was being turned into vegetable gardens and three of the precious lilac trees had been cut down, while the foundations below the veranda at the High Field end of the house had been strengthened. At first Nina heard, or heard about, these changes rather than witnessing them as she had a severe chest cold and spent almost a fortnight propped up in bed. Darya insisted on making her swallow spoonfuls of syrup of onions and brown sugar and, when she developed an earache, held hot onions over her ears. 'Pah,' Cook waved her hand in disgust as she brought through a tray, 'the room stinks. What's the use of having a doctor in the house if he can't be asked to deal with a simple cold? A *feldsher* could do better.'

Nina croakily explained that Dr Vilensky was a surgeon and probably didn't treat colds.

At the end of the fortnight Darya let her out of bed but her chest still wheezed and she tired easily, so her mornings were spent reading in the conservatory, tucked into a wicker chair with mohair blankets. The folding table was put up next to the chair and in the middle of the morning Darya would bring a tray with chocolate, or coffee, and a bowl of dried dates with a slice of bread and honey. The conservatory was warm and humid, good for a weak chest, and it was also quiet. 'The noise,' Darya glared as she put down the tray, 'hammering all day! And the dust. I've had to cover all the furniture with sheets.' One morning her face was clouded with anger. 'It's gone,' she said brusquely, 'the mural of the garden.'

Nina looked up from her book. 'What do you mean?'

'See for yourself.'

Nina walked slowly up to the house and along the back veranda. It was true: the mural of the palm tree in its faded garden was gone. She ran a fingertip over the fresh plaster, tracing where the tree had been. Mamma had sat out here and told them stories about the strange inhabitants of the wonderful garden; she could remember Papa saying that, when he was a child, visitors to the area would stop their carriages at the gates and send a footman running along the drive to ask if they might come in to see the famous painting. But now these things – which had meant so much to his parents, and to Mamma – did not seem to matter to Papa at all.

There was a cough behind her and she swung round to where two of the workmen were carrying a heavy length of wood. 'Why has the wall been covered?' she demanded.

They glanced at each other, then the older one replied, 'For the building work, young mistress. All of this veranda is to be filled in. On Dr Vilensky's orders.'

*

So it wasn't impossible to turn the house into a hospital after all. Over the following weeks the veranda was refashioned into a proper ward for ten beds, with another room at the end for the nurses to work in. The guest bedroom that Papa had slept in after Mamma died was knocked through to the sewing room to make an operating theatre. The windows in the new rooms all opened easily, the floors had been sanded and varnished, the plastered walls whitewashed.

And then the *sestras* came. They stepped out of the carriage wearing ordinary travelling clothes, but after being shown to their rooms – Mrs Kulmana was in a guest room, Miss Chizhova in the room Miss Brenchley had used – they changed into uniforms of grey dresses with white aprons and neat white caps. Dr Vilensky was away but Papa had come up from the fields to meet the new arrivals and it was evident from the way he talked to Mrs Kulmana that she was to be treated with almost as much respect as Dr Vilensky himself. It was hard to judge Mrs Kulmana's age: she had a streak of grey in her coiled brown hair but could have been younger than she looked. She didn't smile very much, which might have been because she was tired from the journey. The younger nurse, a girl not much older than Katya, appeared overcome by shyness, and although she was quite pretty, with blonde hair in a long plait and cheeks pink from travelling, she barely looked up from the ground and didn't utter a word. While they changed, Papa spoke to Darya and Cook.

Mrs Kulmana, he said, would be responsible for the daily running of the hospital and would inform Darya of anything she required. He expected another two maids and a kitchen assistant would be needed almost immediately, and, as soon as patients started to arrive, a washerwoman from the village would have to come every other day, rather than twice a week. Cook was to follow Mrs Kulmana's instructions on preparing food for the patients.

The nurses spent the afternoon checking the contents of the crates against an inventory and Nina didn't see them again until dinner. By this time, however, the household had somehow managed to put together this much information: that Mrs Kulmana was a highly experienced nurse, the widow of a naval officer who'd been under the command of Admiral Rozhestvensky in the Tsushima Straits; and that the younger nurse, Miss Chizhova, was also from a good family. In addition – and this caused a great deal of whispered discussion in the kitchen – the poor girl wasn't shy but mute. Anything she wanted to say she mimed or wrote down in a small black notebook.

Nina doubted this latter information at first but as soon as the two women came through for dinner she saw the notebook hanging from a chain on the young nurse's belt. The conversation that night was much as it had been when Dr Vilensky was present although where the doctor discussed clinics across Europe, Mrs Kulmana compared conditions between hospitals in Russia and Finland. It was obvious that Mrs Kulmana was a serious and intelligent woman and she described how, after the death of her husband, she'd decided to dedicate her life to nursing. She'd trained at the House of Deaconesses in Helsingfors and then returned to Russia to teach nurses at a private hospital in Petersburg. Russian hospitals, she said, were terrible: the nurses, for the most part, uneducated peasants or the roughest sort of townswomen. And some of the hospital doctors weren't much better, many of them still operating in dirty aprons on cracked wooden tables. But such conditions had changed elsewhere and they would change in Russia too. The hospital in Helsingfors, for instance, one of the most modern hospitals in Europe, had started with only eight beds but now had room for forty adult patients with a special wing for over thirty children. There was no reason why the same couldn't happen here. She knew Dr Vilensky well by reputation and regarded him highly: he'd worked in the most advanced hospitals in England and America and appreciated the importance of good nursing. Miss Chizhova – here Mrs Kulmana gave a rare smile – had been one of her students: 'A wonderful student, the best in her year. She's a dedicated and excellent nurse.' The young nurse's pink cheeks grew even pinker. Nina caught her eye and a few minutes later the nurse gave a sweet smile and slipped a note across the table. *I am not a wonderful student, it is Mrs Kulmana who is a wonderful teacher. My name is Leila Grigoryevna.*

When dinner was finished, Papa asked for coffee to be sent through to the study, where he and Mrs Kulmana were to discuss some papers. Nina and Leila got up to leave. As they reached the door Papa called out, 'Nina, you're to help Mrs Kulmana in the morning. Do whatever she asks. Tomorrow will be the start of your training.' She had no idea what he meant but didn't want to spoil his good mood by asking in front of their guests. Leila must have known more, for in the hall she scribbled a note: *Don't worry*, it read, *Mrs Kulmana is a good teacher and I will do what I can to help.*

Papa's plans were made clear the next morning when Mrs Kulmana presented her with a book entitled *Notes on Nursing; What It Is, and What It Is Not*. 'Now,' she said brightly, 'your training as a nurse begins today.'

It was a mistake. Nina gave her back the book. 'Oh, no, Mrs Kulmana,' she smiled politely, 'I'm not training as a nurse.'

A puzzled look passed over Mrs Kulmana's face. 'I thought you knew, Nina Andreyevna. Your father is eager for you to study nursing. He has discussed it with me in letters, and again last night after dinner. I am to train you.'

Why would Papa think she wanted to be a nurse? Her mind returned to the previous evening and to the conversations she'd heard her father have with Dr Vilensky. Nothing they had said had interested her at all.

Mrs Kulmana was handing her the book again. 'I know your father has been very busy lately, which is no doubt why he hasn't mentioned these plans. Or maybe he wanted to surprise you. However, he told me that your governess described you as an excellent student, so I look forward to our lessons. I know you are only fourteen, Nina Andreyevna, and although that is young to start training it is not unheard of. Now, I suggest you take this and begin reading. I have no doubt Miss Nightingale will inspire you.'

If a patient is cold, if a patient is feverish, if a patient is faint, if he is sick after taking food, if he has a bed-sore, it is generally the fault, not of the disease, but of the nursing.

Nina hated everything about this book. She hated its grey cover, its stiff, shiny pages: most of all she hated its contents. Miss Nightingale's passionate insistence on the importance of pure air and water, her praises for the surgical sister – her hands worth three guineas a week – who would drop to her knees and scour a floor because she thought it was not clean enough for her patients, made for dreary reading. How could a woman like Mrs Kulmana find it so inspiring? It was a manual for servants.

She read for the rest of the morning, although she found it almost impossible to concentrate. After lunch, however, boredom turned into nausea when she came to diagrams of the heart and circulatory system. She rested her forehead on the table, feeling light-headed. She needed Mamma, who would have laughed Papa out of his notion for a hospital, just as she had laughed him out of his tempers.

The two nurses dined with them again that night and Papa had another animated discussion with Mrs Kulmana. When Nina rose to leave at the end of the meal he gestured with his hand. 'And how have you found your new student, Mrs Kulmana?'

'She has read diligently all day.'

'I am pleased to hear it.' He nodded. 'Remember, Nina, I expect you to be diligent at all times and to take notes of everything Mrs Kulmana teaches you. You are very lucky to have the opportunity to train under her.'

'Yes, Papa.' But she didn't feel lucky at all.

Over the following days Nina discovered that the young nurse, Leila, felt very differently about nursing books and could settle down to read a chapter on bandaging, or the use of silver clips in reducing bleeding, in the same way she would read a novel. Mrs Kulmana tactfully didn't ask Nina for her opinion of Miss Nightingale's work but did suggest she finish the book in her own time and spend some of each morning helping Leila in the dispensary. Nina shuddered when she first saw the cruel steel instruments in the crates; however, she soon found herself looking forward to helping Leila cut rolls of bandages or place jars of sphagnum moss, chloroform and mercury in a locked cupboard. For although she couldn't speak, and hadn't been able to since having a growth removed from her vocal cords as a young child, Leila was very good company. She was an expert mime and would have the servants, who couldn't read her notes, roaring with laughter. At the same time, she was as passionate about nursing as Mrs Kulmana. She'd had a tremendous battle persuading her parents to let her train as a nurse and knew it was only because of her muteness that she'd won. *I convinced them it was like becoming a nun*, she scribbled, *and as no man would want to marry me, what else could I do with my life?*

Nina would watch Leila counting instruments, folding sheets. She was so pretty and amusing Nina doubted her silence would stop her finding a husband. The truth was she wasn't interested in marriage: what she was interested in was medicine. Nina, on the other hand, knew she would never make a nurse, despite Papa's belief that she would. Where Leila's family had been shocked by her ambition, Papa was obsessed on Nina's behalf. She was, he announced one evening, to study under Mrs Kulmana and then, when she was old enough, she'd go to London to train at the Nightingale School for Nurses at St Thomas's Hospital. On her return she would help run the hospital. As he said this, Nina stared silently at her plate, not daring to speak.

A few weeks after the nurses' arrival, Aunt Elena came to visit. Nina had taken her lunch tray out to the conservatory and as she walked back up the path her aunt watched from the veranda. Nina was wearing a nurse's white apron over her plain navy dress, and as she passed a group of men digging in the garden, they moved aside, but barely touched their caps.

'The men,' Aunt Elena hissed in a low voice, 'why don't they show you more respect?'

'They're new,' Nina replied uneasily, for her aunt's anger seemed to be directed more at her than the men. 'Papa wants the vegetable gardens to be made bigger, for the hospital, and the gardener has brought in workers from town.'

'The way your father runs this estate, without even a steward. And as for the hospital . . .' She bit her lip and lowered her voice. 'He is spending so much money. Your mamma's jewels, Nina, are they still in the safe?'

Nina hadn't seen the jewels since Katya was given her share to take to Nice. 'I believe so.' Where else would they be? Papa wouldn't touch her dowry.

Her aunt leaned close, her eyes suddenly as fierce as Papa's. 'Having failed to save your mother, your father intends to save the world. My fear is that, in tearing this house down, he'll bring you down with it. His plans for you are preposterous. And Dr Vilensky – your uncle has been making enquiries about him. No doubt he's a skilled surgeon, but there are rumours . . .' Here she took Nina's wrist, pulling her the length of the veranda. 'Does he give your father anything?' Her voice was urgent.

What could Dr Vilensky give Papa? 'You mean presents?'

Her aunt spluttered. 'For heaven's sake, girl! Does he give him anything to take? Does he give him medicine?'

In her mind Nina saw the white powder on the slip of paper that Papa took at night. 'No, Aunt, he doesn't.'

'And I suppose you *want* to become a nurse?'

A sour taste came into her mouth. 'Yes.'

Elena dropped her wrist and rocked back on her heels, suddenly defeated. 'Well, dear niece, until you're ready to help yourself, I can do nothing for you.'

She'd had problems sleeping since Mamma died and now was plagued by bad dreams in which there was always snow splashed with blood and, lying on the snow, a person who needed to be bandaged. Sometimes the person was Mamma and she knew that if she did the bandages the right way her mother would be miraculously healed; but her hands didn't know what they were doing, the bleeding didn't stop, and in the end Mamma would lie there as cold and white as she had been in her coffin. Sometimes it was Papa and the bandages were needed to tie him down in case he got away and hurt himself. He always did escape, however, howling into the night.

Mrs Kulmana must have realised straight away that her new pupil was hopeless but she never showed any irritation. Every day she put aside some time to show her how to tie a bandage, or explain some procedure, and then she'd leave Leila to go over it again. Sometimes Papa looked in through the door and would watch as Nina put a bandage on Leila's arm. He didn't know it was wrong and would leave with a satisfied nod. Nina's hands would be shaking and damp. She still went out into the garden with Darya but the housekeeper wasn't very forthcoming. There were no more bedtime stories and Nina knew Darya had taken to walking to the crossroads every morning at first light, to pray to the icon of St Paraskeva; she was often to be found in the icon corner of the morning room as well. But where Darya had shrunk into herself, Cook had expanded. Mrs Kulmana discussed theories of nutrition with her and it seemed that the thought of preparing arrowroot and beef-tea and steamed vegetables gave Cook more satisfaction than any elaborate menu had ever done.

Things continued like this for some weeks. Word spread about the plans for a hospital, and although it wasn't intended that any patients should be admitted yet – Dr Vilensky was still negotiating the purchase of a machine to generate electricity – Mrs Kulmana was soon running an unofficial clinic. One of the cowherds was the first to attend, having cut his arm open on a wire fence, and after that a steady trickle of patients appeared with minor injuries. Nina had tried to stay in the room at first, hanging back by the shelves, but she soon discovered that even that was too much for her and would escape along the hall to her bedroom, or find a tray that needed to be returned to the kitchen.

One morning, however, a boy who'd put an axe through his foot was carried in on the shoulders of his friends and as she slipped out of the dispensary she ran straight into Papa.

'Shouldn't you be watching Mrs Kulmana?' His beard had grown long in recent weeks and he was beginning to look like one of the peasants she and Katya used to call the 'wild men'.

She'd been feeling a little odd all morning and now was too light headed to tread carefully: blood had been welling from the boy's filthy boot and she felt hot and ill.

'Well?'

She leant back against the wall and shut her eyes. 'I cannot,' she began, 'I cannot do it . . .'

Grabbing her by the shoulder, he marched her down the hall and into the study. He slammed the door. 'What can't you do?'

Her knees were weak but it had to be said. She couldn't keep pretending for ever. Mamma's photograph, smiling from the desk, gave her courage. 'I cannot be a nurse, Papa.' She looked straight into his eyes. 'I am very sorry, but I have tried and I cannot do it.'

Papa had never hit her or Katya, not even on the day when he had had to go and plead with both Dmitri and Ivan. Yet now he raised his hand and she found herself staggering back against a chair, clutching her head with shock and pain. She didn't understand what had happened for a moment and then saw Papa standing over her, his face red and his eyes so full of rage that he no longer looked like Papa at all. 'Never say that again.' He clenched his fist hard against her jaw. 'You *will* train as a nurse, for your mamma.'

And that was when she understood that he didn't blame only himself for Mamma's death; he blamed her also. She should have been born a boy.

Four

After Papa left the house, Darya took Nina into the bedroom, then went to the kitchen to get her some milky tea. Left alone, Nina looked at herself in the mirror and knew she hated her father. She had loved him once, but no more. He didn't care about Katya, he didn't care about her. Maybe he had never cared for Mamma, not really.

Her underclothes were damp and she thought she must have wet herself. She slipped her fingers inside the leg of her drawers, and as they came out, covered in blood, Katya's words came into her head: 'Blood is something you'll have to get used to, for your turn will come.' The blood was as red as the blood covering the boy's boot, as red as the blood on Mamma's dress. So this was what it meant to be a woman.

She didn't know what to say, so simply held out her hand when Darya came back into the room. The housekeeper started, then nodded. 'A shock can bring it on.' She showed Nina how to fold a square of cotton and gave her clean underclothes. Then she stood her in front of the mirror again and repinned her hair. 'This should have been a joyful day, Nina Andreyevna.' Her voice was tight.

Nina watched as the bruise came up on her face. She'd grown up seeing various of the peasant children with bruised faces; one of the charcoal burners, a bandy-legged, bad-tempered man, had a daughter who was exceptionally pretty – till he threw her against a tree and shattered her nose.

'Darya?'

'Yes, child?'

'Miss Brenchley said I should write to Katya and say I want to live with her in Nice. Do you think I should do that?' Once she

47

had thought she would never wish to leave; now she wished for nothing else.

Darya shook her head. 'Katya has many problems. Her husband's business is doing badly and', she glanced away, 'the marriage is doing badly too. It's widely rumoured that Ivan Vasilyevich goes with other women. I doubt your sister has been able to keep any of her dowry for herself, and if you went to France, your brother-in-law would want anything you had too. If the marriage ended, you'd both be far from home and destitute.'

Nina felt like she was standing on the edge of a high cliff. 'How do you know all this?' she whispered. But she knew even as she asked: Aunt Elena had friends in Nice. And she knew too that any rumours of scandal involving Katya's husband would be true and that her sister had been a fool to marry him.

'Your aunt told me the last time she was here. She's very worried about you and your sister. She would have you to live with her, but as things are I don't know if your father would ever allow it.'

On the mantelpiece the clock held aloft by a pink shepherdess struck the hour. 'What can I do?'

The older woman spoke close to her ear. 'Pray to God but don't anger the Devil. The master no longer knows who he is and will hit you again. We must try to think of a way of persuading him that you should go to your aunt. And if we cannot do that, we will think of something else.'

A fall down the steps is one way of explaining a bruised face. It wasn't possible to know if Mrs Kulmana was aware that Papa had hit her; but, even if she did know, Nina doubted she'd say anything. Nina was beginning to learn things that Miss Brenchley had never touched on in their lessons. For instance, she knew that Mrs Kulmana was a visionary and that such people might not always feel they can afford to be kind – Mrs Kulmana wouldn't risk the chance of saving many lives for the sake of one spoiled girl. Also, there could be no denying that Nina's 'fall' had brought about an improvement in her attitude towards her studies. She now approached the nursing books seriously because she was afraid of what would happen if she didn't. Leila did what she could to inspire her: encouraging her to try her hand at making splints, mixing poultices, identifying surgical instruments. She even spent a whole evening writing down the story of how she had almost died as a child and how her parents had searched for a doctor who would agree to operate on her throat in order to save her life.

But nothing lessened the dread that descended as Nina turned the pages of *Notes on Nursing*, or alleviated the horror that overwhelmed her one afternoon when Leila leafed through a text on the diseases of the brain and spinal cord, enthusiastically pointing out the illustration of a brain tumour successfully removed by a Glaswegian surgeon. Nina felt hot and faint, the blood drumming in her ears, and only just managed to get to the enamelled sink in time before being horribly sick.

Later they sat together on a garden bench and watched as a tractor crossed Low Field. Picking up her little notebook, Leila scribbled a message. *You should not be a nurse, Nina.* This was so obvious they both began to laugh at the same time, silent tears running down their faces. Then Leila wiped her eyes and wrote again. *What will your father do?*

Nina had told Leila the same story she'd told Mrs Kulmana, about falling. 'He'll be angry with me,' she said.

Leila's fingers stroked the cheekbone where the bruise was now fading, her fingertips as gentle as Mamma's would have been.

For a fortnight, two medical students had been camping under the remaining lilac trees. Georgi Osipovich was tall and serious, with silver-rimmed glasses and dark hair. 'A Jew,' Cook muttered, 'or a Catholic.' The other, Pyotr Yefimovich, was round and blond and enjoyed lounging around the kitchen door gossiping, but only when Dr Vilensky was busy elsewhere. 'Dr Vilensky,' he informed Nina and Leila through a piece of fruitcake, 'is a brilliant surgeon. Which is why the old men who teach us don't like him. He's too good.'

Georgi shook his head. 'Some of our teachers aren't bad but they've no interest in research, or in keeping up with developments. Dr Vilensky is a moderniser and that's what frightens them. He's worked in English hospitals and even spent six

49

months in America with William Halsted, who's recognised throughout the world as a genius.'

Pyotr laughed, brushing off crumbs. 'Although, like many medical men, Halsted developed an unfortunate habit . . .'

But Georgi shushed him and launched into a rambling story about some of the students dressing a skeleton in a lecturer's gown. Later, in the dispensary, Nina asked Leila if she knew what Pyotr had meant about doctors' habits, but Leila just shrugged and turned away.

The young men were invited to dinner on their last night, and it would have been a pleasant evening if it hadn't been for Nina's fear of Papa. He'd barely spoken to her since the scene in his study and whenever he looked at her she sensed his barely suppressed anger. Tonight he gave her a cool greeting then ignored her completely. With the young men, however, he was entirely at ease, explaining how the modern techniques he was employing on the farm would result in surpluses, which would support the hospital. 'A model for Russian agriculture, and medicine,' he tapped the table with his finger, 'all here. For those with eyes to see it.'

Mrs Kulmana was going to Petersburg for a week, to visit an ill relative and purchase the last of the furniture needed for the operating theatre, and the students had accepted the offer of a ride in the carriage to the railway station the next morning. After saying his farewells to Dr Vilensky, Georgi joined Nina on the veranda and told her how much he'd enjoyed his stay and how impressed he was with her father. 'He's ahead of his time,' he commented.

'Yes.' It was raining slightly, and at the bottom of the steps the stableman's dog whined.

'And you are training to be a nurse?'

'That's what my father wants.' She was aware he was studying her.

'But you?'

She said nothing, and he was silent for a moment before coughing self-consciously. 'I hope you do not take it amiss if I say something. A surgeon's occupation is a difficult one: it's not an easy life. But a nurse's occupation – a properly trained nurse, I mean, like Mrs Kulmana and Miss Chizhova – is, so I believe, even harder. I wouldn't recommend it to any of my sisters and, unless it is something you sincerely wish to do, I would caution you against it as well.'

He was right, of course he was right. But what could she do? 'Thank you for your advice.'

He pushed his glasses up his nose. 'It would be a pity to waste your life on something that didn't suit you. I want nothing else than to be a surgeon and if someone suddenly told me I had to become a farmer,' he nodded in the direction of the shivering dog, 'I would feel exactly like that.'

The electric generator for lighting the operating theatre had been ordered and Dr Vilensky was once again making drawings and measurements in anticipation of its arrival. When Mrs Kulmana returned with the last of the steel furniture, and the generator was in place, the hospital would open. In the meantime, Leila continued to run the informal clinic, splinting a broken arm and stitching the forehead of the blacksmith's wife where, so she claimed, a donkey had kicked her. Nina managed to remain in the room by keeping herself busy: filling the enamel basins with clean water, taking bandages from the cupboard, reading Leila's notes aloud to the patients.

Everything had to be kept spotlessly clean, and after Leila had seen her patients, Nina wiped the surfaces with a carbolic spray and put the instruments in the steam steriliser. Once sterilised, the instruments could be handled only with rubber gloves, and Nina soon discovered she was allergic to the rubber, her hands covered in tiny, painful blisters.

The violinmaker arrived one sunny afternoon. There was shouting from the drive, the barking of dogs. This could all be heard from the conservatory, where Nina had gone to hide with a bowl of milk and bread and a novel. She didn't have much time to read these days and, as Papa had gone to the village and Leila didn't need her in the dispensary, she had planned to spend the afternoon by herself. She ignored the sounds from the front of the house, hoping no one would find her.

Not long after, however, Darya hurried in, her cheeks flushed. 'You must come – a man has brought his son on a cart. He's only twenty, a violinmaker. He has an abscess on his brain and is dying.'

Why would anyone bring a patient who was so ill to the clinic? 'Don't they know the hospital isn't open yet?'

'The doctors in town have refused to operate, so the old man has come to beg Dr Vilensky to try to save his son.' She wrung her hands. 'Nina, the doctor has agreed. Leila is preparing one of the wooden tables from the dispensary. The operation must start soon, while there's still light, because Dr Vilensky says the oil lamps might not be enough later. You're going to have to help; he needs more than one nurse . . .'

The milk spilt as she jumped up. It had never been suggested she would be involved in any of the doctor's operations. 'I'm not a nurse! That's Mrs Kulmana's job, Leila's, I can't . . .'

The strong fingers bit deep into her shoulders, holding her upright. 'Listen, the young man is dying. You won't have to do much, just give the doctor the instruments he needs. You know where things are kept and what they're called.' She pulled Nina against her breasts. 'Child, if I could do this for you I would. Now hurry, Leila is waiting – and your father is back. I saw him ride in as I left the house.'

Leila gave a calm nod as Nina entered the dispensary. She was placing surgical instruments in the steriliser and her precise movements could have been those of Mrs Kulmana. After she'd finished she reached for her notebook and scribbled a few lines. *His father is washing him. I'll shave hair. Wash yourself. Clean clothes, house shoes, apron, gloves, mask. Do table with carb. Dr V dressing. Don't worry.*

Nina's legs were shaking so much she could barely stand. She couldn't do this; she couldn't be involved in a real operation. 'I can't,' she said aloud, her voice coming out as a whisper. And then, louder, 'I can't do it.' She leaned back on a bench, her knees completely gone. 'I'll faint, I'll be sick. I don't care if Papa beats me.' He could kill her, it would make no difference.

Leila stopped what she was doing and studied her for a moment, as if she were looking for some clue as to what sort of person Nina might be. Then she spoke silently to herself, something Nina had never seen her do, her lips moving as she reached up to one of the wooden cupboards. Unlocking it, she took a bottle from the shelf where the anaesthetics were kept. Then she opened her notebook, tore out a page, folded it and sprinkled some powder from the bottle.

She scribbled another message. *Take this. Just this once. It will make you strong.*

It looked like the powder Dr Vilensky gave Papa. 'What is it?' Leila wrote again: *Kokaine.*

The young violinmaker was beautiful, his skull polished marble. He lay on his back, a white sheet across his naked body, his eyes closed. He was so very pale it was as if he'd been packed in ice.

And then his eyes suddenly flickered open and he stared up at her, his gaze full of terrible pain. 'Don't worry,' she whispered through the mask, 'we're going to help you. You'll be well again, I promise.' She was going to take his pain away: the thought filled her with joy. Next to her, Leila dropped chloroform on to a cloth, the sickly sweet smell flooding the room, and handed it to her. Taking it, she held the cloth firmly over his mouth and nose, seeing as she did so how the look in his eyes turned into fear as he feebly tried to push himself up. 'Shh!' she whispered playfully, smiling to herself because he would never have to fear anything again. Another look came into his eyes then, an expression she couldn't put a name to, and the eyelids slowly fell shut.

His breathing was soft and rhythmical. From outside the window came the sound of his father praying.

Dr Vilensky stood at the right of the table with Leila next to him, and Nina stood on the other side, close to the counter and the sterilised instruments. 'Take his pulse, Miss Karsavina.'

Her fingers reached for the soft wrist and counted the beats. 'Yes?'

It was easy: she could do anything. 'Sixty, Dr Vilensky.'

'Good. Light could be a problem, so we must work quickly.' As his hands turned the young man's head, foul-smelling green pus poured out of the right ear and into the dressing Leila had put in place. Nina didn't mind the smell: 'The best perfume always grows from the best shit' was what the gardener's wife used to say. Nina almost laughed out loud.

'Notice,' Dr Vilensky was saying, 'that the veins on the right temple are congested. Miss Chizhova and I will wash out the middle ear with antiseptic solution. Miss Karsavina, I will then need a scalpel and clamps, followed by the trephine, the narrow-bladed searcher and the forceps.'

When the scalpel pierced the marble skin the blood spurted red as rubies. 'I'm making an incision approximately one inch above the ear and across to the temple.' It was like watching Cook split a chicken's breast and peel it back over the bone, only where Cook did it with a few deft movements, this took a long time. But Nina didn't mind. She felt warm and strong and could stand here for ever. She checked the young man's eyes: if they began to open she would apply more chloroform.

Eventually Dr Vilensky put the trephine in place. 'In a moment I'll need the searcher, which is introduced for two purposes: to clear away any ground bone, and to ascertain the depth of penetration. When the bone is released it must immediately be dipped in solution and put on the sponge. The searcher?'

Nina handed it to him. He inserted it, working thoroughly around the edge of the trephine. 'A few half-turns and a lift should do it. There . . .'

Nina held the bone with the tweezers, gently dipping it into the solution then placing it carefully on to the sponge, where it miraculously turned into a button of ivory.

'The dura is congested. Miss Chizhova, insert your finger and see if there's a brain pulse.'

Leila slipped a gloved finger into place, but shook her head.

'I didn't think so. I'll now open the membrane and expose the brain tissue. The exposed edge must be covered with idoform to stop further dissemination of the infection. Miss Karsavina, I'll soon need the hollow needle.'

When the membrane was cut, Nina could see something bulge upwards like warm dough, yellowish in colour. 'That's the brain itself,' the doctor explained, 'being pushed out because of the pressure.' He took the needle from her and inserted it slowly into the centre of the bulge. 'Ah!' There was a bubbling sound and an even stronger smell. 'We've located the upper part of the abscess cavity.' He leaned forward, pushing the needle in further, and a stream of pus sprayed out across the front of his apron. He

54

didn't appear to notice. 'We're making good time. Miss Chizhova, you will now enlarge the aperture with forceps so I can remove any necrosed areas of tissue with a scalpel.'

Nina held the dish for the diseased pieces of brain, some as big as horse beans, then Leila washed out the cavity with a solution of boracic acid. The pus, however, didn't stop oozing. The doctor's voice was brisk. 'We'll need the lamps. There must be another cavity and I'll have to drill again.'

Nina and Leila positioned the lamps and Dr Vilensky applied the trephine to the base of the skull. It took longer to drill this time but then the procedure was much the same. There was even more pus and Leila flooded the area with solution until it flowed freely from the upper cavity as well.

'He hasn't needed more choloform?'

Nina shook her head.

'He'll have gone into coma. Now, this will require drainage.'

She handed across the fine glass tubes with india-rubber stoppers and the doctor inserted them into the wounds. 'It was worth obtaining these.' He sounded pleased. 'In most Russian hospitals they're still using decalcified chicken bones.'

Leila dusted around the area with boracic acid and then began to dress the wounds with pads of sterilised gauze. Nina looked at the two irovy buttons sitting on the sponge. The doctor answered her unspoken question. 'It's not always necessary to reinsert the bone, and if he recovered the skin would cover the wounds adequately. But the abscesses were surprisingly deep and it has to be said that recovery is extremely unlikely. If I had had the opportunity to operate earlier it might have been different. As it is,' he pulled down the mask and smiled, 'we have very successfully carried out our first major operation.'

It didn't matter that the young man wouldn't live because inside he was perfect: a carved bowl, an egg blown clean. When all the dressings were in place Dr Vilensky took off his blood-stained apron and went out to talk to the old man, who was still praying. Leila pulled back the sheet and Nina saw how beautiful the young man's body was, the blood still pulsing through his veins. Her fingers reached out to touch him but Leila stepped forward, covering him again with a fresh sheet, and indicated they should clean up.

The floor was slippery with pus and blood and they mopped that up first, then put the instruments into the steriliser and scrubbed the counter with solution, emptying the buckets of bloodied water into the sink. Leila left Nina to wipe the sink itself while she changed her shoes, then came back and took the young man's pulse, writing it down on a chart.

Nina peeled off the rubber gloves. Her hands were covered with red blisters but they didn't hurt at all. She washed the gloves in the sink and left them to dry, swallowing because her throat felt very strange. Leila looked over at her, then scribbled. *Your tongue feels numb – it will go away.*

From outside they could hear the violinmaker's father, speaking with great dignity. 'You have given him one chance where before he had none: that is all any of us can hope for in this life. Now he is in the hands of God.'

Leila wrote again. *You were wonderful. Now go to bed!*

Quickly, Nina leaned forward to kiss her on the cheek. As she turned to leave she noticed the two ivory buttons, sitting unwanted in the dish; Leila wasn't looking, so she slipped them into her pocket.

It was hot. The full moon meant she didn't need a candle so it was easy to carry the quilt across the lawn. In the conservatory she dropped the quilt on the ground and took the pieces of damp bone from her pocket. They were surprisingly smooth, and as she held the discs in her palm they gleamed in the moonlight. 'Look!' She could hear Mamma. 'It's impossible!' But nothing was impossible: they had given the violinmaker his one chance. She put the two buttons side by side on the warm soil at the base of the palm tree, then pushed them down hard with her fingertips, pressing them in deep to where they'd join the seashells brought back from Biarritz, where the Spanish empress, Eugenie, had walked, her silk dress dragging across wet sand . . .

When she woke a few hours later Nina was unable to breathe: there was a button stuck in her throat. Rolling over on to all fours she fought for breath, her mouth wide open as she sucked in cold air over her swollen tongue. The panicky breaths came, one after the other, gradually turning into sobs because she was frightened and because her throat hurt so much and because she was alone in the garden and would always be alone. Mamma was dead; she was not coming back. And the violinmaker, with his marble skull, he was dead too. Remembering the final look in his eyes, now she recognised it for what it was: horror. He had seen his own death coming as she held the chloroform over his nose and mouth. 'You'll be well again,' she had said. 'I promise.' As the sickly sweet smell of the chloroform came rushing back, she began to vomit over the quilt.

Her arms and legs were trembling and her throat and the back of her nose burned. When she finally finished retching, she stood up and stumbled over to the rainwater barrel, splashing the filthy taste from her mouth before drinking handful after handful of cool water. Then she sank down in the wicker chair, where Darya had found her earlier that afternoon.

In the moonlight the conservatory was as big as a cathedral.

She sat there for a very long time, feeling nothing but despair and the pain in her throat. And then she gradually became aware of another sensation, as if all her nerves were on edge. It was like the sensation she'd sometimes had as a young child, playing with one of the half-wild barn cats: the cat would come closer, its nose almost touching hers and, as its animal flesh approached, the skin across her own nose would tingle. Now her whole body felt like that, as if some large animal were very close.

'Nina.' The voice came from above and she stared up into the fronds of the palm tree.

'Nina.' The voice was deep, and although it came as sound she also sensed it as colour. The colour was bronze.

'Nina.' The palm fronds took the shape of wings. There was a face. Eyes that could see everything.

An angel.

'Nina.' It spoke from a long way away, from the top of the conservatory, which was now as tall as the tallest building in the world. Yet it was also very close, whispering in her ear.

'Yes?' she whispered back.

'You must leave and go far away,' the angel said.

Darya found her at dawn. The sky was a pale grey and the roosters were crowing behind the stables. In the half-light the palm tree looked old and sad and Nina knew it was going to die too. She'd seen the gardener's men taking panes from the far wall and now understood that the conservatory was gradually being dismantled, the glass going into the new frames which were being built to cover the seedlings and marrows. The real palm tree would go, like the painted palm tree had gone. It wouldn't survive the next winter.

'So here you are.' Darya looked down, pulling her shawl around her shoulders.

Nina stank of vomit: it had dried across the front of her dressing down and in her hair. She didn't care. 'He's dead, isn't he?' Her voice was hoarse.

'He never woke up. His father was with him.'

'Dr Vilensky knew he wouldn't live.' Dr Vilensky had operated knowing they couldn't save the young man's life. And she had taken *kokaine* and seen an angel. She looked back to where the housekeeper was watching her. 'I have to leave,' she whispered.

'Yes.'

So Darya had known this already. What else did she know? 'Mamma's jewels, Darya Fyodorovna, are they still in the safe?' Every week, Darya collected the housekeeping money from Papa in the morning room, and sometimes the safe was open.

'I think they are, but your father has many plans for the hospital and it's possible he will sell them. The paintings that were taken down, I believe they have been sold already, and the chandeliers are to go as well.'

She would have to act soon. 'If I take my dowry and run away – will you come with me?'

Darya's eyes were unreadable. 'There's nowhere we could go in Russia where we wouldn't be found. You would be brought back here and I would be sent to Siberia.'

Nina looked up at the palm tree, a torn fringe against the morning sky. 'Then I have no choice. I will have to leave Russia altogether.'

Five

It was easy to lie to Papa. 'Aunt Elena has invited me to stay for a few days,' she kept her gaze levelled on his boots, 'so I can go to the dressmaker and have some grey dresses made, like those worn by Mrs Kulmana and Leila.'

He nodded silently and went into the study.

It wasn't until then that she realised they'd always lied to him. 'There's no need to tell Papa,' Mamma would say lightly, or, 'We won't say anything that might worry your father.' Lying by omission. And so it had been easy to invent the story about the grey dresses, while not mentioning the crêpe de Chine dress with pink roses that the seamstress was already working on.

Aunt Elena had come to visit a week after the violinmaker died. They'd walked across the lawn, to where the remaining lilacs had been felled the day before. Elena stared at the raw, broken trees, kicking at the grass with the toe of her boot. Her face was angry under the muslin parasol. 'These trees were planted by my mother, and your mother and I strolled under them arm in arm on her first morning here as your father's wife. It would break her heart to see what Andrei is doing . . .'

'I must leave here,' Nina said, 'and go away.' Her aunt didn't reply, and they walked in silence down the slope of the lawn to the fence at the top of Low Field, where Katya had ruined her lemon dress and her life along with it.

Aunt Elena read her thoughts. 'Your sister is unhappy. I've told your father but he merely replies it's no concern of his.' The pink of the parasol was reflected in her cheeks as she made no effort to hide her contempt for her brother. 'You must understand he has no concern for you either. Dear Andrei would be a saint and he would martyr you to achieve it.'

Nina was going to run away. She would use the code to the safe, which was written at the back of Mamma's commonplace book. She'd checked and the book was still in the glass and walnut cabinet, hidden behind a pair of white porcelain cherubs. She was about to explain her plan when Elena interrupted: 'You know there's only one thing you can do, don't you? You must marry, Nina. A girl as young as yourself must have a protector.'

The long grass waved limply as a line of ducks made their way to the stream. Nina had already made her plans. She had a folding map of London and had decided that Monday and Tuesday mornings were to be spent in the British Museum. On Wednesday afternoons she'd visit Mudie's Select Library in New Oxford Street, which Miss Brenchley had recommended, and on Thursdays she'd attend the National Gallery. The rest of the week would be spent reading; although on Friday mornings she'd treat herself to tea at Liberty's. It shouldn't be at all difficult to find lodgings with a respectable family; in fact she was quite sure that if she wrote to Miss Brenchley on the subject, pretending to enquire on behalf of a friend, the governess would know exactly who to recommend.

It was true she felt a little alarmed by these plans – but only a little. The idea of marriage, however, left her mouth dry. She would marry one day, of course, but it was not possible now – she was only fourteen. That was the age a peasant girl would marry; it was as if her aunt had accused her of something indecent. Maybe she'd heard about Georgi, the medical student. Nina pictured him again on the veranda that last evening, pushing back his glasses. But there'd been nothing between them, they'd only talked. She stammered her embarrassment. 'Aunt Elena, there's no one, believe me. I . . .'

The parasol was a small cloud, her father's sister inscrutable in its shade. 'And it's possible there never will be anyone. The rumours about your father are so wild no respectable man will have you. Those who are kind simply say he's insane, while others claim he is a Bolshevik as well.'

Nina must have looked blank for her aunt reached out and shook her by the arm. 'Don't you understand? Your father has ruined you. You're beautiful but the stories about you are ugly. You no longer attend church or mix with people of your own station. It is said you undress and wash the male patients, even the lowest worker; that you hold screaming men down for the doctor's knife; that you consort with nurses who are little better than prostitutes. That every day you see and hear things that no decent woman should ever see or hear . . .'

'So how can I marry?' she whispered. The British Museum, Mudie's Select Library, the National Gallery, Liberty's: all of these disappeared in the urgency of Aunt Elena's voice.

From the distance came the sound of a man clearing his throat. Elena spoke fast and warm against Nina's ear, the parasol enveloping them both. 'You need to find a man who won't take advantage of you but who needs a wife, just as you need a husband. You're young but you're tall, like your mother and sister, so you look older. What you've been through has made you older too.' The smell of cologne stuck in Nina's throat. 'I know someone, an Englishman. He's in town with a party of friends, staying with the Lavrovs. He's twenty-eight years old, a gentleman with a good position and a private income. From certain things he's said and from what I've observed, I believe he's in need of a wife. An intelligent, understanding young woman from a good family, who'd be a companion to him.' She stepped back and the tip of the parasol dropped to the ground between them. 'Understand me, he's a kind man or I wouldn't suggest this. Such marriages aren't uncommon and they can be most successful: between civilised people arrangements can always be made. I'd certainly hope that both your mother's and Katya's examples would convince you that a marriage based on passion is a far riskier endeavour.' She sighed as if everything was understood. 'He's away on business at the moment, he deals in metals, but there's to be a *bal blanc* so you can meet him there.' Then she added, 'His name is Richard Truelove.'

Two weeks later Nina sat in her aunt and uncle's carriage as it followed the coloured lanterns hung in the trees lining the drive to the Lavrovs' house. I can do this, she told herself over and over, I can do this. She calmed her breathing as the carriage drew up to the large house. Uncle Aleksei helped her to alight, waving back the footman, but her suede shoe stepped on something that crushed. A human skull was thicker than a snail shell but could be crushed almost as easily. The O formed by her lips when she felt the snail beneath her sole could have turned into a short scream but came out as a giggle instead. She covered her mouth.

In honour of the English guests the carpets had been taken up and the walls of the drawing room freshly painted in the French style, white and gold; the windows were hung with rose cretonne. Nina and her aunt went up the sweeping staircase into one of the bedrooms, where there were tables for brushes and combs, a tortoiseshell box for hairpins, bowls of rose water and sachets of lavender. The cross-eyed little maid who hung their coats dusted Nina's shoulders with walnut powder, adjusted a stitched rose, then stepped back clapping with pleasure. For Nina was beautiful in the flowered dress. Not as beautiful as Mamma but a match for Katya, certainly. She'd seen it in the mirror as she was prepared earlier but it hadn't come as a surprise because part of her had been expecting it, her due as her mother's daughter. Not that beauty was worth anything in itself, except as a means of buying escape. She knew that once the skin was peeled away it was only bone that mattered. Mamma's skull would be indistinguishable from the violinmaker's, except for the carefully drilled holes.

'Are you ready, Nina?'

'Yes, Aunt Elena.'

'Then we shall go down.'

As they entered the ballroom it was as if a ripple passed from one end to the other. But she was aware that the admiration was laced with curiosity and pity: she could see the combination in elderly Colonel Balov's eyes as he made a great ceremony of bowing over her hand. The nails of her left hand dug into her palm for her mother could have married a Grand Duke; her great-grandfather had built the biggest conservatory in all Russia.

'The image,' the middle-aged, coroneted woman puffing in front of her was one of Countess Grekova's daughters, though not the one who'd pulled the old lady from Mamma's coffin, 'of dear Irina. My mother, who so seldom leaves the house since her fall, will be pleased to hear it.'

Nina had always thought she would attend her first dance with Mamma and Katya. That they would be there together, the three of them in pretty dresses, laughing and enjoying themselves. She could never have imagined the reality would be this. In the background, Elena was speaking coolly to a woman in an ill-fitting black wig.

'No, my niece isn't sixteen yet but her mother went to her first ball at a younger age – as I did myself – and it seems a pity to keep such a very lovely young woman locked away.'

A moment later Nina was being propelled forward by the elbow, Elena muttering between clenched teeth, 'The ugly old crow will never get her misshapen daughters married, and she knows it.'

There were more greetings and curtseys and then there came the sound of instruments being tuned. Looking up, she saw a short red-faced man with a greying moustache approach with great deliberation – he was English, she could see from his clothes – and she thought numbly to herself that he was much older than she'd expected. He didn't appear to have a clubfoot, or a limp; maybe he had a hump, it was hard to tell. However, her aunt was saying his name and she was breathing again because he wasn't Mr Truelove after all but Mr Stevens. Who was in Russia, he announced jovially, including all those within earshot, because he had an interest in oil. Not gold like some, he added, rubbing his hands as if washing off something undesirable. As a quadrille was called he bowed and presented Nina with a posy of Parma violets selected from a wicker basket.

Long ago, it must have been years and years, she and Katya had had dancing lessons with a middle-aged spinster, Miss Shumina, who said that once you had learned to dance you would never forget; and indeed tonight Nina glided through the *chaine des dames* aware – although there was no pleasure in this for it was purely mechanical – that she danced well. Far better, in fact, than her partner, who was clumsy but didn't mind, obviously enjoying himself. She must be the only unhappy person in the room, she thought. And in Nice, Katya was unhappy too. The unhappy Karsavina sisters, it could be the title of a play. A woman laughed at that moment and she recognised Yelena Pavlovna, an acquaintance of Katya's, dancing with a handsome Englishman whose red hair gleamed under the lights.

When the music ceased, Mr Stevens bowed and her uncle stepped in to introduce her to an elderly couple who were visiting from Moscow, and then to a retired army captain, a thin-faced man with a blotched face. 'Miss Karsavina.' He shot her a wolfish look that had all the force of a slap. If her aunt hadn't warned her beforehand she would have been made uncomfortable by the look but wouldn't have understood what it meant. 'There will be men,' Elena had said slowly, 'who will look at you in a way they would normally not dare, with no respect. You'll see the stories that are told about you reflected in their eyes.' Nina saw it now, and while she might have expected to be disdainful she found she was frightened: it wasn't simply a lascivious look but a cruel one too.

They were all watching, everyone in the room. Young women who'd been friends of Katya's, who'd been pleased to visit the estate with their mothers, slid their eyes over Nina now. She was pitied and despised. She'd seen a man naked; had held his shaved skull in her hands. And worse, she could have shouted, she'd done worse than that – promised him life where there was none. Her eyes pricked, though whether with pity for the violinmaker, or herself, she couldn't have said.

She escaped as quickly as she could, brushing her arm against a fern in a coloured Chinese pot. Gazing in the direction of the gypsy band, she made herself think about something else: the gypsy violinist, for instance; maybe his instrument had been made by the violinmaker. The thought was curiously comforting, like meeting an old friend, but she knew it was unlikely – the gypsy's violin would have been handed down through his family, generations of musicians playing around a fire. The violinist's eyes caught hers and he gave a slight shrug, as if to say don't bother with these people. She nodded a grateful response but he glanced away, not the bestower of sympathy after all, merely dismissing her along with the rest of the guests. She had never felt so alone.

'Nina.' Aunt Elena caught her by the wrist. 'Hiding in the potted plants! Come.' In the background stood the red-haired Englishman she'd seen earlier. 'There's someone who wishes to meet you.'

Aunt Elena hadn't mentioned a hump or clubfoot, it was true, but Nina had assumed this, as something understood. For why else would a man – an Englishman only twenty-eight years old, with a good position as well as a private income – have any difficulty in finding a wife? Men who needed wives but couldn't get them were afflicted in some way, like the Parnoks' son Mikhail, who had a cleft palate and frequently fell to the floor, yelling obscenities and chewing his tongue till it bled. His parents had bribed a timid, penniless young widow from Moscow to marry him and it was widely known she was so terrified by his fits that she locked herself in her room for days on end.

'Miss Karsavina.' Richard Truelove bowed, and she must have managed a curtsey, for he was already leading her on to the floor. His hand was on her waist, one, two, and they swung into the waltz. He was tall, one of the tallest men in the room, and had to stoop to whisper in her ear. 'You dance very well, I couldn't help but notice during the quadrille.'

'I had lessons,' she replied clumsily. 'And my sister Katya and I often danced on the veranda.'

'Bravo! I learned to dance with my sister Anne on the lawn at Cheltenham.'

Looking up she saw he had brown eyes and they were kind.

The dancing was followed by parlour games, and then they sat next to each other at dinner. He asked her about the English governesses she'd had and she described Miss Brenchley in such a way that he chuckled, announcing that her description was his Miss Newton to a 't', only Miss Newton's obsession was mushrooms, rather than birds.

'She'd take Anne and me for long walks in the countryside and make us recite the Latin names of any fungi we found. But only the poisonous varieties; anything edible didn't interest her.'

He enquired about Katya, but not too closely, and she realised Aunt Elena must already have told him something about her family and her life on the estate. Then he explained he'd come to Russia on business.

'I work for a company based in Brighton,' he said, 'and we deal in metals. With metals anything can happen. For example, in London I met an elderly lady, a great philanthropist, who was the widow of an American entrepreneur whose wealth was the result of one simple, but extraordinary, idea he'd had when he was a very young man. In those days, ships that sailed to New York from Europe filled with merchandise had to buy ballast for the return trip. The young man heard someone mention this at a dinner party. All night he kept turning the idea over in his mind and the next morning he raced down to the wharves to confirm the story – and yes, it was completely true. So what did he do? He took out a loan and bought a copper mine and then he approached the captains of the ships and offered to fill their empty vessels with copper. The shippers didn't have to pay for ballast and he didn't have to pay for transport. At the end of the journey the American copper could be sold for less than the expensive European metal.' He smiled at her, very gently. 'Wonderful, wasn't it, to have thought of something so simple?'

'Yes.'

Around the table there were knowing looks and glances, some of them spiteful. But his smile told her he knew it too and she shouldn't mind. Let them look, he seemed to be saying, why should we care? He was shy, she thought, and had had to fight his shyness. Her shoulders relaxed and a faint feeling, like hope, rose inside her. At the end of the evening he asked if he might call the next morning, and she said she would like that very much.

As she sat in front of the dressing table, preparing for bed, her aunt came in. 'So you like him?'

'He seems a good person.'

'Yes,' Elena paused as she adjusted the crêpe dress that the maid had already put on a hanger, 'I believe he is.'

But could she love him? Nina's fingers fumbled with the pearl and coral necklace. Her aunt stepped behind her and smoothly undid the clasp. 'Do you have something to ask?'

'Does it take long, to know if you can love someone?'

Her aunt put the necklace on the dressing table and began to unpin Nina's hair. 'Respect, admiration, these are the things that should be brought to a marriage. You've already said you like him. Do you feel you can respect him also?'

She thought of his story about the ships. 'I think so.'

'Well then. As for love, it takes many forms.' She picked up the hairbrush. 'Nina, don't confuse love with being "in love". Those who fall in love can soon fall out of it. The type of love that is based on respect and admiration endures.' She ran her fingers across Nina's cheek and said lightly, 'I can assure you that Mr Truelove wouldn't expect, or wish, for you to "fall in love" with him.'

*

66

She lay awake for hours. Why wouldn't he expect a young woman to fall in love with him? Maybe he'd been hurt, she thought, like Dmitri. She couldn't know anything about that, but love wasn't the only issue; there was also sex. She'd asked Aunt Elena about love but not about sex because she already knew the answer to that: a husband mightn't expect his wife to fall in love with him, but he would certainly expect her to have sex with him. Having grown up on a farm, sex was no mystery. She and Katya had often watched the barn cats and laughed at the tom's clumsy surprise when the queen angrily spat and swore when he withdrew. The bitches tied on the roof of the shed had to be kept on a short rope to stop them strangling themselves as they attempted to jump down to the dogs. Although it wasn't always like that: once she'd seen the stableman having to hold his best bitch when she refused to mate with the dog he'd chosen. The men had stood around laughing and she'd felt sorry for the little terrier. It had been worse when Papa had the prize mare mated; even now she flinched at the memory of the men's raucous voices and the mare's shivering, sweat-foamed flanks and rolling eyes.

It was different with humans, who could pick and choose, although the ribald jokes that made up much of the women's conversation in the kitchens made it clear that sex didn't always provide women with the pleasure they wanted. Mamma enjoyed it with Papa however – she knew because one night she'd listened by mistake. It had been during a particularly hot summer almost four years ago. She'd tossed under the prickly sheets, having a bad dream, and then got out of bed to find Darya. When she couldn't find the housekeeper in the sewing room, she went along the hall to her parents' bedroom. Mamma always went to bed earlier than Papa, and she'd been about to knock at the door when she stopped, hearing Papa's voice, and Mamma moaning quietly. They were moans of pleasure and grew louder until Mamma cried out words that Nina had never heard her use before. She'd stood listening for longer than she should, then crept away.

She'd known what her parents were doing because at the beginning of the summer she'd watched the new kitchen maid and her lover out on the veranda. Going into Katya's darkened room one evening, she'd seen her sister's shadowy outline beside the window.

'Shhh,' Katya beckoned her, 'they're out there again.'

When she peered past the corner of the shutter she could see the maid and a man sitting with her. 'She says she sleeps out there because of the heat,' Katya whispered, 'but everyone knows it's because she has a lover. He comes up from the village. I've been watching every night. She didn't let him do it at first but now she does.'

'Do what?'

'You'll see.' They'd sat there a long time, the maid and her lover, murmuring and sometimes kissing, and Nina got bored. She would have moved away but Katya gripped her arm. 'Wait.' And then it happened. The man gently pushed the girl down till she was lying beneath him and pulled her skirt up to her waist. Nina almost giggled aloud but stopped because the man was now kneeling and taking down his trousers. He pulled them all the way to his ankles and then he lay on top of the girl, the moonlight shining on his naked buttocks as he moved up and down. He stopped after a few minutes and rolled over to one side, his hand moving down between the girl's legs. She held her hands on his and then there was a low moan and the man climbed on top of her again, moving up and down quickly now till he gasped and they both lay still.

Nina's legs had felt trembly and she found it difficult to breathe as she backed away from the window.

'See?' Katya had said. 'See?'

She'd watched them every night after that, not with Katya but from her own window as she leaned against the shutters. Never again had she felt like laughing; instead the feeling she got was like the one she sometimes had in church when a visiting young priest chanted and she found herself forgetting he was spotty and that his beard and clothes stank, because of the beauty of his voice. It was the same with the maid. Nina didn't know what her lover looked like in daylight, but the girl herself was hard-faced, with thin, bloodless lips; however, at night she was transformed, performing a sacred rite. As the weeks went on the girl sometimes climbed on top of the man, sitting astride him like a Valkyrie, her head thrown back and her throat white with

68

starlight. Once the man pulled her dress and underclothes right off and she sat on top of him naked, her heavy breasts swinging above his face. She cradled his head and he nuzzled up at her nipples like a calf greedy for the teat.

Then one morning the kitchen maid was gone – Cook said she was lazy and had been sent packing. But the mood the lovers had created lasted all summer. In the afternoons, after lessons, Nina felt tired and dreamy, wanting only to read long novels under the trees by the stream, where the bees hummed in the grass and the kingfishers flashed blue and silver over the surface of the water. Katya came with her, and in the privacy of the willows they stripped off their clothes and swam naked over the warm stones. She remembered now how it had felt, the pleasure of the warm sun and being naked in the water. Katya had floated on her back, her nipples like small flowers bobbing on the surface. That was the summer when they tiptoed out and slept in the conservatory at night, dreaming of Africa; the summer Katya believed she understood about love.

The feelings Nina had had that summer had largely disappeared after Mamma's death, and on the nights when she did rock herself to sleep on the heel of her hand, it was as much for comfort as for any thoughts of a lover. Marriage, however, would involve sex; it was inevitable. Mamma had enjoyed sex, and so had the kitchen maid, but they'd chosen their partners. So how did she feel about having sex with the Englishman? He was certainly more attractive than she'd expected, but to do it with a man she barely knew, even though she did like him ... She decided she'd do what the conversations in the kitchen suggested women often did: she'd pretend.

Sex was just something she'd have to deal with. What worried her more was what it led to – very shortly she might become another Katya, her belly swelling with one child after another. Or, like Mamma, die in childbirth. But this, she thought to herself grimly, was her fate as a woman; these things could happen whomever, and whenever, she married. Right now marriage was the price for escaping Papa and the hospital, and however high that price, she had to pay it. It might be the only chance she had.

Six

In the morning her head throbbed. When she didn't touch her breakfast, Aunt Elena looked at her dispassionately and observed she was over-tired. 'That's how you will look,' she said, as Mira and Tatyana stared wide-eyed, 'after your first ball.' She then announced she was taking the girls to visit an elderly neighbour who was indisposed, and would leave instructions for the servants to set the table for tea in the parlour.

After her aunt and cousins had left, Nina stood in front of the hall mirror and studied her face, which looked white and ill, as if she were coming down with something. Mr Truelove must have thought the same, for when she met him in the parlour, half an hour later, he took one look at her then strode to the French doors and flung them open, calling her over to see the beautiful morning.

'Come out into the garden, Miss Karsavina,' he suggested. 'The fresh air will do you good.'

She led the way to the gazebo, but failed to stoop under the low archway and so got her hair hopelessly tangled in a climbing rose. She was clumsy: he must think her a fool. 'I'm sorry, it's because I'm too tall.' She could have wept, although she didn't know what would be worse: if he did want to marry her, or if he didn't.

He gave a tug on one of her hairpins. 'I like you tall. You must promise me you will never bow to fashion and get shorter.'

She knew she was expected to laugh. Instead, she opened her mouth and things started tumbling out so that, without intending to, she told him about Mamma dying and about Papa and the hospital and the operation on the violinmaker. She stumbled over her sentences and repeated herself, sounding more and more stupid and childish, while he stood behind, patiently untangling her hair, so she couldn't see his reaction in his face.

There was silence when she finished, then he turned her around and looked into her eyes. 'Thank you,' he said, 'for trusting me enough to tell me these things. And now that you have trusted me, Miss Karsavina,' he straightened his shoulders, 'I will trust you.'

Aunt Elena returned to find them laughing and joking over their cold tea like old friends, Nina with a piece of blue thread twisted round her finger, symbol of the agreement reached between them. Richard stayed for lunch, and after he eventually left, Nina went up to her aunt's room and found her rising from her knees.

'I've been thanking God,' Elena said calmly, 'for giving me the opportunity to save Irina's daughter.'

The next morning a message came: Papa had left for Petersburg on the train and would be away for four days. He'd call for Nina on his way back.

Nina returned to the estate that afternoon. Mrs Kulmana and Leila were in the dispensary and she found Darya in the rose garden. 'Where's Dr Vilensky?' she asked.

'Gone with your father.' Darya handed Nina a basket. 'Well?'

'We're to be married tomorrow. Aunt Elena spoke about my situation to Father Sergii weeks ago and he's arranged for a visiting priest to give us his blessing. We'll leave straight away for England. I'll tell Mrs Kulmana I've come to collect some of my clothes so that the dressmaker can lengthen them, and that I'm going back to my aunt's early in the morning. When Papa calls for me at Aunt Elena's, she'll say I've come back here. By the time he realises what's happened we'll be far away.'

'Ah.' Darya's black eyes glittered.

The breeze brought with it the smell of resin from the pine trees beyond the stream.

'He's a good man – nothing like Ivan,' Nina added.

Darya leaned sideways and spat across the path, the spit shining like a new spider's web. 'The only difference between men is how far they can piss.'

Darya, however, didn't know all there was to know about

men, Nina realised that now. Aloud she said, 'I've told him Mamma's jewels might still be in the safe but he says I don't need a dowry.'

The older woman shook her head and tutted. 'You will *not* go to your husband a pauper. You're your mother's daughter and you'd be a fool not to take what's yours. Your father will only throw it at strangers.'

'That's what I think too. But Papa will be very angry when he discovers what I've done.' She stepped closer. 'I'll leave a letter swearing you knew nothing about my plans, but he won't believe me.'

'He will not.' Darya gave a humourless laugh.

Behind Darya Nina could see the outline of the palm tree in the ruined conservatory. 'He might hit you, the way he hit me.'

The housekeeper shrugged. 'It wouldn't be the first time a man raised his hand against me.'

Nina shuddered. Sometimes she wondered if it wouldn't have been better to let Papa kill himself when he wanted to. 'Aunt Elena has a purse of roubles waiting. She says she can find you another position in town and that you must go to her when you're ready. Had Mamma lived, this would have been your home until you died. Aunt Elena says she'll help you, as you helped my mother and have helped me.'

There was silence between them for a few moments, then Darya said, 'My brother works on the railway and is often away. His wife's not strong and I know they'd welcome me in their house. When the world changes, Nina Andreyevna, we women must change with it: that is how God tests us.' She took her hand. 'Come, we'll collect the eggs together for the last time. Cook will be waiting.'

At dawn, Nina dressed then tiptoed down the hall to Leila's room. She'd packed a leather travelling case last night, choosing, with Darya's advice, some mementoes for herself and Katya from amongst Mamma's belongings and photographs. Leila had been busy with Mrs Kulmana and Nina wished to avoid her anyway, fearing she'd be implicated in her plans. Now she left a small package outside Leila's door: in it was a note and the pink perfume bottle Mamma had given her for her eleventh birthday.

Then she went on to the morning room and locked the door from inside.

Her hands shook as she pulled the commonplace book from behind the cherubs. If Papa came in and found her he'd beat her. He'd roar she was a thief and would lock her away for ever so she could never escape. The thought made her feel faint with fear. She shouldn't have come back to the farm; Richard hadn't wanted her to come at all. But Papa isn't here, she admonished herself. You know he isn't.

She knelt in front of the safe and, for the first time in her life, tried turning the dial. It barely moved at first, but then she felt it roll under her fingers as she followed the numbers Mamma had carefully copied into the back of her book. 'Don't tell Papa I've written them here,' Mamma had said, playfully putting her fingers to her lips, 'but I can never remember the combination.' It was Papa, however, who had a terrible memory – her mother had wanted Nina to know how to open the safe.

There was a faint click and she pulled the heavy door open. She'd decided during the night that if the jewels were gone but there was money she'd take that instead. It wasn't as if Papa would be left with nothing. There was still Mamma's parents' house in Petersburg – it was rented out to a family but could be sold – and here on the estate there was the furniture, which was valuable, and the china and chandeliers, as well as the silver.

The safe was a mass of documents and papers. Impatiently, she pushed the bundles aside, peering into the depths with a sick feeling in her stomach. Had she left it too late? Was that what Papa had gone to Petersburg for, to sell the jewels? Angrily she blinked away tears: he had no right, Mamma had left them for her. But then she saw something, the corner of a box. Miracle of miracles, they were still there, all three jewellery boxes, tied together with pink ribbon. 'Thank you, Mamma,' she rested her forehead against the edge of the safe, 'thank you.'

'These will one day be yours,' Mamma had said, untying the ribbon and opening the first of the boxes to reveal the pearls she'd worn to the Mariinsky Theatre. Nina pulled the top box out now, pushing back the ribbon and opening the satin-covered case. The pearls gleamed in the faint light. She touched them with the tips of her fingers then quickly opened the others: the diamond earrings and necklace were there, and the emerald necklace and brooch. 'Thank you,' she whispered again.

Pushing the safe door shut she got up off her knees. She was shaking all over, not with fear now but relief. It wouldn't matter to Richard if she had no dowry, he'd convinced her of that, but Darya was right, she didn't wish to be a pauper. Nor could she bear to think that Papa had succeeded in robbing her of everything. She pushed the three boxes into the leather bag and placed the brief letter she'd written to her father under a glass paperweight on the desk.

Darya was waiting outside the kitchen door. The housekeeper took the bag in her left hand, and Nina's hand in her right, and together they walked silently down the steps and across the lawn towards the drive. There'd been a light frost and the grass was hard underfoot, their breath hanging in the air in front of them. A dog set up a desultory barking as their boots crunched along the gravel.

Once she would never have believed that she could leave her home and not even glance back. But she didn't. 'Don't look back,' Darya had advised last night, 'and when I leave I won't look back either. Look to the future, not to the past.' There was no going back; Richard was her future.

As they came to the crossroads Darya sighed audibly in relief at the sight of Aunt Elena's carriage. Nina, however, had never doubted that Richard would be there, just as she didn't doubt they would keep the promises they'd made to each other in her aunt's garden. They would always trust each other and she, unlike Mamma, would never have to lie to her husband. By lunchtime they would be married and by early evening they'd be on the train that would take them away from Russia.

Richard jumped out when he saw them coming and caught her up in his arms, laughing with delight. 'I've been worried sick in case your father came home early.'

Darya passed the bag in to Aunt Elena's maid then turned to face him.

'This is Darya Fyodorovna,' Nina said.

He held out his hand. 'It is an honour to meet you.'

Darya glanced sideways at Nina then took his hand.

'He says it is an honour to meet you,' Nina told her in Russian.

'An honour?' She snorted, but looked pleased all the same.

'What do you think?' Nina asked, a lump coming to her throat.

Darya gave Richard an appraising look. 'It's a pity he isn't Russian, but you could have done worse.' Then she pulled Nina into her arms and held her hard before kissing her forehead. 'Now go, Ninochka. You and I will not meet again in this world, but wherever you are know this: that every day I will pray to St Paraskeva for you and for Katya and for your dear mamma. We will meet again in heaven.'

Seven

Brighton, 1913

A month after Nina and Richard were married they arrived in Brighton, where they took a room in the Royal Albion Hotel. The room, overlooking the seafront and the Palace Pier, had red-and-gold-striped wallpaper and heavy satin curtains to match. On a table under the window stood a tall cut-glass vase full of pale green winter lilies.

'What did you say?' Richard demanded as he held her high in the air. Looking down like this, her husband's hair was a ruby halo and the tails of his white shirt, starched by the *laveuse* in the hotel in Paris, budding wings. 'Tell me!' He tossed her again and the room swayed, not unpleasantly.

'The sea. It sounds like a man. Like a man breathing.' She had lain awake for hours last night, listening to it.

'You're getting drunk up there on the gaslight but I refuse to let you down until you say why you agreed to marry me.'

'Because I wished to leave Russia.' Which was the truth.

'Yes. But why else?'

'Because you danced better than the other Englishmen.'

'Excellent!'

That evening they waltzed the length of the Palace Pier, their feet sliding over sand and grit. Despite the new clothes she'd bought in Paris, Nina still insisted on wearing Katya's old fur coat: England mightn't be as cold as Russia but the cold here crept in deeper, and her bones felt chilled.

'It smells of old dogs.' Richard rubbed his damp cheek against her collar. 'It smells like the stag hounds my grandmother used to keep.'

A group of boys followed as they danced, clapping and singing 'You made me love you' and 'Hold your hand out, you naughty boy'. At the end of the pier Richard threw a handful of pennies to them, and in the coloured lights the copper coins flashed, transformed into gold. Some vanished between the boards and the smallest of the boys wailed like a tin whistle.

Nina had expected Brighton to be another Nice, but the English resort was nothing like its French counterpart. In Nice, the social life of Katya and her circle was made up of luncheon or dinner parties, combined with visits to the painting colony in Antibes or, more usually, the casino at Monte Carlo. In Brighton, however, there was constant public entertainment, and although the season was officially over there were still donkey rides along the front and Italian organ grinders with their green-coated monkeys on street corners. Pierrots performed on the two piers and minstrels, with striped blazers and blackened faces, played banjos on the lower promenade. At her first sight of the minstrels Nina thought they were real African Negroes and was appalled, hanging back on Richard's arm as they rolled their white-circled eyes at her. Richard squeezed her arm and whispered in amusement, 'It's paint, Nina, paint. It's called "blacking up". That's why they're known as white coons. Do you see?' All she saw was that they were grotesque.

There were theatres on both piers and others throughout the town, which members of every social group attended regularly. *It is like being on holiday every day*, she wrote to Katya on a postcard of the Royal Pavilion. *Mamma would have hated Brighton but – despite myself – I suspect I shall enjoy it.* She didn't say much more because she knew Katya was no longer enjoying Nice; or rather she wasn't enjoying married life there. They'd spent a week with Katya's family en route to England and Nina had been startled by the physical change in her sister. Ivan hadn't changed at all, still assuming the style of the young gallant officer, whereas Katya, her hair hennaed and wired in the French manner, appeared far older than her twenty-one years. It wasn't that she'd lost her beauty, but her beauty had acquired what Richard described as 'a bruised look'.

In Nice Ivan had taken the lease on a large but run-down house on a hill overlooking the town. Inside, the rooms were gloomy with dark wallpaper and worn carpets but the garden, wild and neglected – for they could only afford a gardener one day a week – was magical and reminded Nina of the imaginary painted garden she'd grown up with. A gravel path, winding between olive trees and exotic flowering shrubs, led to a greenhouse that contained orchids the colour of blood and deep pits in which the gardener had successfully grown pineapples during the summer. Thirty years ago a famous botanist had owned the house and planted specimens brought from all around the world. An enormous, sprawling monkey-puzzle tree shaded a small summerhouse; nearby was another strange tree with grey-green leaves, and when Nina ran her hand across its pink bark she found it as spongy and soft as thick blotting paper. Katya had been told it was a eucalyptus. Behind the summerhouse there was a black marble fountain with chipped lions, and two fishponds, golden carp hanging in the green water.

On their arrival they'd had tea in the gloomy parlour, then Katya quickly ushered them outside. When they came to the ponds, Nina clapped in delight but Katya frowned. 'I don't trust the nurses, their heads are full of nonsense and I worry every day that my babies will drown.' She stirred the surface with a stick. 'In the summer the water stinks and there are swarms of mosquitoes; we'll all contract malaria.' Catching sight of the look Nina exchanged with Richard, Katya pulled a wry smile. 'You're like an old married couple already. I'm full of worries, I know, but my worries aren't without reason.'

A narrow path led down a slope from the ponds and at the bottom they came to a gap between the cypress trees where they were confronted with a view of the town and the sea. 'The sea!' Nina had seen it in paintings and photographs but could never have guessed at its immensity. It stretched out, further than the eye could follow.

'All the way to Africa,' Richard murmured. There were boats of different sizes with white and brown sails and, on the horizon, something that looked like a mere dot but which Richard insisted was an ocean liner.

She loved the sea. 'I'd come here every morning. I'd bring my coffee and stand here and watch the sea.'

'You get the same view from the top windows of the house,' Katya observed, 'although I barely notice it now. When I first saw it, though, I remember feeling the same.'

After supper, Richard and Ivan retired to Ivan's study and Katya helped Nina hang some of the clothes they'd purchased in Paris. 'Exquisite,' Katya murmured, fingering the coral tailor-made jacket and skirt. 'It's so beautifully cut, it will suit you perfectly.'

'That's what Richard said. He said the narrow style suits tall women.' She didn't tell her sister that the outfit, by Jean Patou, had cost the equivalent of thirty guineas. It was the most expensive item they'd bought but Richard had insisted she have it. 'Thirty guineas is enormously expensive,' he agreed, 'horribly expensive! But we didn't have to spend anything on a wedding gown; there weren't even any guests to feed. You must have the Jean Patou, Nina, it would be a crime not to. It was designed for you.'

Katya sighed. 'I've been a fool in my choice of a husband, and Mamma was the same. You, Nina, have shown more sense. I can see Richard is kind and that's unusual, I think, in a man.'

It was true that Richard was as kind as a woman friend would be. Her cheeks burned as she remembered their second morning in the hotel in Paris, how he'd scratched at the door and come through to find her in floods of tears.

'Oh, Nina,' he'd taken her hands in his, 'what is it? Do you miss Darya?'

She didn't know what to do. She hadn't brought anything with her, hadn't thought, and would have to tear up a petticoat.

'Nina?'

She shook her head, unable to catch her breath. She'd never been so ashamed. He put his arm around her shoulder and as he did so she felt him stiffen slightly. He'd seen it, she knew, the bloodied sheet.

After a moment he said, 'Nina, it's all right, I understand. I have a sister, remember? It's perfectly natural and I know these things can happen.' He hesitated then whispered in her ear, 'There's no need to be frightened. Is it your first time?'

She shook her head violently. 'No. But I have nothing with me, no . . .' She couldn't bring herself to say 'rags'.

'What? Oh, I see. That's no problem.' He kissed her awkwardly on the cheek. 'I'll get something for you. Have a bath, it will make you feel better. I'll be back soon.'

When she got out of the bath there was a brown paper parcel on her bed. Inside were three packets of thick cotton pads and something that looked like a short corset with loops at the front and back. There were also some brown paper bags. It took her a minute to understand, but then relief and gratitude flooded through her: you didn't have to wash anything, the pads could be put in a bag and thrown away.

'I wish I'd never got married,' Katya was saying now. She gave a small shrug, like a real Frenchwoman, as she took a coat hanger from the wardrobe. 'Except, of course, for my babies.'

While Katya helped Nina unpack, Ivan was asking Richard for money. Richard revealed this later as they prepared for bed. 'He suggested I might like to invest a sizeable sum in his ailing business. This was before we'd finished the first cigar. Approaches like that are usually kept until the end of the evening and at least three brandies. I made a suitable excuse.'

'No!' Coming out from behind the screen, Nina hugged her gown around her, furious that Ivan could humiliate her sister like this. 'Katya would die if she knew.'

'I suspect that there's a good deal your sister doesn't know.'

Katya, however, had no illusions about her husband. 'He has other women,' she told Nina matter-of-factly two days later, 'which doesn't make me unhappy, as I no longer love him, if I ever did. No, what worries me more is that he's also *un imbécile* when it comes to business.'

On their first morning in Nice they went down to the town. As it was blustery, Katya advised they remain in the carriage but Nina would have preferred to walk: there were palm trees all along the promenade and the sea swelled and moved and had a smell of its own. She put her head out of the carriage window and felt sea spray for the first time, as she gazed towards the horizon. Africa. Maybe that was where Katya was destined to go: Darya had said she'd travel to a foreign country a long way away. Where could be more foreign, or further away, than Africa? She felt a momentary stab of sadness at the thought of Katya leaving, then found herself smiling at the clumsy antics of a bird caught in a gust of wind. The bird, she knew, was a seagull: she recognised it from Miss Brenchley's books. When she pulled her head back inside Richard smiled at her and she knew she was happy. Only a few weeks ago she had thought it possible she'd never be happy again.

Katya only seemed truly happy when she was with her children. The twins, Marina and Sofia, had thick black curls and ran on sturdy legs, babbling to each other in what sounded like a secret language but was actually a mixture of Russian and French. They plucked at the mother-of-pearl buttons on Nina's new blouses and shrieked with delight when Richard swung them by their hands.

'He'll make a good father,' Katya observed, adding in a low voice, 'I hope you don't fall pregnant too soon, although that's not a matter for us but God.' There was no need to come up with a reply, however, as the baby, Irina, started to bawl from her cot and Katya got up wearily to admonish the young nurse.

Ivan and Katya attended church, and on the Sunday morning Nina and Richard went with them. The Russian community in Nice was wealthy and no expense had been spared on the building, which was a mixture of pink brick and grey marble. 'Stunning,' Richard announced, looking up at the gold domes. Nina privately thought that, compared with the Petersburg churches, it was rather small. 'Is it smaller than the Russian churches in England?' she asked him.

Ivan heard this and grunted. 'There are no Russian churches in England.'

Nina hadn't been to church for a long time, and the thick smell of wax and incense made her feel slightly faint. On the column beside her was an icon of an angel with outspread wings, its left arm raised, though whether in greeting or as a warning she couldn't decide. She'd told Richard about her angel. 'It seemed very real.' She'd had to search for words. 'It seemed – I don't know – to be a *truth*.'

'Cocaine!' he'd laughed. 'My dear wife, will you never cease to amaze me? We'll have to find you a Chinese opium den when we get to London.'

The angel, she realised, wasn't an experience you could readily share.

'How long does the service go on for?' he whispered now beside her.

She saw Katya smile and knew she was remembering Miss Brenchley, who always used to sit at the back with the old ladies – being brought up in the Church of England didn't prepare you for standing through a service lasting over three hours.

'You can walk around the back of the church, or outside, no one will mind.'

Richard did go for a short walk and the service finished soon after he got back. People stood on the white stone steps, talking in the sunshine, and Katya introduced Nina and Richard to her friends. There were curious looks and Nina wondered if news of her elopement could have reached this far; probably not, but there was a sharp interest in the sudden appearance of Katya's younger sister and her English husband.

'Yes, we're very recently married,' she informed one of the more inquisitive matrons. 'We're on our honeymoon.'

The evening before they returned to Paris, Katya purposefully walked Nina around the garden. 'Make sure you keep some of Mamma's jewels for yourself,' she said in a hushed voice. 'Ivan started to sell my share when we arrived and soon there'll be nothing left.' She hesitated. 'If Richard suggests you sell yours, say they're all you have left of Mamma and that it would break your heart to part with them.'

Nina and Richard had left the jewellery cases in a bank in Paris and would put them in another bank when they arrived in England. 'You must keep your dowry intact,' Richard had said. 'It's yours and should be kept safe.' He smiled. 'If we ever fall on hard times we'll know where it is.'

Nina wondered if she should have brought the jewellery with her and offered some of it, the emeralds perhaps, to Katya. But when she said this to Richard he was vehemently against it. 'No! Your brother-in-law would take them from her and throw good money after bad. They're not in danger of starving just yet and I'm loath to help Ivan. Tell Katya that should she and the children ever seriously need our assistance, we'll do what we can.'

Richard had written to his mother from Paris to tell her he was married, and on the couple's arrival in Brighton an angry letter from Cheltenham awaited them. Why was his mother so cross,

Nina wondered – Richard said she'd been desperate for him to marry for years. In his letter from Paris he'd said he was extremely happy and that Nina came from a good family, with a large estate. She sat in the window of the hotel room, re-reading Mrs Truelove's letter, and again found herself frowning over a heavily underlined sentence, _Who is she?_ What could it mean?

She looked over to where Richard was reading _The Times_. 'I don't understand what your mother means when she writes, "Who is she?" You told her who I am.'

He grimaced. 'What she means is that she's mightily put out because she can't look you up in _Burke's_.'

'_Burke's_? What is _Burke's_?'

'It's where you look people up, to see who they are . . .' He lifted his hands helplessly in the air. 'I can't even begin to explain. But what it does mean is that we won't be expected to make an appearance in Cheltenham immediately and so can spend our time more fruitfully here, looking for somewhere to live.'

She put away her mother-in-law's letter and re-read the letter from Richard's sister, Anne. _My dear brother, Your news has taken us very much by surprise. A letter from Paris to say you have married in Russia! I am, of course, delighted for you and look forward to meeting Nina_ . . . The tone was polite but cautious. When she'd pointed this out to Richard he'd shrugged.

'Anne has never managed to wriggle out from under my mother's thumb. I do believe there's hope for her, it's just that things are complicated . . .'

Everything about the English was complicated; it wasn't so much that they were cold, but there always seemed to be – she didn't know what it was – a nervous tension about them. The tension had been there in Miss Brenchley but Nina had grown up thinking this was an idiosyncrasy of her spinster governess: she hadn't expected to find it en masse. Indeed, there was much about England that was unexpected. She'd thought it would all be very familiar, which it was; but it was the fact that it was so familiar and yet, at the same time, so foreign which was disconcerting. It was like looking at a well-known face through a flawed piece of glass so that the perspectives were slightly skewed. Or like the time when she was six years old and had had conjunctivitis in her left eye. She had to wear an eye patch and it was difficult to judge distances; instead of running up and down the veranda steps with barely a look she had found herself clinging to the handrail and feeling for the next step with her toe. Every day in England she felt she had to feel with her toe.

She looked back at her sister-in-law's letter. Richard had shown her photographs of Anne in an album; although there were similarities between brother and sister, Anne's face was thinner, her lips pinched, and Nina had been reminded of Mamma talking about the Streshnev family and how the eldest, Leo, had been endowed with all the good looks, leaving none for his younger sisters. 'They are spiteful,' Mamma had declared, 'because they are plain. It is unfair of a brother to take all the beauty.' In the photographs in Richard's album Anne wasn't plain, but at the same time she wasn't beautiful in the way that Richard was handsome, and maybe, Nina thought, that explained her pinched expression.

For the previous three years Richard had rented a bachelor apartment, which was entirely unsuitable for a married couple and was, anyway, currently occupied by his good friend Charles. Charles, an amiable, pink-faced banker, kissed Nina's cheeks in the French fashion and presented them with a grand silver platter as a wedding present. Richard was expected back at work the next week so they threw themselves into looking for a furnished house to rent. The Brighton houses were nowhere near as fine as Nina was used to: decorated in the English style, they were austere in comparison with Russian townhouses. Each one they saw was impossible for a different reason, but then they came across a property in a square overlooking the West Pier. At the end of a terrace, it was smaller than some of the other houses they'd seen. However, the peacock-blue drawing room on the first floor was well proportioned, with elaborate plasterwork, a white marble fireplace and a bay window encrusted with salt from which there was a clear view over the central lawn to the sea.

'I like it,' Nina said as Richard came into the room. 'While you're at your office I can sit and watch the pier and the waves.' They'd walked to the end of the West Pier on their way here; it was more elegant than the Palace Pier, and this morning a flag flew jauntily from the end.

He sat in the window next to her, twirling his hat in his hands. 'I had a quick look out the back and it's fairly private. According to the owner the next two houses have elderly occupants who've lived here for donkey's years and are seldom to be seen. And you're right about the view, I've always thought it's a pity to live close to the sea and not be able to see it. Let's take it, shall we?'

There was no question of Nina loving a room in her new house in the way Mamma had loved the morning room – this was not that sort of house and in a few years they would move to something larger. All the same, it wasn't an unattractive dwelling and the main bedroom had pretty walnut furniture, pink wallpaper and apple-green satin curtains. The window overlooked a small, neat garden with a single pear tree, which belonged to the house behind. A door from the bedroom led to a dressing room, in which there was a folding bed. On the ground floor, the dining room at the back had blue walls and a heavy oak table and sideboard, while the parlour at the front had emerald wallpaper, a large leather settle and a stitched rug from Persia the colour of rubies.

Despite the house being amply furnished, there were still essential purchases to be made: a yellow Wedgwood tea set, crystal vases, linen tablecloths and napkins, a sprigged Liberty shawl for the drawing room sofa, carved ivory bowls from India. Most of these purchases were made in London.

'You'll love London,' Richard had assured her, 'once you get to know it. It's not as immediately beautiful as Paris or St Petersburg, I agree, but it has an energy and grandeur beyond that of any city I've encountered.'

Nina, however, found London a great disappointment. It was true there were amazing sights so that at moments she could almost believe she was in a city of the future, with the moving escalators, the tube train and the elaborate illuminated window displays of Selfridge's. But at the same time the streets had a bewildering, medieval feel. She was disgusted by how dirty the pavements were and everywhere there was a din: street vendors competed with the sounds of motor cars, bicyclists, wagons, horse-drawn omnibuses. Miss Brenchley had described Bucking-ham Palace and Tower Bridge but hadn't thought to mention there were filthy beggars sleeping in doorways and that the stench of petrol fumes and horse dung was overpowering. And the fog! There were days when it was so thick it was impossible to see across the street; her eyes stung and when she washed her face at night the water was grey.

'You'll find all the world in London,' Richard said staunchly, escorting her to a menagerie in Shadwell which sold wild animals as pets: there were monkeys, snakes, even a leopard. In Whitechapel she spoke Russian with the wary Jewish émigrés who ran the street stalls, and in Soho, which was known as 'Little Paris', they ate at Maxim's. But while French food was all the rage in the expensive restaurants, and French couture was advertised in the smaller shops, everything in the bigger depart-ment stores was 'Russian'. London society had fallen under the spell of Stravinsky and Diaghilev's *Ballets Russes* and Liberty's advertised a 'New Russian Collection' in its windows. The walls of the gallery where its famous materials were sold exhibited designs for the stage and the dancers' costumes – brilliantly coloured drawings and sketches by artists Nina had never heard of: Natalia Gontcharova, Leon Bakst, Georges Barbier. She looked at them in wonder: Dancing Girls, Orientals, Cleopatra's Slaves, A Yellow Fairy, An Odalisque, Baba Yaga the Witch, A Beautiful Daughter, The Old Countess, A Tightrope Walker . . .

'I think they're very good really, don't you?' Richard asked. He was peering at the tightrope walker.

'Beautiful! The colours are so strong, so modern.' But after the theatrical designs there were fashion sketches from English magazines. *The Harem Skirt*, a caption read: *In vivid, oriental colours a narrow skirt is worn over trousers gathered at the ankles in the Russian style, known in Paris as* Modernisme Oriental. *What is savage and primitive is tamed by high fashion.*

It would have been funny if it hadn't been so ridiculous. 'These are theatre designs,' she said to Richard. 'Nobody in Russia dresses like this. Don't they know that?'

He fingered the brim of his hat. 'Well of course . . .'

Turning from him she glared at the sign. '"Savage and primitive": is that what English people think of Russia?' It was outrageous. 'Savage and primitive' from a people who, though they thought themselves so civilised, were more riddled with taboos than any African tribe! Richard was always warning her about things she should – or usually should not – mention. 'Be careful what you say to Mrs So-and-So'; 'An Englishwoman would not be expected to mention "x" . . .'

'I think,' he was saying, 'that Russia is such an immense country that . . .'

'Come,' she said abruptly, 'let's look at the materials.'

The materials were as wonderful as she'd expected and her anger cooled as she fingered silks and velvets amid the sharp hiss of scissors and the heavy thuds as bales were unwound. Unexpectedly, she came across the stuff of Dr Vilensky's waistcoat and for a moment had to grip the edge of the table, conscious only of the smell of pus, and two ivory buttons of bone. The moment quickly passed, however, and she made herself run her fingertips across the blue and green pattern before moving on to a rose velour.

After the materials she looked at silk and satin underwear, Richard discreetly hanging back. There were petticoats in blue, pink and even yellow satin, and the new French *brassières*. In the millinery department large-brimmed hats were trimmed with bird of paradise feathers.

'Your Miss Brenchley would like these,' Richard said.

She tried on a hat in emerald velvet and caught her breath as she turned to the mirror and found Mamma's eyes staring sadly back at her.

The pink house gradually filled with sand and the sour-sweet smell of seaweed.

'You're sure you're not lonely?' Richard would ask when he left for the office in the mornings, and when she replied she had been invited out to lunch or tea he would say, 'That isn't what I meant, you know that.'

What he meant was, was she missing Russia?

She missed Russia terribly, all the time, but that didn't mean she wanted to go back there. Because the truth was that the Russia she missed no longer existed. The Russia she missed was a happy, laughing place where Mamma called from the veranda

87

and Katya took her by the hand. 'Come down to the stream, Nina. Darya has given us bread to feed the fish.'

Russia was a memory, a dream.

'Is there anything we can do,' Richard asked as Christmas neared, 'to make it feel like a Russian Christmas?'

'Christmas died in our house when Mamma died,' she said. 'And anyway,' she patted his sleeve, 'there is not enough snow.' She enjoyed herself decorating a tree with sparkling glass balls and filling the fruit bowls with oranges punctured with cloves and shrunken apples with polished, waxy skins.

Relations with Cheltenham were still frosty, so they had Christmas dinner with the family of one of Richard's colleagues. Compared with the Christmases of her childhood it was a very poor thing, with little sense of celebration.

The youngest of the children, a girl of five with blonde curls, asked Nina what Christmas was like in Russia. 'Are there carols?'

'People sing *kolyadki* – songs which are very old.'

'Do the children get presents?'

'The children look forward to the arrival of Babushka, the grandmother who gives them presents.'

'Oh,' the child pouted. 'That sounds strange. I don't think I'd like that.'

Her mother waved her away.

At home in the evenings they had supper, then smoked Turkish cigarettes that smelt of liquorice. Richard often went out later on and she'd continue to sit and read in front of the fire, wrapped in his blue satin smoking jacket and drinking thick, sugary Turkish coffee, or tea from the silver samovar which Charles had found for her in the back of a curio shop.

In the mornings she was usually awake long before Richard, reading by the bedroom window that overlooked the empty garden. Although it was neatly kept she'd only seen someone in it once, a bent old man fishing about at the base of the pear tree with a walking stick. She'd tapped at the glass but he either ignored her or didn't hear.

'I don't know how you do it.' Richard would yawn as he came through from the dressing room.

'I've never slept much.'

'Never?' his eyes narrow with sleep and admiration.

'Not even as a baby.' Which, of course, was completely untrue. It had been a family joke that Darya had to sprinkle her with water to wake her. But it was true that since Mamma's death she'd only cat-napped.

In the letter she'd left for Papa she'd said she couldn't be a nurse and had fallen in love with a man who was a gentleman, and honourable, and that they were going to be married in Moscow. She'd said this in case her father returned early and telegraphed the border to have her stopped. When she arrived in Brighton she'd written telling him the truth. *I am well*, she'd said, *and happy in England. My husband is a good man and Mamma would have liked him.* She didn't receive a reply and didn't plan to write again. Katya had also written to Papa and not heard back; although that was unlikely to grieve her, as she had more pressing things to worry about, being pregnant with her fourth child. *I pray to God*, she wrote to Nina, *that my fate is not yours. I am weary all the time and the midwife says I have exhausted my strength having the children in such quick succession. But what is one to do?*

'She could be more careful,' Richard gave an unexpected frown, either of distaste or disapproval, as Nina read the letter aloud over breakfast, 'even if she is living in a Catholic country. Most people today show some sense.' Nina ate her toast and wondered what Catholicism had to do with it. 'Catholics and Jews,' she could remember Cook shivering and making the sign of the cross in a lump of dough, 'animals. A decent woman isn't safe from either of them.'

Once a month there was a cream parchment envelope from Aunt Elena. *I hear*, her handwriting looped across the page, *that your father is in good health and the hospital is now taking patients, although I shall never see it because I will never again visit the home I grew up in. Andrei blames me for your marriage and sees no fault in his own conduct. I shudder for his future.* Darya had left the farm the day after Papa's return. *He said she should have stopped you and struck her across the face, splitting her lip and loosening a tooth. On her arrival here I gave her the purse, for which she was grateful, and arranged a seat for her in*

89

a wagon so she could go to her brother, who works on the Trans-Siberian railway.

Early in the New Year, Elena sent on a simple letter written on Darya's behalf by her nephew. She was living happily with her brother's family and was glad to be away from the estate. Every day she went to the market where the vegetables were of an excellent quality although the local butchers all deserved to be flogged as thieves. She hoped Nina was well and remembered to boil the English water. She had put her mark at the bottom of the letter and Nina ran her fingers across it, silently cursing the stupidity of the nephew, who'd failed to include a return address.

Nina wrote to her governess in Persia and Miss Brenchley replied, congratulating her on her marriage ('a necessary escape' was how she phrased it). Her pupil, Angela Mooney, continued to do well, although they had been to a camel race the day before and this had left the poor child tired and over-excited. *I must confess I wasn't much interested in attending the race myself as I suspected that it would prove to be extremely hot and noisy. A moment before it began, however, I was amply rewarded, for I happened to look overhead only to see the most glorious falcon!*

Nina sometimes thought about writing to Leila and maybe sending her a present. But that would risk getting her friend into trouble with Papa and Mrs Kulmana, so she didn't do it.

The business Richard worked for had its main office in Brighton but there was also another, smaller, office near the docks in London, and he often travelled up to town two or three times a week. Sometimes Nina would meet him there for lunch, or they would stay for the weekend at a hotel and attend the latest plays. She loved these visits to London, not because of London itself but because of the fun she and Richard had together. She would put on one of the pretty dresses he had helped her choose – he had a good eye for what suited her and enjoyed having a say in choosing her clothes – and she would come into the room and hold out her skirts. 'Well?'

'Hmm,' he stroked his chin, 'the skirt – is it cut right? What's it like when you turn around?'

She would twirl on the spot and he would break into applause. 'Perfection!'

They saw all the latest plays including Lydia Yavorska in *Anna Karenina*, but soon decided that what they preferred most were revues like *Hullo Tango!*, which they saw twice at the Hippodrome. 'I have to confess,' Richard said, 'that for me it beats the more serious things. I'm sorry if that disappoints you.' It didn't disappoint her at all. She loved going to the revues; it was like going to the circus.

The mantelpiece in the drawing room gradually filled with gilt-edged invitations to afternoon teas, Sunday luncheons, dinner parties. At first these invitations daunted her. In fact when the very first came she burst into tears.

'Oh, Nina,' Richard had said, looking perplexed as he waved the invitation to afternoon tea at a Mrs Smith's in his hand, 'it's only tea. You've been to lots of afternoon teas in Russia and I don't expect it will be that much different. I'd come, my dear, but,' he shrugged, 'well, it would look odd.'

Of course she'd been to teas – but as a child, not as a married woman. And in Russia, not in England. How would she make the sort of conversation Mamma had made? Mamma was always so amusing and clever, making witty comments about books, people, the news. The day before the tea Nina read carefully through all the newspapers, so that Richard laughed and said she was like a student swatting for an exam.

'Mrs Smith will not expect you to be abreast of the latest in current affairs,' he said. 'I can assure you of that.' She ignored him and continued reading.

When he got home the following night, he called to Nina as she came down the stairs. 'How was it? Did you survive?'

She kept her face straight. 'It was terrible.'

'Oh, darling,' his own face fell, 'I'm so sorry.'

'Terribly boring,' she laughed. 'We talked about nothing but the weather!'

That, however, wasn't completely true, as Mrs Smith had also discussed her children, and at one stage took Nina up to the nursery to meet her two youngest daughters, who turned out to be aged twelve and thirteen. The elder of the pair, a short, plump girl with auburn hair to her waist, made a pretty curtsey as they came in, then went back to playing dolls with her sister. Nina had felt her cheeks flush: what would these people say if they knew her true age? She had felt nervous as she went back downstairs, as if the women sipping their tea might all look up and suddenly know her for what she was, but as she passed a mirror in the hall her confidence came back – the face looking back at her was that of a young married woman, not a child. She remembered Aunt Elena's words as they stood at the top of Low Field, watching the ducks make their way to the stream: 'What you've been through has made you older'. It was true. She had gone from childhood to adulthood, avoiding that in-between stage in which the girl upstairs now existed. She regretted the events that had caused this but could no longer imagine herself sitting in a nursery playing with dolls.

Soon there was a flood of invitations, mainly from the wives and mothers of Richard's Brighton colleagues. These women were, on the whole, kind, but Nina couldn't help but notice that they were at a slight loss in the face of her height and foreignness. For her own part she watched them carefully, finding everything they did to be familiar but at the same time slightly different – how they held a fork, drank their tea, sat in a chair.

'Is there something wrong with the way I walk?' she asked Richard one day.

'The way you walk?'

'Yes.'

He looked puzzled. 'What do you mean?'

'Yesterday afternoon, after tea at Mrs Young's, we went for a walk along the front and Mrs Sayles said to me, "I must ask you to slow down, Mrs Truelove, I cannot keep up with your *stride*." And they all looked at each other.'

'Ah yes,' he nodded, 'English women – or at least, middle-class English women – do tend to walk quite slowly.'

'So you think I walk too quickly.'

He laughed. 'I don't think so, no. But Mrs Young and Mrs Sayles are probably not great walkers and might find it difficult to keep up with you.'

They thought she walked like a servant, or a man, and she thought they walked like grandmothers. Why didn't they simply bind their feet?

English women's conversations were also different from those of Russian women: there were all those 'taboos' to start with, so that at the end of one of these gatherings she would have been hard put to say what had actually been talked about. She often sensed that she was somehow misunderstanding what *was* being said, even when it was very simple. It was hard to describe exactly what she meant, but when she said something about it to Richard he waved his arms enthusiastically.

'But my dear, I thought you understood! That's the whole point about English conversation. It's not so much what is said as what is not said; although *how* it is not said is also important. For example, with my clients I worry not when they're being lukewarm in their response but when they're being over-friendly. That's when you know they're planning a deal with someone else. Does that help?'

It didn't help at all; it was terribly confusing. Sometimes one of the women would, cautiously, enquire about her previous life in Russia and she would paint the estate as it had been: the latticework still in place, the lilacs lining the drive, the flower beds not yet dug over for vegetables. On one occasion she went further, sketching the conservatory with the palm tree as well, but on looking up she caught the eyebrows of a peevish woman, the sister of a senior partner in Richard's firm, arched in disbelief. For a moment she was tempted to go on – defiantly adding the sea-shells stepped on by the Empress Eugenie, the white bird that had flown over mountains and sea to bring the seed all the way from Africa – but she had Richard to think of so sipped her sour tea instead.

And, maybe because England was such a small country, they had no idea of the size or diversity of Russia. When she told them her maiden name they believed she *must* be related to the ballerina Tamara Platonovna Karsavina, and would *of course* have met Nijinsky! They seemed to think of Russia as if it were the size of a London suburb, with everyone knowing everyone else.

At first she was also sought after by two other Brighton 'sets'. The 'smart set' – Richard carefully explained the nuances – wore the latest fashions, affecting tight elbow-length silk gloves, even while eating, and had extravagantly coiffed hair. However they did not go as far as the most daringly fashionable women in Nice

– who Nina had seen at the Casino Ruhl wearing evening gowns with stringless day bonnets, and court shoes with long pointed toes. But as Nina pointed out to Richard, her hair was an obvious disappointment, as she stubbornly continued to wear it smooth and simply pinned back, and after a couple of invitations she was abruptly 'dropped'. Richard presented her with a cartoon of herself, with curly wires at angles all over her head.

The 'fast set' also showed an initial interest. The fact that she was Russian was enough to attract their attention, although it was cards rather than culture that absorbed them. They played regularly, particularly 'auction bridge' which, Nina soon discovered, had originally been introduced to England as 'Russian whist'. They invited her expecting some expertise, but Nina knew nothing at all, for Mamma had thought card games boring, an amusement for old ladies. When it became obvious she had little inclination and even less aptitude, the invitations ceased.

Shortly after they moved into the house on the square, Richard had taken her to meet his employer, Mr Lewisham, who lived in a grand house on King's Gardens. 'Mrs Truelove,' a damp silver moustache crawled across her hand, 'I cannot tell you what a pleasure this is. I've been saying to Richard for years that a man in his position, and with such a name after all!' he laughed at his own joke, 'needs to be, nay *must be*, married. But I never expected him to produce such an exquisite flower.' Taking off his pince-nez, he dabbed at an eye with a stained linen kerchief, 'You remind me of my own dear wife.'

A portrait of the late Mrs Lewisham, a squat woman with frizzy hair, scowled at them throughout dinner. The roast beef was leathery as usual – English cooking was shockingly bad – and the talk inconsequential: what this morning's editorial in *The Times* had to say about traffic on the Thames; how it had been reported that the King and his party had bagged almost four thousand pheasants. But as she sat there, Nina felt immensely grateful that Richard and the old man could then go on to discuss zinc, tin, silver, the stuff of their business, without raising their voices or thumping the table.

They dined with Mr Lewisham, or he with them, every month, and continued to attend and give teas, luncheons and dinners.

Every day Susan, the maid, came in and they had also employed an adequate cook, Margaret. Nina still found the role of hostess worrying, however, and at times this must have showed, for after one such dinner one of the guests, a Mrs Laing, loudly announced that she intended to take Nina under her wing.

'My dear,' she said, 'you are new to Brighton and I have lived here all my life. My own daughters are married and living away so I insist you let me be of help.' From them on Mrs Laing attended most of the formal events they held, accompanied by her husband, a calm, small man, who could be counted on to engage even the dullest guest in conversation. She also took Nina to tea parties and meetings of the Women's Guild, and Nina became used to following the sweep of her mentor's skirts into a room, as if trailing in the wake of a large sea-going vessel.

This then was what they termed their 'social life'. Their real life, however, was lived at home, with frequent visits from friends like Charles, the banker, and Lawrence, a quiet, thin-faced historian who was a don at Oxford. Nina had grown up in the company of women and now found herself having to learn how to talk to men. There were no taboos with Charles, who very happily sat with her in the drawing room for hours, gossiping about Brighton personalities. But Lawrence was aloof at first, as if somehow resentful of her presence. He was a distinctive figure in a monocle and long black cape, under which he wore black patent-leather shoes and the tie of his college, Brasenose, with a diamond pin. His reserve vanished, however, when he saw her growing collection of books on the shelves in the parlour and realised she read what he called 'serious literature'. He introduced her to Thomas Hardy's poetry and recommended she read anything by D. H. Lawrence.

Since coming to England Nina had started reading Russian authors as well as English ones. Mamma hadn't favoured Russian novels, describing them as 'overly emotional', and there hadn't been many on the shelves of the morning room. There was a second-hand bookshop on the Charing Cross Road however that had a couple of shelves of Russian works, and Nina followed the elderly shopkeeper's advice on what she should read next. Lawrence had read some of the same novels in translation and would quiz her on how she was finding Dostoevsky or Tolstoy in the original. She tended to agree with Mamma on both these writers, although Chekhov was a revelation. Lawrence had never heard of him and she painstakingly translated a couple of the shorter stories, for which he was extremely grateful. 'There's going to be a college in Brighton soon,' he told her, 'a branch of the University of London. They'll accept women – you should go.'

'He thinks you have what he calls "a good mind",' Richard told her later, 'and says I should hire you a tutor. I told him you were a married woman, not a schoolgirl.' Richard said this in a joking way, but Nina sensed her husband wasn't entirely pleased.

One evening Lawrence brought one of his students, David, with him. David was very pretty and, so Richard whispered to her on the stairs, wrote incomprehensible poetry, which was published in obscure avant-garde magazines. When she sat next to him in the drawing room she was surprised to see he was wearing kohl around his eyes and had a trace of rouge on his cheeks. He had a pleasant smile but he didn't say more than one or two sentences in her hearing.

Sometimes Charles and Lawrence would turn up unannounced and the four of them would raid the larder like children, piling plates high with slices of cold meat, jellied tongue, chunks of cheese and bread, and pickled onions, which had been prepared by Margaret, the cook. As often as not they picnicked in the parlour in front of the fireplace, finishing with port and Turkish cigarettes until Richard – it was usually Richard – suggested a stroll into town. At this stage of the evening Nina would retire upstairs.

The following morning, Susan the maid, who arrived at six to light the fires, would be heard crashing plates and cups together as she picked them up off the floor, muttering loudly about the way some folks did live and how it wasn't any of her business. Richard would remark to Nina, equally loudly, that as Susan was aware it wasn't her business, he did wish she would keep quiet about it. Mamma would have told her to watch her tongue; Darya would have boxed her ears. Nina did suggest this last course of action after Susan allowed the precious samovar to boil dry, causing one side to develop a dent.

'She needs her face slapped,' she hissed to Richard, who looked startled and then roared with laughter. That evening Charles joined them and Richard recounted this story with great delight. 'She's a little savage,' he straightened one of her lace cuffs, 'and would have me beating the servants like a German *hausfrau*. When I told her that if Susan lived in she'd have to have the box room in the attic, my virago here said such a room, while appropriate for a governess, was far too good for a servant and Susan could quite happily sleep on the landing. We'd have been stepping over her!'

He and Charles wept with laughter and Nina removed herself to the kitchen, where she pulled a wing off the roast chicken and ate it angrily over the table, not bothering with cutlery or a plate. They thought she was uncivilised, a peasant. It was true that in Russia a servant wouldn't be given a room of their own but it was also true that the servants were treated as part of the family. Here they hated their employers; the house was full of Susan's simmering hostility and the evil-minded complaints of Margaret. Nina couldn't do something as simple as sitting at the kitchen table with a cup of tea without the woman turning sullen. 'I'm not familiar with on-lookers, madam,' she'd said bitterly one day as Nina watched her (incompetently) preparing salted runner beans. 'None of my previous employers saw any such necessity.' Since then Nina had kept away from the kitchen.

'Sweetheart?' Richard appeared in the doorway.

She left the bones on the table in front of her and slowly licked her fingers. If he thought she was a savage she would act like one.

'Nina, you're not really cross, are you? We were only joking.'

She moved her shoulders in a shrug.

He walked to her side and dropped on to a chair, leaning his head against her chest. 'I can hear your heart.' He looked up at her, 'I do love you, Nina. You know that, don't you?'

'Oh, yes!' She took both his hands, her anger instantly forgotten. 'And I love you too!'

'I believe,' he'd said to her that morning in her aunt's garden, 'that you and I shall be the best of friends.'

And it was true, they were. He was her best friend, and her husband, and she loved him beyond measure.

Shortly after, Richard and Charles went out and she watched them from the drawing room window as they stood on the pavement, appearing to discuss which direction they should go in. Charles nodded his head in the direction of the West Pier, hung with coloured lights, but they didn't go that way and instead walked to the end of the square and turned right.

As they rounded the corner Richard glanced up and smiled, giving a small wave. She waved back. Then she went down to the parlour and began a letter to her aunt. *Just a few months ago I believed I might never be happy again. I cannot thank you enough. I am so content with Richard – we suit each other perfectly . . .*

Eight

The spring of 1914 turned into a truly glorious summer. *It is very hot*, Nina wrote to Katya, *and the sea offers the only real relief. I now have two bathing costumes (both finish above the knee!) and have been swimming on eight occasions. The first time I entered the water from one of the old-fashioned bathing machines – hideous boxes that are full of sand and smell offensive. They are pulled into the water by horses and are operated by an old woman, the 'ducking woman', who pushes the most timid of the children under the waves. I think she would have liked to 'duck' me too but I did not give her the opportunity. After that I launched myself from the beach with much better results. I have been to so many fêtes and garden parties that I have almost lost count. We all began the summer in white muslin dresses (our necks very bare, which, as I think I told you, was considered shocking at the beginning of the season but now does not raise an eyebrow. The dressmaker predicted as much). These dresses have become stained with grass marks and strawberry and orange cordial but no one seems to notice, or mind. There is a recklessness in the air, as remarkable as the heat.*

As well as fêtes and garden parties, there were flower shows, picnics, regattas; so that by the end of a week she had sometimes lost track of what she'd done at the beginning. They also had a number of dusty, exciting outings in Lawrence's new motorcar, which he regularly drove from Oxford. In July he took them to stay in Cheltenham, the three of them making a short holiday of it, going via Glastonbury, where they stayed two nights and attended a music festival. When they got to Cheltenham Lawrence left them with Mrs Truelove. This was the second time

Nina had met her mother-in-law. They had made their first visit one weekend in April, just after Nina's fifteenth birthday, and Nina had found the older woman to be crude rather than formidable. This time they were to take Richard's sister, Anne, back to Brighton with them on the train.

'You'll soon have Anne charmed,' Richard had said. 'She won't be able to resist you.' Where Richard's mother was still completely put out by Nina's existence – her utter foreignness would never be forgiven – Nina was aware that Anne, although wary, wasn't uninterested.

'She wants to like you,' Richard explained, 'but is worried because you're different. Difference doesn't dare raise its head in Cheltenham.'

'It's such a pity,' Anne frowned slightly in the late afternoon sun, 'that you don't have any photographs of your wedding. Fancy the photographer having a fatal accident on the way . . .'

Neither she nor Richard had given any thought to photographs: it had been as much as Aunt Elena could do to have sleeves stitched into the crêpe de Chine dress and to come up with a veil in time.

Nina squinted into the sun herself. They'd arrived back in Brighton earlier in the afternoon and Richard had gone straight to his office, leaving her alone with Anne for the first time. They'd done their unpacking then taken a walk along the front, followed by a stilted afternoon tea at the Royal York Hotel. They were now on the West Pier, near a group of bare-footed flower girls who were laughing and offering posies to passers-by.

'Yes,' she replied, preparing to repeat the lie she'd told the family once already, 'it was a terrible accident. There'd been a hard frost and the roads were slippery; when the horse bolted the carriage hit a tree and the photographer, poor man, was thrown straight into the water. The rivers in Russia are very fast-flowing . . .'

Mrs Truelove had querulously raised the subject of wedding photographs on Nina's first visit to Cheltenham, almost as if demanding proof that the unfortunate event had actually taken place. Nina had promptly invented the carriage accident, although it wasn't a complete invention, of course, for this was how Mamma's parents had died only a few months after she married Papa. Their carriage, complete with horse and driver, had gone through the railings of a bridge into the freezing Neva during one of the Petersburg floods. Richard knew this, and as Nina reshaped the story around the imaginary photographer, she could see him fighting to keep a straight face.

'You little minx,' he'd hissed later as they took a stroll around the Cheltenham garden. 'I thought I was going to explode!'

To hide her own smile now she looked down over the railings of the pier, to where the sea moved heavily, like a large animal, around the struts. A Russian bride, no photographs: no wonder Cheltenham was bewildered. In the garden she'd told Richard the carriage accident was the tamest thing she could think of. 'I was tempted to throw our poor photographer to the wolves!' Richard had flung his head back and roared with laughter.

'Such a pity . . .' Anne was saying again.

There was a faint hint of disapproval in her tone – maybe a carriage accident was too different, too un-English – and Nina pulled her mind back to the question of how to persuade her sister-in-law to like her. Mamma and Aunt Elena had loved each other, but that had been because their personalities were so well suited. 'Your mother is the sister I never had,' Elena would say. 'We tell each other everything.' Nina and Anne certainly weren't kindred spirits, but it would be a challenge to make Richard's sister admire her – in fact it would be her project for the coming weeks. How would Mamma have gone about it? Everyone liked Mamma. As she thought this she remembered Darya saying, 'The world loves your mamma because your mamma loves the world.'

Stepping back from the railings, she reached out and took her sister-in-law's hand in what she hoped appeared to be an impetuous gesture. 'I'm so pleased you could come back to Brighton with us, Anne. Richard talked to me about you as soon as we met; within minutes he was describing how you'd danced together on the lawn.'

Anne smiled quickly. 'Richard and I have always been close.'

Releasing Anne's hand, Nina leaned lightly on her unfurled parasol. 'He's worried because he's had to go back to work, the office has never been so busy, but I've told him we are able to entertain ourselves and he isn't to be concerned on our behalf.

He'd hoped to come with us to watch the motor races next week but you and I can still go together.'

The smile was in danger of fading: Cheltenham might not approve of two women going unchaperoned to the motor races. Nina continued hastily, 'I've been assured that strong colours are to be worn this year, and your green silks will be perfect. And we must make sure our parasols are adequate in size,' she threw an uncertain glance at the one she held, 'for I believe they're expected to be very generous. Richard will be thrilled: he does so want you to enjoy your stay. And on Ladies' Day he can escort us to the dinner. We'll be the envy of the room!'

It was evident that Anne was struggling with conflicting emotions, but then, as Nina had hoped, her brother's handsomeness and her green silks and the prospect of choosing a new parasol won the day. The revived smile was brave. 'I don't expect it can do any harm for us to go to the races. And as you say, it will please Richard. Yes, Nina, do let's go.'

A small corner had been turned and they linked arms and walked back along the length of the pier, chatting quite naturally about how many costumes they would need to cover the entirety of the week.

In the end, Motor Race Week turned out to be an entirely respectable affair, and amidst the crowds watching from Madeira Terrace, Nina and Anne met any number of wives and relations of Richard's colleagues. It was impossible not to be excited by the speed of the cars on the tarred surface, some attaining one hundred miles an hour, and at moments they found themselves clutching each other's arms and laughing like school-girls.

'I'm so glad you've enjoyed yourselves,' Richard announced at the end of the week. 'It's made my days at the office far more bearable, knowing that, although I couldn't attend this year, you two were enjoying yourselves.'

Anne smiled across the dining table. 'It has been enjoyable. I know Mother won't be happy when I tell her, but . . .'

'Then don't tell her,' Richard cut in.

'Richard!'

He held up his wineglass as if proposing a toast. 'In fact, as your older brother, I expressly forbid it. She is elderly and shouldn't be subjected to shocks.' Leaning forward he said, 'Seriously, Anne, I wouldn't say anything about it. You don't need to lie but it isn't always necessary to tell Mother everything, and it will make things smoother for when you decide to come to stay again. Which we hope will be very soon.'

'Thank you, both of you.' Anne busied herself over her plate, two patches of pink on her cheeks revealing the extent of her pleasure.

As they prepared for bed, Richard kissed Nina on the cheek. 'Wife, you are a miracle-worker. You've really brought Anne out of herself. At this rate she'll be kicking over the traces and finding herself a beau. In fact, I've been thinking we might look for one for her and have been compiling a list of Brighton's "most eligible" for the next time she comes.' He whistled happily as he went through to the dressing room, and Nina smiled at herself in the dressing table mirror. He was worried for Anne, she knew, believing their mother wanted her to remain unmarried so that she would stay at home and look after her. 'She'll turn bitter as an old maid,' he'd said. 'There's the potential for that in Anne. And I've seen it happen often enough, the youngest girl staying at home to look after ageing parents. They end up as green and sharp as uncooked apples.'

Nina could see what he meant. There was an edge to Anne that might well become sharp, but this visit had undoubtedly been a success and where Anne had initially been wary she now seemed prepared to approve. As for finding a beau, well, at twenty-six Anne was as good as an old maid already, but she wasn't unattractive; in fact, with her wavy red hair, the exact same shade as Richard's, she was far prettier than her photographs had initially suggested. If Nina and Richard gave it some serious thought they might indeed be able to find Anne a match in Brighton, a widower for example. Mr Lewisham's face came to mind but she shrugged the thought away: he was wealthy, certainly, but must be almost fifty.

On Anne's last day in Brighton there was a most unexpected event – a French pilot landed his aeroplane on the beach. Everyone turned out to look and it was like the motor races again, with the front a sea of coloured silk frocks and parasols. The pilot sat on a deckchair and waved merrily, sipping a glass of wine for the photographers and eating a plate of oysters sent from one of the oyster bars. The next day the *Brighton Gazette* commented on the good humour of the occasion and the courage of the aviator but finished on a typically solemn note – for if a French pilot could perform this feat, ones from less friendly nations might some day do the same.

When Anne's visit came to an end Richard and Nina accompanied her up to London, where she was to stay briefly with her close friend Janet White before returning to Cheltenham. Miss White was twenty-three and engaged to an architect. She lived with her family in Richmond and they lunched with her in a nearby restaurant.

'Mrs Truelove, Anne has told me your sister lives in Nice.' Miss White sipped from her glass of water. 'I was there once on holiday as a child, but can't remember much about it. My parents didn't like it, I do know that. I remember my mother saying it was rather tawdry. But no doubt it's changed . . .'

A voice broke in. 'Why, I've been to Nice recently and thought it very pretty. I was passing through on the way to a Women's Suffrage conference in Italy.'

Nina studied the speaker, Maggie Chaplin, who had to be in her mid-thirties but looked older. Her husband, Frank, was one of Richard's oldest friends, and Nina had met him a couple of times already; his wife hadn't been with him on these occasions and Richard said she was often away, busy with good causes. Today, however, it was Maggie who was able to meet them for lunch whereas Frank, a barrister, had been called to an urgent meeting. Nina rather liked the look of Maggie Chaplin, with her wild greying hair and strong face, but wondered how Anne would react to the mention of women's suffrage. While staying with them Anne had more than once clucked over items in the newspaper about the actions of the suffragettes.

'The vote . . .' Miss White straightened her narrow shoulders, 'which we are in danger of winning at the expense of our dignity.' She shot a look at Anne, who had assumed a pained expression but didn't speak.

Nina didn't say anything either. It was obvious that women should have the vote – why shouldn't they? – but she couldn't understand why everyone in England was so excited about it when there seemed to be no real difference between any of the political parties. There was a lot of talk here about democracy, while the reality seemed to be that there was no great choice at all. What distinguished the ideas of Herbert Asquith from those of Keir Hardie or Winston Churchill? When she'd said this to Richard, who voted for the Liberals, he laughed and answered, 'All the world.' But it didn't seem like all the world to her.

'Oh, I've never put too much stock in dignity,' Maggie Chaplin said cheerfully. 'It just gets in the way. It's like wearing a day dress with a train, a constant nuisance destined to finish up tired and soiled, despite one's best efforts.' As Richard grinned, Nina only just bit back a laugh. Luckily Anne and Miss White, who had in unison ducked their heads over their plates, didn't appear to notice: Maggie Chaplin must have, however, because a moment later she caught Nina's eye and winked.

After lunch they went to Kew Gardens which, despite the weather, was almost empty. Anne threw a crust on to the smooth surface of a pond and one of the white and gold shapes lurking in the water moved lazily upwards. Nina thought of the ponds in Katya's garden. Katya had written to say they would have evaporated completely if the gardener hadn't spent an entire day carrying buckets of water, and that many of the fish had died despite his efforts. Katya's baby was due very soon and she'd suffered throughout this pregnancy with swollen ankles and terrible toothache.

'The fish are fat,' Anne observed, 'from being over-fed.' She folded the top of the paper bag. 'For Richard's tenth birthday he was given a pony named Toffee. All the children used to feed it and it was like a barrel on legs. In the end Father sent it away to a farm for the sake of its health; he said it would be cruel to keep it any longer.'

They proceeded further along the path and Anne took Nina's arm. 'I'm so pleased, Nina, that we've had these few weeks in which to get to know each other. And don't worry about Mother. After Father died she tried matching Richard with any number of the Cheltenham girls – none of whom interested him at all. She was convinced he was in danger of becoming what she called a "confirmed bachelor". It floored her completely when he wrote to say he'd found his own bride. And of course you had to have the wedding in Russia, with your family – I've asked Mother how she'd feel if I married in another country.'

At the thought of Anne, who was so completely English, marrying anywhere else, Nina had to smile. 'Look.' She pointed past her sister-in-law at a shape in the distance. 'What is that?'

Richard, who was ahead with Janet White and Maggie Chaplin, heard and turned round. 'It's supposed to be a Chinese pagoda. I've been told it closely resembles the real thing.'

Pretence, that was what the English excelled at. The Royal Pavilion in Brighton was like a maharajah's palace. Nina shaded her eyes. 'Is it possible to climb to the top?'

'Oh, Nina, you mustn't!' Anne gripped her arm.

'There's a spiral staircase,' Janet White said matter-of-factly, 'which I wouldn't recommend as my brothers say it's quite steep. It would most certainly be uncomfortable in this heat.'

'But with the promise of such a view.' Maggie Chaplin stepped forward. 'I can quite understand if you won't accompany me, Miss White – because of the steepness, and the heat – but you will, my dear, won't you?'

Nina, remembering the wink, replied accordingly, 'I couldn't let you go alone.'

'Nina!' Anne's hand fluttered at her wrist.

'It's a pity, Mrs Chaplin,' Janet White sounded almost rude, 'that there are no longer any tea rooms, where we might await you. But,' she nodded at Richard and Anne, claiming them as her party, 'while Mrs Chaplin and Mrs Truelove undertake their climb, the rest of us can visit the Palm House and then enjoy the shade of the Orangery.'

'The stairs are steeper than I expected, I must confess.' Maggie led the way, the hem of her navy tailored skirt white with dust. Close up the pagoda was disappointing except for the splendid gold dragons; inside, however, it was an impressive spiral of grey metal. 'There's a platform.' Maggie stepped on to it and walked across to an opening that looked out over the wide lawns.

'I don't suppose,' Maggie sounded slightly breathless, 'that you're acquainted with any of the Bolshevists?'

In her mind's eye Nina could see the knife with the red handle hidden under the cupboard. Cook had stopped hiding the knives after Mamma died, either because she'd forgotten or because nothing worse could happen. 'No, I'm not.' She wondered if it mattered.

Maggie smiled. 'Frank's probably asked you already. He thinks everyone from Russia must know all about the radicals, or, better still, be one.'

'Some people say my father is a Bolshevik.'

'But he isn't?'

What was it Papa had said one day that had made Sergei Rudolfoveich so angry?

'I can remember him saying that the Bolsheviks would be justified in their beliefs if Russia continued to fall behind other countries in its grain production. But I don't think that means he's a Bolshevik. I think he's mad. Not,' she added quickly, 'because of what he said about the grain; he might be right about that.'

Maggie's fingers touched her hand. 'You lead the way. I shall take my time.'

Now Nina climbed without stopping. As she laboured up the metal steps she remembered the other thing Sergei Rudolfoveich had said, about Papa becoming a *skhimniki*. But Papa certainly wasn't a hermit, nor was he a *yurodivy*, an innocent, or holy fool – he'd split the lip of Darya Fyodorovna, the only person brave enough to sleep on the floor of his room to stop him killing himself. Maybe he was a Bolshevik after all. She leaned down and briefly ran a finger around the tops of her new shoes, which were rubbing, although not too badly.

Maggie called from a platform below, her voice surprisingly raw, 'Isn't the view splendid?'

But Nina was saving the view for the top. Another turn in the stairs and there she was. She leaned against the railing. It was high, higher than she'd expected, and in the distance there were endless rows of streets and houses. The sensation of falling was almost overwhelming – and exhilarating: you'd go down and down, very fast . . .

'There have been suicides,' Maggie panted from behind, 'which is why they keep threatening to close it off.'

Turning, Nina saw Maggie's hair was awry, her lips blue. 'You shouldn't have climbed the stairs!'

'No, I should not, and if Frank were here he would have strictly forbidden it.' She gestured at the view with her right hand, her left hand clasped to her chest. 'And then I would never have seen all this. You mustn't worry, this happens if I over-exert myself.' Her eyes, however, were frightened.

If Maggie had a heart attack here, at the top of the tower, how would they get her down? It was madness to have climbed this high. 'Sit down.' Without thinking, Nina found herself modelling her tone on Mrs Kulmana's. 'Sit down and rest your head on your knees. We're in no hurry.' She kneeled and loosened the buttons at the neck of Maggie's blouse, then used her hands to fan her.

'You could be a nurse,' the older woman sighed.

'I almost was.' It was like the introduction to a fairy story. 'After my mother died my father decided to turn our house into a hospital.'

There was silence for a moment, and then Maggie said, 'Was that why you said he was mad?' She was beginning to breathe more normally.

'I think he was always mad. Before Mamma died he was mad with love for her, and with ideas about modern farming. If Richard hadn't taken me away I don't know what would have happened. He saved me.'

Maggie lifted her head, her lips pale but no longer bruised. 'Richard seems happier than I've ever seen him before. You have saved each other. Nina, I hope you don't mind my asking, but how old are you?'

They told everyone she was four years older than she really was. 'I am nineteen.'

'Only nineteen.' Maggie smiled. 'You're very wise for nineteen.'

They sat for a while longer, then, after a last look, slowly made their way back down.

'See over there, next to those trees?' At the bottom, Maggie's voice was tired but edged with mischief.

There wasn't anything in particular to see. 'No . . .'

'That's where we would now be meeting our friends – if a suffragette hadn't burnt down the tea rooms.'

'Why the tea rooms?' Nina was surprised at the thrill that shot through her.

Maggie chuckled. '"Why not?" I believe that's what the woman said when the police asked the same question. "Why not?"'

That evening Nina and Richard caught the seven o'clock train back to Brighton, along with parties of people coming down for the bank holiday. 'You've won Anne over completely,' Richard said as they made their way out of the station. 'She adores you and I really do feel your influence will be beneficial. Poor old Anne, you'll help her to open up to the world.'

There was no doubt Nina's project of the past weeks had been a great success, and she'd won Anne's heart as easily as Mamma would have done. In fact it had been easier than she'd expected. Richard went on, 'You were also a hit with Maggie. I expect the two of you will soon be bosom friends. It was a pity about her taking a turn like that because you would've loved the Palm House. The palms are all from Australasia and the Pacific. There was a gardener there, a nice young chap,' he squeezed her hand, 'not badly educated and very polite. I wish you'd met him. He said that in that part of the world there's a tree with stinging leaves. The pain's terrible and lasts for months. It has even been known to drive people insane.'

Where London had seemed unusually quiet, here the streets were crowded, almost festive. People who wouldn't normally speak to each other called hello. A young man in a top hat blew Nina a kiss. 'Is it because of Maggie's heart,' she asked, 'that they haven't had children?'

He didn't answer for a minute and then said, 'I don't know, but I've often thought they'd like a child.' A man tipped his cap and moved aside to let them pass. 'You know, don't you,' he whispered in her ear, 'that I'd be very happy if you chose to have a child one day.' She did know: he'd offered it as a possibility the morning after the *bal blanc*, when they'd agreed to marry. They hadn't discussed it since, however. Richard rushed on, 'Only if it's what you want; there's years yet. Just as long as you know that if you'd like a child, I would be very pleased about it.' He laughed self-consciously. 'A boy or a girl, it doesn't matter. With red hair, like mine!'

Maybe the suggestion should have shocked her, but it hadn't the day he'd proposed and it didn't now: there were things in the world far more shocking than the possibility of a child. She smiled at him and he quickly kissed her hand. Rounding a corner, they saw the domed shadow of the Pavilion.

'Look!' Like the crowd in the centre of the town Richard seemed to be declaring a holiday. 'We could be in India! Would you like to see the Taj Mahal, Nina? Or the pyramids? We could go to Egypt!'

Without thinking she replied, 'I'll never go anywhere like that.'

'Why on earth not? We could go anywhere in the whole world!'

'Darya read it in the cards. Katya's destined to go on a long journey over the sea, but not me.'

'Your sister hasn't even crossed the Channel. Anyway, we could go by land.'

He sounded so like a small boy, she had to laugh.

'And what else did the wise Darya tell you?'

'That I'd live in many houses . . .'

'We'll start looking for our next tomorrow. And?'

'I'd have a long life.' And before he could ask about husbands, 'She didn't finish reading the cards. It was Katya's betrothal party.'

Then there was another crowd and the sound and smell of the sea, fairy lights playing over the water. As they arrived at their front door the railway porter pulled up with their luggage.

'I'll take these upstairs.' Richard dealt with the cases while Nina checked that food had been left under a clean checked cloth on the pantry shelf.

'Everything ship-shape?'

She saw that he was still wearing his jacket. 'There's beef and a rice pudding. But,' she replaced the cloth, 'I do feel rather tired, so if you don't mind I'll simply go to bed and read. If there's enough hot water I'll have a bath.'

He couldn't hide his eagerness. 'I don't mind, if you're tired.'

Glancing away he said, 'I'm feeling quite sprightly myself. In fact, I've been contemplating a walk.'

He'd tell her everything when he returned home, they both knew that, but for some reason his expeditions required this ritual first. 'Go out then.' She shooed him with her hands as she'd shooed ducks from the baby lettuce. 'Don't worry about me.'

Susan couldn't have been in the house long, as there wasn't enough hot water for a bath; instead Nina poured herself some milk and scrambled into bed. Lying there she remembered what Richard had said about having a child. 'If you found a man you liked enough to have a child by,' he'd told her as they stood in the gazebo in Aunt Elena's garden, 'I'd be happy for you. As long as it didn't affect our marriage.'

She pulled her feet up under the sheet. She wasn't sure she would want a child, but she knew one day she'd want a lover. 'I can love you,' his face had been pale but honest, 'but I cannot make love to you. I've tried with women but it isn't possible. You must understand that won't change.' It wasn't that he didn't admire her body – he did, very much – but she saw from his eyes that his admiration was without desire, as if he were looking at a painting or sculpture. And this lack of desire kindled the same response in her: Richard treated her as his closest friend, or younger sister, and she loved him in the same way.

No, one day she would meet a man who would become her lover. Sometimes she tried picturing him as Georgi, the medical student – a more handsome Georgi, with high cheekbones and without the glasses – but even then it didn't work; Georgi wasn't right. She couldn't conjure up the man's features exactly, but in her mind's eye he walked towards her with a masculine grace and she, waiting for him on the bed, was a woman, her body a promise. She would raise her hips toward him, her fingers guiding his; here, she told him, turning her face into the dark heat of the pillow, here. Before crying out, over and over.

It was past midnight when she heard the front door shut. After hanging up his coat Richard usually bounded up the stairs. 'Richard?' She waited, then turned on the lamp and went out on to the landing. 'Richard?' He was sitting on the bottom step, his head on his knees. At first she hesitated, but when he didn't move she ran down. 'What's wrong?' She put her arms around him but drew back at the sour smell of vomit. 'You're ill!'

'I was punched in the stomach, it isn't serious.'

'You've been robbed?'

'Yes.' Then he shook his head, although he still didn't raise it. 'Not really. There was this boy. I got a bit hurt. Not badly, though.' He did look up now, his eyes desolate. 'Nina, I'm such a bloody fool.'

She was awake at dawn and went through to the dressing room. Richard's throat, exposed above the sheet, was as smooth as a girl's, and she remembered how Darya had always checked to see the maids had left the collars on her and Katya's nightdresses unbuttoned, so that their guardian angels could settle there and protect them as they slept. Standing here now she felt like Richard's guardian angel: under the sheet there were ugly marks on his chest and she would happily kill the boy who'd done this if she knew where to find him, taking the knife with the red handle and plunging it into his heart.

'It's completely different for boys,' Richard had told her more than once. 'Girls are in danger of being beaten or getting pregnant; it's a terrible life for them. But there's no risk in it for boys; they do it because they want to.'

There was nothing she could do about the boy, but there was something she could do for Richard and herself. She dressed quietly, used the bathroom, then went down to the parlour, where she took a pen from the desk and wrote on a piece of paper what Darya had read in the cards. Then she put the paper in her bag and left the house.

The sun had turned the sea to blood. There was building work being done on the pier at the end of the square so she walked quickly along the front, a sharp morning breeze catching at her hat. 'There's no hurry, pet, we can wait for it to come to us!' an old man with a dog called out, but she strode past, on to the wooden boards of the Palace Pier. It was windier here, the water below broken into small waves. Along the railings, boys and older men fished in silence.

When Nina reached the end of the pier she turned her back to the breeze and tore the paper into tiny pieces. Then she stepped to the edge and threw out her arms, the wind snatching the fragments of paper and carrying them away. There was a sudden flapping of wings overhead, but it was only a seagull, its eye gold and hungry. She watched it as it battled against the wind, then she turned and walked back toward the shore, strands of hair whipping at her face.

'Take this!' A woman sitting next to a bucket held out a blue mackerel on a sheet of bloodied paper. 'Go on, you take it. And you stick to your decision, mind. Don't you let no one talk you out of it.'

'Thank you!' She felt jubilant as their fingers touched. 'You're very kind.'

As she walked back toward the house Nina saw Susan in the distance, going up the front steps. Susan's eyes would be malicious. 'Surely you haven't been out all night, madam?'

She laughed to herself, thinking of the fish woman. It didn't matter what Susan, or anyone else, thought; she would simply drop her jacket, and the fish, on the hall table and go back upstairs to her husband. Susan could make of it whatever she wanted.

When she stepped into the hall, however, Susan didn't look surprised at all. 'So you've seen the papers?' She rushed forward in her excitement. 'The boys are yelling it in the centre of town. Germany has declared war on Russia and they say it means war for us too. War for certain.'

Nine

Brighton, 1917

The war would be over in six months. That was what many people said at first, but that wasn't how it happened.

> It is the spring of 1917 and Brighton is full to over-flowing with representatives of most of the royal and aristocratic houses of Europe and the families of major financiers and industrialists; not to mention known and, it has to be said, unknown members of the theatrical profession. The result is that even in the winter months the traditional Sunday morning parade along our sea front is a bewildering and most welcome spectacle to those visitors who come from the more war-deprived areas. 'Here', they say, 'is the spirit of Life before the War!' And they are right. Brighton has offered refuge not only to thousands of individuals displaced by the hostilities but also to the memory of How Things Were and the hope that this is How Things Will Be Again. It is of little wonder then that in the New Year we were graced by the presence not only of Queen Alexandra but also the Princess Royal and Princess Maud. And now who should be sojourning with us but Mrs B—— C—— of London, her soldier son with her. On Sunday morning she was to be seen wrapped in splendid furs worn over a dress a lovely shade of . . .

'Is this meant to be a joke?' Richard had asked when he saw the title of the *Gazette*'s 'Fashion on the Front' column the last time he was home. He'd be back today, his first leave in almost a year, and Nina still didn't know the answer.

She continued to turn the pages, but the only news about Russia this morning was a small article on the second page, which said it was widely believed that the Tsar had personally ordered troops to fire on the crowds in Petrograd and that the royal family was now in residence at the palace at Tsarskoe Selo. It was strange reading about these events from such a distance, and strange also that, from this distance, such events seemed inevitable. That women should take to the streets calling for bread, and the next day start calling for freedom. The English ideal of democracy – flawed though it was – had influenced her after all, and she found herself agreeing with the tone of most of the papers, that change in Russia would be a good thing. She just hoped the changes would come quickly and without too much disruption.

There was a knock at the bedroom door. 'Madam . . .'

'Yes, Margaret?'

'I began to clean the grate in the parlour, like you said, but the chimney's blocked. We'll need the sweep.'

Nina checked her wristwatch: it was eight o'clock. 'I'll be down in a minute.'

When Margaret had left, Nina carefully pinned her hair. She'd go shopping later in the morning to see if she could find something nice for supper, and when she came back she'd check the house, which would no doubt be clean and tidy enough, although not up to Darya Fyodorovna's standards. No one knew where Darya was now; Aunt Elena had heard nothing since that first letter, and these days letters from Elena herself were rare, the postal system in Russia having almost collapsed. Elena and her family had suffered badly during the war. Uncle Aleksei survived a serious bayonet wound then died of a fever at Rovno, and Mira's fiancé, Marc, had lost the toes of his right foot and two fingers to frostbite. A letter had got through to Katya two months back, and in it their aunt said that she, Tatyana, Mira and Marc were planning to leave for Finland. The chances were they were in Finland already, away from the events that were altering the face of Russia. Elena hadn't spoken with Papa since Nina's elopement but said she'd heard he'd returned to the farm, having been released from the army after an injury, and that the hospital had expanded enormously to take in wounded soldiers.

In the parlour Margaret was on all fours, peering up the chimney. 'It'll be a bird's nest,' she said, 'for sure.'

The last fire Nina had lit hadn't drawn properly but the

chimney hadn't seemed blocked. Margaret loved to create problems, so Nina ushered her aside. 'Let me see.' Pulling back her skirt, she squatted in front of the grate.

'The sweep, madam, I doubt we'll be able to get him for a fortnight at least.'

'We don't need the sweep but I will need an apron, and some newspaper.' It was what Mamma had always ordered to be done.

Margaret reluctantly brought the paper and Nina screwed the sheets into tight balls, pulling back her sleeves so she could push the paper up the chimney. Then she lit the last of the balls with a match. Nothing happened at first, and it seemed it hadn't caught, but then there was a faint crackling. 'There,' she said, conscious of Margaret's disapproval, 'it will soon clear.'

Not long afterwards Margaret was hammering at the drawing room door. 'Come quick!'

Nina could hear it as she ran down the stairs, a hum that turned into a roar as she entered the parlour. Even from the doorway she could feel the heat, although, eerily, there were no flames in the grate. Over the mantelpiece, behind the clock, a corner of wallpaper had come unstuck and was curling, while behind the wallpaper the whole wall seemed to vibrate.

Margaret was wide-eyed. Nina stepped past her into the middle of the room, where the heat was intense. At one side of the grate there was a lump of something, moist and white: it didn't look like bird's nest. As she watched, another lump joined it. It couldn't be – but it was. White-hot brick. Turning, she pushed Margaret aside and ran along the hall, outside, and down the steps on to the pavement, where she stood and watched the column of black smoke belching skywards.

'You need the firemen, missus!' a man laughed, and she couldn't suppress a smile for it was wonderful, the angry column of smoke coiling against a leaden sky. She watched a few minutes more, ignoring the tut-tutting of passers-by, then slowly went back inside to where the parlour was all heat and roar, the wall by the chimney hot to the touch. Standing close to it she closed her eyes.

When she opened them again Margaret was staring. 'Shall I call the fire brigade?' she asked stiffly.

'Certainly not, it will burn itself out.'

And it did, the roar gradually abating. Margaret went for a bucket and mop and Nina looked around the room, which would need a good cleaning again, with the carpet rolled so the floorboards could be washed.

'I have to go out now,' she said as Margaret returned. 'There's the shopping to do.'

The bucket clanged against the grate.

Nina walked quickly. For Margaret the chimney fire would be 'the final straw'. They'd had a few 'final straws' already, but Nina wouldn't protest this time. She knew that for Margaret the wages offered by the munitions factory in Lewes Road would finally prove too tempting. The truth was that Margaret should have gone long ago. Susan had departed at the first opportunity, taking a job on the trolley buses. Margaret had stayed out of complacency and because Richard had doubled her wages. 'I can't leave you completely alone,' he'd said to Nina. 'You must see that.'

She hadn't seen why he had to go at all.

A milk wagon pulled by a pair of heavy horses trundled past and three office girls raced it, holding their hats and laughing as they ran. 'You choose!' one called to another. 'Where will we go tonight?'

Did men and women understand something different when they spoke about choosing things, making a choice? 'I had no choice.' Richard had said that, the day the first silver Zeppelin appeared over the English coast. 'I couldn't put off volunteering any longer.'

He'd volunteered without telling her and they had had their first real row. She had never before felt really angered by anything he'd said or done – but to do this without any word or discussion. She'd screamed and thrown a jug on the kitchen floor. 'You do not care for me! You couldn't do this if you cared!'

He'd stared down at the jug, pushing the pieces with the toe of his boot as if puzzled by how they had got there. Then he said, 'This isn't about you and me, Nina. It isn't about us.'

What was it about? Honour? Glory? Patriotism?

He'd gone to the training camp and she'd cried herself to sleep every night till the day he'd telephoned to say he'd been assigned as an aide to a general in the War Office.

When she heard that she felt happier than she had ever felt in her life. As soon as she put down the receiver she ran up the stairs, past the curious Susan, and danced ecstatically around the bedroom.

Remembering this now as she crossed the road she smiled grimly. Her euphoria had been premature, for it wasn't long before Richard started talking about putting in for a transfer. When she'd demanded to know why, all he could say was that he felt guilty. 'It doesn't feel right,' he said, 'to be safe when others are not.'

It was so ridiculous, it made her angry. And the stupidity of his mother, who'd sent a telegram from Cheltenham, *Very proud STOP Have done right thing STOP Nina must come to Cheltenham to live STOP*

Nina had been furious when she read this but had replied as tactfully as she could. *It is my hope*, she wrote, *that my sister Katya and her family will leave France for the safety of England and I could not impose so many young children on you.* Mrs Truelove must have agreed, for the approach wasn't made again.

As for Katya, Nina had repeatedly urged her to come to Brighton, but Katya continued to reassure her there was no need to fear for their safety. Nina also suspected from the tone of her sister's letters that Ivan's business was doing much better with Ivan away in the army and Katya managing things with the help of an elderly but able accountant. She'd had a letter from Katya three weeks ago, before the mutiny in Petrograd, full of gossip about the murder of Rasputin. *The mad monk is said to have come to his end in the house of Prince Feliks Yosopov himself. The rumours about his mode of death are so wild it is impossible to know what is true and what is not, but what is certain is that Alexandra wept for him publicly, accusing his assailants of murdering a saint. I have heard people here openly refer to her as 'Rasputin's whore' and it is whispered she is a German agent as well. Russia is in chaos.*

On a corner an inexperienced soldier struggled to get a comrade's wheelchair over the kerb. Nina had left Russia to escape a hospital and Brighton had turned into one. Many of the larger houses had been commandeered and on the King's orders the Royal Pavilion had become a hospital for Commonwealth soldiers, the chinoiserie boarded over and the royal apartments transformed into wards crammed with metal cots. The patients gazed up at crystal chandeliers and painted ceilings and there were stories of unconscious men who'd woken and believed they were dead and in heaven, the pale nurses angels. At the very beginning of the war the patients in the Pavilion had all been Indian soldiers, and day trippers paid twopence to take the trolley-bus in order to stare over the walls at the exotic, turbaned figures. Now the Pavilion accommodated mainly limbless patients, or those suffering from limb injuries.

Coming to the public library, Nina hurried up the steps. She'd been working here as a volunteer for two years and usually came in three or four mornings a week. The war had made the nurse's uniform respectable and a number of officers' wives were now working in the hospitals. It had been suggested to Nina more than once that she should do the same. The library was her refuge, an excuse for not getting involved in these other activities. She wouldn't be in this week, of course, because of Richard's leave, but she'd promised to bring a list of dates she'd be available over the next month. At the top of the steps she pushed open the heavy wooden doors and walked across the vestibule to the reading room, where she recognised a soldier from one of the hospitals. Private Flynn walked slowly across the parquet floor, clutching a book between his thumb and first finger, the only fingers remaining on his right hand. It would be a romance novel, she knew that. Many of the soldiers read romances. The private's left hand, which had no fingers at all, was still heavily bandaged, and inside the blue flannel uniform his body was stick thin.

Mrs Tucker, a recent volunteer, was at the counter sorting cards. She gave a brief nod and Nina wondered how old she was – twenty-three? Twenty-four? She was pretty, with a halo of tight blonde curls, and dark lashes. Her first name was Vanessa. She scandalised the older volunteers by wearing heavy colour on her lips and sometimes smoking a cigarette in the office during her break. According to Lydia Barnes, the deputy librarian,

Vanessa was having an affair with a young Canadian pilot. 'Her husband, Major Tucker, is much older than she is. He isn't at the Front and he's in no danger, whilst a pilot . . .' Lydia, who was forty and lived with her widowed mother, had stood very straight. 'I hope you don't think me terribly improper, but I cannot find it in my heart to truly blame her. All those brave young men. The war, I must confess, has changed the way I think about some things.'

The war had relaxed some attitudes, whilst hardening others.

Nina found Mrs Hunter, the librarian, in the hallway outside the office, anxiously studying the ceiling. There'd been problems with the roof over the winter and ominous damp patches had begun to appear across the ornate plaster. Mrs Hunter had begged for repairs to be made, but there was a long wait because the men who usually did this work were all in the army. She looked down again as Nina approached.

'Ah, Mrs Truelove . . .'

'Good morning, Mrs Hunter. I've brought the list with the dates I'll be available.'

'Yes. Thank you.' She took the paper absently. 'I hope Captain Truelove's leave is enjoyable. Will you be going anywhere?'

'He only has ten days. He'll spend a week here and then go on to Cheltenham to see his mother.'

'What a pity it's so short, although I know you're sometimes able to meet him up in town. And it's nice he'll be able to see his mother. Cheltenham, how lovely . . .' Her gaze crept upward again.

Nina walked back out through the vestibule and down the steps. She must make sure Richard's leave was as enjoyable as possible. Arguing with him about a transfer was pointless and only made him more determined. The first thing to do was to find something interesting for supper: there might be some fish, or perhaps ham for a soup. There were growing protests about scarcities but the truth was that food was readily available if you had the money for it. Somewhere in her basket was the shopping list . . .

'Oh!' She'd missed the bottom step.

'Whoa!' A man caught her by the sleeve, breaking her fall.

Her heart pounded as she found herself looking up at an

officer in an Australian uniform – Lieutenant O'Connor. Harry. He smiled down at her. He had red hair, almost the same colour as Richard's, but where Richard's eyes were brown, the Lieutenant's were a piercing blue.

'Thank you.'

'It would be a pity for you to end up injured too, Mrs Truelove.' He gently released his grip on her jacket.

She glanced quickly away, smoothing her skirt. 'I'm so sorry. I wasn't being careful.'

Bending over, he picked up the basket and handed it to her with a smile. His face was not as classically handsome as Richard's, but more boyish. 'There are enough walking wounded in the world.' His left arm was in a sling under his greatcoat, badly broken, she knew, as the result of an accident in which the truck he was in went off the road just outside Paris. She'd met him twice now at Mrs Laing's, the first time a fortnight ago and then again last Friday. Mr Laing was a major in the Royal Scots Greys, and these days Mrs Laing's energy went into providing entertainment for the officers being treated at the various Brighton hospitals. Nina often attended these events and had met a number of the Australian and New Zealand officers, who were very popular in Brighton. Indeed, everyone seemed to like the ANZACs, with their drawling voices and good humour. It was said they were brave fighters but hated following orders.

'Thank you.' She slipped the basket over her arm. 'You're on your way to the library?' He'd been coming to see her; she'd told him on Friday that she worked in the library.

'I'm going to collect some books for the chaps in the Pavilion. I was hoping you'd advise me.'

If only he had come five minutes earlier. 'I'm afraid I'm going shopping, but there'll be someone to help you.' She couldn't resist adding, 'I will see you at Mrs Laing's again?'

'Of course,' he replied. Nina's cheeks felt warm and she found herself smiling. Then she caught sight of Lydia Barnes watching them with interest as she came down the steps.

Lieutenant O'Connor followed her look. 'I had better let you get on with your shopping. I look forward to the next time we meet, Mrs Truelove.' He held out his hand.

She took it. 'Goodbye, Lieutenant O'Connor.' As she walked

away she could still feel the lingering pressure of his fingers, and found herself wishing it wasn't Vanessa Tucker who was on duty at the counter.

The next morning Nina sat in the window of the bedroom, sipping her tea and cursing herself for not having held her tongue last night. So much for tact and diplomacy – only a few hours after he arrived she and Richard had had their most bitter argument ever. It began immediately after supper and she'd never seen him so angry. 'I won't discuss this with you further,' he'd said, his face red, 'as you completely refuse to make any effort to understand that I have to at least *try* to do the right thing.'

'Stop it,' she told herself now as her eyes pricked. 'It's not going to happen.' Maggie Chaplin had assured her of this the last time they spoke on the telephone. 'Try not to worry too much, Nina,' she'd said. 'Frank and I both feel Richard won't be allowed to go to the Front. He's far too experienced and more valuable where he is.'

She wished her friend was here to talk to now. She usually managed to see Maggie every three or four months, but sometimes it was longer because Maggie was very busy lecturing to women factory workers all around the country about accidents and safety. Cradling the cup in her hands, Nina looked down into the old man's garden; she still thought of it as belonging to the old man although he no longer lived there. Just after Richard had left for the training camp she'd glanced down one afternoon and been surprised to see the old man beckoning. As she stood outside the scullery door he called softly over the wall, 'They say you are a German lady and that the police will come for you soon.' His voice was immeasurably sad and he spoke with an accent she didn't recognise.

'I am from Russia,' she called back, 'and have papers to prove it.'

'Good. I am glad for you.'

'Thank you for telling me,' she called, but he didn't reply.

The policeman had rung the doorbell the next night. 'The authorities have been informed that a person of German birth is resident in this house.' His face was red with embarrassment, not, she sensed, because of the role he was playing but that a respectable-looking woman could be guilty of such a thing, German birth.

'I am Russian,' she said calmly, and brought him in to see the documents Richard had had prepared for her. 'Here is a solicitor's letter, verifying my marriage certificate, and my Russian passport.' Aunt Elena had purchased this for Nina on the day before her wedding, for one gold rouble. 'And here are letters from my husband and his employer.'

The next morning the policeman returned with an official form, identifying her as a 'Resident Alien', which she had to carry whenever she left the house. She was aware of course that there were English people who would have said that being Russian wasn't much better than being German. Indeed, before the accounts of German atrocities in Belgium began to circulate, letters in many of the newspapers suggested that Germany was England's natural ally and the real enemy was Russia. Not long after the policeman's visit it was reported in some papers that trains were moving Russian battalions across England at night, and this led to a spate of outraged correspondence about the dangers posed by bloodthirsty Cossacks. Richard shrugged it off, saying the letter-writers were simply ignorant, but when she sent cuttings to France, Katya replied that she wasn't surprised, for everyone in Nice said the English were deeply suspicious of Russia and would be happier fighting the Tsar than the Kaiser.

As Nina watched from the window, a small boy appeared in the garden, throwing a ball. She'd never seen the old man again after their one conversation. A few weeks later two women had moved into the house and children's voices floated up through the branches of the pear tree.

'Good morning.' Richard came through from the dressing room. He hesitated, then walked forward and kissed her on the cheek. 'I'm sorry about last night.'

'You needn't be.' She put the teacup back in its saucer and lowered her voice conspiratorially. 'Margaret has handed in her notice.'

'Oh dear.' He ran his hand through his hair. 'The chimney fire?'

'The last straw.'

'Shall we advertise?'

'No, I can shop and look after the house myself.'

'You're sure?'

'Yes. And I will begin this morning by going out to buy something for your lunch.'

'Hang that.' He smiled. 'We'll eat out and then find ourselves a tea dance.'

'A what?'

'You'll see.'

The tea dance was held in a small hall. It was packed with people of all types and ages: middle-aged women dancing as couples, and ordinary soldiers and their girls. Richard was the only officer and Nina was overdressed, but it didn't seem to matter as everyone was laughing and friendly.

'Do you think this is what it will be like after the war?' Nina asked over the noise.

'No. It will go back to the way it was.'

Thinking of Russia, she shook her head. 'The world's changing.'

'You are an optimist.' Putting his arm around her waist he whirled her back into the crowd.

That night it was Nina's turn to stay with Alice Evans, whose husband had died of malarial fever a month ago in Alexandria. Alice was expecting a child any day now, and the officers' wives took turns to stay with her.

'This hasn't been thought out properly,' Richard complained as they walked arm in arm. 'What if I hadn't been here? How would you have got yourself across town at night? There isn't always a cab.' The sky was perfectly clear and the full moon meant they could see where they were going. It also meant an increased danger of air raids.

'I would have walked,' she replied, 'like we're doing now.'

He snorted. 'Yes, I suppose you would.'

There was a woman waiting by the window, anxious because she was expected home for dinner. 'Alice is asleep. She's been very poorly today, crying for her husband. We've told her he'll live on in the baby and that her duty now is to think of the child, but I'm not sure she even remembers that she is going to have a child.'

'There's a telephone?' Richard asked uneasily.

The woman looked surprised. 'If there's a problem, Mrs Truelove can ring the bell at number eleven. The boy will go for the midwife.'

'Shall I come back?' he whispered at the door.

'Don't worry, I'll be home in time for breakfast.'

After they'd gone, Nina went upstairs to check on Alice. Her breathing was regular but she tossed and turned, muttering nonsense so it was surprising she didn't wake herself up; maybe she'd been given a sleeping draught. Nina listened for a while and then went down to the library, where there were shelves of books, all of them on painting or architecture. Pulling down a large volume on monuments and castles, she came across a drawing of Glastonbury Tor, which they'd seen on one of their trips with Lawrence. Lawrence had died at the end of last summer and she often found herself thinking about him. After declaring himself a conscientious objector, he'd been forced out of his university post; a humiliating tribunal followed and he was sent to work on a farm outside Oxford. He'd had a heart attack while bringing in hay. She remembered how, just before the tribunal, she'd said in a letter to Richard that she thought Lawrence was very brave. *What he is doing is immeasurably brave*, Richard had replied, *and I would never have the courage to do it myself. You of all people should know that.*

Richard was too hard on himself.

Sighing, Nina glanced at her wristwatch. Two weeks ago she'd spent the afternoon here and Alice had slept most of the time; tonight would no doubt be the same. She went through to the kitchen and turned on the gas ring to make some tea, which would have to be black – although there was a small jug of milk in the pantry, a note sitting next to it read, *IMPORTANT. Please leave ALL milk and food for Mrs Evans.* Looking at this, Nina thought how efficient they were, these wives and daughters: collecting reading material to send to the trenches; finding boots for the Indian soldiers; knitting socks. The Red Cross was an army in itself. Her sister-in-law, Anne, spent much of her time working for the Red Cross, and on her last visit her eyes had shone as she described the efforts of the Duchess of Westminster, who'd turned her beautiful villa in Le Touquet into a hospital. 'Can you imagine anyone being so generous? It's even said that she raises the morale of the new patients by greeting them in evening dress!'

Nina had had to turn away, suddenly imagining Papa dressed for the opera and greeting a wounded soldier on a stretcher. The English were so bizarre. It was an absurd, even grotesque thing to do. Why could Anne not see this?

There was no doubt, however, that the war had been the making of many women and that Anne herself was transformed almost beyond recognition. Her work had given her confidence and largely freed her from her mother. Not only that, but she was no longer in danger of being an old maid, having very recently become engaged to a hospital chaplain, the Reverend Jeremy Gregory. Anne was happy – and now it was Richard who was in danger of becoming bitter.

Back in the library it was chilly, and Nina pulled a rug over her knees, telling herself it was morbid to think about things too much: Richard wouldn't get a transfer, the war would end and they'd be content again. She thought of how they'd danced this afternoon, people nodding at them approvingly – and then she allowed herself to imagine that Harry O'Connor had been there too, watching in admiration as she laughed and danced, swirling past with flushed cheeks. For he did admire her, she had no doubt about that: she'd seen it in his eyes as they parted company outside the library, and at Mrs Laing's suppers.

The first time she met him, she'd noticed him because of the colour of his hair. She'd come into the room and, out of the corner of her eye, caught sight of a tall man with red hair. She'd swung round, half thinking it was Richard, only to see a young Australian officer talking to Miss Marshall, a rather serious young woman who taught the piano. A little while later Mrs Laing introduced them, and Nina found herself talking to him as if she knew him already.

She remembered now how his face had been alight as he described Sydney Harbour, which he declared to be the most beautiful harbour in the world. 'When the troop ship left Sydney,' he said, 'there was a pageant for the Red Cross and

Elizabeth and her court were carried across the harbour in a barge. There were dozens of girls dressed as mermaids. The girl playing Elizabeth wore a powdered wig and an ivory dress with a silver ruff. It was ridiculous, really, Queen Elizabeth in Sydney Harbour, but it was moving at the time.'

The next day in the library Nina had found a book about the Commonwealth and looked for an illustration of Sydney, but the only pictures were of kangaroos, which were very strange animals indeed. She doubted they would live in a city, unless they were kept as pets.

The second time, they had sat next to each other at supper and she'd asked about his studies at university. 'I read European history,' he said, 'and German.' He emphasised the last part as he said it, and she could see heads turn around the table. His blue eyes were fixed on her face and she felt he was somehow testing her.

She kept her voice steady. 'So you are fluent in German?'

'Fairly, yes. German is close to English in many ways.'

A matron opposite tutted, but the Australian officer next to her laughed. 'And it's a jolly good thing that Harry here *is* so fluent, with all the translating he does.'

The plates were being changed, the conversation changing at the same time, so it wasn't until after the meal that Nina was able to talk to Harry properly again.

'What is it that you translate?' she asked. 'Is it documents?'

He pulled a face. 'I don't translate; I interrogate German prisoners.' He shrugged, giving a small smile. 'They were all waiters before the war and tell me how much they enjoyed working in London and how fond they were of their customers. We get on famously.'

He was smoking a cigarette and she saw it shake in his hand. Then he said, very quietly and quickly, 'My grandfather, my mother's father, was German.'

There was so much sadness in his voice that she had been tempted to reach out and touch his hand. Closing her eyes now she imagined the scene again, her fingers reaching out and lightly brushing his cheek, his lips . . .

'Oh!' She jumped as a loud banging came from the front of the house. As she hurried into the hall the banging came again, not from upstairs but from the front door. It wasn't Alice.

Going through to the porch, Nina dimmed the lamp and turned the latch, peering past the chain into the darkness, where three figures stood on the doorstep. 'Thank heavens,' a woman said in an annoyed voice. 'We thought you must be asleep and that we'd have to wake Alice with the bell.'

Nina undid the chain and the woman pushed past, followed by a younger woman and an elderly porter with a trunk. 'In the hall will do,' the second woman said quietly, removing her gloves and giving the man a coin from her purse. Her thin face was pale and she looked tired.

The older woman's cheeks were flushed, the tip of her nose red. 'How is she?' she demanded over her shoulder.

'She's been asleep all the time I've been here.'

'You're not English.' The woman turned to the hallway and called, 'Where are you going, Nell? Hadn't we better unpack?'

The young woman was obviously used to this. 'Yes, Mother,' she answered softly from the stairs, 'but I'd like to see Alice first.'

Nina stepped forward. 'I'm Mrs Truelove. And you are?'

'Why, Mrs Evans, Alice's mother-in-law. We sent a message this morning but the train was greatly delayed.'

Nina hurried back through almost deserted streets. Mrs Evans hadn't invited her to stay, not that she would have wanted to. No, she'd go home and Richard would be furious because she'd had to walk back alone. She thought how she'd amuse him with her description of Mrs Evans's face when she saw there was only bread and some cheese for her supper: she'd positively glared, as if she suspected Nina of eating everything in the larder!

The stars shone overhead and the cold reminded her of the morning she'd left the estate, trudging hand in hand along the drive with Darya. And then one of the stars arced across the sky, followed by another and another. They weren't stars at all but searchlights – further along the coast a raid must be taking place. She stopped to watch, wondering if Richard was doing the same from one of the upstairs windows. Harry might also be watching, from the house he was sharing with some of the other officers.

'Quite a show, isn't it?' The special constable stepped out of a doorway. 'Not so pretty if it's overhead, mind, and they're dropping their wares. Do you have far to go, miss?' Before Nina could reply, he suddenly shouted, 'First floor, lights!' and huffed across the road.

When she got home she was relieved to see Richard's coat on the stand. She hung up her own coat then ran lightly up the stairs, to where a light shone from under the bedroom door. He'd be so surprised to see her and to hear about her evening. As she pushed the bedroom door open, however, she froze, her hand still on the doorknob. The bedside lamp was on, she could see it in the wardrobe mirror, but the rest of the scene was incomprehensible, for there was a naked man, no two of them, on her bed.

Who were they? What was happening?

As the confusion of arms and legs sorted itself in her mind, she understood that one of the men was Richard. The man with him had a shock of blond hair; he was on his hands and knees and Richard was kneeling behind him, his eyes closed. Richard's face looked terrible, red and contorted, as he moved back and forth, breathing in loud grunts. The man beneath him braced his arms, his member hanging from him impossibly large and red. His mouth was open as he gasped for breath, and then his eyes opened too, meeting hers in the mirror.

She stood where she was, staring back, until her body took over and she silently stepped backwards, out of the door and across the landing. She managed to turn and make her way down the stairs, although by the time she reached the bottom her knees were trembling so violently she had to hold on to the newel.

Overhead she could hear Richard cry out.

She put her hands over her ears; she wasn't meant to hear. When Richard told her about the boys he met on his outings, he talked about 'larking around'. Or he might say he'd met a nice boy, 'a funny boy who gave me a kiss and a cuddle'. She'd pictured it all as a sort of boyish game. What happened between a man and a woman was no mystery to her, but she hadn't realised that the same things could happen between two men.

When she woke, her back ached and her mouth was dry and foul tasting. Light was coming between the curtains and at first she thought she was on the sofa in the morning room, but the curtains were red, not turquoise, and there was no desk. She was in Brighton, and this room was the parlour. Shivering, she tried to huddle deeper into the cushions but it was no good, the room was cold and it all came back: Richard had been with a man, in the way that a man went with a woman.

Richard had told her everything, she had thought; there were no secrets between them. But now she could see how absurd that was, and how absurd she had been in believing it. He had told her only so much and no more. Liar. She tried the word out in her head, but it didn't ring true. How could he tell her what really went on between him and the boys he met? And how could she really have believed that his sexual life was made up of nothing more than games? She had turned eighteen, she wasn't a child. 'It is hard to explain,' he had said, over three years ago now, in Aunt Elena's garden. 'Many people find it difficult to understand and so they think it is wrong. I freely acknowledge it is a mystery but I do not believe that that makes it wrong.'

Nina had accepted that – it had been an enormous relief, that they were to be just friends – but now that she knew what it really meant, how did she feel about it? She turned this question over in her mind. What she had seen had shocked her because it was unexpected. But it wasn't of its nature more shocking than what happened between a man and a woman. No, what she resented was that Richard had brought the man to her bed and that he had not come down to her. She had waited last night but he'd left her here alone, without even a rug or a blanket. Maybe he was angry, she thought, feeling angry herself at the injustice of it, for it wasn't her fault Alice's mother had appeared. It was wrong of him to humiliate her like this, leaving her to sleep like a servant while he spent the night with a stranger in her bed.

She went along the hall to the downstairs lavatory on numb legs. The water from the taps was ice cold and her hands felt raw. After splashing her face she did what she could to tidy her hair before going through to the pantry to get a box of matches and the tea caddy. She was alone and unwanted in her own home and her hands shook as she lit the gas.

'So you're the housekeeper?'

Water spilt from the kettle as she swung round. He was

standing in the doorway, holding his coat and wearing an enlisted man's uniform. He was younger than she'd thought last night, no older than she was.

They stared at each other, then she carefully put the kettle on the ring before turning back to face him. 'I am his wife.'

A startled look came into his eyes. He appeared to weigh her in his thoughts, then gave an ugly smile and said, very slowly, 'You Belgian bints must really like big cocks. Though I couldn't put me hand on me heart and swear to the Almighty he's the best fuck I ever had – how 'bout you?' He pulled a mock sad face. 'Too good to talk to me? Well, his lordship's sleeping like a baby, so you can go on up and get yourself some leftovers if you like.'

He pulled on his coat and walked away down the hall, leaving the front door open behind him so the sound of the sea swept into the house.

Ten

Alice Evans didn't have one baby but two, twin girls. On her way to the library the following Tuesday Nina met Mrs Laing, who confided that despite the births Alice was still so sunk in sorrow no one knew what to do with her. It seemed very wrong, selfish even, after the blessing of two healthy girls. When spoken to she didn't reply but simply stared at the wall, barely acknowledging her daughters' existence, so that in exasperation her mother-in-law had named her granddaughters herself, believing names might somehow make the poor babes more real to their mother. The elder of the pair, marked by a pink ribbon tied at the wrist, was to be known as Patience, while the younger, marked with mauve, was Hope.

'Which is very appropriate, under the circumstances.' Mrs Laing started as a seagull screamed overhead in the rain. 'And your husband, I've heard he's applying to be released from his duties in London. He'll be bitterly disappointed if they turn him down. I will remember him in my prayers.'

Nina bowed her head under the umbrella. The last time she'd prayed had been the night Mamma died.

'Mrs Truelove, it's good to see you back; we've been very understaffed.' Mrs Hunter unlocked the heavy doors, saying something about how the damp patches on the ceiling had spread and buckets had been put out as a precaution. Nina followed her across the vestibule but the older woman stopped short in the doorway. 'Oh my God!' It was raining in the middle of the library. 'The books!' she screamed. 'The books!'

Together they dropped their umbrellas and ran to pull sodden books off the centre shelves, hugging volumes of the *Encyclopaedia Britannica* and *Mrs Beeton* against their coats and piling them in dry corners. Lydia Barnes arrived a few minutes later and Mrs Hunter shouted at her to telephone for help.

While the men stood on ladders and hammered boards across the ceiling, Nina spread old newspapers over the parquet floor and trod them down before covering them with dustsheets. The library was only open from noon on Tuesdays anyway so Mrs Hunter pinned a notice to the front doors, declaring it closed for the rest of the day. She then produced headscarves from a drawer. Nina caught sight of her reflection in a window: she looked like one of the village girls who came to help roll bales of hay or carry lunch to Papa. The men would clap and call obscenities as they walked through Low Field. Sometimes the girls called back.

Despite the devastation, Mrs Hunter seemed happier than she had been for weeks: the worst had happened. 'Mrs Truelove,' she bustled up, carrying her coat and hat, 'I cannot tell you how grateful I am. Between us I believe we've saved most of the volumes that were in danger.'

Nina couldn't help looking up at the planks covering the ceiling, and Mrs Hunter followed her gaze. 'The foreman assures me it will hold, as a temporary measure. The rain appears to be clearing and if we have a few dry days there'll be time for the slates to be replaced. But I'm determined that things be done properly and am going to the Town Hall this minute to discuss the matter in person. Miss Barnes, as deputy librarian, will come with me. I expect we'll have to persevere with this matter for the rest of the afternoon and I would be grateful if you would agree to take my spare set of keys and lock the library after the work is completed. The men will also need advice about where to move some of the shelving. It must be done today so we can open again tomorrow – I'm determined we won't lose more than one afternoon. There's a new packet of Lipton's in the office cupboard and,' she added generously, 'in the top right drawer of my desk a tin of arrowroot biscuits.'

There was a small mirror on the back of the office door. Nina tidied her hair and rubbed at a dirty smear across her right cheek, wondering as she did so what Harry O'Connor would think if he could see her now. Just as quickly she dismissed the thought – it was nothing more than schoolgirl nonsense.

A gust of laughter came from the other side of the door. 'Billy-boy, you be careful with them there books!'

A wave of resentment went through her and she remembered how angry she'd felt as she walked up the stairs after the young soldier had left the house that morning. But the anger had drained away as she looked down on Richard asleep under the blankets, his arms flung wide and a sweet smile on his face. She realised he hadn't known she was there the previous night and that if he had known he would have come down immediately – he was no coward. No, he didn't know and she would never tell him. 'But,' a small voice whispered, 'you still have every right to be angry. He told you you could take a lover and have a child, but that's impossible and you know it. What gentleman would become involved with a married woman?' The ugly look on the young soldier's face came into her mind and then she shivered as she saw another face behind it: the wolf man sneering at her at the *bal blanc*.

'Ma'am?' The mirror swung towards her and she stepped quickly back as the foreman came into the room, cap in hand. 'Pardon me, ma'am – I did knock but you cannot have heard for all the commotion. We're about to move some shelving and thought we'd best ask you first, if you don't mind.'

'Of course,' she said quietly. 'I'll come now.'

When the foreman knocked again it was past six o'clock. The library looked miserable with the shelves gathered around the walls and dustsheets over the floor. The men packed their tools then Nina locked the doors and followed them down the steps. At the bottom she found herself behind a group of giggling factory girls, josting and teasing each other.

The girls turned towards the centre of town and Nina turned in the direction of the sea. There was a slight breeze and she hugged her coat around her. The clouds kept covering the moon and it was dark, the light from the blue-painted lamps dim.

'Cooee!' Some soldiers shouted up ahead, their voices echoing across the low waves. And then from behind the echo there came something else, a low hum. The soldiers heard it too, stopping and looking up at the same time she did. It was closer now, a determined buzz. Suddenly a spotlight appeared from nowhere, raking the sky and marvellous to see. Then there was another and another until the sky and sea were full of dancing lights. In the wonder of the lights she forgot what they were searching for so it was a shock when the soldiers sent up a shout as a cigar-shaped shadow appeared from behind a cloud. The shout turned into a cheer and suddenly she felt like cheering with them because it was a magnificent sight, the great shape suspended so high up with the sweeping lights playing over it and the clouds behind.

The Zeppelin was still a fair way from the coast, heading west, when a bright light raced towards it and there was an explosion. 'Star-bombs!' someone yelled. 'Our boys are firing at it!'

A small crowd had appeared from nowhere. 'Let's kill Germans!' a boy called from a man's shoulders. There was laughter and then a shared intake of breath as another star-bomb streaked towards the aircraft.

When the explosion came the giant shape seemed to shudder. 'Hooray!' The soldiers were dancing up and down, a war dance, but then from the back of the crowd there were angry cries of 'Lights out!' Nina quickly glanced round but there were no lights in the windows behind them. The crowd surged towards the road and between shoulders she could see the dark shape of a cyclist being pulled off a bicycle. There was the sound of breaking glass as a bicycle lamp was thrown to the ground.

'Leave me alone!' The voice was that of an older, middle-class woman. 'Take your hands off me!' she called crossly.

It was widely believed that German spies signalled to enemy aircraft, and for a moment Nina feared the woman would be hurt; at that moment, however, the crowd's attention was attracted by a change in the Zeppelin's course. It stood still in the sky, as if hesitating, then slowly moved round so that it was no longer pointing along the coast but directly at them. The hum changed too as it changed direction, two or three star-bombs now frantically streaking in its direction.

'Run!' Nina had to brace her feet as people pushed and ran in every direction, leaving her alone again except for the soldiers. 'Come on!' one of them yelled, 'Come on!' He and one of his companions jumped down from the top of the low wall overlooking the beach, but the other stayed where he was.

'We're going to be killed anyway!' he shouted. 'I'd rather die in Brighton than fucking France!' His companions yelled something then raced off, jumping over the abandoned bicycle.

The man on the wall was laughing, and Nina laughed too as the clouds parted and she saw an elderly man in a long, dark dressing gown loping along the pavement: the world had gone mad. As he drew close she could see he was barelegged and barefoot, his breath coming in great ragged gasps. She watched him go then turned back to the approaching Zeppelin. 'I'm here!' The soldier was waving his arms wildly. 'Here, you bastards! Here!' The moon disappeared and it was dark again.

'Mrs Truelove!' A voice shouted into her ear and she was grabbed roughly by the sleeve of her coat. 'Are you trying to get yourself killed? Run!' She resisted for a second but then the air filled with the howl of sirens and she was running with him, her boots slipping as they crossed the road. He stopped on the corner and she fell heavily against him, feeling the cast on his arm under his coat. 'Do you live far away?' he yelled.

'No.' She could barely breathe.

'One minute? More?'

She looked around quickly, unsure of where they were. 'One minute.'

'Then come on!'

He was half dragging her as they ran up the street towards the house. 'Here!' she screamed. 'Here!' tearing her glove off and groping wildly for the key.

They collapsed into the hall and she held him by the hand, feeling her way along the wall to the dining room. 'The table.' She fell to her knees and he followed clumsily. A flash came from behind the curtains as the air outside exploded and the whole room lit up. He was breathing heavily, and without thinking she reached out to find his face, turning it towards her and running her fingertips down to his lips.

He held her fingers fiercely against his mouth before pushing her hand away. There came the smell of a match striking and then there was a shock of red hair and a pair of blue eyes looking urgently into hers.

'Are you sure?' he shouted over the sirens. And then, 'Mrs

Truelove – Nina – I'm leaving Brighton tomorrow, you must know that!'

Slowly, she reached out again.

Eleven

On a warm day like this the windows of the Royal Albion overlooked a sea front crowded with wounded soldiers, some sitting on benches clutching crutches, others in bath chairs. Under the grey or navy blankets many were missing one or both legs. A small boy still in skirts pointed at the occupant of one of the chairs and Nina saw the woman with him shake her head and take his hand to hurry him along.

'You'd like some tea, madam?' The little waitress discreetly picked a flower petal off the cloth and rolled it between her fingers.

'Yes. And a plate of sandwiches.' A small group of Australian soldiers had gathered around one of their comrades and she found herself watching although she knew Harry wouldn't be there. She hadn't seen him since the night of the Zeppelin. 'I'll have to go back to my digs,' he'd whispered, stroking her face, 'or I'll be missed, and I have to leave for London early in the morning.'

The doctors had become concerned that his arm wasn't healing properly, and had arranged for him to be seen at Guy's Hospital. He was being sent to barracks in Horseferry Road. That had been ten days ago. Reaching into her bag, Nina took out the letter that had arrived in this morning's post. It was the second letter she'd received from him and she'd already read it half a dozen times. *I am beginning to feel I know London as I travel between the barracks and the hospital. There are queues for the x-ray machines and emergency cases must take precedence, but yesterday my arm was finally x-rayed and I will be called in again when the X-rays have been seen by a surgeon.*

In the meantime I continue to exist in something of an official limbo. I am able to spend some of my time exploring London and I was wondering if you would like to come up for lunch. I will quite understand if you cannot . . .

Across the road one of the Australians was pushing a chair. The occupant's left trouser leg was folded neatly at the knee and he pointed forward with a swizzle stick, as if commanding a charge. What if Harry's arm didn't heal; what if he lost it?

The waitress put the tray down with a bang. 'Sorry, madam.' She smiled apologetically. 'Earlier on some of the ladies were discussing the Zeppelin. Did you see it?'

'Yes, I did.'

She giggled. 'We were hiding under the tables here, like sardines. I don't know how much damage would have been done, or people killed, if our lads hadn't chased it away. We were lucky, my pa says.'

'We were . . .' Nina could still hear the surprise in his voice, overcoming desire. 'I didn't know. Shall I stop? Do you want me to stop?' Holding her hand over his mouth, she'd pushed him deep inside, crying out in Russian, words she'd learned from the fields and the kitchen.

'Will there be anything else?' the waitress asked.

'Some notepaper and an envelope.' She'd write to Harry now, saying she would meet him.

The train passed fields, a clutch of thatched cottages, a church spire. Behind her reflection were those of the other two occupants of the first-class compartment, a middle-aged couple who'd barely spoken since the journey began and who now sat deeply immersed in their reading. The book Nina had brought, an English translation of *Crime and Punishment* which Lawrence had given her before the war, sat unopened in her lap. She continued studying herself in the glass. 'I know,' Richard had said that morning in Aunt Elena's garden, 'that I can trust you to be discreet.' Who was it that Mamma had described as 'the height of indiscretion'? It had been Olga Ivanovna. Nina had sat on the floor doing a jigsaw puzzle and heard Olga Ivanovna light a cigarette and say to Mamma, 'I am not a fool, Irina, and although I enjoy myself I am careful not to endanger my marriage.' It was the word 'endanger' that had captured Nina's interest, and she imagined a princess, in danger of being carried off by an ogre. Mamma saw her listening and waved her out.

In the kitchen, however, she found Cook talking about the robust gardener who accompanied Olga Ivanovna's carriage everywhere while her wealthy merchant husband was away on business. 'She says it's too dangerous to travel with only a coachman these days, because of the revolutionaries.' Cook pummelled the dough. 'Well, revolutionaries must often surround that house, for they say that when the master's absent the gardener spends more of his time harvesting indoors than he does out.' The women laughed, but that night Nina had been too frightened to sleep, fearing revolutionaries would surround their house also. Mamma came through and asked what was wrong, and when Nina told her, Mamma stroked her forehead and said Cook had only been joking. When Nina asked why it was then that the gardener stayed inside, rather than tending the gardens, Mamma said he was no doubt a carpenter as well and had many small jobs to do. The next morning, however, Nina had heard Mamma make the comment about Olga Ivanovna's indiscretion to Papa, adding, 'It's not enough that she makes me privy to secrets I have no desire to know, but even our kitchen is intimate to all her business. I won't invite her again.'

'Excuse me, but do you mind if I open the window?' The man opposite had lowered his book and was about to stand up.

'I can do it.' The window opened easily. 'Is that enough?'

He was scrutinising her over the top of his glasses. 'Thank you. I hope you won't think me terribly rude, but am I right in thinking you're from Russia?'

His wife looked at him, raising her eyebrows slightly.

'I am Russian.'

He puffed his cheeks, not trying to disguise his excitement. 'I cannot help wondering what your feelings might be about the great changes happening in your country.'

'Arthur,' his wife frowned fondly, 'don't agitate yourself. Not everyone shares your interest in politics.'

'This isn't simply a matter of politics, my dear,' pulling a silk handkerchief from his pocket, he made as if to wipe his forehead, then waved it in the air instead, 'but of world history. As it said in the *Manchester Guardian*, we might be witnessing the birth of democracy in one of the largest nations on earth. There is bound to be an effect on the rest of the world. Although it is still possible, I suppose, that the old order will prevail . . .'

'No,' Nina found herself shaking her head, 'no, I think the time has come for change in Russia.' It would mean change for all the people she knew, Papa and their friends and neighbours, but it would be a good thing for Russia to have a proper parliament, and more modern ideas.

'Well then,' the man nodded as if everything was settled to his satisfaction, 'I'm glad to hear you say that. Democracy is, I believe, a sacred thing. The greatest gift Britain has given to mankind.'

'Not that I would call our own country a democracy,' his wife added, 'with half the population still unable to vote.' She sounded like Maggie.

'Quite right.' He patted her hand and smiled at Nina. 'Let us hope, madam, that your extraordinary and wonderful country will teach *us* a lesson about universal suffrage.'

Fleet Street was crowded, the road full of carts and automobiles and the pavements a mass of umbrellas. After getting out of the cab, Nina walked too far along the pavement then realised she'd missed the door and turned back. She'd never before been inside a public house and hesitated at the doorway before closing her umbrella and stepping into the interior, which was dimly lit and fogged with tobacco smoke. A shrill scream from the direction of the counter made her start; there was a large red and green parrot on a perch, bobbing up and down as a man in a bowler hat bobbed in front of it.

'Well of course things will change with the Yankees!' a soldier in Canadian uniform shouted at his compatriots. He bumped against Nina and touched his cap. 'Pardon me, miss.'

Further in, the tables were taken up with men in suits and a few women. There was a low hum of voices. Nina stood self-consciously, searching the room for Harry, and finally saw him sitting at a small table in a corner, reading a newspaper. There was a lamp on the wall behind him and in its light his hair burned red. A jolt of panic went through her as she squeezed her way past the tables.

His head came up, blue eyes wide as if surprised to see her there. 'Good heavens.' Part of the newspaper slipped to the floor and he bent over to pick it up before pushing himself out of the chair. 'I thought it would take you much longer to get here from the station.' They shook hands awkwardly and as they did so Nina saw that although his arm was still in a sling the cast was off.

'Oh, your arm!' Relief flooded through her.

'Yes.' He looked down at it. 'I got a message to go to the hospital yesterday morning and the surgeon said he could see nothing wrong with the x-rays at all and there was no reason to delay in sawing off the plaster. So off it came. It will be some weeks before I get the strength back.'

He'd be returning to France, but that was all right, she reminded herself – as a translator he wouldn't be in the front line. Looking up, she saw a muscle jump in his left cheek and said quickly, 'You must be very relieved.'

'There was one stage when I thought – well, you think all sorts of things, tuberculosis of the bone, all that. Would you like some tea?' He held the chair for her and she sat down. 'It should be possible. I'll ask.'

He went over to the counter and she tried to calm herself by looking around. At a table across the room three women in their twenties were engaged in earnest conversation. She wondered if they worked for a newspaper. They all wore dark tailored jackets and had smooth bobbed hair: 'Nihilists' was how Mamma would have described them. Nina didn't look much different herself, in a simple white blouse, navy skirt and navy linen jacket. There was a mirror on the wall behind the women, and her own face stared back, pale under her hat, while behind her Harry leaned on the counter. Despite his colouring he was physically very different from Richard. He wasn't as tall, his build was slighter and his clean-shaven, heart-shaped face wasn't conventionally handsome. 'Had you imagined this could happen?' he'd asked as they kissed goodbye in the dark hall, still hungry for each other. 'Had you dreamed it?'

'Yes, but I thought it was only a dream.'

He whispered into her hair, 'I saw you walking through the

town and followed you to the sea front. I knew I was leaving and wanted to speak to you again, just once.'

Blindly, she'd searched for his mouth.

'I've ordered tea.'

Her cheeks were burning and she glanced away as Harry sat down. 'I hope you don't mind coming here,' he said. 'I know it's not really suitable but I've always wanted to see Fleet Street. Before the war I planned on joining a newspaper and had fantasies about working in London one day. I still do.'

Nina hadn't allowed herself to imagine anything like that. Her voice came out slightly hoarse. 'I wanted to thank you, for telling me about your grandfather that evening.'

He frowned slightly. 'I felt worried later, that I could have embarrassed you.'

'No!' She shook her head. 'No. Tell me about him now.'

Reaching inside his jacket, Harry took out a packet of cigarettes and some matches. 'He was one of the kindest, most civilised men I've ever met.' He struck a match.

'How did he get to Australia?' she asked quickly.

'The same way everyone gets there, by ship.' He gave a low laugh, avoiding her eyes. 'He came over as a ship's carpenter on an English ship, met my grandmother and stayed. She was working in a lace shop in Sydney and he went in to buy a lace collar to send to his mother. My grandmother sold him the collar and they were married three weeks later.'

'And he taught you German?'

He drew on a cigarette and smiled for the first time. 'English was his great love as a language. He decided when he was twelve that he wanted to see the world and that the English merchant navy offered the best opportunity, so he taught himself English from a school textbook and a dictionary. He came to London when he was seventeen. He adored English literature. England for literature, he used to say, Germany for music and Australia for women and dogs – he bred cattle dogs. He played the fiddle brilliantly, it's where my mother and Ruby – my sister – get their talent from. They're both professional musicians. My mother's a pianist and Ruby's a violinist; she trained at the Conservatorium in Sydney.'

Behind them the parrot screamed. He nodded in its direction.

'We have birds like that in Australia. I wonder how it feels, living here?'

'Your tea, sir.' A waitress had brought a tray. They waited silently while she set the table.

When she left, Nina asked, 'Were there problems when the war started, because of your grandfather?'

He ran a fingertip along the edge of the table and she saw he had a musician's fingers, long and well shaped, the nails carefully filed. 'Within a week someone threw a rock through the window of my parents' music shop. There was a note wrapped around it saying, "Your father was a filthy Hun and so are you." I was home from university and had gone in with Mother to open up. When I passed the note to her I could see the blood drain from her face. She was absolutely white, and then – and this was completely unexpected – she put her hands to her mouth and said, "*Mein Gott!*" My grandfather had taught her some German as a child but she hadn't spoken it in years. It's a funny thing, language. Later, when we were at home and talking about it with Ruby, Mother wept with laughter; there she was, being accused of being German, and the first thing she says is *Mein Gott*. Ruby thought it was the most hilarious thing she'd ever heard.'

'Is Ruby your only sister?'

'Yes. And I've a younger brother, Edward, who's thirteen – young enough not to be involved in this, thank God.' He suddenly reached across the table and looped his fingers around her left wrist. 'You've got wrists like Ruby, I can do this with hers. You remind me of Ruby in some ways.'

She watched his fingers circling her wrist, fascinated by the intimacy of the gesture and the welcome sensation of his touch. She didn't want him to stop. After a moment she said, 'Is she younger than you too?'

'Older, by fifteen months. Her hair's the same colour as mine and very long. People often think we're twins. How many siblings do you have?'

All she was conscious of was their fingers, curling around each other's; she could have been saying anything. 'One sister, Katya. We're both tall but her hair isn't as dark as mine, or her eyes. We look like sisters – we both take after our mother – but no one would think we were twins.'

'My father's dark and so is Edward.' He smiled. 'My mother jokes about aboriginal blood. Ruby and I take after my mother's mother, who's Irish. My father's father was Irish as well, of course.'

'You're Catholic?'

'Officially Papists but you wouldn't know it; we're not a family of real churchgoers. Both my grandmothers did sometimes take us when we were children, and ever since I've had a weakness for candles.' He gently let go of her hand and reached into his top pocket. 'I'd like to give you something. I bought it in Cairo and was going to send it to Ruby for her birthday, but I can find something else for Rubes in London.'

Opening the folded brown paper, Nina found an intricate gold bracelet decorated with scarabs. It was beautiful. 'Thank you.' The metal hung heavy and cool across her wrist and they both studied it. 'What was it like,' she heard herself ask, 'in Egypt?'

'The evacuation?' He shrugged. 'It was hell for the men there and I was lucky to have arrived in the very last stages. It was appallingly hot. I thought I was used to heat from Australia but I'd never experienced anything like it. And it was filthy. The place was crawling – we were crawling – with lice and flies.'

Her eyes left the bracelet and she looked at him. 'I thought it would be wonderful, Egypt.'

He nodded. 'It was, despite the dirt and the heat. To come from a young country like Australia and see something like the Pyramids, something built thousands of years ago. I carved my initials in the base of one of the smaller ones. A group of us went on camels – they're bad-tempered beasts, the stories are all true – and it was so childishly rewarding, to carve your initials into something that old.' He abruptly put out the cigarette. 'Shall we have our tea and then explore? We can find some lunch on the way.'

As they left, the parrot was being watched by a small crowd as it slowly drew a cork from a bottle. Outside it had stopped raining and Nina didn't have to open her umbrella but took Harry's arm when he offered it, conscious of the warmth and closeness of his body. He lightly put his hand on hers. 'I had a quick look at a map this morning and thought we might go by the Inns of Court before walking down to the river.' They made their way along the crowded pavement and then turned down a side alley, which led into a quiet courtyard. Two barristers in wigs and gowns walked past. 'Isn't it amazing?' he whispered. 'Like stepping back into the Middle Ages.'

The central lawn had been dug over for vegetables, and as the sun came out from behind a cloud it shone on an elderly gardener who was bent over, pulling weeds. Nina was reminded of the old man who'd beckoned to warn her that the police were going to call. 'Why did you say all the German prisoners were waiters?'

'Oh yes.' He laughed. 'Well, I'd only been in France two weeks when some British soldiers brought in three German prisoners; they simply strolled in with these men, chatting with them in English. It turned out that all three had been waiters in London and had taken the decision to give themselves up. When I asked why, one of them said he couldn't bear the thought that he might have to shoot one of his favourite customers. I didn't think their story could be true at first but then an English officer came in and recognised one of them. They obviously knew each other quite well and when the German asked after one of the officer's friends, and was told he'd died at Arras, he broke down in tears. "I was not at Arras," he sobbed, "but what if I had been? I could not live with myself, thinking I had killed Mr Henderson. He always asked for soup!"'

Nina and Harry had a light lunch in a small café. On leaving, they walked down to the Thames. The sun had come out again and they leaned on the damp railings and watched the river. A barge with sailors went past and one of them waved; he looked very young.

Nina watched them go. 'It must be terrible for your parents,' she said, 'for you to be so far away.'

'Yes.' He paused. 'I expected my mother to be upset, of course, but I thought it was the right thing to do, to join up. I thought it would make things easier for her somehow. Anyway, I told them what I'd done over dinner – and it was strange: Mother said she understood, but my father didn't say anything, he just sat there, silent. And then, after dinner, he asked me to go outside with him and said that the events in Ireland had changed the way he viewed things, the way he thought about the war. He said he thought I'd made a mistake. I didn't know he felt like that, he hadn't said anything. Oh well.' Harry stood up straight again. 'Shall we keep walking? There was something in particular I was hoping to talk to you about.'

A little way along they came to a small lawn and some benches. A grey-uniformed nanny rocked a perambulator in one corner but otherwise they had the area to themselves. There was a bench under a beech tree, just dry enough to sit on, and the sun shone through the leaves overhead.

'I'm glad you came today,' Harry began. 'Nina, I don't want to spoil things, but we mightn't have another opportunity to talk for some time . . .' She felt him give a small shrug. 'It's so difficult to discuss some things – it would be easier to say nothing at all.'

She was frightened of what he might say. 'Please,' she whispered, 'there's no need . . .'

'But there is.' He laid his cap on his knees and ran his hand through his hair. They sat for a minute and then he said very quietly, 'Your relationship with your husband is completely your own business but there are things you need to know. Someone very close to me, someone I love – not a girlfriend, mind – well, she got very badly hurt, and I wouldn't want anything like that to happen to you. I feel some responsibility towards you and so I'm going to talk to you now as if you were my sister. I hope that nothing I'm going to say will offend you in any way.' He took a deep breath.

After he'd finished talking there was silence and then he said, 'How old are you, Nina?'

She almost said twenty-two but stopped herself. 'I am eighteen.'

'Eighteen,' he murmured. She felt him look at her. 'Shall I tell you what it was like, the first time I made love?'

Across the lawn the nanny was asleep on her bench, her chin on her chest. Nina quickly wiped her eyes. 'Yes.'

They were sheltered from view, no one could see, and he put his arm around her. 'It was in April 1912. I'll never forget that because the next day the news about the *Titanic* sinking was in the papers – it seemed such a tragedy, all those lives lost. I was seventeen and somehow I felt as if the whole world had changed and I'd grown up.'

'Was she beautiful?' Nina whispered.

'She had pretty eyes and a lovely laugh.' He ran his fingertip over her lips. 'I enjoyed talking to her.'

Nina had never known you could want someone as much as she wanted him now. 'How many women have you made love to?'

'Thousands. Now do you want to hear this story or not?'

She nodded.

'Bella was thirty.'

'Thirty!'

'Shh. She'd had a terrible time. Her husband had died three years before – she'd gone into labour with their first child and he'd tried to get back home over a flooded creek. His horse lost its footing and he was swept under a bridge and drowned. Bella was left with a new baby, a little girl, and had to make ends meet by giving singing lessons. She had a good voice. I knew her because she often came into the shop to buy sheet music and I worked there during the holidays. One day she came in and said she was moving to Geelong, where she'd accepted a position as housekeeper. She wanted us to crate her piano for her, so Dad sent me to do it.'

'And?' It was almost unbearable.

'I crated the piano.' Harry pulled Nina even closer. 'It was hot and we were both perspiring, and her dress – it had lilies of the valley on it and she smelt of lilies too – was clinging to her. The room was almost empty, nearly everything was packed but for the gramophone, and she put on a record and started to dance, all by herself in the middle of the floor with the sunlight slanting in through the shutters. She bent to take off her shoes and I could see her legs were bare. It was a wonderful moment and we both knew it. I put my arm around her waist and we danced; then we were in the bedroom, naked. I still can't remember how we got there.'

He was silent and Nina held her breath, watching: the woman dreamy with desire, standing in front of the naked boy. They stood in the sunlight, both of them perfect.

'She hadn't been with anyone since her husband died and I

think it represented the end of mourning for her; she was going on to a new life. A year later she married the man she went to work for, a widower with two children. She sent me a Christmas card and sounded very content. It seems like a lifetime ago now.'

Nina turned her face up to him and his lips instantly met hers. She wanted him so much, she wanted him for ever. They kissed for a long time, lost in each other, and then he spoke quietly against her cheek. 'My darling, we'd better start moving if you want to catch your train.'

If she started to cry now she would never stop. Instead, she took his arm and they walked across the grass.

'The story about the waiters – it's not all like that, you know, questioning prisoners,' she heard him say.

'No,' she replied. 'I don't suppose it is.'

They headed back in the direction they'd come. It couldn't be happening, she kept thinking, it couldn't be over. He was saying something.

'I won't come to the station in case we run into anyone you know.'

It started to rain again and as they emerged on to Fleet Street they saw a cab approaching. Harry hailed it, and before Nina knew it he was helping her in and the door was shutting. He spoke through the open window. 'You will write?'

Nina couldn't speak, her throat tight. He squeezed her fingertips. As the driver flicked the reins he walked quickly alongside. 'Your husband,' his face was drawn and anxious, 'Richard – he is good to you, isn't he?'

'Oh yes,' she called back. 'We have an understanding!' But the rhythm of the cab quickened and she couldn't see him any more, his face lost in a sea of uniforms and umbrellas.

Twelve

The war will be over within the year, Katya wrote, *that is what everyone here believes. The involvement of the Americans will mean the inevitable defeat of Germany. Meanwhile the talk in our community is of nothing but events in Petrograd where, it is said, the streets were lined with black limousines as government officials and their families fled. I weep for the Emperor and his family, and for Russia. The newspapers here talk about democracy but they know nothing of the Russian character or history. The provisional government is made up only of Liberals and Bolsheviks – how is that democratic? I take refuge from these dark thoughts in the running of the business and in looking after my darling babies.*

Katya had enclosed a letter from Aunt Elena, addressed to the two of them. Their aunt and her family were already in Finland before the Petrograd riots and Elena had posted her letter only days before they were due to embark for Canada. *Soon the country we knew will no longer exist,* she'd written. *Neither I nor my daughters – nor you, Katya or Nina – will ever see Russia again.*

Before leaving, Elena had gone to the farm. It was widely rumoured that while he was in the army Andrei had single-handedly captured two German officers; although Elena didn't know if there was any truth in this, for she had only seen Papa from a distance. She paid a baker to drive her there in his cart but when Andrei saw her walking down the drive he mounted his horse and rode away across High Field.

From what I could see, your father, that grand gentleman, is wilder than ever. I went into the house – the house where I was born and lived until the day I married – and had I not known it for what it was I would not have recognised it. The furniture and paintings are all gone and the only room fulfilling its original function is the kitchen; the rest is all hospital. There were wounded soldiers everywhere and many more outside in rows of tents.

Mrs Kulmana is still in charge and I found her very civil. She told me that Dr Vilensky had left a year ago to run one of the biggest military hospitals near Moscow, where he specialised in neurological operations. (I already knew this.) She spoke in the past tense and when I asked if he was still in Moscow she would not meet my eye and replied she was not sure. No doubt there was some falling-out with the authorities. Your Uncle Aleksei had made enquiries about him when he first arrived at the farm – for why would a doctor wth any reputation come to such a place? – and the stories were that although he was a brilliant surgeon, he was known to be addicted to the drugs he prescribed to his patients. (When I left the farm my baker-driver solemnly told me there had been a scandal in Moscow. These days a baker might be as well informed as a duke and for all I know his story is true.) I asked Mrs Kulmana how my brother was and she replied his injuries had healed and the hospital relied on him for its supplies, which he procured by bartering produce from the farm. So I must assume he is not entirely mad. I asked her to tell him his daughters were both well and that my daughters and I were about to leave on a long journey. She promised to pass on this information but it was obvious that we both knew it would not be received with any great interest.

My baker had promised to return for me by lunchtime so I spent the rest of my time trying to find traces of what had once existed. The flower gardens are all gone but there remains one climbing rose, a white one, on the north wall. It was a favourite of your mother's. I had quite expected the stables to be filled with beds but the outbuildings are still kept for animals and I was surprised by the amount of hay stored there and the good condition of the horses. The conservatory is a sad thing, mostly reduced to frames for seedlings. Mrs Kulmana has recruited a number of young nurses, many of them from rough backgrounds, though they appeared clean and hard-working enough. But there were also young women from good families, for it seems the dedication of our Empress and her daughters has made the nurse's uniform fashionable. I recognised a couple of the farm hands, older men, and your old cook is still there. She wept when I told her that you were happy and living in England

*and asked to be remembered to you. Her husband still works on the
farm but their eldest son was killed early on in the war. I asked if she
had any news of Darya but she said there had been no news of her
since before the war started.*

*After that I left. I walked up the drive and did not look back. The
home I had known was no more, it no longer exists. At least your
mamma saw none of this.*

As Nina carefully folded the letter she wondered where Leila
had been when Aunt Elena visited. She had to have been there
somewhere; she would never leave Mrs Kulmana. Putting Aunt
Elena's letter aside, Nina picked up the last letter she'd had from
Harry. Three days after they'd met in London he'd written to say
he expected to leave for France soon, and a week later she
received a letter saying he could be embarking at any time. With
this letter he'd enclosed a photograph of himself on a camel; in
the distance there was a pyramid. Taking out the photograph
now, Nina studied it closely. Harry's face was shaded under his
hat and it was hard to make out his features, but he looked older
than his twenty-three years. Maybe the photograph told the real
truth, for they were all older inside. She looked at the picture for
a few minutes, remembering what he'd told her as they sat on the
London bench. 'There are things you need to know,' he'd said.
'About diseases which women, as well as men, can catch. And, of
course, pregnancy. But there are precautions you can take. The
girl I knew who got hurt, she had an affair with an older man,
who was married, and she fell pregnant. He refused to acknowledge that the child was his and she had an abortion, an
operation to get rid of the baby. It was a dreadful thing to go
through and she could have died. I saw her after the operation
and it was very shocking to see her so ill.'

It was his sister, Ruby, he was talking about. He hadn't said so
but Nina could tell from his voice. She'd felt angry at first, not
with Harry for telling her these things, but because she'd been
left ignorant about them – why had she and Katya never been
told that it was possible to avoid pregnancy? But then she'd
remembered the conversation between Katya and Darya in the
kitchen, when the betrothal cake was being prepared, and

understood. In many ways Darya, perhaps even Mamma, was as ignorant as Nina herself had been.

She laid the photograph back in the metal box in which she kept Harry's letters, then put on her jacket and hat. More often than not she was spending all day at the library, as it was suddenly short of volunteers: Vanessa Tucker, for example, had stopped coming. 'Has something happened to Mrs Tucker?' she'd asked when she noticed Vanessa's name crossed off the roster.

'It is all too possible,' Lydia Barnes blinked, 'that something has happened to *him*. No one, of course, can ask, but she sent a message saying she is no longer available and Miss Finlay saw her in church last week and said she is thinner and has lost her bloom entirely. Once that happens it never comes back. We must fear the worst has befallen her pilot.'

The following weeks passed slowly. Harry was somewhere in France, questioning his prisoners – she'd had two letters – and Richard was in Paris. Alice Evans's mother-in-law was taking Alice and the twins to Gloucester, and Nina went to see them before they left.

'She doesn't want to leave Brighton, but what else can we do?' Alice's sister-in-law, Nell, said in a low voice. 'It's difficult for her but I do believe she is trying. Don't be alarmed if she doesn't acknowledge you.'

The elder Mrs Evans overheard. 'The plain truth is that she's in danger of losing her wits entirely.' She made it sound as if her daughter-in-law had carelessly broken a necklace and lost the beads down the floorboards.

The twins slept peacefully in their cots, their hands curled tight as ferns. Across the other side of the room their mother's grief had eaten her away to the bone, so that her hands, clutching at the green coverlet, were those of an old woman. Nina sat beside the bed and Alice stared at the wall without seeming to hear anything that was said. When Nina finally rose to go she felt dispirited and light-headed and had to hold on to the doorframe. When she looked up again Alice was watching her, her mouth forming into an ugly shape as if she were going to howl. ''Oodbye.' She formed the words painfully. ' 'Oodbye.'

*

153

While the news in the papers was about Baghdad, there was some new gossip in Brighton about the Zeppelin. 'There was a lady cyclist, signalling in Morse code,' Mrs Laing informed the Women's Guild. 'I was at the Pavilion this morning and heard it from the Matron, who was told by a nurse who knows a special constable. Unfortunately the woman escaped in the crowd. When the police examined her abandoned bicycle they discovered Ordnance Survey maps cleverly concealed in the frame. Matron told me all about it. She – the spy, I mean – was wearing bloomers and the shape of a pistol was clearly discernible under them. No doubt that is why she escaped.'

Mrs Burton-Smith, Secretary of the Guild, was hostess for today's meeting. 'I have been told, on very good authority, that there are known cases of the mothers of prisoners of war being forced to spy. They're told that if they do so their sons will be treated well. If they don't, the poor lads will be tortured and then executed.'

'You mean British mothers?' Mrs Laing frowned.

'Why, yes.'

Mrs Laing straightened her shoulders. 'I find it difficult to believe that any British woman whose son was willing to sacrifice himself for his country would be feeble enough to betray it herself.'

Mrs Burton-Smith fanned herself with her hand and sought refuge in Nina. 'I'm so excited about the prospect of the Tsar and his family coming to England. Indeed, my sister-in-law believes a petition should be got up, declaring that the Pavilion would be a fitting residence and would make the Russian royal family feel at home after all they've been through.'

'The Pavilion?' Mrs Laing was almost sharp.

Mrs Burton-Smith shifted in her chair. 'Because of the domes.'

'I do not believe that the residents of Brighton would agree to the Pavilion becoming home to a foreign royal family. If the Tsar is to come to England it would surely be appropriate for him to purchase his own residence. I know I would wish to do so, under the circumstances.' She nodded at Nina. 'I know you won't take that amiss, my dear. Now, on the subject of the Zeppelin, I hear you had your own adventure that day.'

'Adventure?' Nina's fingers felt for the bracelet.

'Oh yes, I heard all about it. You deserve to be commended for not panicking in what must have been the most difficult circumstances. It is dreadful that nothing was done earlier about the library ceiling, despite Mrs Hunter's warnings that it was in danger of collapse. I will be attending a luncheon with the Lady Mayoress on Friday and shall make sure she is aware of your exertions.'

As they collected their outdoor jackets, Mrs Laing took Nina by the elbow and peered into her face, not unkindly. 'I didn't like to say anything earlier for fear of embarrassing you, but you seem very quiet and pale, not your usual self. I understand the recent events in Russia must be very distressing – I know how I would feel if revolutionaries overran England – but it is our duty to look after ourselves so as not to cause our menfolk unnecessary concern. Maybe you need a short break, Nina, a change of scene.'

'I've been invited to Hampstead to stay with friends, the Chaplins, next week.'

'I'm glad to hear it. I have always found that a few days in town works as an excellent pick-me-up.' Doing up her buttons she said, 'Have you heard the news about Constance Jones, from Hove?'

'No.' Nina had only met her once.

'She's engaged to one of the New Zealand officers, Captain Freeman. The poor man's leg has healed short, by a full three-quarters of an inch I'm told, and he's to return home. Dreadful, for a man to be crippled like that. They'll be married after the war but naturally Miss Jones is very worried about him returning at the moment, because of submarines.'

Three-quarters of an inch seemed a small price to pay. Nina looked at Mrs Laing in the mirror as they pinned their hats. 'When do you think the war will end?'

Mrs Laing opened her mouth to reply, then closed it again. Her shoulders sagged. 'I do not know,' she said. 'That is beyond me.'

Nina travelled to London the following Tuesday. Maggie had been held up at a meeting and so it was Frank who met Nina at the station. Her small suitcase was stowed in a guest bedroom and now she was sitting in Frank's study. She looked around the room. She usually enjoyed her stays with the Chaplins – they'd become her closest friends in England – but because of the nature of her marriage she'd never been able to talk to them completely freely, and now she couldn't speak to them about Harry either. 'Don't tell Nina any secrets,' Katya used to say. 'First she'll tell the kitchen and then she'll tell the world.' Well, now her life was a mesh of secrets, whereas someone like Maggie didn't appear to have any at all.

Hearing Frank return along the hall, Nina sat up. He'd offered her supper but she pretended she'd eaten on the train: the truth was she didn't feel like eating and had felt slightly off-colour all week. He came in. 'As I was saying, Nina, it is not a fact Maggie readily acknowledges, but if I did not go to my club she would not be privy to half the political gossip she is privy to now.' He sank back into his armchair. 'All these machinations about the Russian imperial family, for example.'

The room was very stuffy. 'It is believed they'll come to live here – I mean Brighton,' Nina replied.

He sat forward. 'Oh dear no, Nicholas won't be coming to England. I have heard from a reliable source that Lloyd George would allow it but our King doesn't want his royal relatives here. It is said he fears that the resentment that much of the British public feels toward them will colour feelings about the monarchy in general. He cannot be seen to be closing the door on his own cousin, however, so the guilt will be allowed to fall on the shoulders of the government. They will simply say that the mood of the people was against it. Everyone wins, except for the Tsar and his family, who will be exiles in their own land. No doubt their circumstances won't be too uncomfortable.'

Would the King really do that to his own cousins? Well, the emperor and his family were unimaginably wealthy and there were many places they could live in Russia, enormous estates. Nina watched as Frank poured tea from his cup into a saucer and bent forward to offer it to the elderly terrier, Bumble, who nosed the dish and started to lap. 'I share my ration with him,' Frank patted the dog's rump, receiving a low growl in return, 'because it keeps away the distemper. He's been with me fourteen years has the old boy, and he was an excellent ratter in his prime. Not good with children, unfortunately.' He looked at her own untouched cup. 'You're quite sure, are you, that you won't have a bite to eat?'

'I'm sure, thank you.'

He frowned. 'You must be careful not to become anaemic. I was speaking to a doctor last week and he said many more cases of anaemia will arise because people have taken against the new bread. He's been assuring all his patients that it is full of iron and highly beneficial to the digestive system.'

Nina took an envelope from her pocket. 'I've brought you this to read. Richard has a question for you.'

'Where is he at the moment? Although I suppose that's top secret.'

'He's been in France but he's back now. He telephoned yesterday and I told him I was coming here. He sends his best wishes.'

Frank put on his glasses. 'Richard's letters have always been a delight. The ones from Russia were so superb Maggie and I thought he should write a book.' He took the letter out of its envelope. After a minute he chuckled and read aloud: '". . . a Hindu officer from Bombay, who brought me a pot of real curry – delicious but so hot my eyes unmanned me, much to his amusement – attempted to explain his religious beliefs, which are somehow bound up with seeing the infinite in the finite. His reasoning was far too abstract for my poor brain to follow. I have always thought of Hinduism as a violent religion which, until the intervention of the Raj, demanded the barbaric practice of 'sati', in which a widow was burnt in a cage following the death of her husband. How the poor wives must have laboured to keep their spouses alive! Just think if you were expected to throw yourself on my funeral pyre . . . He said that this custom was not widespread across all India and he also told me about another practice, during a Mohammedan era, called 'jauhar', in which the wives of warriors expected to die in battle were burnt first so as not to experience the indignities of capture! When I protested he reminded me of Homer's *Iliad* and the dreadful suffering of the Trojan women, knowing they and their children were to be enslaved . . .'"

Frank smiled. 'Have you read *The Iliad*, Nina? You should. Having to read it in Greek killed the joy for me when I was a boy but I've just finished reading a new English translation done by a professor in Edinburgh, and have enjoyed it enormously. It's on my desk in the library if you're interested. Maggie keeps saying she's going to read it, but with all her work we both know she never will.' He went back to the letter. '"He is an amazingly well-read fellow, knowing not only the Greeks and our own Victorian poets and novelists but also your countryman, Tolstoy. He is a great supporter of Mahatma Gandhi who, he informed me, was a staunch member of the Vegetarian Society during his period as a student in London. He is very keen to be put in touch with the Society and I had to disappoint him by confessing I know nothing about it. Now that I think of it, however, Frank and Maggie might be able to put him in contact with someone. If you speak to them could you ask about this?"'

Frank hummed and nodded to himself. 'I do know someone: Berenice Oliphant – she must be ninety and was probably a member when Mr Gandhi was in London. Her husband was a thin little man who secretly . . .' Looking up, he stopped and removed his glasses. 'Good heavens, you look completely done in. To bed with you Nina; Maggie might not be in for hours and will be cross if I've kept you up.'

He escorted her to the bottom of the stairs. 'Watch your feet, I heard Maggie tell Ellen to put a warming pan in. And there's something I forgot to ask – does the name Lenin mean anything to you?'

'Lenin?'

'Some colleagues from the Fabians were discussing him yesterday. There's some confusion here as to whether he's a Bolshevist or an Anarchist.'

She couldn't stop herself yawning, hanging on to the banister. 'I've never heard of him.'

'No matter.' He waved her up the stairs. 'If he's of any consequence we'll know soon enough.'

Nina went down to breakfast the next day to find Frank had already left to go to court. Maggie, as usual, was full of her war work. 'The conditions are dreadful,' she confided. 'The girls are at great risk from the chemicals and there are so many accidents.' She watched as Ellen left the room with a tray. 'The truth is,

Nina, that the newspapers don't usually report the accidents, but there are many of them. For instance at one factory there was an explosion and a terrible fire; there was some confusion with the authorities and the police refused to unlock the gates, with the result that the women inside were burnt to death. The ones outside could hear them screaming for help.'

Nina's teaspoon shook against the china eggcup, and she had to look away from the pile of broken shell, feeling suddenly nauseous.

'Frank is concerned that the work upsets me, because of my heart – and I confess it does, who wouldn't be upset? – but it is vitally important that information about safety should be made available. "Upset" is the wrong word anyway; I'm not upset, I'm angry. A young woman we know, her mother used to "do" for Frank in his bachelor days, approached me recently and asked about munitions work. I advised her to join the WAACs instead. There are all sorts of wild rumours about the WAACs, that there are secret plans to send women into combat one day, quite ludicrous.' Giving a rueful smile, she nodded in the direction of the door. 'I didn't persuade the young lady concerned, but Ellen overheard our conversation and since then has been unusually thoughtful. I fear that soon Frank and I will be forced to get our own breakfast.'

Her eyes fell on Nina's uneaten toast. 'You've barely eaten a thing. If Frank were here he would be extolling the virtues of brown bread! Are you feeling all right?'

'Yes, I'm just a little . . .' A second wave of nausea hit her and her throat burned. The servants' lavatory was next to the scullery: jumping up, Nina clamped her hand over her mouth and ran down the hall and into the kitchen. Ellen, drying a plate, stepped towards her, her eyes wide in surprise.

'I . . .' A mouthful of tea and bile spurted on to the flagstones, splashing over Ellen's boots.

'Bugger me!' Ellen stumbled back. Nina turned away, and the next mouthful went down the back of a kitchen chair. The heaving went on, although her stomach was empty, causing her to double over in pain. She gave a long sob and looked up as a tea towel was pushed into her wet hand.

'Sorry, madam.' Ellen's face was red. 'I shouldn't have sworn like that. It was me own fault for not getting out of the way faster.'

'You couldn't help it, Nina,' Maggie said as she wiped her face and hands with a flannel soaked in rosewater and propped her up on the sofa in the library. 'You probably caught something on the train up.'

'I'll feel better soon.' She wasn't well; she shouldn't have come.

'Of course, you just need to rest. I was going to suggest we go into town as I need some new shoes, but I have two letters to write and then I'll take them to the post office.' She nodded at the tray. 'The tea is lemon grass. Very good if you're slightly liverish. Frank won't be back till later this afternoon but Ellen is in the kitchen and will come when you ring. If you like the tea there's a pot made up that can be freshened with boiling water. Now, is there a book I can bring from your room?'

'I forgot to pack one.' Nothing she read lately held her attention.

'If you want a novel you'd do best to look on Frank's shelves.' Maggie waved in the direction of those closest to the door. 'My books are over here. And on this shelf,' she pointed to one with a large mother-of-pearl shell sitting at the front, 'you will find what Frank calls "the ladies' books".' She laughed. 'He says some of them are far too shocking to be seen by men, and he is quite right.'

Nina drank the strange-tasting tea, which did at least stay down, then fell asleep on the sofa. When she woke the sun was coming through the window and the house was silent. She lay where she was for a while, watching shadows from the plane tree play on the flock wallpaper, then stood up and wandered over to Frank's desk, where he'd left the leather-bound *Iliad*. Opening it, she read, *the mother bird lamented for her babies as Cronus's snake gulped them down, the mother fluttering over him* . . . She let the pages fall shut and looked at the two volumes next to it. One was a collection of short stories by someone named Radclyffe Hall and the other was essays by another writer she didn't know, Emma Goldman. She opened this at the bookmark: *Can there be anything more outrageous than the idea that a healthy, grown woman, full of life and passion, must deny nature's demand, must subdue her most intense craving, under-mine her health and break her spirit, must stunt her vision, abstain from the depth and glory of sex experience until a 'good' man comes along to take her unto himself as a wife? That is precisely what marriage means. How can such an arrangement end except in failure?*

She jumped as Maggie bustled in, clutching a large brown-paper bag. 'Forgive me for being so long but I found some new shoes in a little shop around the corner from the post office. They are exactly what I wanted and half what I would have paid for them in Oxford Street.' She sank into an armchair. 'You look better. What have you got there? Ah, *Anarchism and Other Essays.* The Russian Jewess writes heady stuff, but like most Anarchists she's hardly practical. That's the problem with the Anarchists, they have these splendid ideas about social freedom and individual free will but no idea as to how they would work in the real world. I wish you and I could have gone to one of Prince Kropotkin's lectures together; I've never met him but Frank says he's delightful. No doubt he'll be going back to Russia soon. Now,' she bent forward to pick up the bag, 'I'll try these on so you can see them.'

'Yes,' Nina said, smiling, 'I'd very much like to see your shoes.' It was impossible not to love Maggie, who was so busy trying to save the world but could still find time to take pleasure in a new pair of shoes.

Ellen gave in her notice as she prepared supper. 'She is to join the WAACs as I feared.' Maggie stirred her bowl of soup. 'It's all my fault, Frank.'

Nina's cheeks burned. 'I'm afraid I'm to blame.'

Frank looked puzzled. 'You, Nina?'

Maggie gestured with her left hand. 'It's nothing. Nina was slightly unwell this morning, that's all. No, it's my fault for saying what a wonderful idea the WAACs is and how it has far more to offer a young woman than munitions work or service. Ellen isn't stupid and decided this was sensible advice. And I am pleased for her, really, it's just that good servants are difficult to come by these days and we live such busy lives.'

'We shall advertise immediately,' Frank said. 'I'm sorry you haven't been feeling well, Nina, though I'm not surprised. You looked poorly last night.' He nodded at Maggie. 'I told Nina that she mustn't go along with any prejudices about brown bread. It's full of iron.'

A piece of woody carrot bobbed on top of the soup; Nina pushed it to the side of the bowl. A blob of oil floated next to it.

'My dear,' Frank said, 'is the soup all right? I know it tastes a little strongly of yeast but I am assured that yeast . . .'

Nina stood up in time to be sick across the table.

As Maggie led her into the bathroom she continued to sob. 'I'm so sorry, we can't leave Frank to clean it up.' She felt completely humiliated.

'Why not?' Maggie took a flannel from the washstand. 'Women clean up after men all the time. Anyway, Frank won't clean up, Ellen will. Sit on the stool.' She wiped Nina's hands. 'Just to cool you down – I don't think any went over you.'

'I don't think so.'

'No, it went over the table instead!' Maggie laughed. 'I will always remember how you looked after me at the top of the pagoda. "My little nurse", that's how I thought of you then. So now you must let me look after you.' She patted the flannel down Nina's cheeks. 'This isn't something you caught on the train, is it?'

Maggie was so kind. 'I'm sorry, Maggie: I haven't been feeling well for the past week. I shouldn't have come. I'm being such a nuisance.' Nina couldn't bear to think of Frank back in the dining room.

'You are not a nuisance. You are our friend and we are concerned about you.' Maggie hung the flannel over the wooden towel rail. 'Come on, let's go through to your room.'

In the bedroom they sat on the edge of the bed. 'Now,' Maggie took Nina's hand in hers, turning it over as if she could read the palm. 'I will ask Ellen to make some more of the lemon grass tea and I will bring you the essays to read from the library. There's water for a bath if you'd like one.'

Nina rested her head on Maggie's shoulder. 'You are the dearest of friends.'

Maggie squeezed her hand. 'I hope so, because you are very dear to me. And it is because you are so dear that I feel I must ask you this. Is it possible, Nina, that you are pregnant?'

Thirteen

As soon as Maggie said it Nina knew it was true.

'It might just be a cold, of course,' Maggie was rocking her gently, 'but the signs are all there. Every week there's at least one girl who asks to talk to me. Sometimes they think their symptoms are the result of the chemicals they work with and they can be months pregnant – or, in more than one case, even in labour – before they realise they're with child. Is it possible, Nina?'

'Yes,' she whispered. As they'd sat on the bench in London, Harry had said, 'That night – I hadn't been expecting anything like that to happen and it was all so wonderful. However, I wasn't as careful as I should have been . . .'

Maggie said into her hair, 'Do you have any idea of how far gone you might be? When did you last have your time of the month?'

'Seven weeks.'

'Seven weeks since you had your last period?'

'No.' The crêpe of Maggie's dress was damp under her face. 'I am seven weeks gone.'

There was a crunching underfoot: Nina was on the snow-covered path, explaining to Miss Brenchley about the young man who had fallen over the waterfall, and his name slid easily into her mind. 'Kyril,' she said aloud. The young man who had loved Great-Aunt Adelaida was named Kyril. 'I always liked the sound of his name,' Mamma had said, 'perhaps because of the way Adelaida said it when she told the story. She used to sound so sad.'

Opening her eyes, all Nina could see was darkness, but from the distance there came the sounds of morning traffic. She'd slept in. And then she thought, I am pregnant. The thought didn't bring any emotion with it; she didn't feel sad or angry or frightened or happy. She felt nothing at all.

'The important thing is not to starve yourself,' Maggie said when she came down for breakfast. 'I've heard some women say the secret is to eat little and often, so I'd suggest starting with the lemon grass tea. And,' she clapped her hands, 'you can have a spoon of honey; we've a comb from a farm in Wiltshire, from one of Frank's clients. I'll ask Ellen to bring it through.'

Nina looked quickly away from the thin slice of toast on Maggie's plate. 'Please. I might be able to manage that.'

Ellen brought in the honeycomb and Nina sipped the tea slowly.

Maggie fiddled with her knife. 'I've told Frank about the baby. I hope you don't mind.'

'I don't mind.' The grandfather clock in the corner clicked loudly. She'd seen Frank wind it up once, not on this visit but on a previous one. 'I always feel that one turn too far and the whole spring could go,' he'd said. 'It's got a kick like a donkey, enough to break your wrist.'

'Good.' Maggie positioned the knife at the side of her plate. 'And Richard. How will he feel, do you think?'

Maggie knew: she knew Richard wasn't the father. Nina studied the flower pattern on her cup, not daring to lift her eyes. 'Richard will be delighted, he's been looking forward to having a child.'

'He has?' Maggie couldn't disguise her relief. 'Of course he has. It's just that you never know – men can be strange about these matters, particularly with the way things are, with the war.' She leaned forward on her elbows. 'I'm so pleased for you. I had thought maybe, well, one thinks all sorts of wild things when these big events come along. And what can be bigger than a baby?' She laughed. 'Now, you must let me help you plan a layette . . .'

Nina half listened, realising that Maggie and Frank had probably guessed the truth about Richard long ago. Perhaps their secret wasn't so secret after all.

After breakfast they sat in the garden, where it was sunny. 'There are a lot of nests this year,' Maggie observed. 'The world is full of new life – it makes one hopeful for the future. I've been thinking of putting in a pond here, when the war is finished.'

Her friend's words brought to mind something Nina hadn't thought of in years. 'I remember Mamma telling me that as a child she was taken to a garden where there were fish that were very old, from the time of Catherine the Great. They were marked with gold rings and came to be fed at the sound of a bell.' She felt as though she were a pond herself, with memories suddenly rising to the surface.

'Like the swans at Wells Cathedral. But how do you think the fish hear the bell underwater? Now, Ellen is preparing some broth for lunch, and what I suggest is that you sip it with a teaspoon while reading a book. That will take your mind off it and the small spoon will fool your stomach. Tell me,' she patted Nina's knee, 'what do they do in Russia, to tell if the baby is a boy or a girl?'

What everyone did, surely. 'They look. The midwife or the doctor looks at the baby when it's born and . . .'

'No,' Maggie laughed, 'before the baby's born! In England there are all sorts of ways of trying to guess the sex. Mostly nonsense, but fun. For instance, you can tie your wedding ring on a strand of your hair and see which way it turns. It's clockwise for a boy and anti-clockwise for a girl. Or is it the other way round?'

Eventually Maggie went back into the house and Nina opened the book of Emma Goldman's essays, which Maggie had very kindly said she could keep.

There are to-day large numbers of men and women to whom marriage is naught but a farce, but who submit to it for the sake of public opinion. Marriage is primarily an economic arrangement, an insurance pact. It differs from the ordinary life insurance agreement only in that it is more binding, more exacting . . . love is free; it can dwell in no other atmosphere. In freedom it gives itself unreservedly, abundantly, completely . . . Love needs no protection; it is its own protection. So long as love begets life no child is deserted, or hungry, or famished for the want of affection. I know this to be true. I know women who became mothers in freedom by the men they loved. Few children in wedlock enjoy the care, the protection, the devotion free motherhood is capable of bestowing.

'Oh!' She stopped reading and looked up at the blue sky overhead, an unexpected wave of exhilaration going over her. It was like stepping off a cliff top, stepping into space. That a woman could think – could write – such things! These were the ideas coming from Russians: ideas that would change the world. And she would be part of that change: herself, Richard and Harry. And the baby.

She was going to have a baby.

'Nina,' Maggie called, 'here's the broth. My dear,' she put the tray down and knelt on the grass, 'you're crying. Don't cry, darling, everything will be all right, I promise you.' She put her arms around her. 'You're not alone, you know that. You are loved and you are not alone.'

Nina kissed Maggie on the cheek and wiped her eyes. 'I'm not crying because I'm sad, Maggie. I'm crying because I'm happy.'

Maggie and Frank wanted her to stay longer but she remained only the four days as planned. 'You mustn't worry about me,' she said. 'I'll come again soon.'

Maggie sat next to her in the cab. 'When you do come back you can stay as long as you like; you're welcome to have the baby here, you know that, or I will come to you. The sickness will soon pass and there's so much to look forward to in the future.'

'The future.' As Maggie and Frank waved goodbye from the platform Nina said the word aloud so that the woman sitting opposite in the compartment looked up from her knitting, her hands frozen but her mouth still counting stitches.

When she got home that evening Nina had a bath then put on her nightdress and dressing gown and went down to the kitchen to brew another pot of lemon grass tea. She also half filled a bowl with some of the dried fruit Frank had purchased for her: the combination of tea and fruit did help to keep the nausea at bay. Now she took a tray through to the parlour and sat in the chair next to the empty fireplace. The chimney fire seemed a very long time ago now.

Yawning, she pulled a cushion under her head; in the morning she'd make up a list of things to do. First on the list would be letter-writing. Maggie and Frank already knew her news, so she needed to write and tell Richard. He'd be surprised, she thought, but happy. And then she'd write to Katya. And to Harry. She'd tried planning this letter on the train . . . *My position is a happy and comfortable one and you have no need to feel any concern on my behalf. I do hope, however* . . . Her mind stopped there, not daring to form into words whatever it was she hoped for.

'Nina!' The front door slammed. 'Nina!'

It couldn't be – Richard was coming into the room, carrying his bag and a bunch of flowers. 'My dear, you're half asleep. No, don't get up.' He kissed her forehead then sniffed suspiciously at the tea. 'What the devil is that? Don't tell me, something from Maggie.'

He'd never arrived like this before. 'The war,' she whispered, not moving from the chair, 'is it over?'

'What?' He dropped the bag on to the settle and gave a short laugh. 'God, no, I'm afraid it's nothing like that. Just some unexpected leave. I rang Frank to see if you were still there and he told me you'd left.' He shrugged out of his coat. 'Stay where you are, you look tired. I'm going to make myself some real tea.'

After quickly tidying her hair in the mirror, Nina followed him through to the kitchen. 'I'm so pleased you're here.'

'Good, I'm pleased to be here too.' He was putting the flowers in a milk bottle on the table. 'I'll fry an egg if there is one. Have you eaten?'

'I have. I'll do the egg for you.' She wasn't sure, however, that she could.

'I can do it. You really do look done in; Maggie and Frank must have been keeping you up. You go ahead and have an early night; I'll sit down here and write some letters. I owe both Mother and Anne.'

He bent his head as he lit the gas under the kettle and she saw his hair wasn't exactly the same colour as Harry's, but a little darker. And then she saw there were strands of grey weaving through the red, not just one or two but many. It came as a jolt: when had this happened? Her eyes moved to his face. 'Richard? Is something wrong?'

'You mean apart from everything?'

She felt herself stiffen. Had he done it then, got transferred?

167

Was he here to tell her he was going to France?' Her throat was tight. 'What is it? What's happening?'

'Nothing is happening at all. Not a bloody thing.' He blew out the taper and looked up at her apologetically. 'I'm sorry, there's no reason you should have to put up with my bad temper. Bad-tempered and bloody ungrateful, that's me. You see I've been told I won't be moved from the War Office. My experience is invaluable, or so they say, and I am not to apply for a transfer again as it is a waste of my time and other people's. So there you go. I should be grateful but I'm not.'

She felt immense relief at his news although she did pity him as he seemed so dejected. 'I'm sorry,' she said, 'that you're unhappy.'

'Unhappy?' He nodded slowly. 'Yes, I am unhappy. Though that makes me sound like a disappointed schoolboy, doesn't it? "Not allowed to fight in the war, Richard was deeply unhappy."' He sighed. 'It isn't something that's easy, or even possible, to explain. It's not that I *want* to fight, Nina, you must understand that. I have no interest in killing anyone, or in being killed myself. No, it's about – proving myself. That sounds pathetic, doesn't it? Even selfish. But it's about being part of something that is bigger than any of us. I will always feel I sent other men to do what I might not have been capable of doing myself. I will feel that I haven't deserved my own stake in the future, that I served no purpose.' His face was drained.

Could he really believe this? 'But, Richard, what you're doing is immensely important . . .'

'How important it is has nothing to do with it!' He went over to one of the cupboards and said quietly, 'Forgive me. I promised myself we wouldn't argue.'

He was too hard on himself. She looked at the flowers he'd brought, so delicate but full of life and colour. 'Richard,' she heard herself saying slowly, 'I have some news.'

'Do you? Is it good?' He put two cups and saucers on the table.

'I think so.' She took a breath and looked straight at him. 'I'm pregnant, Richard. I'm going to have a baby.'

His cheeks flushed deeply but he held her look. 'A baby? You . . . I had no idea that you . . . Good heavens, this *is* news, isn't it?'

He'd be happy again. They would all be happy. 'Yes, it is.'

'You're sure?' he asked quickly.

'I think so, yes. Maggie had to tell me.'

'So Maggie knows?'

'And Frank. They're very excited. Maggie says you'll make an excellent father.'

He paced to the sink and then back to the table. 'Nina, this is such a surprise. I had hoped that one day . . . you know that. But to come home and hear this. I hardly know what to say.'

'So it is good news?' she teased.

'Good?' He grinned. 'It's excellent, it's superb! I'm stunned, you know that, completely stunned.' Coming around the table, he took her hands in his. 'I've been feeling so low, and then to hear this. Thank you, Nina. A baby!'

'With a very good chance of having red hair, just as you asked.'

He started. 'Good God. I was joking, you didn't have to – really . . .'

She laughed as the kettle began a low whistle behind them.

'You're sure you can't eat anything?' He sprinkled salt over his fried egg and bread. 'You must eat, you know.'

'I know, for the baby.' The smell of the food made the bile rise in the back of her throat.

'For you and the baby. Did Maggie have any advice?'

'About the sickness? She advised small meals, often.'

'That sounds sensible.'

'Yes.' She had to look away from his plate. 'Maggie knows a great deal about babies.' Maggie was so excited about the baby, but Nina couldn't remember her ever having said anything about wanting children herself. But there was her heart problem, of course. 'It's a pity she and Frank haven't had a child.'

'Yes, maybe she didn't feel she could . . .' He stopped and then said, 'Do you know when it's due?'

'December, I think.'

'The poor little blighter will think it's a cold world. I wonder what he'll make of snow?'

'He? What makes you so sure it will be a boy?' she joked.

'A girl or a boy, it makes no difference to me – as long as he, or she, is healthy.'

He was his old self again, his eyes bright. She thought of Alice's baby daughters asleep in their cots, their small fingers curled tight. That was how the baby was curled inside her now. She hoped it knew it was loved. She loved all of them: the baby and Richard and Maggie and Frank and Katya. And Harry: she loved Harry. Tears of happiness pricked her eyes. She only wished she knew where Darya was, so she could write and tell her. And Papa? But there would be no point, even if the letter got through.

Richard sipped his tea. 'There's a lot to think about, isn't there? Names, for instance. Have you thought about that? What if it's a girl?'

It was like a guessing game, or the charades they'd played with Charles and Lawrence in the days before the war. 'I don't know. I've always liked my mother's name, Irina.'

'And a boy? I wouldn't suggest my father's name, Herbert, because I know he never liked it himself. "Bert," he used to say with a frown, "it makes me feel like a shopkeeper." Boys' names are difficult; there are lots of pretty names for girls, but for a boy . . .'

'Kyril. My mother thought it was a lovely name.' Or Lawrence, she thought; if it was a boy maybe they should name the baby after him.

'Kyril? It's very Russian. Well, there's time to think about these things. Good heavens – my letters to Mother and Anne! I knew they'd be disappointed by my news, but now – well, this will certainly cause some excitement. I'll write to them immediately. You don't mind, do you? I know that people sometimes don't like to say anything, but with everything that's happening around us it seems only right to pass on good tidings. We can say it's early days yet.'

'And I must write and tell Katya, and Harry.'

'Harry?'

She almost said 'the baby's father', but stopped herself in time. 'Yes, he's an Australian – a lieutenant.'

'But what do you mean to tell him? That you're pregnant?'

'Yes! What else?' He could be so funny.

He was staring at her. 'Sweetheart, you can't tell him. Surely you must know that.'

It was her turn to stare back. 'I don't understand.' Was this another taboo?

'Well, he wouldn't thank you for a start,' he said gently. 'Nina, no man wants to hear he's got a married woman pregnant. Besides . . .'

She sat up straight in her chair: what could he be thinking? 'Harry does care about me.'

A small frown played over Richard's face. 'My darling, who wouldn't care about you? But you can't have anything more to do with him; you must see that. It wouldn't be fair on him for a start.'

This was madness. 'Not fair to tell him he is to have a child?'

'It wouldn't be fair on any of us, the child included.'

What was wrong with him? He didn't seem to understand at all. 'Richard, I didn't set out to become pregnant, that's just something that happened.'

'What did you set out to do then?'

The sudden coolness in his voice unnerved her. 'We're both free to do as we wish, that's always been agreed. If we met someone we liked, or loved . . .'

He said very quietly, 'I told you I couldn't *make* love to you; I never said I couldn't love you.'

'I didn't say that!' He knew she wasn't saying that.

He ran his hands through his hair. 'What would it achieve, to tell him? You say he's Australian?'

'Yes.'

'He'll return to Australia. What good would it do for him to know he has a child back in England?'

'He has a right to know.' Her fingers went to the bracelet. 'And he mightn't go to Australia; before the war he'd hoped to work in Fleet Street.' She'd only dared to half think this till now.

He was silent for a moment and then said, 'What have you told him about me?'

'Nothing. I simply said we have an understanding.'

'And what did your – what did Harry make of this?'

'I don't know.' He had to understand; she would make him understand. She leaned on her elbows. 'Richard, the world will be a different place. The war will change things and there are so many different ideas now about how we might live our lives. Maggie gave me a book by a Russian Anarchist, Emma

Goldman, who lives in America. You must read it. The things she says, the things that are happening. Look at Russia . . .'

She jumped as he slapped the table with the palms of his hands and stood up. 'Maggie and her tomfoolery! We are not in Russia. We are not Anarchists. This is England, and do you really think England, or the rest of Europe, is going to change for the better after this wretched war? That it is going to solve anything or make the world freer or happier or kinder? Because I can tell you now that it will not.' His eyes desperately searched the room. 'What is this, Nina? You'll have a child. You're loved. What more could you want?'

Could it be possible he really didn't know? Because if he didn't . . . She looked up at him. 'Passion,' she said quietly. 'Sex. Do you expect me to live without those things for ever?' That had not been part of the agreement they'd come to in the garden.

He avoided her eye. 'I would have thought a child would satisfy your needs.'

A hot stab of anger went through her: it was not right to deny her like this. 'My needs are no different from yours.'

'And you plan to have them satisfied how? By carrying on a long-term affair with a man who is content to fit in with our "understanding"? What sort of gentleman would agree to that?'

She was standing up now, holding the dressing gown tightly across her chest as she faced him. 'More of a gentleman than the soldier I met here one morning. Although he did compliment me on having a husband with a big cock.' The words fell out of her mouth like pebbles.

His face was ghastly.

'Richard, I . . .' She shouldn't have; she should take it back.

But he held up his hand. 'You're right to be angry. It was unforgivable of me to have brought him here and unforgivable of him to have spoken to you like that. I had no idea. You're not to blame. Well,' he blinked, 'this has been an evening of surprises, hasn't it? I think we've both said enough for now; tomorrow our thoughts might be clearer.'

She stood frozen. She shouldn't have said it, but at the same time he had to know she couldn't half live her life. He couldn't ask her to do that.

When he got to the doorway he swung round. 'You're young,

Nina, sometimes I forget just how young, and maybe I've also forgotten how long it takes to learn not to confuse sex and love. But I promise you, many marriages have the first without the last; while many others have neither. I'm sorry if I've disappointed you in some things, but I still consider us – or myself at least – to be lucky in our marriage.' He looked down at his hands. 'I don't think I'll write to my mother or Anne now; I'll leave it till the morning.'

A few minutes later she heard the front door close behind him.

Early the next morning she retched into the downstairs lavatory and the ugly expression on the boy's face came into her mind. *Not the best I've ever had.* She tried to brush the memory aside.

When her stomach finished heaving she turned on the tap at the sink, her mouth sour as she sipped from her hand and spat. Hopefully Richard hadn't heard: she didn't want to wake him. She made herself put on her jacket and hat then walk quietly along the hall. No sounds came from upstairs.

On the street she felt heavy and sick. There'd been a saying in the kitchen, 'Sick in the stomach is sick at heart,' and there was no doubt she was both. From behind came the sound of running feet and a boot boy dashed past, beating a wooden hoop with a stick. ''Eaper Weaper, chimney sweeper, had a wife and couldn't keep her. Had another, didn't love her. Up the chimney he did shove her!' Snatching at the hoop, he bounded up the steps leading to the French Consulate. '*Allez!*' A maid opened the door. '*Vous êtes en retard, allez!*' He yowled as she clipped him lightly round the head.

Crossing the road, Nina walked along the front; a ship lazily shadowed her on the horizon and she slowed to watch it, remembering the ship they'd seen from Katya's garden. 'You're like an old married couple already,' Katya had said. Nina's nails dug into her palm: Harry might not want to have anything to do with her once she told him, but she did have to tell him, surely Richard could understand that? And if he didn't? The picture of Mamma's jewel cases came into her mind, but she pushed the thought away; it wouldn't come to that. The ship gradually disappeared and she turned away from the sea and walked into town. It was only seven o'clock, but by the time she got to the bakery there'd be a queue.

Not only had she been able to buy a loaf of bread but also a small cake. 'Though it has no icing,' the girl had warned, 'because of there being no vanilla because of the submarines.' The thought of the cake made her feel nauseous again, and as she stood on the top step she fumbled with the keys to the front door.

'Mrs Truelove?'

Turning, she found a policeman standing at the bottom of the steps, staring up at her.

'Yes.'

He hesitated, glancing a few doors down to where a servant was watching them while polishing the brass letterbox. 'This is a private matter, ma'am.'

Her fingers shook as she pulled the key from the lock. 'I can assure you my papers are . . .'

'Papers? It's nothing like that, Mrs Truelove.' He followed her into the hall. 'Your husband is Captain Truelove?'

'He is.' She put her shopping down on the floor, treating it gently because of the cake.

When she stood up again he was watching her very oddly. 'May I ask you, ma'am, if Captain Truelove has red hair?'

He sounded like a madman. 'What is this about?' She looked in the direction of the stairs, wondering if she should call Richard.

'May I ask you, Mrs Truelove, if Captain Truelove is missing?'

'Missing? No, he isn't missing, he's here.' As she said it, a wave of panic went through her: Richard had had his transfer refused and had come to Brighton without permission. He was absent without leave.

'You're sure about that? You've seen him this morning?'

As she chewed her lip, her eyes went to the coat rack, but Richard's coast wasn't there. Why wasn't it there?

'Mrs Truelove,' he was saying, from a long way away, 'I am afraid I have very bad news . . .'

Fourteen

There were voices. 'She's to be left alone until tomorrow or, even better, the day after. If anyone tries to insist, ring the Chief Inspector and tell him I have left strict instructions.'

'The constable said it was a matter for the military police now.'

'Well, Mrs Laing, they too will have to take no for an answer.'

'Don't fear, Dr Williams, I am experienced in handling the army. Now, if we can prop her up for a moment.'

There was the sound of water in a bowl and then her face was being wiped with something warm.

'Here, drink this, it will make you sleep.'

She drank it.

A woman sat on a chair, reading. Past her the curtains were open and there was a blue sky, empty of clouds. The window was open an inch or two at the bottom and from the distance came the faint sound of the sea.

When Nina swallowed, her throat burned.

'You're awake.' The woman got up and stood looking down at her. 'You've slept for a whole day, Nina, since yesterday morning. Here, have a sip of water.'

She gulped greedily. As she pulled her legs up, the sheet was cold under them. 'The bed's wet.'

'Is it?' Maggie hurriedly checked under the blanket. 'Oh, that's all right, it's only to be expected. We'll turn the mattress once you're up.'

There was a smell too: she had soiled the sheets. And then she remembered what else she'd done. 'Maggie,' she wailed, 'I killed Richard!'

Maggie was holding her. 'My poor girl, my poor girl . . .'

Later Maggie took a clean nightdress from a drawer. 'We haven't spoken to the police yet ourselves. Frank rang here yesterday morning; he had an address to give Richard and Mrs Laing answered the telephone. Nina, it's an appalling thing, unbelievable, and at such a time.' She sat on the edge of the bed. 'The baby's all right, you know, there's been no blood, you haven't had a miscarriage.' She looked away. 'Mrs Laing spoke to the military police yesterday evening and she says the man who killed Richard has a history of violence and is known to the police in London. They expect he'll try to hide there but are confidence he'll be caught soon.'

It wasn't happening, not really. Richard couldn't be dead like Mamma. It was a terrible dream and she'd wake up and Darya would come in. 'It's my fault. He would never have gone out if we hadn't argued.' She hesitated. 'I said terrible things.'

'My darling, we've all said terrible things. We've all said things we later regret,' Maggie replied.

But she *was* guilty. 'Maggie,' she whispered, 'the baby isn't Richard's.'

'I know.' Maggie glanced away.

'It will have been one of the young men who killed him. The young men he met while he was out.'

Maggie was silent but no doubt she knew that too.

Fifteen

Where Mamma had been carved from ice, Richard was birch-wood, smooth and pale. Nina looked away again, then made herself look back. He was in his uniform and there were no marks on his face. According to Mrs Laing there was only one wound, where the knife had entered his heart, and the doctor had said death was instantaneous.

'Your husband would have bravely attempted to defend himself,' Mrs Laing said. 'With the blackout, the streets are a haven for ruffians.'

His hair gleamed red in the light from the parlour lamp.

Nina whispered, 'Forgive me.'

Frank was in the drawing room. Nina sat on the sofa while he busied himself at the grate. 'I hope you don't mind my setting the fire – ridiculous in mid-May and horribly extravagant – but there is a slight nip in the air.' He put on some more coal, then said, 'To tell the truth, I found myself doing it without thinking. Mrs Laing has a mysterious source of coal and the shed appears to be half full. She has also filled the pantry.'

'I must pay her.'

The flowers Richard had brought had been put on the mantelpiece; she couldn't bear to look at them.

Frank waved his hand. 'I've already dealt with that. She has also suggested something about a roster of officers' wives, but I believe Maggie has managed to steer her away from the idea. Still, it's good to know people are willing to help.'

'Thank you.' In three days Nina had become an automaton: one half of herself said the things that needed to be said and the other half watched.

'There are no thanks required, none at all.' He closed the coal scuttle.

Charles, she thought dully, they must contact Charles, who was in France.

The door opened and Mrs Laing came in, followed by Maggie carrying a cup and saucer.

'Here you are, Nina. Mrs Chaplin has made you, what do you call it again, lemon grass tea. It smells frightful but I am not against these things if they help: copper greatly alleviated my sister's arthritis.' Mrs Laing sank on to the sofa. 'Before I forget, the dressmaker is coming tomorrow afternoon, for the mourning. She did very well for Alice Evans, although Alice never wore what was made for her as she stayed in bed all day. Luckily you have a good deal more grit. And a message has come from the military police – they would like to have a word tomorrow morning, around ten o'clock. A corporal brought the message, a very polite young man. He assured me the visit would be brief. A Captain Stewart will be coming, but don't worry, I will stay with you throughout the interview as I'm used to the army's way of handling things.'

Frank coughed. 'That's terribly kind, Mrs Laing, but I have already told Nina I will accompany her, should an interview be suggested. As one of Richard's oldest friends.'

Maggie and Mrs Laing went downstairs to check on supper. Nina watched them go then turned to Frank. 'The military police,' she said quietly, 'what will they want?'

Frank breathed on his glasses and wiped them with a small silk square. 'I expect they'll want some details. Such as what time Richard left the house.' Putting the glasses back on, he studied her over the top of them. 'Speaking from a professional point of view, Nina, I wouldn't feel the need to say too much. It isn't as if you have any information that will help them with their enquiries. In fact you could be asked questions which will, quite naturally under the circumstances, be upsetting, so I would recommend you give some thought now as to what you wish to say.'

She stared at the closed curtains: day had been turned to night. 'Is there anything in the newspapers?' Frank had gone out earlier to buy *The Times* and the local papers.

'I don't think the authorities have released much information. In yesterday's *Gazette*,' he picked it up, 'there was a short entry, saying that a soldier had been stabbed.' He hesitated, then added, 'It says it occurred in a house in Edward Street. Does that mean anything to you?'

In a house: she could feel the walls shift around her. 'I've never been there. I know it's a poor area.'

'Well, we shall see.'

Captain Stewart was a short, dark man with a thin moustache and quick eyes. Frank brought him up to the drawing room. 'Captain Stewart, this is Mrs Truelove.'

'Captain Stewart,' she said, 'please sit down.'

'You're not English, Mrs Truelove?' But he didn't seem surprised.

'I am Russian.'

'Ah yes. Mrs Truelove, let me say how sorry I am about your tragic loss. I have only a few questions to ask and I won't take up much of your time. I understand Captain Truelove's family lives in Cheltenham?'

'Yes. But they haven't heard about my husband yet.'

'We've tried ringing,' Frank offered, 'and a telegram has been sent. Mrs Truelove and her daughter must both be away.'

The Captain took a notebook and pencil from his top pocket. 'If you give me their address before I leave I'll contact someone in Cheltenham and have them go round. The neighbours might know where they are.' He wrote something in his book. 'And you, Mr Chaplin, you knew Captain Truelove well?'

'Mrs Truelove and my wife are good friends. And Richard and I both went to Sherborne.'

Nina glanced over at him but he kept his gaze on the captain.

'Good rugby players. When is the funeral, Mrs Truelove?'

'We cannot set a date until we've spoken to Richard's family.'

'No.' He kept the notebook open. 'I hope you understand there are some questions I must ask. You might also have questions you wish to ask me.'

'Mrs Laing said you know who killed my husband.'

'We believe him to be a Jimmy Reed, a very violent and

dangerous young man. He's well known to the police in London, in connection with various activities.'

Out of the corner of her eye she saw that Frank didn't move.

'I don't suppose, Mrs Truelove, that your husband had ever mentioned this young man to you?'

'No.'

Captain Stewart smiled sympathetically. 'No, why would he? Now, do you know what time your husband left the house?'

'I think it must have been around eight o'clock. He went for a walk.'

He made a note of the time. 'Eight.' Without looking up he said, 'What time did you expect him back?'

'I didn't think he'd be long. I was very tired myself, having just got back from four days in London with Mr and Mrs Chaplin, so shortly after Richard went out I went to bed.'

Shifting in the chair, the captain put the notebook on his knee. 'Did your husband often go out for an evening walk, Mrs Truelove?'

'He enjoyed walking.'

'And he often stayed out late?'

'Sometimes.'

'Was he in the habit of carrying much money on his person?'

'Not a large amount of money, no.'

He asked a few more questions, about the direction Richard usually took and how often he would go out, and then unexpectedly closed the notebook. 'Mrs Truelove, thank you for your time.' He stood up. 'If there are any developments we will let you know.'

'Is that it then, Captain Stewart?' Frank stood as well.

'I think so.' He put the notebook and pencil back into his pocket. 'For now.' He gave a nod and followed Frank to the door. 'There is one thing.' He turned around. 'Mrs Truelove, I'm told that in the morning you were unaware that your husband hadn't returned . . .'

She held her hands in her lap. 'I thought he was sleeping late.'

'Pardon me – I do not wish to be at all indelicate – but you hadn't noticed he hadn't come to bed?'

'There's a cot in the dressing room, Richard would sometimes sleep there rather than wake me. I have problems getting back to sleep.'

He nodded. 'That would explain it. Goodbye, and thank you for your time. Mr Chaplin, could you let me have the Cheltenham address?'

Frank led him out of the room.

'The hem will need taking down, but apart from that it's a good fit.' The dressmaker tugged the waistline. 'And the pleating will grow with you.'

Downstairs the telephone rang, and a few minutes later there was a gentle knock on the door and Maggie came in. 'That was Anne. Frank spoke to her. She'd just got back to Cheltenham when the police called; they told her the news. She is, of course, deeply distressed. Her mother is in Bath, visiting a cousin. Anne will go there and tell her personally as soon as she is able.'

'Thank you.' In the mirror Nina's head was a pale oval floating above the high neckline of the black dress. She felt a firm push in the small of the back and turned obediently, lifting her arms.

Later she went down to the parlour. As she was about to open the door, Frank came out.

'He looks so peaceful,' he said, 'I keep expecting him to wake up. Oh dear.' He wiped his eyes, speaking quickly. 'There's a message from Mr Lewisham, asking if he might call, and I've asked Mrs Laing to organise a decent woman for the house. I hope this will suit you, Nina. She says she knows a Mrs Fay Proctor, who'll do very well. Now Anne has been contacted we can get on with the arrangements. There's a lot to do.' He hesitated. 'Anne asked what happened and I told her it was a robbery.'

'Yes. Frank, what more will the police want?'

'I don't think we can tell at this stage.'

'Captain Stewart frightened me.'

'Oh, you mustn't let the Captain Stewarts of the world frighten you.' He gave a rueful smile. 'There's no doubt his manner is somewhat brusque, but that's how the police work. They are practised at unnerving their suspects. Not that we are suspects, of course.'

'There'll be a court case, won't there?'

'Only if they catch him, Nina, and it isn't at all certain they will.'

Frank climbed the stairs and Nina went into the parlour. There was the smell of flowers and varnish. The windows were open at the top and the curtains moved gently in the breeze. The sea was very loud today.

'I'm sorry,' she said aloud over the coffin. 'Forgive me.' She'd promised the young violinmaker he'd be well; she'd promised Richard they would be happy. She would never promise anything to anyone again.

Fay Proctor, a short, stout woman with brown eyes and curly iron-grey hair, started work the next morning.

'Mrs Laing has informed me about your delicate state,' she said. 'She thought it right under the circumstances. I've got a fillet of witch for lunch – it's inferior to plaice, I know, but poached in a drop of milk it'll stay down a treat, you'll see. My eldest had the same problem and I had her eating normal after the doctor had her half out of her wits, what with saying she must drink a glass of ox blood every morning or lose the bairn. "I can't keep an egg down, Mam," she said, "so how does he think I'll keep down a glass of blood?" Stupid old fool. Excuse my language, but it does make you wonder.'

'She says she's only interested in temporary posts,' Maggie explained over lunch, 'because of her family. She sometimes helps her daughter out by looking after the grandchildren. But I said that would suit you for now, Nina.'

Nina let them talk around her. She felt distant from everything, as if she were watching from behind a pane of glass.

'I'd keep her if I could.' Frank nodded approvingly at his plate. 'After lunch, Nina, we do need to sit down and make some serious plans. The vicar wants to meet you and there is the matter of which hymns to choose. And then there's the carriage and horses. Pall-bearers too.' She must have winced, because he lowered his knife and fork. 'I do apologise. Maggie's always telling me that I rush in with no sensitivity whatsoever, but it's just that that's what I'm best at, organising.'

'It's not that.' Nina avoided looking at the food in front of her, fighting the urge to gag. 'Please, Frank, you do it. I don't know about English funerals. They're very different, I think. I wouldn't know what to do.'

Maggie went with Frank to the post office and Nina answered the telephone when it rang. It was the Reverend Gregory, Anne's fiancé. She'd never spoken to him before. 'I'm sorry to add to your grief,' he was saying, 'but Mrs Truelove had a heart attack, some three hours after Anne told her the news. Anne could only speak a few words to me on the telephone – this, on top of your husband's death, has knocked her for six – but her mother's condition is extremely serious and she won't be able to leave her to come to the funeral. I'm so terribly sorry, for all of you. I'm going on to Bath now and then I'll come down to Brighton to attend the funeral on Anne's behalf.'

Nina sat on the stairs and wept uncontrollably because she wasn't going to wake up from this nightmare, and because Richard's mother had lost her son and her heart had been broken by it.

The funeral was a tawdry thing. 'The Church of England', Nina remembered Richard saying after taking her to see Westminster Abbey, 'is about being English, rather than about religion. It lacks passion, and the Anglo-Catholics are no better; worse in fact, as they simply play at it. Passion doesn't come naturally to the English.' Maybe that was it: the English lacked passion whereas Russians were ruled by it. Papa, Mamma, Katya – their lives were all marked, channelled, by passion of one sort or another. And Nina herself? She ran her hands over the belly already swelling beneath the black poplin.

'Nina,' Maggie came in, 'shall we go through? Fay and her niece Violet are dealing with the door and coats. People are already here.'

She hung the veiled hat over the back of the mirror and smoothed her hair.

The Reverend Jeremy Gregory had arrived the previous evening, taking a room in a hotel. Over supper he'd told them that Mrs Truelove was in a critical condition and it would be some days before they knew if she'd survive. Now he sat with

Nina in the drawing room as Maggie and Frank saw the last of the mourners out.

'Do tell me if there's anything I can do,' he said.

'You could open the curtains. Please. I hate sitting in darkness during the day.'

He gave a small smile as he stood up and went over to the window. He was a tall man, as tall as Richard had been, with an attractive face and kind hazel eyes. As he crossed the room Nina saw that he walked with a slight limp and remembered Anne saying that that was why he wasn't in the army: he'd injured his leg falling out of a tree when he was a boy. He pulled the curtain cords and the room filled with light.

'There,' he said, 'that's better.' He came and sat down again. 'The officers from London were all very decent. Major Ellis isn't at the War Office, is he? He said he didn't know Richard personally but had heard only good things about him.'

'I don't know. He gave me his condolences, that's all.' She'd felt the major watching her from across the room: in his mid-thirties, he was one of those men who manage to create an impression of being physically larger than they actually are. He reminded her of someone but she was too numb to remember who it was. It didn't matter.

'He was quite chatty for someone of that rank. He asked me about your being Russian and whether I knew if Richard had spent much time there. I said I didn't think he'd been there any great length of time. Captain Williams and Captain Scott said they worked with Richard.'

'I've met Captain Williams before, we had dinner with him at a restaurant in London once.' There had been potted palms with lights in them, and an orchestra dressed in uniforms with gold brocade. She and Richard had danced and people had smiled and nodded. The atmosphere had been so gay it had almost seemed as if there were no war.

'There was somebody from the military police. He didn't come back here.'

She looked down at her hands. 'Captain Stewart. He is in charge of the investigation.' She put the captain from her mind and thought instead of how Richard would have approved of the Reverend Gregory as a brother-in-law: he would be good for

184

Anne and she would be happy with him. 'The service was different from the ones I'm used to,' she said. The scene in the cemetery had been much the same, however; the empty sound of soil on wood.

'I went to a Greek Orthodox funeral when I was studying botany at Cambridge. I had a Greek friend whose family lived in London, and his uncle died. It was very different from the funerals I'd been to – more powerful, I felt, because it maintained a greater distance. There was no attempt at intimacy and somehow that felt right. I probably shouldn't say this, but I've never felt entirely happy with the Anglican service.'

She'd forgotten he'd studied botany. 'My sister lives in Nice, in an ugly house in a beautiful garden. The trees were planted by a famous collector – I don't know his name – many years ago. There was one particular tree, with soft pink bark. It peeled off like tissue paper.' Richard had stood with her in the garden and they'd looked out over the sea together, all the way to Africa.

'A eucalypt. The bark comes in numerous colours – greys, creams, pinks – and in New Zealand it's the fashion for ladies to dry it and tear it into small pieces to make collages. A parishioner once showed me a landscape her sister-in-law had sent and it was surprisingly effective.'

Where were they, when Richard had told her about a tree that could send you mad? It was after Kew; he'd met a young gardener, 'not badly educated and very polite'. 'Some plants are poisonous,' she murmured.

'Yes, but they might also be the source of important medicines. There are thousands of plants that are as yet unknown to botanists and many of them might have powerful medicinal properties.' He stopped. 'Anne tells me I let my passion for plants run away with me, but they are such wonderful creations.' Hesitating, he said, 'I'm sorry I never met Richard and that you and I have met in such tragic circumstances. I cannot tell you how devastated Anne is. She adored Richard; the first afternoon we met she told me all about him, and you, how fond she is of you. She's bearing up very well but it's going to hit her hard later. It would have helped her if she'd been able to come to the funeral. And now her mother . . .'

'Tell her,' Nina looked down at her hands then back up again, 'tell her there is also some good news. I am going to have a baby and Richard will live on in his child.'

He gave a small gasp, then said, 'May God bless you.'

The day after the funeral Nina wrote to Katya and to Harry, simple letters in which she said that something terrible had happened, that Richard had gone out at night and been stabbed and killed. And then she told them she was pregnant. 'In the midst of death there is life,' she wrote. 'I do not understand any of this. I am numb.'

Sixteen

The major who'd attended the funeral called the following day while Maggie and Frank were out taking some papers to the solicitors. Fay showed him into the drawing room.

'Mrs Truelove, it's very good of you to see me with no warning.' Holding out his hand, he said, competently but with a heavy accent, '*Ochen rad vstretit'sa snova*.' He released her hand. 'I've surprised you.'

'I am not often greeted in Russian, Major Ellis.'

'I'm very much a beginner. I visited Archangel some time ago and have been to Moscow. I find your country exciting and beautiful, Mrs Truelove.' He put his head on one side. 'You must be wondering why I'm still in Brighton, but, you see, there's concern at the War Office about the circumstances of your husband's death, and I've been working with Captain Stewart on the case. In fact I was expecting the captain to meet me here; no doubt he'll arrive soon.'

'Please sit down.' She shouldn't have agreed to see him without Frank. 'Russia', she heard herself say, 'is very different from England.'

'Indeed. Do you mind if I smoke, Mrs Truelove?'

'I don't mind.'

He tapped the cigarette end on the side of the packet. 'You met your husband there, I believe?'

'Yes. He worked for a company that imports minerals.'

'That was in 1913?'

'Yes.'

'And you haven't been back since?'

'No.'

'Nor your husband?'

'Neither of us have been back.'

He nodded thoughtfully. 'You must have been following events closely in the newspaper?'

'They are events that will change Russia for ever.'

'And they are events of which you approve?'

He was from Army Intelligence: the realisation hit her like a slap. Her fingers found the edge of a cushion. 'I believe in democracy, Major Ellis.'

'Democracy. Yes.' At the same moment the doorbell rang and he gave a small sigh. 'That will be the captain.'

Captain Stewart opened a notebook like the one he'd been writing in the other day. 'I must thank you for agreeing to see us, Mrs Truelove,' he said. 'And I hope you will accept my apologies if any of the questions I ask today cause you pain. As I'm sure you appreciate, however, we do need to be able to ask for information that might not at first seem relevant to you but which might, in fact, be of immense help to us.' He gave a small frown. 'I also feel I owe you an apology; after coming away from our brief interview the other morning I realised that I couldn't have made my intentions clear. I had meant you to know that you should avail yourself of the opportunity to ask certain questions that must have been troubling you.'

It was like crossing a fast-running river on slippery stones. 'There's no need to apologise, Captain. You were most helpful.'

'Oh?' He threw a surprised look in the direction of Major Ellis. 'But you didn't ask me, Mrs Truelove, about what actually happened to your husband – how, please forgive me, he was murdered.'

She sat slightly higher against the cushion. 'I know what happened: Richard was robbed and his assailant stabbed him. My friend, Mrs Laing, spoke to your surgeon. I was hoping that you'd come here to inform me that the man in question is in custody.'

He looked away first. 'I wasn't aware that any of these details had been passed on to you. You will also know then that this took place in a house on Edward Street?'

'I didn't know that.' She managed to keep her eyes on his face.

Major Ellis sat forward. 'Mrs Truelove, I can assure you that it is with the greatest regret that Captain Stewart is raising these matters at all. But it's possible that your husband's death might have far-reaching implications – implications concerning the war effort – and so he has no choice but to touch on some painful issues.'

She knew she should ask what he meant, but didn't dare.

'Yes, Mrs Truelove, if there were any other way I would not raise these matters with you, but when the case comes to court it will become public knowledge anyway.' Something in the way the captain said this made it clear it was meant as much for the major as for Nina herself. 'Yesterday my men conducted interviews in and around Edward Street and Carlton Hill and your husband's description was recognised by a number of people as being someone who had frequented the area over a period of years. From well before the war, in fact.'

She took a breath. 'Richard was a striking man and people would be likely to remember him. He came to Brighton some fifteen years ago and knows – came to know – the town well.'

The captain's eyes narrowed and she was reminded of the gardener's terrier, sniffing out a rat in the barn. 'Mrs Truelove, do you have any idea of what sort of area Edward Street is?'

'I've never been there, Captain, but I believe it's very poor.'

'It isn't the sort of place where one would expect to come across an officer in His Majesty's Army.'

She couldn't stop herself from glancing in the direction of the door. 'My husband was going for a walk . . .'

'Mrs Truelove, what I have to tell you is, I'm afraid, going to come as a shock, and if I could somehow protect you from this information, I would. As I have already said, however,' here he half turned in the direction of his companion, 'if this case comes to court it will become public knowledge.'

The major shrugged. 'Go on.'

'Mrs Truelove, I hope you will be able to forgive me. It is my duty to say it because we are at war and national security must be put above individual considerations. You see, it is sometimes my painful obligation to inform wives such as yourself that their husbands have been involved in activities which are not worthy of them – activities which are, in fact, reprehensible.'

The silence was filled with the ticking of the clock.

'As I have said, your husband was murdered in a house on Edward Street. He was found in a room that was being rented by Jimmy Reed. Mrs Truelove – I have to ask you this – do you know what a prostitute is?'

A wave of something went across the room. What the something was it would have been hard to say, but it was as if an invisible hand had come in and rearranged the position of everything by a fraction of an inch, so that while the surface looked the same everything was different.

They were watching her. 'I have been told . . . yes.' Her throat was tight.

'Jimmy Reed is known to the police as a male prostitute.'

She said nothing.

'Mrs Truelove, your husband's body was found naked in his bed.'

The brutality of his words indicated how much danger she was in.

He was still speaking. 'I know that this will come as a terrible shock – that you might not fully understand. I am afraid your husband has been guilty of the greatest betrayal . . .'

She was standing on the path leading to the Low Field, and Aunt Elena's voice was clear and hard, '. . . every day you see and hear things that no decent woman should ever see or hear.' By marrying Richard she had thought to step back inside the charmed circle, but once outside, that circle was closed for ever. It had been a pretence all along: neither she nor Richard had ever really belonged. And it had been tiring, although she hadn't realised it at the time; it had left both of them exhausted.

'No,' she said quietly.

'Of course you will find this difficult to believe, but it is my sorry duty to assure you it is the truth.'

'Richard didn't betray me.' She spoke clearly. 'My husband was completely honest with me, Captain Stewart. I knew he went with young men.'

The expression on his face almost made her laugh. It felt as if a great weight had been lifted: she was free to say whatever she wanted. It was wonderful. To her left she heard Major Ellis. 'Mrs Truelove, I don't believe you fully understand . . .'

But she did. 'I understand', she cut in, 'that my husband had sex with young men and paid them for it. He did not betray me; indeed, he told me everything.'

'Dear God . . .' Captain Stewart spluttered.

The expression on Major Ellis's face remained the same, however, and she knew who he reminded her of: Dr Vilensky. He would probe with his questions as calmly as the doctor probed with a knife. 'You weren't appalled by his behaviour, Mrs Truelove?'

'My husband didn't choose his nature.'

'That's a very understanding, and liberal, attitude. An attitude which would not, I feel, be understood by the majority of people. One would expect an English woman in your position – a lady – to be disgusted by any suggestion of moral degeneracy on her husband's part.'

On the mantelpiece the flowers were wilting in their vase.

'Mrs Truelove?'

She looked back at him. 'You were saying an English lady would be disgusted; but I'm Russian, Major Ellis, and maybe that is the difference. There are, I think fewer – how should I put it? – taboos in Russia.' How many had been broken here today?

'Maybe.' He bowed his head slightly, as if conceding a point. 'In your husband's work at the War Office he frequently dealt with sensitive information. Did he ever talk to you about that?'

'He never told me any details of his work, but I was aware he saw important documents.'

'And are you also aware that army personnel who see such material in their line of duty are also vulnerable to blackmail – should their personal lives conceal secrets they could not afford to have disclosed?'

'I suppose so, although I'd never thought about it.' She thought about it now. 'As my husband was completely honest with me, Major Ellis,' she said slowly, 'there was little danger of him being blackmailed.'

He raised a finger, as if impatient with a child who'd missed an important point. 'But it isn't just the relationship between a husband and his understanding wife that must be considered here. Mrs Truelove, are you aware of the laws in England concerning male homosexuality? I have no knowledge of the law in Russia, although I am aware that in other European countries

– France, for example – the laws can be different. But in England male homosexuality is illegal. Were you aware of that?'

She'd known there would be gossip and humiliation but had never imagined there were laws about such things. She shifted in the chair. 'No.'

'The *Manual of Military Law* makes the seriousness of such offences quite clear. The act of sodomy – the most serious form of indecency – carries a minimum sentence of ten years' imprisonment. The maximum sentence is life.'

He was lying: it wasn't possible, even in England.

'So, you see, your husband's actions endangered not only himself but also those around him. It's popularly rumoured that the Germans have a "black book", a list of the names of prominent British men and women – hundreds, possibly thousands of them – whose perversions have made them vulnerable to blackmail, even to the point of betraying their country.' He glanced at the captain. 'Personally I think these claims are wildly exaggerated, but even half a dozen names, if they were the right ones, could do the war effort an immense amount of damage. Your husband gained a reputation for efficiency and he was frequently given access to material which would be of great significance to the enemy.'

Nina clasped her hands to stop them shaking. 'Do you have any evidence he was being blackmailed?'

'We don't, but you can see why there's reason for concern.' The major leaned forward. 'Can you think of anything that might indicate that your husband was worried? Was there anything in his manner that might have suggested something of this nature?'

She shook her head.

'Did your husband keep a diary, Mrs Truelove? We've already searched his quarters in London.'

'He didn't.'

'Did he have many personal papers here? Letters, for example?'

'There's a drawer of letters from the bank, that's all. Mr Chaplin has taken most of them to the solicitor's office.'

Major Ellis studied the floor for a moment and then said,

'Your husband had made a number of attempts to be transferred from the War Office. Why was that?'

A wave of revulsion went over her. 'Because he felt guilty, Major Ellis, that other men were risking their lives when he was safe in England.'

He remained unruffled. 'Has anyone with German sympathies tried to befriend you? You might have become suspicious about their allegiances as the result of something they said?'

She swallowed. 'No.'

'You say your husband told you everything. Did he tell you the names of the men he was involved with?'

She shook her head.

'Do you know if he had sexual relations with any other soldier? Did he say there were other homosexuals in the War Office?'

Her mouth was dry and she had to wet her lips. 'He never suggested that. He only told me he had relations with young men he met while he was out.'

'So you knew why he went out the other evening?'

'I thought he'd gone for a walk.'

The major picked up his cigarette again and nodded at Captain Stewart.

'Mrs Truelove,' the captain said, 'after your husband's "walks", did he sometimes return injured?'

'No.'

'Maybe his knuckles were bruised, as if he had hit someone?'

'No.'

'Was he ever violent towards you?'

She could have spat. 'He was not that sort of man.' Her knees were weak, but she managed to push herself up and stood facing them. 'I think you had better go.'

The two men stood as well and she saw them glance at each other. The major nodded and Captain Stewart said, very slowly, 'Mrs Truelove, according to what Reed told someone else, he stabbed your husband in self-defence after being subjected to the most bestial and degrading form of attack.' His voice was bland. 'He said your husband raped him. I take it you know what that means?'

She had never heard the English word said aloud before but

she'd grown up hearing the whispers in the kitchen about what men sometimes did to women, forcing them . . . Her face burned. 'He is a liar as well as a murderer.'

'Oh, many people are liars, Mrs Truelove.' Captain Stewart took another notebook from his pocket and turned to a page. 'We've interviewed the boy who rented the room next to Reed's.' He held the book out as if daring her to take it.

It was open at a carbon copy, written on squared paper. It was signed and dated at the top with an underlined heading that read *Interview with Eddy Holmes.*

Last night, round eleven, I got home and Jimmy Reed, who had room 6, came running in. He had blood on his shirt and all over and was mighty upset. I asked what was up. He said he had met an officer, a captain, who had come up to him on Carlton Hill and asked if he was a bugger. Jimmy told him he was game for a trick because he needed the rent money, but he was no quean. The officer asked if he had a room. Jimmy said aye and the officer said he would pay generous though he didn't say how much. When they got back to the room the officer told him to take his clothes off and get on the bed. Then he took his trousers down and told Jimmy to suck him off. Jimmy said he would but he should not spend in his mouth and the officer said, 'I'm not after that.' Jimmy sucked him for a few minutes and then the officer took his tool out of his mouth and pushed Jimmy over on the bed. He said, 'Now I'm going to roger you, but don't worry, I'll pay you for it.' Jimmy said he would not let him because he had been rogered before and it had hurt something terrible and he got the clap. Then the officer hit him very hard around the head and the next thing Jimmy knew he was being rogered. The officer was very rough and Jimmy shouted at him that he was a dirty bugger and cried for help, thinking I was in the house, and the officer hit him hard again and said if he didn't shut his mouth he'd throttle him. Jimmy had a knife under the bed and he reached for it and stabbed the officer once. I asked him if the officer was hurt bad and he said he was dead. He said there was money in the officer's wallet and that he was running away. He asked me to come but I said I couldn't because of my mother, who is poorly. This is all as I remember it, the God's Truth.

It was as if they'd stripped her naked and beaten her in the street. Her teeth chattered.

Captain Stewart pulled the notebook from between her fingers. 'In court he will claim self-defence.'

Her knees gave way and she sank back down into the chair. 'He's a liar,' she whispered again. Her jaw locked.

'I beg your pardon, Mrs Truelove.' Captain Stewart looked down at her, his voice heavy with contempt. 'I couldn't catch what you said.'

Seventeen

'Financially you are secure,' Frank had assured her. 'Richard's income from the trust will pass to you. It wouldn't be wise to be overly extravagant but, provided you are sensible, you should have nothing to worry about. There'll be things to deal with in the future – for example, the lease on this house runs out next year and you'll need to decide whether you wish to stay on – but there's plenty of time to think about that.'

He blew on his fingertips. 'As for any court proceedings, I shouldn't worry too much. It wouldn't surprise me if the military police don't pursue the case with any great vigour. It angers me greatly to think Richard's murderer might not be brought to justice, but there are other people to think of and nothing must be allowed to undermine your health, or your child's. A court case would be extremely distressing for everyone. If this Jimmy Reed isn't apprehended you must trust in divine judgement, for he will, finally, meet his maker. We are all judged in the end.'

What judgement, she wondered, would be made of her?

Frank had to go back to London after a fortnight but Maggie stayed on and Fay Proctor agreed to stay also. 'I thought of my own girl and how she had all her family round her when the bairns were born, and then I thought of you, newly widowed and a foreigner – begging your pardon – and I knew I couldn't walk out.'

Nina finished her omelette and ate a slice of brown bread. The nausea had abated over the past week but other symptoms had appeared: her mouth flooded with saliva and she'd taken to carrying one of Richard's large handkerchiefs, folded into her pocket or sleeve. Fay noticed and said she'd been the same herself.

'Each pregnancy I drooled like a mad dog; it'd run down my chin if I weren't careful. Don't worry though, after a week or two it'll dry up. My daughter wasn't like it, mind.'

Maggie was out shopping so Nina had eaten her lunch sitting on the window seat in the drawing room. Sometime over the past month the building work that had been taking place on the West Pier for almost a year had finished, and this morning a Union Jack flew proudly from a flagpole over the roof of the new concert hall. She pushed the plate aside and took a folded letter out of her pocket. It was from Harry and had been written a fortnight ago. She wondered dully whether he'd yet received her letter about Richard's death and the baby.

Unlike Egypt we are not allowed cameras in France. If, today, I could have taken any photographs, what would they have been of? We have passed through what once must have been beautiful villages. In one there was a medieval church, its roof gone, and most of the walls, but the central arches were completely intact, as delicate and natural-looking as young saplings.

Outside the entrance sat an old peasant woman, all in black but for an apron so heavily embroidered that in places it was all the colours of the rainbow and as thick as my thumb. When I complimented her on it she smiled and pointed, saying, 'Ma mère, ici, et sa mère, ici . . .' and so on, it apparently being the work of generations, just like the church . . .

The letter was signed, *With love, Harry.*

There was a knock at the door. 'I've come for the plates, if you're finished.'

'Thank you, Fay.'

Fay loaded the tray. 'I got some nice sausages this morning. Mr Gibbs, the butcher, his eldest son Tom is home and says there's to be a big push in the south.' She blew her cheeks out. 'They have to do something, don't they? It's nonsense, a few yards this way and a few yards back and a thousand men dead in the meantime. If they can't agree to a treaty they'll have to give a good heave-ho or this war will go on till doomsday – only there won't be enough men to keep it going that long, so they'll be sending bairns.' She stopped at the door. 'I could do toad in the hole for supper.'

'Yes, thank you.'

A few minutes later the telephone rang and Fay reappeared to say it was Miss Truelove.

'It's happened.' Anne was tearful. 'A blessing, as it was during her sleep. Last night she asked after you and the baby. She was wandering in her thoughts and believed the baby had already been born. "Is his hair red?" she asked. "Is he a Fergusson?" Daddy's family had brown hair and she always said Richard and I were more Fergussons than Trueloves. I didn't think it would do any harm, Nina, to humour her, and so I said the baby was indeed a boy and had a thick head of red hair, like his father.

'Now remember, you're not to come to the funeral. You've been through enough and must think of the baby. The two of you come first. Dear Jeremy will be here to help me.'

Nina's hand shook violently as she replaced the receiver. 'Hypocrite,' she admonished herself. 'Liar.' In the midst of her own grief Anne was so concerned for her, for the woman who had caused her brother's death, and now her mother's. If she ever knew, ever guessed . . .

She needed to get out. The seamstress had delivered an outdoor jacket and Nina took it off the hanger for the first time, along with her veiled hat. On her way out she went through to the kitchen. 'If Mrs Chaplin gets back before I do, tell her not to worry. I'm going to the bank and then I'll do some shopping – the walk will do me good.'

The sun was bright, but there was a breeze, and white-capped waves out to sea. As she hesitated briefly on the pavement she remembered, before the war, watching Richard and Charles from the window: Richard had looked up at her, smiling, and given a small wave. Now she walked to the end of the terrace and turned right.

An hour later she'd found Edward Street. On the corner a group of barefoot boys playing marbles froze as she approached. 'There was a murder recently,' she said through the veil, 'in a house here. An officer was killed. Do you know which house it is?' They stared at her, silent, and then the smallest stood up.

'The next corner.' He pointed. 'Ma Taylor's. The front door has boards because it were kicked in by the coppers.'

'Thank you.' She handed him a penny.

'Be careful, lady,' he called after her. 'They're rough as old nails up there.'

His friends hooted.

The house was narrow and three-storeyed. The front door was boarded, and there was rubbish and filth strewn across the side path. Halfway along she stopped; she could go back, she didn't have to do this. But then she remembered Captain Stewart's words, 'It isn't the sort of place where one would expect to come across an officer in His Majesty's Army.'

She continued straight to the end of the path, took off her gloves and knocked loudly on the side door.

A woman answered. 'Yes?' She looked to be in her early thirties. Her face was hard, and even at this hour she was heavily rouged and powdered: the tight blonde curls were a wig and, like Nina, she wore black.

'Are you Mrs Taylor?'

She stared without saying anything.

'I am Captain Truelove's wife.'

Frowning, the woman moved aside. 'You'd better come in.'

The hallway was a relief after the path. There was the smell of damp but also a heavy cut-glass light shade, and although the brown oilcloth was old and stained it still shone.

'Through here.'

The front parlour had a large sofa and two armchairs. An oak sideboard stood against the wall. The curtains were still drawn, and in the half-light Mrs Taylor looked younger. She stood in front of the fireplace. 'What do you want?'

Nina had come because Richard had, and because it was her fault. She glanced around her.

'Go on, have a good gawp. What were you expecting – a zoo?'

'I would like to see where it happened – the room. If it's convenient.'

'Convenient? No, it's not convenient.' On the mantelpiece were two photographs: in one, three small dark-eyed children stood gathered around Mrs Taylor, who sat in a high-backed chair; the other was of a man in uniform. The second frame was edged with black crêpe. Mrs Taylor followed Nina's gaze and her voice softened slightly. 'Thousands of men get killed every day. How it happens doesn't make much difference as far as I can see. Dead is dead. What's the use of being a hero when it means your children will starve? What's the use . . .'

A hammering came from the back of the house. She sighed. 'Go on then, sit down.'

There was something hard under the cushion: a child's rattle. Nina weighed it in her hand, feeling the smoothness of the wood, then laid it carefully on the arm of the sofa. Letting her gaze travel around the room, she saw that though it was poor it was clean and attempts had been made to make it pretty. It was a room a woman took pride in.

A man's voice was loud and overbearing. Nina listened for a moment and then stepped out into the hall, crossing quietly to the bottom of the staircase. She stood there briefly, then made up her mind and tiptoed quickly up.

The light wasn't on on the landing and she had to peer to take her bearings. There were two doors. Taking a deep breath, she tried the first and found herself in a bathroom: there was a small frosted window and she could make out a rusted bath in the middle of the room, and a sink and lavatory. She was suddenly desperate to empty her bladder. The smell of damp and mould made her falter but she knew she wouldn't be able to hold it. When she'd finished, she didn't attempt to pull the rusty chain.

Back out on the landing she could still hear voices. The next door had a large number eight painted clumsily on it in black. Taking hold of the banister, she hurried up the stairs to the next half-landing. The door opposite the stairs was number seven so the other, unnumbered room must be six. She stood and listened, trying to quiet her own breathing. When she tried the handle, it turned. Inside the room was pitch black; reaching forward, she groped for the light cord, found it and pulled.

The small room was empty except for a narrow metal bed frame with no mattress, a cheap dressing table, the top drawers open and empty, and a green-painted chair. The walls were covered with stained pink paper and the floorboards were bare. There was something wrong with the room but at first she didn't know what it was. Then she saw there wasn't a window: a larger room had been cut in half to make two smaller ones.

She made herself look back at the bed. He died there, she told herself. He died on that bed. But the words didn't seem to connect with the room: she was here, but she couldn't imagine Richard ever being here. She couldn't imagine him coming into this miserable place with a man he'd met on the street. A man who would rob and kill him. Suddenly she was angry, angrier than she had ever been in her life: Richard had got himself killed. How could he have been such a fool, to come to this disgusting place? They were right to say no gentleman would ever be seen here. He should have been ashamed of himself; she was ashamed for him. 'Disgusting.' She tried the word out loud, and it echoed in the empty room. 'Filthy.' And then the next sound she made was a sob, and the next, and she imagined herself holding him in her arms and stopping the blood with her hands. 'You won't die,' she would have kissed his face, 'I won't let you die.'

'Here.' The woman, Mrs Taylor, was holding out a small glass to Nina, who was sitting in the chair. 'Go on, it's not poison.'

It was raw and burned her throat.

Mrs Taylor looked down at her. 'I tried to stop you,' she said dully. 'Because it couldn't help, could it?'

'It was my fault, I'm to blame . . .'

'Aren't we all? All of us guilty as ruddy sin. Well, coming here should make you feel you've suffered enough.' She sank down on the metal edge of the bed and folded her hands in her lap. 'They won't come back. They're dead and gone and that's it.' She could have been a woman sitting in church.

Nina swallowed another mouthful.

'That was the landlord, giving me a week's notice – not that I could pay any longer, all the tenants disappeared and owing. The MPs got rid of them; vicious they were, kicking down the front door, and rough with the lads – gave a couple of them a good going-over. I thought one was set to lose an eye. The bugger says the door's my responsibility and he'll add it to the bill. So I guess that's that.'

'Eddy Holmes,' Nina said. 'What's he like?'

Mrs Taylor half looked at her. 'Harmless. Soft in the head is Eddy.'

'And Jimmy Reed?'

She snorted. 'Where Eddy's soft, Jimmy's vicious.'

'And a liar,' Nina said slowly. 'Would you say that?'

The woman's eyes were immediately calculating. 'I might.'

Very calmly she put down the glass and took out her purse. 'This will pay for the door, and a bit more.'

On the way out, one of the dark-haired children from the photograph was sitting on the kitchen step, a filthy doll in her lap. Her mother pushed her with the toe of her boot and the child sullenly let Nina pass.

Eighteen

Every night sleep eluded her. She sat up reading till late, then tossed and turned, going over that last evening with Richard and imagining how it could have been different. If only she hadn't said she was going to write to Harry. Or, having said it, if only she'd laughed the argument off, as Mamma would have with Papa. Then Richard would have sat and written his letters and not gone out to Edward Street. Maggie said Nina wasn't responsible for Richard's death but she was: not entirely responsible, but partly responsible, and that was enough. Just as she was partly responsible for the operation on the young violinmaker. 'And,' she whispered to herself in the mirror, 'for Mamma's death, for if you'd been born a boy Papa would have been content.' She tried to smile at herself as she said it, but found she couldn't because it was true.

Katya had written: *Your news is too terrible and I ran out into the garden and threw handfuls of gravel against the wall like a madwoman. With each handful I shouted, 'Why us? Why us?' because I do not understand what our family can have done, to experience so much unhappiness. And you least of all, Nina, for where I did not choose wisely or well, you did. Richard was a good man and a good husband and the two of you loved each other and were happy.*

That much was true but Nina wondered how Katya would feel if she knew the whole truth.

After Mrs Truelove's funeral, Anne came straight to Brighton. Maggie brought them tea in the parlour then left them alone. 'I haven't been back to Cheltenham since Mother's illness,' Anne said, 'but I felt I must come here first, to see you.' She sat on a chair and wept. 'We are all there is of the family now, the two of us. But I'll marry Jeremy and you'll have Richard's baby. Then we'll be a proper family again.'

On the second day Nina and Anne went to Richard's grave to lay flowers and Anne suggested that the next afternoon they go to the Downs. 'When Richard first came to Brighton his letters were full of descriptions of walks he'd done, of how beautiful the Downs were. Let's go, for him.'

The following day she and Nina stood on a windswept hillside watching a small child with a kite. Shading her eyes, Nina watched him struggle to keep hold of the string. She could remember as a child watching a boy in a hat and sailor suit running along a path pulling a red kite behind him. Where would that have been? In Petersburg, most probably, in the park near her grandparents' house. Even though she'd never met her mother's parents she'd come to know their house and the streets around it so well that as a young child she believed she had known them. 'My mother used to bring me here,' Mamma would say when they went to the park. 'Her uncle taught her the Latin names for flowers and the head gardener named a rose after her.'

The kite tugged at the end of its string and the woman with the boy – Nina assumed it was his mother – threw out her hand in warning. 'Don't let go!' she'd be calling. 'It will fly away!'

When she was growing up Nina had thought the threads that bound a family were the strongest things there were: unbreakable, invisible bonds of steel. But with Mamma's death the threads didn't break, they simply slipped through her hands, like a kite slipping through a child's fingers.

'The larks,' Anne was studying the sky, 'I wonder if they still catch them for the hotels? I remember we saw trays of them in the market before the war.'

Nina had forgotten about going to the market; Richard had taken them very early one morning. Overhead the skylark's song was perfect – pure and unblemished. Maybe it was singing with happiness: the humans had taken to killing each other and had lost their appetite for innocent birds.

Anne took her arm. 'You're tired, Nina. We'll go back to the trap.'

As the horse moved into a trot the Downs rolled past, ancient and peaceful. 'What is that?' Anne called to the driver, pointing past the edge of her parasol. In the distance was the squat brick erection they'd passed on the way up.

'That's the *ghat*, that is,' he called over his shoulder. 'Built for the Indian soldiers. It's the way they do things in their country, burn the bodies, so their spirit can go straight up to heaven I guess. Can't say I blame 'em. Not that I've got anything against a Christian burial, the prayers and the like, but I don't fancy the thought of being worm food meself.'

A faint smudge of smoke hung in the blue sky over the *ghat* and Nina couldn't stop the tears from running down her face. Why hadn't she thought to bring Richard here? He wouldn't have wanted to be closed in, under the ground; he deserved to be free, like the skylarks. But it was too late now.

Anne took her hand and they travelled on in silence.

On the morning of Anne's departure they stood together in the hall, putting on their hats in front of the mirror. All in black, they were like two old women. Nina remembered back to the first time Anne had come to stay and they had gone to the motor races in their bright silk dresses and straw hats and enormous parasols. That was only three years ago, but it might as well have been a different world. It *was* a different world, the world before the war.

Anne pushed a strand of red hair into place and smiled sadly into the glass. 'I'm so glad you met Richard. You made him very happy.' Hesitating, she said, 'Nina, I haven't wanted to ask, but did you have the opportunity to tell him about the baby?'

Her throat was tight. 'Yes.'

Her sister-in-law's eyes were dark under the brim of the hat. 'Thank you! It will always console me to know that before his death Richard knew he was to be a father.'

The day after Anne left a letter came from Harry. Nina had morning tea with Maggie and then went into her bedroom and sat weighing it in her hands: it felt very light. Then she took the opener and slowly cut through the envelope. There were two sheets of paper inside. Unfolding them, she read: *Your letter has torn me in two. My dearest darling, you have lost someone you loved deeply – that comes through in every word you've written – and who I know will have loved you. If I could do anything to change this I would, for I would keep all harm and unhappiness away from you for ever. I grieve for you both, you in your loss now and Richard, who cared for you and loved you.*

And yet at the same time there is joy because you are pregnant with our child. How can grief and joy exist together? What is the fabric of this world, that I can sit here in the midst of war and weep and laugh at the same time? That while there is death all around I find I am the father of a child? Our child – I never dared to imagine such a thing. For you do know how much I love you, don't you? I fell in love with you at Mrs Laing's first supper . . .

'Oh,' she whispered aloud, putting down the letter, and then, 'No!' For surely she had no right to feel happy.

Maggie was to return to London. 'I don't like leaving you at all.'

Nina would miss her, but Maggie was needed elsewhere. She shook her head, reaching out to straighten her friend's collar. 'And who would take over your work in the factories? Fay will be here every day, and one of her nieces, probably Violet, will sleep over at night. And no doubt I'll see a lot of Mrs Laing.'

'No doubt.' They were standing in the bay window and Maggie was looking through opera glasses. 'I'll come down as often as I can,' she said, 'and of course I'll be here when the baby is due. When does Anne plan to be back?'

'She has her mother's estate to sort out, and her fiancé, Jeremy, is now based in Cheltenham . . .'

'You don't want her here?' Lowering the glasses, Maggie leaned forward to peer through the window.

Nina followed her gaze, resting her cheek on the window frame and watching a group of young girls walk along the front in the direction of the pier. The paint around the window was peeling, and as she moved her face she felt flakes stick to her skin. 'I worry about her being in Brighton in case Captain Stewart calls, or she hears something.'

Maggie looked at her. 'Nina, it's been weeks now, and Frank always says that if the police don't apprehend someone within a few days of the crime it's unlikely they ever will.'

'But they know who they're looking for in this case,' she drew a circle on the window with her fingertip, 'and Anne won't be able to cope if it comes to court.'

Maggie gave a small shrug. 'We all find ways of coping, don't we? You and Richard did, and Frank and I . . . Think how much ordinary people go through. Anne is much stronger than you think: in fact there's something about her that's quite steely. Now,' putting her arm around Nina's shoulders, she nodded in the direction of the sea, 'I've been wondering what's wrong with the view and have only this minute seen what it is. The bathing machines, where are they?'

'The army took them away and destroyed them. There were complaints but it was too late.'

'Ridiculous! Whatever did they do that for?'

'No one seems to know.' She rested her head against Maggie's. 'Fay says there's going to be a big push in the south. Our butcher told her.'

'The butcher is probably as well informed as anyone.'

What was it Aunt Elena had said, about a baker being as well informed as a duke? On the front the girls they'd been watching came to the pier and unexpectedly broke into a run, one of them waving her hat in the air as if celebrating a small victory.

It was becoming more difficult to buy food, and to save Fay from having to shop for her lunch Nina took to going to a hotel each day. Under normal circumstances such a routine might have aroused criticism, but these were not normal circumstances and Mrs Laing, for one, energetically congratulated her on her regime.

'You are to be praised, Nina, for your good sense. There are those who would say that a woman so recently bereaved, and in your condition, should remain secluded in the house and not parade herself on the street, but I have no truck with that degree of delicacy; pregnancy is a completely natural state and nothing to be ashamed of. No, a proper luncheon every day is what you need, and on top of that a short walk is excellent exercise. It shows you're putting your child – and thereby your husband's memory – first and not moping, as Alice Evans did. Everything about Alice was excessive – it came as no surprise to me that she had twins. I have no such fears about you.'

No one seemed to know much about Alice. Mrs Laing had had one letter from Alice's sister-in-law but all it said was that they took each day as it came.

There'd been a break in the warm weather, with a week of rain, but today it was all sunshine, the sea flat and calm. Nina had lunched at the Royal York Hotel and was now walking back along the front. A naval boat was a little way out in the water and she thought about how life had been the first summer she'd spent in Brighton, before war was declared. The paddle steamers had made regular trips, and there were yachts and fishing boats. It had all been so very different. It would never be the same again: nothing would be the same again.

Coming to one of the shelters she felt hot and breathless and sank down on the wooden seat. As soon as she stopped moving the baby woke and she could feel its slow but purposeful movements. Did you enjoy our walk? she dutifully asked it in her head. Can you hear the sea? The movement stopped and she could have cried, feeling that the baby had turned against her. It was absurd, of course, but because she barely slept she felt tired and emotional much of the time; she also found it difficult to concentrate. Maggie had telephoned yesterday evening and during the conversation had berated Mrs Pankhurst for travelling to Russia to inspect the women soldiers there. 'A "Women's Battalion of Death", it's called. Can you think of anything more dreadful? Ridiculous woman, just when the public was beginning to accept the WAACs.' After finishing her lunch today, Nina had asked for a copy of *The Times*, meaning to search for any news of this, but then found she couldn't keep her mind on any of the articles she read and had sat gazing out of the window instead. Mamma would have disapproved of her reading a newspaper in public anyway. 'Like a man in a coffee shop,' she would have said. Miss Brenchley had told them that ladies should always wear gloves to read a newspaper and it was not a task to be undertaken in a light-coloured dress.

'One, two, three . . .' A group of boys were playing at hide-and-seek around the sacks of rubble deposited by the army as a defensive wall. Nina remembered how Richard had fumed the first time he'd seen the sacks. 'Perfect shrapnel.' He'd prodded one of them. 'You'd think someone, somewhere, would have had more sense.' She hadn't thought about that, the night of the Zeppelin. 'Are you trying to get yourself killed?' Harry had shouted.

Maybe that was what she had been trying to do.

'Mrs Truelove, surely you aren't alone?' It was Mr Lewisham, taking off his hat. 'My dear lady, might I intrude for a few minutes? I am just on my way to a business luncheon but am in no great hurry, and seeing you sitting here by yourself,' his voice trembled, 'without dear Richard by your side . . .'

His guest for lunch, he was saying, was a lawyer from London who represented the interests of a large company based in Glasgow. He'd already acquired a second warehouse and might soon have to consider a third, which meant having to explore various means of transport: only yesterday he'd arranged the purchase of a lorry. Drawing out a large kerchief, he wiped his brow; if only Richard were here to help – he found himself thinking this every day – so many of his problems would be solved. It would be one of the great regrets of his life, that Richard wouldn't be rejoining the company after the war to share in its success. Another regret was that his own dear wife had not lived to see the King's Gardens house.

'What is the point, I keep asking myself, in having a substantial house – even, some might say, an imposing house – if it is not decorated appropriately? I have found a retired painter and managed to purchase enough paint for the woodwork, but there is still the matter of the walls. And the arrangement of furniture could be improved. The truth is, Mrs Truelove, that King's Gardens lacks the woman's touch.'

'Yes,' Nina murmured. When she could escape Mr Lewisham she'd go home and splash cold water over her face and arms; she was burning up.

'Had my dear wife still been alive she would have made all the decisions about the house and I wouldn't have been involved but for complimenting her on her choice of wallpaper. She had an eye for wallpaper, as no doubt you do yourself. In fact – and I hope you do not mind my saying this, but I can assure you it is meant as the highest praise – you remind me of my wife in many ways. And to think of you, like so many young widows at this sad time, condemned to a lonely life. I know what it is to be lonely. Lonely, yes, but not poor. No, I am not a poor man . . .' His voice cracked with emotion and seemed to come from a long way off. 'My dear,' a hand gripped hers, 'Mrs Truelove . . .'

She was too hot; she had to get home. She managed to get to her feet but had to catch hold of the side of the shelter as a wave of dizziness threatened to sweep her away.

'A summer flu is always the worst,' Fay said, 'for being out of season.'

Lydia Barnes had brought a basket of miscellaneous books from the library and Nina sat in bed reading *By Way of Reefs and Palms: Travels in Australasia and the Pacific* by Herbert Palmerton, Esq.: *In the North of the great state of Queensland we find the wonders of the tropical jungle's prolific plant forms; the brighter, richer hues of the blooms and flowered foliage, and the gayer colours of birds and butterflies; the people of many strange callings and wayfarings, the sandalwood traders, the hunters of the dugong and the gatherers of bêche-de-mer; the picturesque aboriginal villagers who give stirring exhibitions of war dances, spear and boomerang throwing. Here also there are fruits fit for the platter of an oriental banquet, mangoes, guavas, tamarind and wilder ginger . . .*

Her mouth was full of ginger syrup now. 'I found a crystallised piece in the pantry,' Fay had explained, 'so I soaked it and boiled it with sugar. I'd prefer a boiled onion to ginger but there are no onions to be had. It comes to something, doesn't it, when there's not an onion to be bought in Brighton?'

Nina swallowed another teaspoonful and went back to the book. *The southern cities of Sydney and Melbourne are charming but those of an adventurous mettle will find what they seek in this vast country's northernmost regions. Here, in the denseness and beauty of the forest, sportsmen will discover that handsomely feathered fruit-eating pigeons, as pretty as parrots, make excellent table birds, while floriculturists will marvel at strange, snake-like epiphytes clinging to the trees and the huge cables of lawyer vines shading dainty and rare orchids below . . .*

Was Bathurst in Queensland? She had no idea. *I am not asking you to come to any decisions now*, Harry had written in his last letter. *But I do believe you would find Australia exciting and that there is a future in the New World that no longer exists in the Old – Europe is a charnel house.*

He'd written to his sister Ruby and told her about Nina. *It will put my mind at rest to think that, should anything happen to me, my family would know about you and that, should you ever want or need, you and our child would be assured of finding a home there. Please keep their address safe . . .*

'You've finished the syrup?' Fay was gently taking the cup from between her fingers.

'Thank you.'

'Here now, I'll put that book on the side. You go back to sleep and I'll bring your supper later.'

Nina dreamed she was in a forest, surrounded by palm trees and other trees she didn't recognise, heavy with dark vines. She walked under them, marvelling at the bright colours of the flowers, but after a short distance her boots became heavy from the wet grass and she took them off, and her stockings. I can't walk through the forest in bare feet, she thought, so she scrambled down the nearest slope, following the sound of the sea. At the edge of the sand there was a line of palm trees, and she stood under one of them, watching as a group of children played. They called to each other, laughing and hiding till there was only one child left, a beautiful child in a long white shirt and with curly red hair. She watched as the child played alone, happily scooping water out of a rock pool.

Eventually she walked across the sand. 'Hello,' she said, and smiled. She was full of love. The child looked up, curious but not smiling, and a stab of panic went through her. 'But you know who I am?'

The red curls shook and the child stood up and backed away.

'I am your mother!' She held out her arms.

'No you're not!' The eyes were angry and frightened. 'Go away! You are not my mother. I don't know who you are.'

Nineteen

The war was going badly. It was whispered in all the shops, discussed on street corners. In London a Zeppelin raid had smashed the windows of Swan and Edgar's, while the General Post Office sustained a direct hit. Behind the GPO, St Bart's was also damaged, and a synagogue. There were rumours that St Paul's was on fire – German aircraft regularly used its dome to guide them to the centre of the city – but Maggie had telephoned and said this wasn't the case.

Nina looked down from the bedroom window to where, a fortnight ago, a man had come and cut down the pear tree. 'They'll be digging a vegetable garden,' Fay observed, but nothing had happened, the ground was simply waste. Behind her on the mantelpiece the clock chimed twelve. Soon she'd go to lunch, but today she wouldn't buy a newspaper, because there was one word she couldn't bear to see in print again: Ypres. Everywhere, Ypres, Ypres, Ypres. And what made it even more unbearable was that she hadn't heard from Harry in almost three weeks. In his last letter he'd said they'd arrived at their destination and were settling in, but she didn't know where that destination was.

Getting up, she wandered restlessly through to the dressing room. Richard's cot was still in its place, but soon she'd have it moved so the room could be turned into a nursery. The walls would be sky blue, the curtains gold velvet: Richard would have liked that.

'Mrs Truelove?' There was a knock at the bedroom door. 'Mrs Truelove?' Violet had the morning off from the factory and was filling in for Fay.

'I'm through here, Violet.'

'There's a gentleman to see you, ma'am. An officer, I mean. His name is Captain Stewart. Shall I show him up?'

Her heart sank – she hadn't heard from Captain Stewart for a while now, and her first instinct was to refuse this visit, but she couldn't bear for him to know he frightened her.

'I was passing and thought I would call in for a few minutes, to let you know how our investigations are proceeding. I assume you are curious?' His eyes lingered on her belly.

'Yes, I am.'

He gave a faint smile, and this time she wasn't reminded so much of a terrier as a cat, playing with a mouse. 'Unfortunately these things do take time. We haven't apprehended Reed yet, but we undoubtedly will. Even when we do catch him, however, there is still the question of his guilt.'

She felt the baby move jerkily and tried to relax her breathing. 'He confessed to his friend.'

'Indeed, but until proven guilty he is innocent, and at this stage we cannot say without doubt that he is the murderer. That will be a matter for the court to decide. When it comes to court.'

She didn't say anything.

He watched her for a few seconds and then said, 'Because of his friend's statement we've put our efforts into locating Reed. But I've found myself wondering, as one must always wonder about these things: I don't suppose, Mrs Truelove, that anyone else would have wanted your husband dead? There isn't anyone who might benefit from his death?'

Nina felt like throwing something at him: the man was a complete fool. 'I can assure you my husband had no enemies. He was very well liked, and respected.' She emphasised the last word. 'There was no reason anyone would want him dead.'

'You're sure?'

'Completely.'

'Ah well, it does no harm to ask. Thank you for your time, and please do feel free to contact us whenever you wish.' He stood and she rang for Violet, but instead of moving towards the door he took a step in the direction of the bay window. 'What a summer's day for England! With heat like this you could think yourself in a foreign country.' He smiled over his shoulder. 'Somewhere very hot – Australia, for instance.'

She felt the blood drain from her face as he turned and followed Violet from the room. They knew about her and Harry. Of course they knew. The censors could read any letters coming out of France, and no doubt it was easy to arrange for hers to be read as well. Her letter about Richard's death, and her pregnancy, they'd read that. And all her other letters, pathetic as they were.

A cold shiver passed through her, as though she'd walked over a grave. 'I don't suppose anyone else would have wanted your husband dead?' He meant her. He meant she'd wanted Richard dead because of Harry.

There was a tap at the door again. 'Ma'am, should I bring a cup of tea?'

'No.' She needed fresh air. 'I'm going out, Violet. I'll go to the grocer's. Bring me the list and I'll see what's available.'

As she opened the front door, however, the postman was standing there. 'Sorry I'm so late.' Tipping his cap he handed her a brown army envelope.

'Thank you!' But even as she took the letter she could see it was far heavier than usual. There'd been a mistake, she thought, this wasn't for her. But it *was* for her: *Mrs N. Truelove*. The writing wasn't familiar, however; the letter wasn't from Harry. Reluctantly she turned it over and read on the back, *Major F. Jones*. She stood completely still in the doorway for a few moments, and then slowly turned back into the house, where, without taking off her coat or putting down her basket, she walked up the stairs past the startled Violet and shut herself in the bedroom.

Twenty

'Mrs Truelove?' A figure sat near her on the bed. 'Violet called me. She's been very worried.'

Death had a smell to it. The smell of a blood-soaked mattress, of pus oozing from a man's ear. On the battlefield the corpses would bloat and burst, like the body of the cow the stream washed into Low Field.

'Lying here in your coat for hours she says.' A hand shook Nina's shoulder. 'I have to know what's wrong. You're exhausted through crying – have you had bad news?' Fay's face came close and a glass was pressed against her bottom lip. 'Take a sip of water.' The water ran across her mouth. 'Come now, ma'am, it's a warm day and there's the bairn to think of.' She opened her mouth and swallowed. Fay sat staring down at her. 'I'll call the doctor, shall I? Or Mrs Laing?'

Nina shook her head.

'I have to do something, with you in this state. I can't have the responsibility of not getting help if it's required.'

The letter was still clenched tight between Nina's fingers. She pushed it at Fay, who took it and asked, 'Who's Major Jones?'

There was too much death and she was to blame. Everything she touched died.

Fay read aloud. '"Dear Mrs Truelove, I do not know how to begin this letter except with the words 'forgive me'. For I am writing with the worst of news. My good friend, Lieutenant Harry O'Connor, asked me to write to you in the event that anything happened to him . . ."'

Fay read the rest in silence then pulled Nina on to her lap, her fingers stroking her hair. The only sound was from a wasp in the window, buzzing angrily as it searched for a way to get free.

Twenty-one

They were both dead, Richard and Harry. Nina sat and looked at herself in the dressing table mirror, no longer knowing who she was except that she was someone who'd lost them. They were gone. You could reach out your fingers and touch the face reflected there but you would never touch either of them again. You would never talk to them or laugh with them. And you would go on getting older and older and would feel their loss just as acutely every day; it would never end.

She touched her reflection now as she sat in the bedroom in Cheltenham, smearing her fingers slowly across the glass. Darya Fyodorovna used to tell the story of a woman from her village who, on waking one morning and finding her daughter and grandson dead in the bed beside her, had a fit causing one side of her face to freeze so she could not smile or frown. The same should happen to her; it seemed wrong that she should still be wearing the same face.

'Nina.' Anne knocked and put her head around the bedroom door. 'We'll have tea on the lawn.'

She sat back from the mirror. 'Yes.'

'I still can't quite believe you're here.' She listened. 'That's Helen with the tray. I'll see you downstairs.'

It had been Fay's idea that she should come to Cheltenham. 'Have you thought about going to your sister-in-law's to have the baby? And then, after the babe is born, come back to Brighton. It will all be different then, when you're a mother, you'll see. You're making yourself too upset here.'

Although she'd known Harry was dead as soon as the postman handed her the envelope, she'd cried out against it with every part of her being. He couldn't be, it must be a mistake. Another letter would come, *I'm so sorry you've been worried . . .*

Harry hadn't wanted her to worry. In his letter Major Jones said Harry let her think his role was mainly that of a translator, *but that, unfortunately, was not the whole truth. It was true he was often called on in this capacity when not in the front line, but he was a soldier and a soldier's duty is to fight. He didn't want you to worry.*

He'd died instantly, when a sniper's bullet hit him. *This was not in the heat of battle but on waking in the morning and standing up in the trench. Such a simple act. Who would think that such a simple, natural act could be dangerous? It is something one is not supposed to do, but we all do it. I am not lying to you when I say he did not suffer. I have spoken to those who were with him at the time and they said his death was immediate. He fell down instantly and it was as if he were asleep. There were birds singing in the trees and a faint breeze and he looked completely at peace.*

A wave of emptiness passed over Nina, as if she were being sucked into a black pool. Part of her wanted nothing more than to go with the blackness, but she resisted, because although Richard and Harry hadn't survived, she had, and it was her duty now to look after the baby.

Nina spent the mornings in Cheltenham on the lawn in a wicker chair, under the trees where Richard and Anne had learned to dance.

'There were Chinese lanterns,' Anne said, 'made of stiff varnished paper. They were such bright colours: pink, yellow, orange, green. Father bought them in London, in Chinatown. Richard loved them and suggested hanging them in the trees. By the end of the summer they were in tatters and Mother insisted they be brought down. The gardener carried out a ladder . . .' She stopped abruptly and looked away, the memory evidently too painful.

Nina imagined a young Richard dancing across the lawn, his head thrown back as he laughed. And then there was the crack of a rifle and he was on the ground, his eyes open and his face peaceful. In the trees the birds went on singing as if nothing had happened.

Anne's fiancé Jeremy often came to afternoon tea or supper. 'He works terribly hard in the hospitals,' Anne said, 'with the wounded soldiers, and civilians. But the worst place is the mental hospital; I don't know how he bears it. Not that he tells me much about it – it's not something one can discuss.'

They were sitting in the summerhouse. Anne had entwined her arm in Nina's and in the silver jug they were reflected as twin black figures. The back door shut and Jeremy approached across the lawn, his limp giving him a slight rolling motion. He stopped on his way to inspect some roses.

'Confess,' Anne called to him. 'They are wonderful.'

'Roses,' she said to Nina, 'are not Jeremy's favourite flower.' She smiled as he joined them.

'It's not that I don't like them, it's simply that . . .'

'They're not exciting enough for a real botanist.' Anne moved so that Jeremy could slide around the table and sit between them on the bench. 'We were at Mrs Bewick's for luncheon last summer; we'd only known each other a few weeks and our hostess was showing off her prize roses – whereupon Jeremy whooped with delight, fell to his knees and pointed out this tiny plant, a weed to anyone else, which he announced to be a rare specimen.'

Jeremy laughed self-consciously. 'It isn't often, in our English gardens, that one comes across something truly unusual. Of course there are other areas in the world, around the equator and the tropics, where there are thousands of plants that have never been written up at all.'

'It's a pity, then, that mine is not a complexion made for India, or Africa, or any other country with a hot climate. With your colouring, Nina, you would no doubt survive the tropical sun but I would simply burn to nothing.' Laughing, Anne took the cloth from the jug in front of them and poured lemonade into glasses.

Nina looked up at Jeremy. 'Would you really like to go to those countries?'

He glanced at Anne. 'I suppose I would. When you've read about the flora, such places do sound exciting.'

Nina's head, reflected in the jug, was a bubble about to float free. 'I've heard there are plants that can make you go mad. I believe there are plants like that in Australia.'

'Oh, Nina,' Anne remonstrated.

'No, Nina may very well be right,' Jeremy said. 'Some plants produce very powerful toxins.'

'I read that in the north of Australia the rainforests have vines as thick as a man's arm and there are strange water plants as well, weeds and coral.'

A plant had more chance of surviving than a man did, or maybe the same. Maybe there was a God and he was a gardener who pruned and weeded indiscriminately.

'Ah, but coral isn't a plant, you see, although people naturally think it is. It's actually clusters of small animals.'

Nina pulled her thoughts back to the book. 'And sea cucumbers? Are they plants or animals?'

'Good heavens,' Anne exclaimed, 'sea cucumbers! How do you know about such extraordinary things, Nina?'

'There was a book, in the Brighton library.'

'If you're interested, I have a text which might appeal to you,' Jeremy said. 'I must find it. We could look at it together – it's not often I find someone interested in these things.'

'Oh dear!' As Anne proffered the plate of brown bread smeared with margarine, a slice slipped to the ground. Frowning, she clumsily pushed it under the seat with her shoe. 'The birds will deal with it later. Well, all I can say is that with all this talk of poisonous trees and animals that look like plants, I'm very grateful to be living in Cheltenham and not the north of Australia.'

Fay sent on any post and Katya wrote every week. *We are all aware of a tide of ill feeling rising against our small community here and Ivan reports similar feelings in the army as rumours spread that the government in Petrograd will fail to honour the payment of war bonds. Many French people will suffer large losses if this proves to be the case. In his last letter Ivan said he increasingly feels that the future lies outside Europe and believes we should join his cousin Vasily in Mexico after the war. (It is a good thing he has no cousin in Kathmandu or he would be threatening to drag us off there!) Do you remember Darya*

*telling our fortunes with the cards? She said I would go on a long
journey. Shall we do that, Nina, all of us leave Europe behind
and go to Mexico?*

*The twins are peevish today as it is hot, and I have promised
to take them to the sea front. I think of you constantly and pray
for you and your baby, and Richard in Heaven, every day.*

As she read this, Nina remembered Darya saying she would
pray to St Paraskeva for them daily. Prayer, it seemed, was of
little avail.

The midwife, Betty, was a woman in her sixties. Her hand ran
over Nina's swollen belly approvingly. 'Not too long to go now.
You must continue to eat properly and take some light exercise,
and try not to dwell on things. Your sister-in-law tells me she's
looking for a nurse and I've given her some names. Everything's
being looked after.' Before she left, she busied herself with her
bag. 'How much do you know about childbirth, Mrs Truelove?'

Nina was heavy and tired. 'What do you mean?'

'Do you know how the baby will be born?' She hoisted the bag
up and sighed. 'Do you know where it comes out?'

'I grew up on a farm in Russia.'

The midwife grunted. 'I wish all women in England grew up
on farms.'

'My mother died . . .' Every night she had the same dream, in
which the red-haired child didn't recognise her.

'I never knew my mother, she died having me,' the midwife
replied. 'I've had five sons myself, none of them at the Front,
thank God. I'll look after you and you look after the baby by not
worrying yourself unnecessarily.'

The baby came before everything else; her own safety was only
important for the baby's sake. 'You will be safe,' Nina
whispered, but didn't dare to add, 'I promise'.

Maggie telephoned often and came to visit. Anne showed her the
bedroom which was to become the nursery. 'The cradle is to be
delivered, and look here, on the mantelpiece.' She pointed to the
photograph of Richard in his uniform. 'So that Baby will know
what Daddy looked like.'

'Nina, are you sure you're all right here?' Maggie asked when

Anne eventually left them together in the drawing room. 'Don't you think it would be easier if you came to us? We would love to have you, you know that. I can't bear to think that you've lost Richard *and* the father of your child, and that you're here with no one to talk to . . .'

'Anne has lost Richard and her mother, and wouldn't understand.' Besides, even though Nina loved Maggie, she knew that talking wouldn't help.

'I suppose you're right.' Maggie's voice was doubtful. 'And you'll stay on here for some time with the baby?'

'I'll stay until the war finishes. Not necessarily in this house – Anne has hinted they expect to marry within the year – but I might as well stay in Cheltenham.' She took an envelope from her pocket. 'I've written to Frank, asking him to tell the solicitor I won't be renewing the Brighton lease when it comes up.' She'd also asked him, should anything happen to her, to open her metal box and destroy Harry's letters to her and the ones she'd written to him, which Major Jones had returned.

'You're not going back to Brighton at all?'

'Only to supervise the packing when the time comes.' She checked for sounds from the hall and lowered her voice. 'Captain Stewart came to see me again. He knew about Harry and I'm sure they'd been reading our letters. I think he knew Harry was dead when he came. I didn't hear till later that morning, but I think he already knew.'

Maggie gazed out of the window. It was raining and the garden looked dismal. 'The English can be very vicious. There's a streak of real cruelty in us.'

'I've written to Ruby, Harry's sister: three letters, at different times, to make sure one gets through, and I've given her your address so Anne doesn't see the reply. When it comes will you telephone and tell me what she says?'

'Of course.'

'I've been thinking a lot about the future, Maggie. I'm not sure yet, but when the war is over I'll probably go to Katya in Nice – Anne will soon have her own family to think about. And from Nice I might go to Australia.'

Her friend looked blank. 'What?'

'I'm not sure yet but Katya's husband is talking about them going to Mexico, and my aunt and her family are in Canada.' She made herself smile. 'If I go to Australia we will be spread around the globe.'

'You mean to *live*?' Maggie's eyes filled with tears and she quickly looked away. 'I had never thought . . . You know how much I would miss you, don't you?'

Nina did know, and her resolve almost faltered. But Europe was a graveyard, stretching on and on for ever. It wasn't a safe place for a child.

Jeremy brought the book he'd promised. 'It's taken me a while to find it. As is the way of these things, it was at the bottom of the last trunk I unpacked.'

Sitting next to her, he opened the book across his lap. *The Flora and Fauna Marvels of the Pacific* was large with gold edges, and reminded Nina of Miss Brenchley's bird books. She hadn't heard from the governess since the beginning of the war and had no idea where she was now.

'There's a section on Australia.' He turned the pages. 'See,' he pointed to an illustration of a tree, 'I remember we discussed *Eucalypti* in Brighton. And look at some of these flowers, "Bottle Brush" and "Kangaroo's Paw". What remarkable names, like something from a children's book.' He smiled unselfconsciously, like a child himself.

'What do you think it would be like in Australia? To live there?' She'd become as slow in her thoughts as she was in her movements.

'Paradise,' he said, 'from my point of view. There's still so much to discover. That's one of the joys of botany, there are so many discoveries yet to be made.' He turned the page and they were looking at animals. "The Amazing Marsupial",' he read the title aloud. 'Kangaroos, aren't they extraordinary? And here, the duck-billed platypus. When the first settlers sent a preserved specimen back to England the scientists here believed it to be a hoax.' At the bottom of the page there was an illustration: *One of the Native inhabitants. The Aboriginal today exists as our ancestors did many thousands of years ago.* The old man stared out of the page at them. He was very black and had long white hair and a beard. His eyes were sad.

'And aren't these birds splendid? Budgerigars, parakeets, parrots.' Jeremy said softly, as if to himself, 'The miracles of God's creation.'

The red and blue parrot was like the one Nina had seen in the public house in Fleet Street. The recognition caught her unprepared and she had to turn away quickly, wiping her face with the back of her hand.

'Dear Nina,' putting the book down on the floor, Jeremy caught her hands up in his, 'if you need to talk, if there is anything I can do . . . I know how hard it can be to keep faith in Christ's compassion and love . . .'

Anne came in but stopped when she saw them. 'What's happening?'

'Nina is a little upset. I was about to tell her how wonderful I think it is that she's come to Cheltenham. It's important for the two of you to be together at such a time.' He released her hands.

'Yes,' Anne said, 'Jeremy and I are both pleased you are here.' She sat down on a chair, facing them. 'Is it the police investigation you're worried about, Nina? I've been concerned about that myself; we haven't heard a thing. I've been thinking I should write and ask for news. Will you help me, Jeremy dear, with the letter?'

He nodded. 'We'll need to contact the officer in charge. What was his name, Nina?'

'I don't know.'

He frowned. 'The military police captain: he was at the funeral but didn't come back to the house afterwards. Captain Stirling, wasn't it, or something like that? He's the person to write to.'

'That's what we'll do then,' Anne said. 'Was his name Stirling, Nina?'

'I'm not sure, more than one officer came to see me.' Her fingers found the scarab bracelet. 'With the baby so close I don't want to think about any of it. Frank will contact them, I have asked him to deal with all my affairs . . .'

'But surely, Nina . . .' As Anne's voice rose, Jeremy gently put his fingers to his lips. 'It can wait,' he said soothingly. He picked up the book and carefully placed it back on Nina's lap. 'You can keep this, Nina. And we won't write to Brighton yet if the thought upsets you. Of course we won't.'

After Jeremy left, Anne watched him from the window. Without turning around she said, 'He is so kind. It worries me sometimes, that people might take advantage of his kindness.'

Nina was beginning to get a headache. 'Yes,' she said, rubbing her temples. It was true that Jeremy was kind, and it probably was one of the dangers of being a kind vicar, that people would take advantage.

Pulling her shawl around her, Nina closed this morning's copy of *The Times*, where it was reported that the Winter Palace had been stormed by rebels and Kerensky had fled. At last Russia would be out of the war.

Sitting here on the summerhouse bench it was chilly; the leaves had turned, and while the garden was red and gold now, within a few weeks it would be dead and bare. Fay had forwarded on three letters from Brighton and Nina looked at the envelopes on the table in front of her without interest. One was from the bank, the second was from Lydia Barnes at the library and the third was in an unknown hand with no return address. She opened this one first, drawing out a badly printed pamphlet on grey paper. There was no letter with it, but paragraphs had been underlined in blue ink.

Homosexualism is the weapon used by the Germans against the people of Britain within their own shores. Those displaying moral weakness are identified and turned into sodomites and lesbians (the most unnatural of 'women' who often display the symptoms of insanity and neurasthenia, symptoms readily identifiable in those who show no shame at all in the title of 'Suffragist'), these German urnings thus undermine the collective morality of the Nation with their diseased and degraded practices. The symptoms are readily identifiable to those who have some experience of the world (and are not too wearied by it) but others often fearfully ask, 'How are we to identify those who hide their corruption, very often, under the guise of a respectable and frequently (because corruption can breed a putrid wealth) even lavish lifestyle?' The answer is simple: 'Do not be afraid but look clear-headedly at the ranks of the Pacifists, Fabians, Socialists, Suffragists, Internation-alists and Jews, for sheltering in these putrid miasmata there will be found the perverted and unnatural.'

In the lower ranks these vices are also to be found all too readily, for many of the lower orders are already Venereally-Diseased, feeble-minded and morally degenerate. Indeed it is for just these reasons that upper-ranking sodomites frequently descend into the alleys and by-ways of the cities' slums, where there is a cesspool of corrupted choice awaiting them . . .

'Oh!' Pushing herself up, Nina manoeuvred clumsily past the table, then crossed the lawn in the direction of the pile of leaves the gardener had raked into a corner. It was a disgusting, vile thing, as disgusting and vile as the man who'd sent it; she pictured the captain's face as her fingers ripped the paper to shreds. When she reached the pile she dropped the pieces on the ground in front of her and savagely pushed them underneath the damp leaves with the toe of her boot.

'There,' she said aloud, trying to calm herself as the baby moved inside her, 'all gone.'

Breathing deeply, she turned to go back inside the house, and as she did so the first hot spasm of pain went through her.

Twenty-two

'Push! If you want your baby to live you must push!'

She was crushing the baby's skull.

The push turned into a scream that would never stop.

'What is it?'

'Luminal. She'll sleep now.'

A voice spoke into her ear. 'God has saved your son. And you. God has saved you both.'

'I'll hold him for you.' A dark shape stood against the light. 'Dr Harrison says he's never seen so much hair. It is just the colour of his father's, and mine. And his eyes are so blue, just like Mother's – he is a real Fergusson after all.'

The doctor rinsed his hands. 'You're badly torn, but without the forceps we would have lost your son. There's no sign of infection.' He picked up the towel. 'You caught us by surprise. I'll have to leave instructions that you're to be watched carefully.'

A little while later Anne came back in. 'Dr Harrison left you some more morphine, Nina. Is the pain very bad?'

'No.' She didn't dare move for fear of crying out, but she deserved the pain, for almost killing the baby. 'How is he?'

'Unfortunately he kept us awake last night. I've barely slept. Betty is feeding him. She says some newborns can't tolerate cow's milk, but he seems to be taking it without a problem.'

Nina had heard them saying she couldn't feed him herself because of the Luminal and morphine. She'd failed him twice already.

'I wish Mother could have seen Richard's son before she died.'

When Nina woke again the room was dark, but despite the darkness she could clearly see a young man sitting on the chair near the window. He didn't say anything and she didn't recognise him. He sat there for a long time. Eventually she fell asleep.

'Who was the man in my room last night?'

The little maid, Jane, picked up a glass. 'A man, madam? Here?'

'Yes, he sat in that chair for a long time.'

The girl looked frightened. 'No one was here.'

She was stupid, or a liar, or both.

'Jane tells me you had a dream, Nina, about a man being in the room. No doubt it was the morphine.' Anne pulled open the curtains. 'I'll bring the baby through now, just for a moment.'

He was so beautiful. The love she felt for him filled her entirely.

'He has a rather ugly rash on his face, which is a great pity, but the nurse says it's common and many babies look even worse. I suppose it wouldn't do any harm to put him next to you on the bed for a little while.'

'No!' Nina shook her head fiercely. 'No!' She would drop him. She would drop him on the floor and his head would break open like an egg.

The voices were whispering. 'On her hands and knees, like a bitch about to drop a litter. Helen downstairs looked out of the kitchen window and saw her crawling across the lawn. Fair gave her the jeebies, she said. Miss Truelove, she looked set to faint, and then the Reverend arrived and saw the lot. Helen said that if that doesn't put the poor man off getting married, nothing will.'

There was someone in the chair again, but this time it was a woman, not a man. Nina watched the woman, who was gazing out of the window. Then the woman turned and saw her. 'You're awake,' she said. 'I didn't know.'

At first Nina thought it was Mamma, but then she saw it was Maggie.

Maggie came and sat on the edge of the bed. 'Dearest, what a surprise! I'm so sorry I wasn't here.'

'I was in the garden.'

'But you're safe now, Nina, and so is your beautiful son.'

She didn't know, then, that Nina might drop him.

Maggie took her hand and gave a small smile. 'Anne says he doesn't have a name yet.'

He did have a name, it was just that she couldn't think of it. 'I'm tired.'

'Go back to sleep and we'll talk again later.'

She pretended to sleep, but after Maggie left she opened her eyes. The young man was back in the chair and she saw he was naked and his body was wet; his hair was streaming water. She knew who he was now. 'Kyril,' she said aloud.

He studied her. 'Will you name him after me? You are the only one who remembers me now.'

'Yes.'

'He needs another name too, to keep him safe. What is his father's name?'

'Richard.'

'You are lying.' His voice was sad.

'Harry.'

He nodded. 'Kyril Harry. You must make sure he is named those names and no others.'

When Maggie came back Jeremy was with her. 'Dear Nina . . .'

'I've remembered his names.'

'Names? Oh, I see.' He smiled gently.

'He must be named now.'

Jeremy turned to Maggie. 'I'll call Anne, shall I? I'm sure she'd like . . .'

She reached out and clung on to his hand. 'His names are Kyril Harry.' Two magic stones dropping into a pool.

'Kyril? Is that a Russian name? It would be very unusual in England, but I've always liked the name Harry, in fact it was my grandfather's . . .'

'Both names! He must have both!'

'Of course.' Maggie bent over and smoothed back her hair.

'They are excellent names, Nina. I like Kyril very much, very much indeed.'

There was someone in the chair again. 'Kyril?'

'Pardon, madam?' The voice was alarmed.

She raised her head and saw it was the little maid. 'Where is Darya Fyodorovna?'

'Who?'

'Tell her to come to me, after she's finished with Mamma.'

The maid ran from the room to call her.

'And how are we today, Mrs Truelove?' The doctor was wearing glasses to hide his eyes. Maggie was standing behind him but didn't seem to notice anything strange: Nina was the only one who could see it.

'I am very well, thank you.' She spoke clearly, the way Miss Brenchley had taught her.

'I hear you've been having bad dreams.'

The question was a trick. She wondered if he could see inside her head. 'Dreams . . .'

'About a stranger being in the room. And about your mother being here.'

'My mother is dead.'

'And you've been dreaming about her?'

'Yes.' Although she hadn't.

'As I've assured your sister-in-law, it isn't uncommon for women to have disturbing dreams after a traumatic birth and even, on occasion, to become slightly disoriented in their waking thoughts. But the realisation that they are now a mother, responsible for their child, is usually more than enough for them to pull themselves together. I don't think there's any call for more Luminal or morphine. Do you feel well in yourself, Mrs Truelove?'

'Very well. Thank you.'

'I am pleased to hear it.'

Maggie left the room with the doctor and returned a few minutes later. 'How are you really feeling, Nina?'

So she could read her thoughts. Nina kept her eyes on the bedpost, so Maggie couldn't see inside. 'Well. But I am tired.'

This time the figure in the chair was wearing a long cloak and at first she thought it was a woman. However, when it spoke the voice was a man's: 'Do you really think names can keep him safe from me?'

He had a wild beard and looked like Papa but she had no doubt about who it was: God. There were flames dancing in his eyes and when he spoke the flames darted out of his mouth. 'You should have died like your mamma, but you're evil and crawled away like a snake.'

She wanted to scream but no sound would come out.

'You stink with evil. Everything you touch dies. Soon the baby will die too.' Something bulged under his cloak, and when he saw her looking he sneered and said, 'Got a big cock, haven't I?' She knew she was filthy to look but she couldn't turn her head away. Then the figure in the chair was no longer God but a woman, Mamma, and Nina knew she was responsible for her death. And the young violinmaker was standing behind Mamma, and Richard and Harry and another man she had never seen before but knew to be Alice Evan's husband. There were others: Uncle Aleksei and Lawrence and the peasant girl whose face was broken by her father. They all watched her, not accusingly but with sadness because they weren't evil and were sorry for the baby and how much he would have to suffer because of her.

'He's beautiful, Nina. Five days old and so perfect.' The trickster went on, 'I've been holding him in the nursery and he's lovely. Would you like to take him?'

It was cunning, this one, expecting her to say no. Opening her mouth a sound came out, 'Yes.'

The trickster showed its pointed teeth. 'I'll go and get him.'

It came back. 'Look,' it said, 'here is your dear Mamma.' It held out the rag doll, which would be full of rats' filth and feathers. 'Look at your mamma, Kyril.'

She opened her arms but then the horror was too much because they had tricked her and it was him, he was real, and they had almost tricked her into taking him. Her love for him was the most powerful thing in the world and it surged through her like a wave. 'No! No! No! No!'

'And you say she did this to her arms with a sharpened hair pin?'

'Yes. We hadn't thought of her doing anything like that. If she had got to the baby . . .'

'And she was screaming things – obscenities?'

'Terrible things – words I have never heard any woman use. She calmed down, very suddenly, and said she had cut her arms to let the evil out. She also said . . .'

'Go on, Miss Truelove.'

'That she was going to kill her baby.'

'She said that?'

'She said, "If the baby comes anywhere near me he will die."'

'I'm most dreadfully sorry, Miss Truelove, but you know there is no choice, don't you, under the circumstances. I'm sure you will agree. It is very distressing, but the good thing is that your nephew has you to look after him, and because he's so young he will not even miss his mother.'

They put the thing around her and tied it behind her back so her arms were tight and she could feel the blood pumping, pumping.

'Is this really necessary?' a voice kept demanding. 'Is this really necessary?'

Twenty-three

'What did I tell you yesterday, you bad girl? Dirty mouths get washed out with soap.' As the nurse-devil undid the straps, the pain surged through her arms like white fire and she howled. Her bladder emptied, and that was hot too.

'You can lie in that, missy, 'twill make no difference to the wet pack.'

Her arms were useless, and they laid her naked like a rag doll, then began to roll her back and forwards in the wet sheets so that they got tighter and tighter.

'There you go.' The block of ice was forced on to the top of her head and tied roughly. It burnt as much as fire. 'We'll be back later. Sleep tight.' There was laughter, and then the lights went out and the key sounded in the lock.

She lay in the silent darkness. The skin all over her body burned and itched unbearably but there was no way she could move a muscle, and although she fought it the usual panic began, that she wouldn't be able to keep breathing. The panic slowly turned into a great heat and the ice began to melt, trickling in cool rivulets down her face as her body became tauter and tauter, straining against the tightness of the sheets.

And then it happened again: the miracle.

The tautness went and all the anger and evil flowed out of her, to be replaced by a blessed peace.

Later someone came and unwound the sheets and smoothed her hair, murmuring, 'Good girl, good girl.' She relaxed into a perfect sleep.

The sun was warm on her face.

'Why don't you ever look up at the sky, missy? The clouds are beautiful today, like feathers.'

But she had to watch her feet, in case she tripped.

'Some of the soldiers at the Front saw angels in the clouds. That's how they knew we would win the war.'

'Is the war over?'

'No.'

'I saw an angel once.'

'That's a surprise.'

'I trusted it, but maybe I shouldn't have.' Though she didn't really think the angel in the palm tree had been evil.

'You're going to start helping out in the vegetable garden. Because we all have to eat here, don't we? And it won't matter if you don't look up, because you'll be doing the weeding.'

'Nina.'

'Yes?'

'How are you feeling?'

'Tired.'

'I hear you've been working in the garden all day. Without pause, in fact.'

'Yes.'

'Do you like that?'

'Yes.'

'Why?'

She was surprised he didn't know. 'It stops me thinking.'

'I see.' He smiled. 'Maybe I should try it.' His eyes looked into hers. 'So you don't feel responsible for the deaths of anyone any more? Or for the war?'

'Yes.' But then she felt sorry, because he was as tired as she was. 'We are all responsible.'

'Ah. Collective guilt. Shall we begin there then?'

'Begin what?'

'Talking.'

'Just talking?'

'Just talking.'

Her hands felt through the leaves as if they knew without her looking where the pods were hidden. On the other side of the canes she could hear Lulu singing quietly in her pretty voice. Behind Lulu, Agatha was turning over topsoil with a shovel, her skirts hitched daringly high above her boots. Agatha would be leaving in a few days. She was known as 'the Honourable' and lived with her parents in a castle in Scotland. She was a Socialist. 'Not that that has anything to do with my being here,' she said cheerfully. 'It's in our family, the madness. We all do it, regular as clockwork. My father says that's how he knows we're his and that if we were entirely sane all the time he'd suspect my mother had been up against the pantry wall with the butler.' She told Nina she hoped to go to Russia one day and that it had been in the newspapers that a group of avant-garde young women artists in Moscow had travelled naked on a tram.

Nina squeezed open one of the smaller pods and offered it to Agatha, who picked the sweet peas out with muddy fingers. 'It's like being in the trenches, this. My brothers all say the worst thing is the mud, followed by the smell. Did you see what I found?' Reaching down, she picked up something white. 'A wee bird's skull.'

It was so delicate and yet strong. And light: Nina weighed it in her hand and it was like a feather.

'Alas, poor Yorick . . . Shall I wash it in the watering can, so you can keep it on your windowsill?'

'No. Thank you.' Nina laid it gently under the pea vines. 'It should stay here.'

'Why, Nina . . .' In front of her she could see a pair of brown boots and a hemline damp from the long grass. She looked up and Maggie looked back at her. 'You have turned into a gardener.'

Nina held out her hands, which were cracked and stained and strong. They were her tools.

'What do you grow?'

Turning, Nina led the way through the narrow paths of runner beans.

'It's like a forest in here!' Maggie laughed but sounded nervous, and Nina slowed down; it was easy to get lost if you didn't know your way.

'Frank sends his love. And Charles wrote and asked that his

greetings be passed on. And Mrs Laing and Fay Proctor. Do you know how long you've been here?'

'Eight months.' Dr Astor had told her yesterday. She had thought it was longer.

Maggie looked hot in her jacket, and was carrying a bag. 'Shall we go back to the lawn and sit in the shade?'

Nina hesitated: the weeding wasn't finished.

'Please, Nina, I'm hot.'

As they walked across the grass Nina said, 'You come to see me, Maggie, but I don't think Anne has ever been. Maybe she came at the beginning and I don't remember.'

'No.'

They sat on a bench and Nina looked at her hands. 'I have asked Dr Astor and he promises me Kyril is well.'

Maggie patted her knee. 'Oh yes, completely well. There's no need to worry about Kyril, I promise. He is a strong, healthy baby.'

Nina started to breathe again.

'What's that, around your neck?'

Her hand went to the vial of pink medicine. 'Luminal.'

'And do you use it often?'

'Not now.' In fact the last time she'd opened it she'd found it was almost empty. But it helped to know it was there.

'It is all right here, Nina, isn't it?' Maggie clutched at her bag. 'It has a good reputation, we checked that. Dr Astor seems a very kind man, and progressive in his thinking. Are the nurses kind too?'

Not always, but she knew from some of the other patients that things were far worse elsewhere. 'Yes. Are the bills being paid from my account?'

'Frank arranged everything with your solicitor, you have nothing to worry about.'

'Thank you. For all you've done.' She sat in silence then, hoping that Maggie would be rested enough to leave soon so she could go back to the garden.

The war ended and bells pealed in all the churches. At the hospital they rang the bells in the small chapel and the nurses clapped their hands and laughed and tossed their caps in the air.

Dr O'Neill, who was older than the others, looked on. 'It's like Bedlam in here.'

Nina glanced at him.

'And that's just the nurses.'

So he thought she was cured.

'Do you think the world will be different?' she asked.

He shook his head. 'I would like to think so, but I cannot believe it.'

'There were celebrations at first, of course. We saw effigies of the Kaiser being burnt, but the crowds weren't as big as you might expect. Everyone's too emotionally exhausted to celebrate and already there are worries amongst the returning soldiers about employment and housing.' Maggie had flung open the suitcase to reveal half a dozen new dresses. 'We expect you to be out by Christmas.' She held up a navy blue dress, and as Nina fingered the material it snagged against the rough skin on her hands.

'Not one of them is black, and,' Maggie smiled, 'they are all fashionably short. Nothing too extreme, but you are my friend and I want you to be fashionable.'

'Your friend is a madwoman.' She had thought she had caused the war. The truth was they had all caused it.

Maggie unfolded a dark green and red shawl and handed it to her. 'It's to do with the body's chemistry, you know that, don't you? Apparently the ancient Greeks referred to it in their medical writings. I cannot read Greek myself, but Frank assures me this is the case.'

Nina held the soft shawl to her cheek. 'Dr Astor says it is one of the only forms of mania that can result in recovery, but I mustn't attempt to have another child because it is certain I would go mad again after the birth, and next time it might be even worse.' Lowering the shawl she said, 'I used to think my father was the mad one, but it was me.'

Maggie quickly hugged her. 'You are not mad.'

Nina rested her head on her friend's shoulder. 'Maggie, is Kyril well?' She hadn't held him in her arms, not once. She ached to hold him, the ache echoing inside her like waves in a hollow shell.

Maggie said, 'I believe he is very well.'

'But you haven't seen him?' In the garden she'd learned to cultivate patience.

'No. I've been in Scotland a great deal.' Maggie moved away. 'I almost forgot, there's a letter for you in my bag, from Katya. I've been writing to her regularly, we're old friends now. But there were no replies to your letters to Harry's sister, I'm afraid. With so many British ships lost she might never have received your letters. Maybe you should write again?'

Nina pictured Ruby in her mind, a woman with long red hair. Harry had said they were as close as twins. But she wouldn't write to her again until she was out of this place and had Kyril back.

There was the sound of shouting and together they looked out of the window, to where an elderly couple pushed a young man in a bath chair. 'Bang bang!' he screamed.

'Is he shell-shocked?'

'We're all civilians here. He went like this when he was about to be conscripted.'

'Poor boy. Who is he shooting at?'

'God. At first it was Satan, but I heard one of the nurses telling him he must have managed to shoot Satan by now and he replied that he had – but that now he must kill God, who is even wilier than Satan and hides in the trees.'

Two weeks later Maggie came again.

'I think you might be able to leave very soon,' Dr Astor said before Nina went through to see her. 'Possibly by the end of next week. But you need to speak to your friend alone and come to some arrangements.' He played with a pencil, studying it through thick glasses and avoiding her eyes. 'Mrs Chaplin has things of a personal nature to discuss with you.'

Maggie sat on the edge of her chair. 'Frank is sorry he couldn't come but he's at a funeral. The sixteen-year-old son of one of his colleagues, William Hastings, died last week of the influenza. His family is devastated; they had just one other son and he was killed at the Somme.'

The world was awash with pain. 'Is it really turning into an epidemic?'

'Most definitely. This morning at the station I saw two women wearing masks and nobody seemed terribly surprised.' Maggie forced a smile. 'That dress does suit you. Do they all fit as well?'

'They do. Thank you. You must tell me how much they cost and I'll repay you. I owe both of you a great deal, for everything.'

'My dear, we can discuss that later. I was only concerned in case they were a little short but it seems they are *à la mode*.' She looked away. 'Has Dr Astor told you what I've come to talk about?'

'He said there were arrangements to be made, for when I leave here.' Standing up, Nina walked over to the mantelpiece. 'Anne hasn't contacted me – there's been no letter, nothing.' She took a breath. 'So I assume there's some problem between us.'

'I've discussed with Dr Astor all that's happened and he has said to tell you everything, Nina. There's no point in hiding things from you . . .'

She'd never heard Maggie sound frightened before; she hadn't thought anything could frighten her. Picking up a small ebony elephant from the mantelpiece, she turned it over blindly in her hand. 'Anne's had Kyril for almost a year and must love him and feel that she's his mother. I can understand she mightn't want to part with him and that she might be concerned I'm not fit to care for him. She must have been very shocked when I went mad – I know what it's like, I've seen enough examples here. It *is* shocking, and frightening. No doubt I was saying – and doing – dreadful things.' She looked up. 'But Kyril was never in any danger from me. I feared he'd die because I was being punished by God; I never intended to hurt him in any way.'

'I know, Nina, but there's more to it than that.'

How could there be more?

Maggie's voice shook. 'I fear that we – Frank and I – have let you down very badly.'

Nina took a breath. 'I know you've always tried to do your best for me.'

'Tried, yes.' Maggie pulled a wry face and glanced away. 'To begin with, Anne was deeply shocked by your breakdown. She clearly found the birth itself very stressful, and when I arrived I thought she seemed very shaky indeed. Coming on top of that, your collapse was extremely difficult for her to cope with. And then, a few days after you were brought here, she had a visit from the military police. I wasn't there, unfortunately, I'd just left for London.'

The elephant cut into the palm of Nina's hand as she closed her fist around it.

'It wasn't Captain Stewart, but a colleague based in Cheltenham. When he called at the house he met Jeremy – Anne was upstairs with Kyril, but she came down in time to hear at least some of what he said. I know this because Jeremy later told Frank over the telephone.'

'How much do they know?'

'Jeremy knows where Richard died, and how. I'm not sure how much of the conversation Anne overheard, or fully understood. But she did hear the officer telling Jeremy that Richard had been corrupted and . . .'

'What?'

'He said that Captain Stewart blamed much of Richard's corruption on you. That he thought . . .' She bit her lip.

'I have to know.'

'He said Captain Stewart had told him you were the most perverted woman he had ever met.' Maggie stood up. 'Nina, they can say things like this because they are stupid and ignorant and frightened. You refused to deny Richard. What you did was brave and noble – you are one of the bravest people I know – but this is all beyond the understanding of someone like Stewart.'

Nina bowed her head. 'So Anne hates me.'

Maggie sighed. 'She has to put the blame somewhere. I've spoken to her once on the telephone, and found her very cold, and confused in her thinking. Since then, she has refused to speak with me again, but Frank had three or four telephone discussions with Jeremy. It was very difficult, Nina, for him to know how much he should say, or how he might defend you. Jeremy's concern, naturally, was for Anne – he wished to protect her from the truth as far as possible. We knew Kyril was quite safe and so we thought it best to leave things as they were until you were well again; there was nothing we could do anyway, as the doctor in Cheltenham had written letters for Anne saying you were not capable of looking after your child and that she should have complete care of him.' Her voice faltered. 'She was horribly jealous of course, you must know that, Nina.'

'Jealous?'

Maggie's cheeks flushed. 'It was very obvious.'

Maggie was wrong; there'd been nothing for Anne to be jealous about. 'Anything I do must be in Kyril's best interests. He's being well cared for, that is the important thing. I must make sure I'm completely well so that I can leave here, and I must persuade the doctors to support my case so I can get Kyril back.'

Maggie was silent for a minute; then she said in a quiet voice, 'We received a letter from Jeremy a week ago. My darling, I am so sorry – it was written as they were about to embark on a ship leaving England . . .'

It was like a physical blow to the chest.

Maggie was speaking quickly. 'Jeremy said they were married last month and he'd persuaded Anne they should leave; he doesn't expect them to return to England. In his letter he said Anne would be devastated if the full truth ever came out in court. He wants to protect her from any scandal, and Kyril too. Nina, forgive me, we never anticipated anything like this.'

'It's not your fault.' She rested her forehead on the cool marble. 'Where have they gone?' She felt as though she were on a ship herself, lost and alone in the middle of an empty ocean.

'The letter didn't say. But Jeremy indicated they were leaving on the Thursday morning. The letter was posted from Plymouth, so Frank immediately made enquiries. There are very few ships carrying civilians as yet, but there were two leaving from Plymouth on the Thursday.' Maggie's voice broke. 'My dear, it's all so far. One ship was leaving for Cape Town . . .'

'And the other?'

'The *Marathon*'s destination was Sydney, Australia.'

Her whole life had been leading to this. Everything she had ever done – laughing with Katya in the conservatory, dropping a bracelet under a table, watching the carpenter oil a coffin, burying two buttons of bone, seeing an angel, dancing on the pier, watching the Zeppelin – every little act had led here, to this point in time.

Had Darya seen it in the cards? Had it all been spread across the kitchen table? If so, the kindest thing might have been to pick up the red-handled knife and put an end to it then and there.

She had been the only one with no sense of purpose. Mamma had kept the family together, Darya had looked after Mamma, Katya cared for her children. Miss Brenchley, Mrs Kulmana, Leila, Dr Vilensky, Papa, Richard, Harry, Maggie . . . all of them had a purpose, a direction. Her purpose had been to escape from Russia, but she hadn't thought any further than that. It was as if she'd been a piece of flotsam, adrift.

In the corner of the drawing room a small group of patients half-heartedly put up dusty Christmas decorations. There would be decorations on the ship, and Kyril would reach out for them: Anne would hold him in her arms and he would laugh and reach forward with fat fingers. His hair would glow gold in the light of the lamps. And then they would arrive in Sydney Harbour, the most beautiful harbour in the world – for she was sure that was where Anne had taken him. There would be people waiting on the dock, a woman waving . . .

It was unbearably stuffy, the fireplace smoking with damp pine cones. Picking up the green and red shawl, Nina went down the hall and out through a side door. The sky had cleared of clouds and there were stars and a full moon. She'd known it was a full moon tonight because the nurses followed the night sky like astronomers, or sailors. 'It'll be bad tonight,' they called to each other along the corridors, 'with the moon.'

She felt hot and took off the shawl, bunching it in her hand. Without thinking, she began to follow the slope of the lawn in the direction of the vegetable garden, her shoes crunching through the gleaming snow: they'd be soaked and she would have to stuff them with paper before she went to bed. The garden gate was ajar and she pushed through; where there had been high rows of peas and beans all was now empty, the snow sparkling on the top of the long mounds. She remembered holding the bird's skull in her hands, the wonder and delicacy of it. Her own head was beginning to throb.

The walk back to the house took longer, and by the time she was inside the pain in her temples was coming in waves. She got to the first landing, then had to cling to the banister.

'What's wrong with you, missy? Good God, your hem is all

soaked, and your shoes. Have you been outside dressed like that? It seems to me that people who can't display some basic common sense should be back on a locked ward.' A hand was clamped to her forehead. 'You're burning up! Come on.' An arm gripped her round the waist. 'Before you catch your death.'

Her hair was wet and wild in her eyes but she didn't mind because she'd come a long way, from the other side of the world. '*Smotri*, Kyril! Look!' Kissing him on his fat cheek she held him up in her arms so he could see the shore. But Kyril was laughing and pointing at the sky instead.

The captain, a kind man – they had all been so kind – called, 'There'll be someone to meet you no doubt?'

'We are expected.' She scanned the shoreline and there it was, against the water's edge, the palm tree. And under the palm tree a woman stood waiting, a woman with long red hair: Ruby. Ruby raised her hand and waved and Nina immediately felt at home and at peace.

It had been a long journey, over a lifetime, but now it was over.

Book Two

1933

One person's fate is forged by the angels, using tiny silver hammers; while the Devil forges another's, using the butt of an axe.

Proverb

Twenty-four

Brisbane, August 1933

'Snakeskin, from Foy and Gibson's, and the shoes to match, though I haven't worn them today.' May Trimble stroked the side of her new handbag then suddenly smacked a plump hand – luckily not the one clutching the candy-pink Chinese fan – across her mouth. 'Oh, I am so sorry, Mrs Gregory, I didn't think!'

No doubt this would become an anecdote with which May would entertain the next meeting of the Toowong branch of the Women's Guild. Anne could hear her now: 'Ladies, you will never believe what I said to poor Mrs Gregory – such a dear thing, a real lady – quite unthinking on my part . . .'

Anne raised her eyebrows in feigned bewilderment. 'Why, Mrs Trimble, should snakeskin cause me offence?'

Her guest shifted uncomfortably on large buttocks, unsure how to proceed. 'Well, snakes,' she was in distinct danger of trailing off and losing her moment altogether, 'I mean, they're very close, aren't they? In kind.'

'Close?' Anne threw an innocent glance around her sitting room.

'Close.' May Trimble's eyes also darted around the room but failed to find anything to settle on. 'Close to . . .'

'Yes?' Anne urged helpfully.

'To crocs!' Catching herself too late. 'Croc-o-diles, that is . . .'

'Ah.' Anne sank back, allowing herself a composed smile. 'I see. But you have no need to feel concern at having mentioned your handbag to me. I can quite understand how you feel about it, and your shoes. I remember buying my first snakeskin bag in London – no, I am wrong, it was Paris, on a short trip with my mother, many years ago now. And it was certainly most exciting.

245

I would not wish to dampen your enthusiasm about your new purchases. Where was it you said you discovered them?'

'Foy and Gibson's, the summer sale.' An underarm wobbling, not so much with the effort of the fan but with her hostess's wider experience of the world. 'Paris. With your mother. Yes, well. It must have been. Exciting, that is.'

'Very. At that age Europe always is, don't you think? Now, some more tea?'

Later, Anne walked May Trimble down the path.

'Your oleander, Mrs Gregory! Your jacaranda!' The pink fan pointed in the direction of the large tree, heavy with purple blossom. 'It's all so delightful, so – English!'

Anne had been in Australia for fifteen years now and still missed England with every fibre of her being. On their arrival in Sydney she had felt as though she were sailing into a nightmare – although Sydney was bliss compared with what was to come. She could still remember Mrs Horsefield, Secretary of the Anglican Ladies' League, beginning to explain. 'You see, Mrs Gregory, Queensland is not New South Wales. And North Queensland, where it has been decided your good husband should have a parish – oh, I can barely bring myself to go on. You do it, Gwendoline.'

Mrs Gwendoline Marsh was less sensitive. 'It's the wilderness,' she said, popping a Henzo Cough Diamond (advertised as guarding against the Spanish Influenza) into her mouth. 'It's worse than the outback: it's the back of nowhere.'

The journey on the *Marathon* had been a nightmare. Kyril was fretful the whole time and this, combined with the debilitating heat and the bitter knowledge that they were exiles, had left Anne exhausted. A sense of dread had descended on her as they came through the heads into Sydney Harbour and, given the choice, she would have opted to go below. Jeremy, however, was anxious to see everything and she was determined not to disappoint him.

'One of the natural wonders of the world!' he'd exclaimed, waving his arms almost wildly. 'And I just caught a glimpse of something overhead, a large sea bird of some sort, a good omen surely. Look, little man, your new home!'

Kyril had taken hold of Anne's pearl necklace – he was always pulling, demanding attention – and as she attempted to prise it from his fingers she felt the thread snap. He screwed his face into a howl and she could have done the same; not only because of the pearls but because Kyril was always howling and because this was not home and never would be.

On land it got worse, for the Reverend Jeremy Gregory was something of a let-down. There were so many marriageable daughters, because of the war, you see, and they had been led to believe, those church matrons who eagerly made up the welcome party, that the reverend was unmarried. '*Mrs* Gregory?' Mrs Horsefield kept repeating, 'There was nothing about a wife.'

They spent a month in Sydney, and during that time the parish which Jeremy had expected to take up, in a leafy suburb of Sydney itself, suddenly became unavailable, the Archbishop deciding Queensland's need was more urgent.

'You'll be old before your time,' Mrs Hastings, who was deaf, shouted. 'The climate up there ravages a white woman's skin. Never step outside without a veil and gloves. Mercolised Wax, it's the only thing that might save something of your complexion. Also Sanatogen, and Clement's Nerves and Brain Tonic, because your nerves will suffer, there's no doubt. You'll need Dr Morse's Indian Root Pills, for the heat is no friend to digestion. Also Rexona Medicated Soap, which is good for tropical ulcers. There's cholera up there and typhus, malaria too. If you take my advice you'll stay inside the house for the best part of the day, although there's no escape from the heat and that's what makes for thread veins on the face, especially in someone of your colouring. The nose goes first. Make sure they've got you a couple of reliable mission girls – some of the aborigines can be turned into half-decent housemaids – or even better, Kanakas. No danger of them going walkabout, they've got nowhere to walkabout to – that's why they were brought over from the Islands. Excellent workers if you train 'em right. Whatever you do, spare yourself as much as possible.'

'Port Douglas will be an enormous challenge.' Jeremy had been genuinely enthusiastic, and Anne found herself hating the Archbishop, the old hypocrite, who'd managed to convince her husband he was being offered an opportunity when in reality they were simply getting rid of him.

'I know it's not what you were expecting, darling, but the Archbishop is, I'm sure, quite right in saying this is my calling. And I can't help feeling very excited at the thought of the tropics. The botanical life will be amazing. If we stayed here in Sydney it would be almost as if we'd never left Cheltenham.'

Sydney was brash and vulgar, Anne thought, with none of Cheltenham's refinement, but nothing she'd seen, or even heard, there had prepared her for the reality of North Queensland.

It was worse than anything she could have imagined.

In summer the heat was sheer horror, and with it came the wet season, which should have offered relief but was simply another form of torture. Every afternoon a grey wall of rain moved across the coast, thundering like hooves on to the iron roof of the miserable timber house. The humidity was such that the walls and window frames warped and widened, letting the water in so that within weeks their leather shoes and the bindings of Jeremy's books succumbed to ruinous green mould. The house was built on wooden stilts topped with beaten tin plates, because of termites and poisonous snakes, but that didn't stop it from being infested with beetles and cockroaches. Spiders were a constant danger and geckos scurried across the walls, naked and pallid as ghosts.

From the front there was a view of the ocean, which Jeremy announced magnificent while Anne could barely look at it because it was over this same ocean that the *Marathon* had brought them. 'Such a view!' the visiting farmers' wives, red and hungry for a glimpse of something different after the endless acres of their vast inland properties, would exclaim in envy. 'To see something that moves!' The women's bodies swayed while their husbands shook their heads, not bothering to brush the flies from their lips. 'Pity about Port Douglas, though – time was when it looked to become a thriving sort of place. Cairns winning the railway for the tin mining, that was the death knell.' The farmers and their wives took the steamer south, sometimes not returning for months, or even years.

A series of lackadaisical native girls tended the house, cooking in an outside kitchen over a wood stove and doing the laundry in a tin shed, which housed a bench, a copper boiler and two tin tubs. Baths had to be taken in a tub in the kitchen, with hot water from the boiler carried inside in buckets. The privy was a shed over a hole in the ground, and there was a very real danger of venomous spiders or snakes. There was a second privy for the servants, dug a little further along the path, and one morning one of the girls ran out screaming there was 'a real badfella snake' inside. Jeremy took the rifle and killed it.

The girls washed, cleaned and cooked. They also looked after Kyril, who, like Jeremy, didn't suffer from the heat. Anne did suffer: she was easily dehydrated and had terrible headaches. Not that she became a recluse, however, for she refused to let Jeremy down, or give the Sydney matrons the satisfaction of hearing she'd been broken. There were times when she thought she might go mad, opening her mouth and screaming at the unfairness of the world, at her ruined life; screaming at Jeremy, whose talents were being wasted collecting useless plant specimens and talking to the natives. But no matter how strong the temptation to scream and tear her hair and pound her fists against the rough wood walls, she didn't give in to it, not once.

Instead she did all, and more, than could be expected. She always looked after her appearance and made sure to set an example to the drab wives of the white parishioners, whom she visited by buggy. There was one store to supply basic foodstuffs and hardware, but if she wanted clothes or furniture she had to wait for the annual trip to Brisbane or order from catalogues. Her experience with the Red Cross during the war was invaluable, and she organised the Sunday school; rotas for tending the sick; church teas.

She also prayed on her knees on the wooden floor, every morning and every night, asking God that when the next fortnightly post came it would bring the long-awaited letter announcing they had finally been given a parish in the south of the state (she'd long given up on Sydney).

'Is there anything about us leaving?' she would say to Jeremy as he opened the letters addressed to him.

He always shook his head. 'No, darling, there's nothing like that.'

It came like a blow each time and she would have to turn away, hiding the extent of her disappointment.

But while no message came from the Archbishop's office, there were scientific papers and journals, and after the first of Jeremy's pamphlets on North Queensland flora was published in London by the Royal Botanical Society, there were letters from botanists around the world. In the evening Jeremy would sit up late by the oil lamp, reading and composing replies to London, Rome, Lisbon . . .

And so life dragged on, for three long years, until the visit by the Reverend Mr Jamieson and his wife from Cairns. They'd all taken the buggy to the church and were getting out when a small group of camp blacks appeared out of nowhere and approached Jeremy. Anne had known for some time that Jeremy had an interest in the aborigines' language (if it could be called that – she constantly had to rebuke the servant girls for speaking to each other, and even to Kyril, in incomprehensible grunts). He had started compiling a list of aboriginal names for local plants, and although she'd often seen this list, written in a big ledger in his study, she hadn't taken much notice of it. This morning, however, the aborigines approached and instead of waving them aside and conducting his guests into the church, Jeremy smiled and spoke back to them in their own language. They jabbered at him, hands waving, eyes rolling, and in front of everyone – the Jamiesons, his parishioners, herself – Jeremy jabbered back.

One of the camp women, a big woman known as Ethel, ambled over, bare feet trailing through the dust. She grinned insolently. 'Your husband one clever bloke, Missus Gregory.' She spat a stream of tobacco over the church's picket fence. 'He talk our lingo pretty good, eh? Look like youse got yourself a real clever one there.'

Anne was too shocked to speak, but not so shocked that she missed the appalled look that passed between the Jamiesons. There was silence, and then Mr Jamieson casually brushed at the lapel of his coat. 'Well, well. No wonder your good husband is so happy to remain in Port Douglas, Mrs Gregory. What might represent purgatory to most is obviously paradise to those with a passion for plants, and native dialects.' His wife coughed delicately into her hand.

The Jamiesons left on the steamer the next morning, and that evening Anne confronted Jeremy. 'Why are you learning their language?' she asked.

He looked surprised. 'Darling, I've told you what a wealth of knowledge they have, put together over thousands of years. Old Bob is like a walking botanical encyclopaedia, but – unfortunately for me – the encyclopaedia is all inside his head, not in the King's English but in Kuku Yalanji.' Putting down his pen, he suddenly gripped her hand. 'I can't tell you how exciting it is, Anne. Everywhere I look there is another plant I've never seen described. Do you know, I sometimes think to myself that this is how the Hebrews must have felt, when the Lord led them to the Promised Land! This has been my opportunity to make my name as a botanist, to establish a reputation throughout the scientific world. I've already been nominated for membership of the Royal Society, and in the future – who knows? A Society medal isn't an impossibility.' He stopped himself, giving an embarrassed smile. 'I know I sound vain, but I do genuinely believe God gave me these interests, and put me in this place, for a reason. I'm fully aware that I'm not the world's best clergyman, but by being here I can, in my own way, help reveal to the world the miracles of God's creation.' He dropped his gaze. 'And you are so good to put up with it, Anne. I know you miss having friends to talk to, and shops.'

Although Anne kept her complaints to a minimum, Jeremy could be in absolutely no doubt about how much she hated her life here. And yet that knowledge was not enough to make him want to go elsewhere. All her desperate homesickness, all her loneliness and misery and longing for some company, society, culture – he could reduce all of that to nothing more than 'missing friends and shops'. Her exhausting daily battles with heat and humidity and dirt and snakes and insects; the constant nagging fear that there'd be an accident, or that one of them would become seriously ill, without a proper hospital for hundreds of miles – all that counted for nothing. All that did count was his scientific reputation, his ambition. He knew she waited for every post in the hope there'd be news they could leave, but the truth – she couldn't shrink from the knowledge any longer – was that he had done nothing about trying to find a parish elsewhere. The sacrifice was to be all hers. He was content and therefore she was condemned to rot in Port Douglas.

She managed to keep her voice even. 'And what about Kyril?'

He laughed. 'Oh, there's no need to worry about Kyril, he's a very happy chap. He's coming along nicely with his ABC, I find him a bright pupil, and when the time comes for school, why, we'll send him down to Brisbane.'

So Kyril was to escape, but not her.

While Jeremy worked on his pamphlets or wrote his correspondence in the evenings, she usually sat and sewed or read or wrote letters home. This evening, however, she sat alone on the veranda overlooking the sea. The warm air buzzed with the sound of cicadas, the sky blazed with stars, and far away on the horizon were the lights of a ship. The coral reefs made these treacherous waters for shipping and there'd been numerous wrecks all along the coast. Anne felt shipwrecked herself. It seemed she had had no choice in charting her own life and had been flung here by a wave of misfortune and chance.

She'd felt so grateful to Jeremy for marrying her. It had taken all her courage to stand in the Cheltenham drawing room, the precious ring cupped in her outstretched hand, and tell him he was under no obligation to honour their engagement. Richard had been disgraced, pulling her down with him, and she would release Jeremy from any obligation he might feel. He had slipped the ring back on her finger, vowing to stand by her for ever, and the rush of happiness and relief she had felt at that moment had overwhelmed her.

Then and there he'd sat her down and said that the danger of scandal was such that as soon as the war was over they must leave England for good – surely she must see that. All she had seen was yet further proof of his goodness and how much he cared for her. 'I will follow you to the ends of the earth.' She had said those very words.

Now, however, on a veranda phosphorescent with fireflies, she saw that her brother's death had simply given Jeremy the excuse he'd wanted. She remembered that afternoon in the summer-house in Cheltenham, and Nina, as usual, fixing her attention on Jeremy. 'Would you really like to go to those countries?' she'd asked. And Jeremy had replied, 'Yes, I suppose I would.'

It was what he'd wanted all along. And when it came down to it it was Nina who had made it possible for him because it was through her influence that Richard had fallen. Anne had stood in the hall, listening as the man from the military police said frightening, unimaginable things. 'Captain Stewart said he has never met such a degraded woman,' he told Jeremy. 'He puts the blame for Captain Truelove's fall into degeneracy squarely on his Russian wife. He has told me – I may as well be forthright, Reverend – that she openly boasted that she encouraged her husband in immoral acts . . .'

Anne had known there was something weak in Richard. She'd always sensed it there, in the kernel of his being, but she had so much loved his laugh, the shape of his hands, the dearness of him, her dear older brother, that she had allowed herself to ignore it.

Out at sea the ship's lights twinkled in the blackness and she thought back to the twinkling coloured lanterns in the garden, and how she and Richard had danced those summer evenings, just the two of them, stumbling over the grass and laughing. She'd spun round and round, her skirts flying, and Richard had caught her in his arms as she staggered giddily, laughing and calling her his 'whirling dervish'.

One evening at the end of that summer Richard and the gardener had carried out ladders to start taking down the tattered lanterns. She'd opened the French doors and walked quietly across the lawn. The gardener had been coming down the ladder – Richard was steadying the bottom – and then, as the young man had stepped off the bottom rung, she'd frozen as she saw her brother reach out and gently run his fingers down the other man's face. Nothing more than that, a simple touch, but there was something about the way it was done – in the quiet dusk, the two of them very still and close to each other – that had made her feel giddy.

Richard was weak, horribly weak, but the love of a good, decent woman should have enabled him to overcome his weakness. Instead he'd fallen prey to a she-snake.

She'd been unsure of Nina at first. Mother had loathed her from the start, predicting that a foreign wife could never make Richard happy, but Anne had vowed to herself to be as fair as possible. When she first met Nina she couldn't help being shocked by her strangeness: she hadn't expected her to be *so* Russian, *so* different. Everything about her was foreign: her features; her height; her mannerisms; the way she spoke, walked. It all jarred and felt wrong. Despite this there was no denying she was beautiful and that Richard seemed happy. And so, for his sake, Anne had pushed aside her reservations and decided to give her new sister-in-law the benefit of the doubt.

And then she'd been won over by her too. It was obvious of course that that was what Nina was setting out to do: win her over. 'Oh, Anne, your green silks will be perfect, especially with your lovely hair!' 'That cream bonnet suits you so well, it sets off your complexion.' The patent effort Nina put into this was flattering in itself. When they went out together the admiration Nina aroused was evident: heads literally turned. Yet she was so apparently oblivious to this that, in her company, Anne began to feel that the admiration was as much for her.

After Mother's funeral she'd gone straight to Brighton, in no doubt at all that she did love Nina. Grief had broken down any lingering reservations: Nina was her dead brother's wife, her dear sister. They had stood on the Downs side by side and listened to the lark's song, so perfect and yet so distant, as if it came from another world.

When Nina called to say she was coming to Cheltenham, Anne had barely been able to speak for gratitude. Richard's child would be born in the house in which he and she had been born, and she would be able to stay close to Jeremy, who had just moved down from Newcastle. It had seemed such a generous act on Nina's part, so thoughtful. There was so much they would be able to do together, preparing for the baby. So many plans . . .

She'd tried to ignore her early misgivings. However, the truth was that from the moment she arrived Nina was cool and detached, and no matter what subject Anne raised – anecdotes about Richard's childhood, the decoration of the nursery, the state of the weather – her sister-in-law seemed disinclined to engage in conversation. At first Anne had told herself this was only to be expected, given her loss and condition, but she hadn't been able to ignore the fact that when that awful woman Maggie Chaplin came to visit Nina talked eagerly to her. They would sit waiting for Anne to leave the room, and as soon as she did their voices lowered as they huddled together, their faces close as they shared secrets. She had felt so hurt and excluded. Nor, finally, had she been able to ignore how Nina's attention revived whenever Jeremy appeared.

When she first noticed this she was actually pleased. Her sister-in-law seemed so depressed and unlike herself: it was a relief to see the old Nina come back to life. But then . . .

She'd berated herself when she realised she was becoming jealous. It was ignoble, horrible under the circumstances. Nina couldn't help being beautiful and Jeremy was just being Jeremy, concerned and kind. And he was, after all, doing it for her sake.

That wasn't what the servants thought, however. From the kitchen she'd overheard Helen and Jane giggling in the scullery. 'Me mam thought I was laying it on thick when I told her Mrs Truelove was every bit as good as Theda Bara in *A Fool There Was*. "I swear to God," I said, "a real vamp, she is."'

'Shoosh, Helen!'

'It's true. Don't tell me you haven't seen the reverend looking at her, dreamy-eyed like he can't get enough, and her in the family way. A vicar's only flesh and blood. And there's poor Miss Truelove, red and pinch-faced beside her.'

She'd fled upstairs to weep in the bedroom. It was demeaning, listening to servant tittle-tattle; but that didn't mean it wasn't true.

It *was* true. She knew Jeremy had started to look at Nina in just the way they described, while for her part Nina was winning him over with flattery, in the way she'd previously won over Anne. Was coral a plant? she'd asked, her eyes large in her face. He was so clever, so learned, to know these things. Sea cucumbers, vines as thick as a man's arm . . .

And then she'd walked into the parlour and found them passionately holding hands: it had been like a knife going through her heart. Nina didn't love her at all. Anne had loved Nina, but the cruel truth was that their friendship had been a sham. And it was obvious Jeremy was besotted, it was written all over his face. Mother had been right all along. She'd been right about Nina and she'd been right when she'd warned Anne that men weren't to be relied on. It was ten years ago, at Father's funeral. 'Your father had a mistress,' Mother suddenly blurted out as they walked together along the cemetery path, 'for twenty years. She was a seamstress in Hounslow. Every Christmas he'd give me something she'd made and never once noticed I didn't wear it. I have a trunk full of clothing made by his whore. Men can't be relied on, Anne, always remember that.' She'd felt faint at the time, hearing Mother talk in this way and realising she'd never really known Father. Neither of them had referred to the matter again.

Yes, men were weak and unreliable, while women – some women – were treacherous. Nina had made Anne admire her, trust her, love her. And then thought nothing of betraying her, and Richard's memory. Anne had watched Jeremy reluctantly release Nina's hands, and the bile had risen into her mouth. She had never felt so lonely, so bitter.

Sitting in the tropics, Anne smiled grimly to herself. Jeremy hadn't found Nina so alluring when she'd gone mad; she was on the floor spewing obscenities. 'Got a big cock, have you?' she'd screamed as he came through the door, her hands rubbing at the place between her legs. The look on his face had been one of such utter horror and revulsion that Anne had almost laughed aloud. She'd forgiven him then, for having fallen victim to Nina's flattery, and had exulted in believing he'd learned a lesson he would never forget.

A flying fox flapped overhead and she brought her mind back to her present situation. For a start, Kyril should be sent away as soon as possible. He was mixing too freely with the native servants – at this rate he'd soon be babbling in Kuku Yalanji as fluently as his uncle. She kept the child at a distance, she knew, not only because he reminded her of his mother, but because he reminded her even more of his father. His hair, gleaming in the sun, was just the same shade as Richard's. He was too much like Richard altogether, and as he grew older any sign of weakness would need to be watched for carefully and dealt with. So Kyril would go to boarding school and she and Jeremy would go on living here – for how long? She saw gruelling decade after decade stretching into the future. And then, one day, Jeremy would retire and finally agree to move somewhere civilised: somewhere where there was a university, no doubt, so he could give lectures and speeches and be congratulated on his life's work by admiring students.

He'd asked to be sent to here.

Maybe not in so many words but he would have indicated that, with his great interest in botany . . . And if he ever did feel a twinge of conscience he could quickly salve it by telling himself he'd done the noble thing in marrying her and taking her away from England and that he was, anyway, doing God's bidding.

She was seeing her husband clearly for the first time: his ambition, his selfishness. Hot tears filled her eyes but she wiped them roughly away. She must not, could not, give in to weakness. Richard had given in to weakness, it had betrayed him, destroying his life and hers.

The Anne who eventually stood up and went back inside was a different Anne from the one of a few short hours ago. That Anne had still been part Anne Truelove; now she was all Anne Gregory. A creature of iron, forged by the fires of social disgrace, bitter disappointment, and the North Queensland wet.

And so life went on for another three years, and would have continued to go on, had Jeremy lived.

When Old Bob came with the news, Anne had thought he was lying and that Jeremy was lost in the rainforest. Then she'd become convinced the aborigine had robbed and abandoned her husband, and demanded his humpy be searched for Jeremy's gold watch. When it wasn't found, a search party was put together, including two black trackers, and they'd followed Old Bob on horseback to the Daintree River.

It took a week of slaughter along the riverbank before they found the crocodile that had taken him. 'His watch, Mrs Gregory.' One of the men stood on the top step and handed it to her in a linen handkerchief. 'We found it inside the brute.' The other men stood silently below, their hats in their hands, while inside the house the aboriginal girls began a high-pitched wailing.

Up until then she hadn't let herself believe Jeremy was dead, not until she felt the weight of the watch in her hand. But when she did feel it she knew it was a sign from God, who didn't, after all, intend that she should spend the rest of her life in Port Douglas.

That life seemed an eternity ago now, and as May trundled heavily along Coronation Drive in the direction of the tram, Anne gave a small wave from under the jacaranda tree. She made a charming picture standing there, she knew, and had had her portrait taken in the same spot two summers ago, the timber house with its iron lacework along the wide veranda forming the backdrop. She had sent copies of the photograph back home last year, tucked inside Christmas cards printed in Birmingham and illustrated with red robins hopping across snow.

Friends had written back complimenting her on the magnificence of her flora and the youthfulness of her appearance. *The southern climate obviously suits you*, wrote one, *for while we shrivel in the cold you are blooming in the heat!* Anne loathed the heat, but it was undoubtedly true that it didn't seem to have done her any harm, not physically at least. She rubbed her hands with lemon at night, smoothed her face with lanolin cream, and looked younger than most women her age. It would have been different if she'd borne children in Port Douglas, of course, but, thank God, she'd been spared that.

'Post, Mrs Gregory!' As the boy handed her an airmail envelope she recognised the handwriting of her old friend Janet White, now Janet Hindley. Janet's letters were a great source of news about events in London, but Anne always made sure her own replies were equally engaging, and as she wandered back up the path now she began to compose her response. She would be able to describe the mah-jong afternoon Mrs Parker had organised at the Blue Bird Café, and how attractive the afternoon tables had been with their decorations of pink and white sweet peas. She looked forward to hearing the Sistine Soloists at Lennon's Hotel next week and could pass on the news (given to her this morning by May Trimble, whose husband was in building) that another skyscraper was to be erected on the corner of Queen and Edward Streets. *So it seems we are to be the next New York!* Then there was the Milanese silk she was pondering, available in either nigger or navy. She could also tell her friend about Miss Mary Clapperton, *who, Mrs Hewitt informs me, is to marry the youngest son of an English lord, though Mrs Hewitt cannot remember which particular lord this is.*

As she walked back into the hall, Gladys emerged from the rear of the house, wiping her hands on her apron. 'Mrs Gregory, I done the polishing – I mean, I polished the table.'

'Good, Gladys. Where is Kyril?' As if she didn't know.

Gladys fidgeted on her feet. 'Down the back garden.'

Kyril was always slipping out into the garden. But that would stop when he started work next year: the discipline of a bank was just what Kyril needed.

Gladys went on, 'He did his piano practice earlier, Mrs Gregory. It was a real pretty tune, but sad too. Shall I be getting on with tonight's tea?'

She bit back her irritation. 'Supper, Gladys. Supper, not tea. Yes, do start on it.' Going through to the sitting room, she opened the letter from Janet with the ivory opener, unfolded the onion-skin paper and began to read. As she did so, her cheeks burned. Anne had had dozens of letters from her friend over the years but none of them had begun like this: *My Dear Anne, I am at a loss as to how to begin. Something has happened – an extraordinary encounter, which took me much by surprise. My only concern was to protect you, and of course the boy. I do hope you feel I have done the right thing . . .*

'Mrs Gregory!'

'How many times do I have to tell you to knock?' The letter shook between her fingers.

'Please, Mrs Gregory, I got something important to show you.'

She had no choice but to put Janet's letter down and go out into the hall, where Gladys was pointing dramatically upward at an oddly shaped stain. 'It's the ceiling, Mrs Gregory.'

'I can see that. The roof is leaking again.' It had been repaired only a month before, and was undoubtedly annoying, but she would deal with it later.

Gladys, however, was shaking her head. 'It's very dark. I'm not so sure that's rainwater, ma'am.'

Anne took a deep breath. 'If it isn't rain, then what is it?'

'I thought I heard someone slitherin' up there last week.' The wretched girl's face took on a satisfied grin. 'That's blood, Mrs

Gregory, there's no doubt. It looks like we got ourselves a carpet snake and he got himself that possum what's been keeping everyone awake!'

As she stared at the stain on the ceiling, Anne could clearly see the outline of a woman's face, and knew that the woman was none other than Nina Karsavina, the Russian witch responsible for Richard's downfall, her own exile, six years in Port Douglas, and now for the horror in her ceiling.

Twenty-five

From where he was sitting, on the bench under the umbrella tree in the back garden, Kyril could hear the commotion from within the house and guessed it was about the snake. He'd known about the snake for some weeks: lying in bed at night, he listened to it flow across the rafters like a breeze rustling leaves. He'd enjoyed the sound of the snake, but no doubt when Fred, the gardener, arrived Aunt Anne would tell him to catch it and kill it. He didn't know how Fred would catch the snake but he did know how he'd kill it, because he'd seen him kill a red-belly black snake that had been hiding in a pile of leaves. Fred had called for Norm, who was mowing the lawn next door, and Norm had held the snake down with the back of a rake while Fred chopped off its head with the shovel. The blood had spurted and the body of the snake had danced in the air when Fred picked it up by the tail. 'An abo,' he'd held it out to Kyril, 'now he'd think that was good bush tucker. Give that to a blackfeller and he'd reckon it was a tasty feast.'

'That's right.' Norm kicked the bloodied head on to the shovel with the side of his boot and winked. 'He'd have it with a gin. A gin with tucker and a gin at night, that's what keeps an abo happy.' The two men had laughed as if this were a great joke, but Kyril had felt superior to both of them, because he knew a lot more about aborigines than they did and also knew Old Bob wouldn't have needed to call another man to help him kill a snake. He wouldn't have needed a shovel either, but would have picked it up by the tail with his bare hands then snapped it fast as a whip, breaking its back.

For a moment the thought of Old Bob made him almost happy, but then it was as if a wall came down, pushing the happiness away. It was over nine years ago that Uncle Jeremy had died and they'd left Port Douglas. He hadn't seen Old Bob since. 'He as good as murdered your uncle,' Aunt Anne had said. 'He took him to the river, knowing there were crocodiles.'

Kyril had often heard Old Bob warn Uncle Jeremy it was dangerous along the riverbank, but Aunt Anne said he'd tricked him anyway because you couldn't believe a word the blacks said. So it was Old Bob's fault that Uncle Jeremy had been killed, and it was wrong, very wrong indeed, to have fond memories of him. The thought of how Uncle Jeremy died – the crocodile holding him underwater with its terrible jaws until he drowned – made Kyril feel as if he were choking.

He eased his breathing by pulling his thoughts away from the terrifying scene and instead allowed himself to think about Milly and Daisy and Prudence, the girls who'd looked after him when he was little. In the afternoons they would go single file down to the creek and fish with string nets for yabbies or turtles, which they carried back up to the kitchen in a tin bucket. There'd been stories too: the girls were mission-educated, so often the stories were the same ones he heard Aunt Anne tell at Sunday school, about the life of Jesus. But there were also other stories, secret stories they remembered from their families, before they'd been taken to the mission, and these stories were the exciting ones, told in whispers. About the big mountain, Manjal Dimbi, and about Kubirri, the good spirit who came to the people in the shape of a man with a bright, shining body and taught them which plants were poisonous and how they could be made safe to eat. Kyril had loved the stories, begging the girls to tell them over and over, and they'd done as he asked, laughing that he was becoming one of them. 'Youse a good little kid, Kyril. Youse one of us!'

Sometimes Uncle Jeremy would come down to the water with them, carrying Kyril high on his shoulders. The girls would shyly point to various plants and name them. Kyril could still run over the names in his mind: *bikarrakul, yibuy, wuymbariji, jilngan, jun jun* . . . Uncle Jeremy would ask the girls what the plants were good for and they'd giggle, then become serious, saying this one was good for eating or that one was good for toothache and healing wounds. Some of the plants were harmful but could still be eaten if all the poison was washed out. Their mothers had known how to do this but the girls didn't because they'd been taken away from their families before their mothers could teach them. If you didn't know how to do it properly and ate the plant you'd die. The plant everyone was frightened of was *mili*, the stinging tree. 'Him bad plant.' The girls would shake their heads and frown. 'You keep away from that bad plant, Kyril.'

Today Kyril couldn't stop himself chanting native words over in his mind, *bana, kakan, marrakan*: water, dilly bag, canoe . . . The words were a guilty, fragile connection with a time when the world had seemed a golden place. He pulled himself up abruptly – it had only seemed like that because he'd been a little kid and didn't know any better. When he thought now about the colour of the girls' hands, combing his hair, washing his face, tickling his feet, he felt slightly sick.

The voices inside the house had stopped. Soon he'd go inside and wash. His fingers were getting red and cracked again, from washing them too much Gladys said, but Gladys was ignorant. You had to wash because of germs. He always wore gloves when he was gardening, but you couldn't wear gloves all the time. There were germs everywhere: you could only see them with a microscope, and for that reason he always carried two handkerchiefs in his pockets, one for turning doorknobs with. You could have it folded in your hand and no one would see. It wasn't always easy at school, he went to Church of England Grammar, because boys sometimes noticed things like that, but usually it was all right, and it was better to be safe than sorry.

Aunt Anne said it was germs that had killed his mother. He hadn't known his mother was dead, but when Uncle Jeremy died Aunt Anne told him about his mother too. They'd been standing on the veranda of the Port Douglas house, watching the tin trunks and the tea chests being loaded on to the wagon that was to take them to the steamer. 'It's time you knew,' his aunt said slowly. 'You're old enough now. Your mother died, Kyril, when you were a baby, shortly after she gave you to me. So now you know. You and I are the only family left. The only ones. Never forget that.'

Standing on the veranda, he'd felt desperately sad because Uncle Jeremy had died and because he was leaving all his friends in Port Douglas, but he hadn't felt sad to hear his mother was dead because she hadn't wanted him anyway. He certainly didn't feel sad about her death now he was older, because he knew that not only had she given him away, but she'd also been a Bolshevist. Russians were treacherous – they'd betrayed the Allies. There'd been a report in the newspapers last week that they'd discussed in class: two Russians had been arrested in Shanghai, where they were trying to start a revolution. When their hotel room was searched the police found sixty thousand roubles hidden in a suitcase. Mr Knowles, the history teacher, had been very solemn as he said it was possible there were Bolshevists in Australia with similar amounts of money and that Russia was willing to pay whatever it cost to take over the world. The whole class had voted that anyone in the pay of the Russians should be hanged for treason, and for a few tense seconds he'd expected them all to turn around and point at him, because he was half Russian. But that was silly, because they didn't know his mother was Russian, he'd never told anyone. They didn't even know he had a Russian name. He hated his name and was always being teased about it: when challenged, he told people it was Irish. Having a surname like Truelove made his first name even worse.

No, he wasn't sad about his mother, not at all. But he was sad about his father, Captain Richard Truelove, who'd been an officer in the army and died a hero in the war. His father had imported metals, and when Kyril turned sixteen at the end of the year and left school, he too would join the world of business by taking a junior post in the Commonwealth Bank in Queen Street. He'd been interviewed by the manager, Mr Warren, who said that if he worked hard he might one day be a bank manager too.

A sudden pain went through Kyril's chest and he leaned back against the wooden bench. He'd had a horribly tight feeling in his chest when Aunt Anne first told him he'd be working in a bank. It would be difficult avoiding germs in the bank, all that money handled by people, kept in their pockets. But that wasn't the only reason he'd been worried about it – it was also because he'd secretly hoped to stay on right till the end of school and then, maybe, do further studies . . .

Uncle Jeremy had studied botany at Cambridge, and in Port Douglas he'd written pamphlets and books. These were all on a shelf in the parlour, though Kyril had only looked at them a few times because Aunt Anne didn't like them to be touched. But that didn't matter, as he could also read them in the big public library in town, and he often did so. It always struck him as a small miracle that although Uncle Jeremy was dead his words lived on and anyone could pick up his books and listen to what he had to say: *The flora of North Queensland is, I believe, the most exciting in the world and those of us who daily open our doors to find such wonders are remarkably privileged . . .*

Closing his eyes, Kyril could still hear his uncle's voice. 'Isn't it amazing, Kyril, to see something as remarkable as this on our very doorstep? You are so lucky, little man!' The common name for the plant they'd been looking at was 'the Shy Plant', and it truly was amazing, for when you touched it the leaves immediately moved, closing in on themselves. He'd jumped when his uncle first showed him. 'Is it an animal?' he'd whispered, bewildered, and his uncle had laughed. 'No, Kyril, it's all plant, and when you're older I'll explain the chemistry that allows it to move so quickly.'

Uncle Jeremy had been a good teacher. He'd taught Kyril how to read, painting jolly, brightly coloured letters on pieces of stiff card so that the lessons hadn't seemed like lessons but more like games, and learning to read had taken no time at all. Because it was Jeremy who had taught him to read it meant even more to Kyril when he read his uncle's books in the library in town.

The public library wasn't the only library where Kyril had seen these books, for one day he'd gathered up his courage and gone into the university library in George Street, to see if they were there as well. This was a year ago, but because he was tall he looked like the other students and no one had stopped him. He'd found Uncle Jeremy's books on the shelves of the botany section and while he was looking at them a grey-haired man in an academic gown had come up beside him. 'Pioneering works, those,' he'd said. 'I'm glad to see you tackling them. First year, are you?'

Kyril had felt ill: he shouldn't be here – they might call school, or even his aunt. He'd fought to control his breathing. 'I'm sorry,

I'm not a university student and I know I shouldn't be here. But these books, sir, they were written by my uncle.'

'By Jove.' The lecturer peered at him. 'Is that right, you're the Reverend Gregory's nephew?'

'Yes, sir.' The man was smiling broadly now, so it seemed all right to add, 'I lived with him in Port Douglas.'

'Did you now. And what's your name?'

'Kyril Truelove.'

The man put out his hand. 'Well, Mr Truelove, I'm honoured to meet you. You are welcome to come to the library to peruse your uncle's work whenever you wish – tell the librarian Professor Hayworth said so.' He rocked back on his heels. 'Should I expect to see you here as a student in the near future, Mr Truelove? Do you see yourself as a botanist?'

Kyril had never thought of it before. He felt his cheeks flush. 'I don't know, sir.'

'Think about it, my boy. And if you are interested, do come and talk to me in the department. You'll find a list of room numbers by the front entrance.'

Kyril had thought about it, a lot. He hadn't said anything to Aunt Anne, of course, but when she told him he'd be going into the bank he had to say something. 'I'd thought,' he'd said, 'that I might be able to stay on at school, Aunt Anne. I'm doing so well, all the masters say so. And after that . . .'

'Yes, Kyril? After that?'

'That I might go on to further studies.'

Slowly, she nodded her head, as if thinking about this for the first time. 'In which subject?'

He swallowed. What he really wanted to say was music, but she would never allow him to pursue music professionally, he knew that. Music was something he would have to do in his spare time. But going to university to study botany was possible, surely, because of Uncle Jeremy?' 'Botany, Aunt Anne, like Uncle Jeremy.'

'Ah,' she said, looking away, 'like your uncle.' When she turned back her voice was sad, as if he'd disappointed her. 'I'm surprised, Kyril, that you have been thinking like that, for you know you will need to work for a living. Where would a degree in botany take you? The disciplined environment of the bank will suit you very well, and, if you think about it honestly, I'm sure you'll agree. To go to university purely to study a subject out of personal interest would be very self-indulgent indeed – even, some might feel, selfish.'

Selfishness was one of his weaknesses, he knew. His asthma was another weakness. He was also liable to daydream, and daydreaming led to silly ideas – such as going to the Conservatorium in Sydney, or to university. Aunt Anne said that if you indulged in such daydreams they eventually took over and all your weaknesses would come out.

That was what had happened to his mother: before she died she'd gone mad and been locked away in a mental hospital.

Despite the heat he shivered, pushing his hands deep into his pockets. He felt breathless again: being locked in a mental hospital would be far worse than going to work in a bank. He had to make sure that nothing like that ever happened to him.

'You must be strict with yourself,' Aunt Anne had warned him, 'if you are to do your duty and not let yourself, and others, down. It's in your blood, Kyril, but you must fight it. Self-discipline is the answer.'

Sometimes, however, you could deceive other people into thinking you were being disciplined when you were really indulging yourself. In his heart he knew his piano practice was like this. People praised him for his dedication, but the truth was that when he played he left things like duty and discipline far behind, losing himself in the music. However, his teacher, Miss Milne, said he didn't let himself go enough. 'Let yourself go, Kyril!' she'd urge. 'Music isn't simply about technical excellence. You need to allow yourself to *feel* as well. I know you can do it, don't be frightened.'

But he was right to be frightened, having had a stark warning of where letting himself go could lead only a few weeks go, when Miss Milne had taken some of her pupils to a concert by the ABC Symphony Orchestra from Sydney. 'You'll enjoy this,' she'd said to him, 'you'll see.'

He'd never heard music like it before: the pieces played that night were modern works by composers like Arthur Benjamin and Alfred Hill. They weren't at all like the music he was used to, and at first he simply felt lost. Then he was exhilarated. That it was possible to write, and to play, music like this. That a famous orchestra, with a conductor as respected as Bernhard Heinze, could perform such pieces in public.

The last piece that night was *The Lark Ascending* by Vaughan Williams. Miss Milne had told him the composer had written it before the war and then revised it. 'The world before the war meets the world after it,' she'd said. 'There's the beauty and simplicity of nature tempered by the knowledge of what terrible things can happen, what terrible things mankind is capable of.'

The violinist had been a woman, with red hair the colour of his own. 'Truelove,' Jim Wilson had hissed from two seats away, 'is the violinist your cousin?'

The wave of emotion that swept over him as she played was beyond anything he'd ever felt before. He closed his eyes and let the sound pour and wash over him, and then flow away. He was buffeted this way and that by sound that was pure feeling: sadness, love, grief, happiness. He was torn by loss – the loss of his uncle and his father – and by joy, the knowledge that this was what it meant to be alive.

The audience's applause at the end was bemused rather than thunderous but the red-haired violinist didn't appear to notice. She stood still and alone in the centre of the stage, her head bowed, her hair a burning halo under the lights, and he knew that she too had soared. He didn't applaud at all – the music and the performance were beyond that – but as soon as he stepped out on to the street, the exhilaration burst out of him. 'Yes!' He punched the air, because anything was possible and he had never seen it before. 'Yes!'

'Why, Kyril!' Miss Milne laughed, sounding surprised but glad. 'I take it that you enjoyed the performance?'

'It was sublime!' He'd never felt so happy, so free. Jumping up, he grabbed a lamppost with both hands and swung around it. 'I'm free! We're all free!'

It was true. He had shed all his usual fears and worries. Anything was possible; he could do anything. He knew that although he played the piano well, and was capable of playing even better than he did now, he would never play as well as the violinist had done. But that didn't matter, because what he really wanted to do was write music. He already had a portfolio of pieces he'd put together: Miss Milne was the only person who knew about them but she said he had a strong talent and was good enough to go on with his studies, even to go to the Conservatorium in Sydney. This was what he should do, he knew that without a doubt. Going to university and studying botany would be very rewarding, but music was his real love and was what he should spend his life doing. And it was possible, because anything was possible. He would not work in a bank. The problem was that he had never really tried to explain how he felt to his aunt but once he did, once she understood how he really felt and how much it meant to him, then everything would be different. Why had he never seen this before?

'I'm free!' he shouted.

'You're drunk, mate!' a good-natured voice shouted back.

'Drunk on music!' he replied. Throwing back his head, he let out a Red Indian whoop. And then another one and another one.

As he stopped for breath, Jim Wilson's voice, heavy with distaste, carried across the pavement. 'You're mad, Truelove.' Wilson thrust his hands into his trouser pockets. 'Completely barking. I've always suspected as much. One day they'll lock you up in the loony bin and throw away the key.' Turning on his heel, he walked off.

The concert audience had spilled out on to the pavement and frowning faces were turned in his direction, people muttering and staring. He heard a woman's voice: 'Shame!'

Miss Milne stepped forward. 'Come, Kyril,' she said quietly. 'Let's go.'

They were all glaring at him now, shaking their heads.

'Kyril,' Miss Milne said firmly, 'it's over, we must start for home.' She took him by the arm but his legs had turned to jelly so he had to lean on her as she pulled him away. 'It's all right, Kyril, come on.'

Jim Wilson thought he was mad; they all did. People who went mad in public were put in a straitjacket and locked up in a mental hospital for the rest of their lives. By the time they reached the corner he was gasping for breath and shivering violently all over. 'You're ill, Kyril. Do you have a fever?' Miss Milne asked. He just had time to push past her before he threw up violently into the gutter.

Miss Milne had taken him home in a cab and he'd spent the next four days in bed, supposedly suffering from gastric flu. On the fifth day he got up, feeling as weak and fragile as if he had had a serious illness. As they had afternoon tea, Aunt Anne read from a review in the *Brisbane Courier*. 'The orchestra's performances have been very badly received,' she observed. 'It says here that "Brisbane audiences have not been appreciative of the Symphony Orchestra's latest offering and it is not difficult to see why when 'modern' is a euphemism for decadent. Regular classical concert attendees are not to be fobbed off with such a discordant offering, with 'jazz' masquerading as art . . ."'

She frowned slightly. 'How did you find the concert, Kyril?'

His mouth was dry: what if one of his aunt's friends had been outside the theatre? Jim Wilson's mother sometimes attended their church. 'I don't know really. I was feeling so strange, because I was ill, that I didn't take much of it in. I think I was delirious.'

She gave him a long look but didn't say anything more about the concert, and he found himself yet again cursing the weakness in himself, the weakness he'd inherited from his mother. His music came from his mother, he knew that. One day some visitors had listened to him play and later Kyril heard one of them say to his aunt, 'Are you also a talented musician, Mrs Gregory?' She didn't say anything at first, but then replied, 'No, he doesn't get that from my side of the family.' He'd inherited it from his mother, so it must be connected to weakness. His aunt knew the connection was there – he could see it in her face sometimes when he'd been practising – and so he usually tried to practise when she was out, or busy with Gladys.

But although his mother had been weak and selfish, his father had been strong and had sacrificed his life in the war. Kyril very much hoped that one day he'd be as strong as his father. So he would go to work in the Commonwealth Bank – and when he did he would give up his music altogether. His eyes watered shamefully at the thought, but he'd made up his mind about this as he lay in bed in the days following the concert. His dream of going to the Conservatorium was childish and fanciful: he wasn't good enough for anything like that, and anyway, he had seen very clearly where such self-indulgence would take him. He had been mad there on the pavement. At the time it had seemed like freedom but really it was insanity. The image of the red-haired violinist suddenly came back into his mind, as if she was watching him sadly, but he blinked her away. Maybe some people had the self-discipline to cope with the emotion music brought with it, but he didn't. No, giving up music would be his first real act of self-discipline.

His decision had been painfully made, like cutting out a part of himself, but there was no denying it also brought an immense sense of relief, because it showed he could fight against his own nature. Aunt Anne had only told him a little about his mother's madness but that little had been more than enough. 'It is not something one wishes to discuss in detail, Kyril,' she'd said. 'But you should know it was very shocking. She was acting in a way no lady – no human – should ever act. She was on her hands and knees, like an animal, shouting the most disgusting, vile things.'

Sitting on the garden bench now, he shuddered. Last year in English they'd done *King Lear*, and 'O! that way madness lies; let me shun that' had become his grim motto. The other boys had laughed at Lear's madness and the antics of Edgar as mad Tom, 'Poor Tom's a-cold!' Kyril hadn't laughed, however, for he knew the same germ was in him.

And his interest in plants? No, it wouldn't be necessary to sacrifice that as well. The masters at school were always saying it was healthy to have a hobby – some of them collected stamps or built matchstick boats – so he could keep up an amateur interest in botany. It would be his way of honouring Uncle Jeremy's memory.

As he thought this his eyes settled on the Moreton Bay fig and he felt himself frown. He'd seen Aunt Anne a bit earlier, standing under the jacaranda but looking in the direction of the fig. The Iver sisters, who'd moved into the street at Easter, had had their fig cut down and Fred said they'd done it because their Chinese cook refused to move with them if it stayed. 'They think figs are bad luck, Chinks do,' Fred said. 'They say evil spirits live in 'em.' Fred said Chinks were almost as bad as the aborigines, though neither were as bad as Jews.

Thinking about Fred made Kyril remember the snake, and he suddenly imagined himself trying to save it, before Fred arrived.

There was a trapdoor in the ceiling of the laundry room, and if he climbed up through it . . . He'd stood on a ladder once when some work was being done and had seen what it looked like up there. The carpet snake, bloated with possum, would be sleeping curled around the base of one of the rafters. It would be heavy and sluggish and not, surely, too difficult to catch. It would be terrified, of course, and might try to bite, but if he moved quietly and quickly enough he could be on it before it knew what was happening. He saw himself silently edging through the darkness to where the snake was sleeping and then, quick as lightning, gripping the enormous creature's neck with one hand while unlooping its steel-like coils from the rafter with the other. He would then drop it into the hessian sack he'd brought for the purpose. When he released it into the garden it would realise he didn't mean to harm it and would slide gratefully away.

But even as he pictured this he knew it was impossible. There was no way he could get into the roof without his aunt knowing, and the whole exercise wouldn't be that simple anyway: Old Bob might know how to catch a snake, but Kyril didn't, not really. As for the reptile feeling grateful – well, he'd listened out for the snake at night but the snake hadn't known he was there, didn't know he existed at all. And even if it did, it wouldn't care.

No, he told himself sternly, it was stupid, weak even, to feel sorry for the snake. Fred would catch it and cut off its head with a shovel. He would do this because that was what had to be done with snakes, even the ones that weren't dangerous to people, only possums. 'If every snake that got seen got killed,' Fred had said after killing the last one, 'there'd be no more snakes left in the world. And the world would be a far better place then, wouldn't it? Stands to reason.'

Fred was right, the world would be a better place. In future Kyril would try to be more like Fred, strong and not sentimental or weak. Work and self-discipline would guide him through his life and this way he would be in no danger of letting himself, or anyone else, down.

Book Three

1990

Be not forgetful to entertain strangers:
for thereby some have entertained angels unawares.

Hebrews, 13:1

Twenty-six

Mountview Psychiatric Clinic was a forty-five-minute drive from Brisbane city centre. When Julia Truelove told anyone about the time she'd spent there as a patient she laughed it off. 'I was crazy as a teenager,' she'd say over a glass of wine, 'crazy as a coot.' But if they asked – as they sometimes did, embarrassed but curious – why she still went to visit, she replied without hesitation, 'I go there to think.'

Mountview was originally built as a friary, its grounds designed for thinking, or rather for meditation, by Anglican friars sent over from England a century ago. A working order, they rolled up their sleeves to reveal muscular forearms, tied their habits to reveal sinewy thighs, and sometimes more. There were still women who told their grandmothers' stories about how the local girls would gather to watch the young friars build their new home. 'See, they didn't wear anything underneath,' one confided, 'like Scotsmen in kilts. Nan said they were enormous, those young English friars, hung like horses. The girls all reckoned it was because those parts never got used.' Here she winked. 'Although from the tales me nan told they weren't as unused as they should have been. Can't blame them, though, can you, young blokes like that? If God had wanted them to be celibate he wouldn't have given them the equipment, that's what I say. I don't believe the Lord condones waste.'

Gripping the wheel this morning, Julia remembered the first drive up from Brisbane, twenty years ago, when she was just fifteen. Despite what she said to anyone now, her teenage craziness hadn't been a laughing matter. She'd sat sulking in the back seat, the cuts she'd made on her arms hidden under bandages, while in the front her mother, Hazel, couldn't help thrusting her hands nervously against the dashboard. 'Go slowly, Kryil,' she pleaded, 'these bends are so dangerous.' Dad drove on in silence, his shoulders set and angry as he negotiated the Holden around the steep curves.

When they'd arrived at Mountview her parents had gone through to talk to the doctors and Julia had escaped into the garden. So a pattern was established, and gradually she learned to listen to the hum of beehives, follow the grain of the sandstone walls with her fingers. That first visit she was admitted as a patient for three weeks, and there followed two years of fortnightly sessions with Dr Dorothy Jenkins, a senior psychiatrist. Before or after the sessions she usually spent some time in the garden: in summer retreating into the shade with a sketchbook and in winter sunning herself against the stones alongside the frill-necked lizards. Her mouth would turn sideways against the warmth as she whispered the ugliest words she knew. 'Shit,' she muttered against the sandstone. 'Fuck.' The dirty words tumbled out.

Over the years the drive up the range became easier as the roads improved, and these days Julia could usually do it in twenty minutes: the friars would have believed such a quick journey would require a miracle. They'd used horses to drag the stone blocks and had baked the bricks themselves. It had taken two years to finish the building and then they had set about constructing an English flower garden, a prayer to a gentle, tea-drinking God set against a backdrop of his sturdier native creations: ironbark, stinging trees, bat's-wing coral, pink bloodwood. The friary had only been in existence for twelve years before something happened, no one was sure exactly what – a shake-up in the mother community, rumours the Brisbane hierarchy couldn't quash – and the original English friars were recalled to Somerset. The Australian recruits were summarily dispatched to a community in Adelaide.

After the friars' retreat a rich grazier, Clarence Pride, bought the property from the Church for his delicate wife, Janette, who supervised the garden's expansion, putting in large banks of pink and red roses, the cuttings shipped especially from the Royal Botanical Gardens in Sydney. When she died Mountview became a hotel and then, in the early Fifties, the headquarters of a motorbike club. Finally it became a psychiatric hospital, now Mountview Clinic.

Julia knew all this because last year the local history society had published a booklet tracing the building's history and had asked her permission to use a detail from one of her early etchings, 'Woman in the Garden', for the cover. The woman sitting on a bench and staring forlornly across the lawn was her mother.

Turning right off the highway, the little Honda Civic began the familiar climb and Julia quickly reached for her sunglasses, the sun slicing between tall trees. She hadn't planned to come up here today – what she'd planned to do was make enquiries about letting out her house, it would be crazy to leave it empty for a year – but then the post had arrived and she didn't feel like talking to an estate agent after all. Instead she'd rung Mountview and asked if Dr Jenkins was expected. Dorothy had recently retired but she still spent most of her time at the clinic, and the receptionist this morning had said she had no doubt Dr Jenkins would be in. And so Julia had left the rest of the post unopened and jumped into the car. 'Damn,' she said out loud now. Because it was ridiculous that getting a passport in the post could throw her like this. But the moment she opened it everything had flooded back: the feelings from that morning all those years ago when she was twelve years old.

It had been the first day of the summer holidays. For years holidays had always been spent at the same place, a cluster of small, brightly painted fibro holiday cottages north of Brisbane. Mum would pack food and clothes and Dad would load the Eskies and fishing gear into the back of the station wagon and off they'd go. Julia used to get carsick and Paul would sit next to her on the back seat and play games like 'I Spy' for the entire drive to keep her mind off it. He was seven years older than she was, so they didn't fight like other brothers and sisters.

They'd arrived late in the evening and unpacked after dinner. She was exhausted, Mum having to help her undress as she sleepily held rag-doll arms in the air, but as she put her head on the pillow she still remembered to bang it four times. Because that was when she was going to get up; at four o'clock in the morning. Before anyone else was awake she'd get up by herself and go straight down to the water. Paul had told her about banging her head like that. 'It works', he'd said, 'every time.' And it had worked; she woke up and there was a faint light coming through the closed venetian blinds. Her clothes were folded on the chair and she started to pull on jeans and a T-shirt. Mum wouldn't want her going out alone this early, she knew that, and Dad would be angry if he caught her. Dad got angry easily because he was a bank manager; Mum had been his secretary in the bank before they got married and she said it was a big responsibility, looking after other people's money, and that Dad was very good at his job. But even the thought of Dad catching her wasn't going to make Julia chicken out now; she'd been planning this first morning for weeks.

Ten minutes later she was running triumphantly over the clumped wet grass, down the slope past the acacias towards the beach and the jetty. The jetty was where she'd spend most of the coming fortnight. She'd swim off the point and then lie on the salty, bleached boards; later in the day, when it was really hot, she'd crouch in the shade below, smoothing the grey-gold sand into the shape of a castle. In the evening, when it was cooler, she'd walk with Mum and Paul along the beach.

This morning, however, she was determined to see a sleeping stingray.

As she neared the jetty she slowed down and looked around. She'd expected there to be a few fishermen along the water's edge, but she was completely alone except for a pair of cormorants silhouetted against the mangroves further along the beach. She watched them for a moment then walked carefully out on to the boards, hunched low so as not to frighten the rays.

When the tide was low you could see the outlines of where the stingrays slept during the night. Lozenge. She said the word in her head. It was the only word she'd come up with so far to describe the shapes sculpted in the sand. She knew it wasn't really the right one, not right like in the dictionary, but it was right in other ways, in the way it felt and sounded, the sound filling the deeper hollows left by a stingray's body then flowing into the shallower areas left by the wide wings and the tip of the tail. She liked the way some words and sounds flowed into shapes, but that was the sort of thing you could only think in your head, not tell anyone else. She'd learnt that back in fourth class. 'What are you doing?' Jim Matthews had asked one day, not in a nasty way at all, but as if he were asking a real question. She'd answered without thinking, 'I'm listening to the leaves – the sounds they make are the same shape as the shadows they make on the wall. Look!' But he hadn't looked at all. Instead his face had taken on an ugly, stupid look and then he'd turned and screamed across the shimmering bitumen of the playground, 'Julia Truelove loves leaves! Julia Truelove wants to marry a tree!' So she'd learnt.

Coming to the end of the jetty, she gently knelt, then stretched her body flat on the smooth planks. Folding her hands under her chin, she stared down into the green-blue water, letting her eyes adjust until she could see the shifting shadows on the bottom. The shadows made changing patterns, and as she watched them she knew she didn't really expect to see a stingray. She also knew that the shapes left by the stingrays were somehow as real for her as the rays themselves. No, the main reason she'd come here was for the adventure of getting up so early.

She lay there for a long time, feeling content and dozy as she listened to the sounds of the water, and watched the play of light and dark over the sandy bottom. But then one area of light and shade took shape and she sucked in her breath, clutching her hands tight together as the stingray lazily flapped its wings, sending up little clouds of sand, then drifted towards her, rising through the water till it broke the surface, its flecked back gleaming in the sunlight. It looked straight at her, as if it were laughing, and then it was gone again and she was left dazzled and blinking.

It had happened; she had seen one after all.

She stayed where she was for a while, reliving the moment, then her ribs began to hurt from the wood and she slowly pushed herself up. A stingray! She spread her arms wide like the stingray's wings. She wished there was someone to tell, but she was still alone except for the cormorants and, closer, a pelican bobbing self-consciously along the water's edge. A stingray! She ran the length of the jetty and took the slope in jubilant leaps, shouting in her head, I saw it! And it saw me! I saw it!

She didn't see the dark shape hiding in the bushes until it was on top of her.

The scream rising in her throat stopped as a hand clamped across her face and she was rolling over and over in the sodden grass, flailing and kicking wildly until she finished up lying on her back, looking straight up into the sky. Her captor held her tightly from beneath and then a voice said into her ear, 'I am the bunyip.'

Her mouth was uncovered and she shrieked with fright and relief. 'Let me go!'

'Shh! You'll wake everyone up. Now – I am the bunyip!' The hands tickled her till she choked with laughter and rolled off him, scrambling to her feet and weaving back and forth as Paul stretched out his arms. 'I am the bunyip!'

'I saw a stingray – so go away, you, you stinky bunyip!' They hadn't played a game like this for a long time.

'Shh! The bunyip wants his breakfast!' As her brother chased her up the steps, she caught sight of their reflections in the window, two red heads gleaming against the pale sky.

After breakfast they went back down to the jetty. She carried two old blankets to sit on and Paul carried the wicker fishing basket. They sat on the end, their legs dangling over the water, and Paul took out two hand lines while she cautiously picked up a handful of prawns. They were cold and green, not pink like the cooked ones. Taking care to avoid the sharp bits at the front, she twisted off the first prawn's head then pinched the tail and pulled the soft body from the shell.

'You want to do it?' Paul pulled a hook from the end of the cork reel and held it out.

'OK.'

'Watch your fingers.'

Starting with the thick end, she threaded the prawn on to the hook. Lacing live worms on a hook was disgusting, but she didn't mind using prawns because they were already dead and it didn't matter. Paul took the baited hook from her while she stood up, then handed it back to her, along with the cork reel. She held the reel in her left hand and began carefully swinging the line, with the hook and weights, in her right, the way Dad had taught her. One, two, three: she was always surprised by the way the movements had become automatic, the line flying smoothly between her open fingers and thumb, disappearing with a faint plop into a small circle of ripples a fair distance out from the jetty.

'Well done,' Paul whispered as she sat down beside him. A few minutes later he threw his own line out, grinning at how far it went, and then sat and quietly started telling her about the dance he'd been to at the YMCA two nights before. The band had arrived so late people thought nothing was going to happen, but then a van had screeched to a halt outside and everyone helped the band members carry in their equipment. Julia loved it when he talked to her like this, as if they were the same age and she knew all the people he knew. He hadn't done it for a long time, months and months, and she'd been worried they might never talk like this again. He'd become so quiet and different since leaving school, staying in his room by himself for hours, even on the weekend, playing the guitar and listening to records. Her favourite group was the Beatles, all the girls at school were mad about the Beatles, but Paul preferred the Rolling Stones. But he didn't only stay in his room to play music, she knew that; it was also because he was worried. He was working in the office of a local newspaper, running errands and making the tea and coffee in the hope that one day they'd agree to train him as a journalist, but there was no guarantee that this would happen. Dad said working in the newspaper office was a big mistake, it was a dead-end job and he should take a post in a bank. But Paul was determined to work for a newspaper, even though it was very hard to get a cadetship. He used to laugh and joke a lot, but he didn't laugh much these days and sometimes Julia thought he'd changed for good. This morning however he was his old self again.

'Some of the girls were wearing wigs,' he was saying, 'and early in the evening they swapped them, and their dresses, and their boyfriends couldn't tell who was who. And later there was a blackout halfway through and all the girls started shrieking because the boys were kissing them in the dark.'

She'd never been to a dance. 'Did you kiss anyone?' She felt shy, wondering if he'd mind her asking.

'Dozens!' He winked. 'I ran around the room and kissed as

many as I could. It was dark, though, so they didn't know it was me.'

It was hard to tell whether he was joking. Paul had a number of friends who were girls, but he didn't have a girlfriend yet. Mum said he was very sensible not to get involved in dating too young, but sometimes Julia worried that Paul hadn't been able to get a girlfriend because of his red hair. Everyone said men should be tall, dark and handsome. Paul was tall – he was six foot three inches, the exact same height as Dad – and he was as handsome as Dad too. Dad had blue eyes, as did she and Paul, and Mum always said that the girls in the bank had thought he was good-looking. His hair was going grey at the sides now but he wasn't bald like a lot of fathers and he wasn't fat either because of the work he did in the garden. Gardening was Mum and Dad's hobby, and they had one of the most beautiful gardens in Brisbane. Dad knew a lot about plants because his uncle had been a botanist, and Mum, who was a good drawer, did lovely designs in coloured pencils. They'd planned the garden together and often worked on it early in the morning before it was hot. Sometimes people stopped in front of their house and took photos over the low brick wall. Julia felt proud when that happened but Dad complained it was an invasion of privacy.

Anyway, Dad worked in the garden and also went swimming, so he looked a lot younger than many of her friends' fathers; all the same, she couldn't help wondering if he'd be even more handsome without red hair.

Other people soon joined them on the jetty; there were little kids swimming up at the point, their mothers shading their eyes and watching from the beach in case of sharks, while a car cautiously backed a boat on a trailer on to the concrete ramp leading into the water. Paul got one nibble on his line but that was all, and after an hour or so he clambered up and headed in the direction of the cottage to get them some cold drinks.

He was away for ages and her shoulders were starting to burn. Eventually she wound in her line, and Paul's, and fastened the fishing basket. Peering up the shope, she shielded her eyes with her hand; Paul wasn't to be seen, he must have forgotten. Which meant she would have to carry everything in by herself. She decided to leave the blankets where they were and take the basket for now.

Julia trailed crossly up the slope and was inside the door before she heard Dad's raised voice. She froze: if she'd realised they were having a row she would have waited in the shade outside, but it was too late for that now. She hated the rows. One good thing that had come from Paul staying in his room all the time was that he and Dad didn't see each other much, so there hadn't been as many arguments.

This was a bad one. It must be, because Mum usually busied herself as if nothing was happening, but this morning she was sitting at the end of the table in her pink apron, crying. Dad was standing with his back to Julia, leaning on a chair, and Paul was facing him across the other side of the table. Paul was very pale and she could see he was shaking. It was horrible, seeing him like that.

Dad was saying, in a very loud voice, 'I was willing to do my duty, and so was my father. What about your mother and your sister? Don't you feel any responsibility towards them at all?'

'That is so much bullshit.' Paul's voice shook as much as his body.

Julia's knees went weak. She could see her father's face in the mirror on the far wall, and his jaw was jutting. She pleaded with her brother in her head: Please stop, please stop. She tried to say this to him with her eyes, but he didn't look at her, only at Dad. She knew Paul and his friends swore, but he never swore in front of their parents, and to say something like that to Dad . . . She was glad Dad was standing on one side of the table and Paul on the other, because otherwise he might have hit Paul. Not that he'd hit Paul before, or her, but he might now. She quickly looked at Mum, to see how she'd reacted to Paul swearing, but it was strange because Mum didn't seem to have heard at all. Then Julia saw that her mother was staring at something on the table, a small book with a dark cover. There were torn pages sticking out of the book and other torn pages scattered across the table. Who had ripped up the book, Paul or Dad? Maybe Paul had done it and that was what had made Dad so angry.

'How dare you use language like that in front of your mother! I don't understand what's got into you. To even think of running away when there are decent men from all over Australia already doing their duty. How can you look any of your friends in the eye? I certainly couldn't tell any of my colleagues that my son was trying to sneak out through the back door, leaving their sons to stand up for their country. Don't you care what people think?'

Paul made a horrid sound, as if he were going to cry. Then he looked back up at Dad and said, very quietly, 'Fuck you anyway. You've just ruined my life.'

There was silence, no one moved, and then Dad exploded. 'Get out! Go on, if you're going to go, do it now! And you can take this with you!' He picked up the torn book and threw it, hitting Paul's arm.

Paul looked down at the book but didn't pick it up. Then he turned and walked out to the little sunroom where his bed was and shut the door behind him.

'Oh, Kyril.' Mum sounded frightened, her eyes wide. 'Are you sure? What if . . .'

Dad thumped his hand on the table and Mum jumped. 'This is a decision he'll regret for the rest of his life! How will he ever live with himself? And if you can't live with yourself . . .' His voice went funny as he said this, and in the mirror he suddenly didn't seem handsome any more but old, like a really old man, and Julia felt so sorry for him she wanted to run up to him and give him a hug. He rubbed his face with his hands, like he did when he came home tired after work. 'I just don't understand, Hazel, I've tried but I feel I've failed . . .' Catching sight of Julia, he swung round. 'What are you doing there?'

'I was getting burnt, I came in for a drink . . .'

'This is not the time to get a drink, Julia, you could have used the tap outside.'

She hesitated. Should she stay or go?

'Go outside when I tell you!' He stepped forward, his blue eyes blazing again, and she half dropped the fishing basket, watching in horror as everything flew out across the floor, prawns and fishing reels and the tin with all the weights and hooks.

'Now look what you've done!'

Spinning around, she bolted down the steps and along the side of the cottage, to where you could push into the space between the frangipani tree and the fibro wall. Crouching there, amongst the dead flowers and snail shells, she hugged her knees and rocked herself as she cried.

A little while later Paul left. She saw him cross the lawn to the back gate and he was carrying his suitcase, which meant he was going back to Brisbane. She didn't run after him but stayed where she was, her head throbbing, because something terrible had just happened – although exactly what, and why, she didn't know.

After a long time she pushed her way out. She knew she should go down to the jetty for the blankets but she didn't care. Dad had driven Paul away, shouted at her, and the holiday was ruined. She would never forgive him.

She went in the back door and found Mum, her face red and puffy. The packed fishing basket was on the kitchen counter, the little torn book sitting forlornly next to it. Julia listened but there were no sounds from elsewhere in the cottage, so Dad had probably gone out. If he'd gone fishing in a boat with some of the other men he'd be away most of the day. He could stay away for ever.

Her mother was staring out of the kitchen window.

'Why did Paul tear up the book?' Julia asked her. The pain in her head was making everything look strange, like when the television screen went fuzzy.

'What?' Mum turned round. She slowly untied the apron then slipped it over her head. Her voice was heavy and flat. 'It was Dad who tore it up. Paul sent away for a British passport. He's eligible for one, you both are, because of Dad being born in England. I'll make us some tea.'

Julia had never seen a passport, but she knew you needed one to go on holiday to a different country. Had Paul been going to do that? But he would have told her, surely? 'Is Paul going somewhere?' Is that what Dad meant, about running away?

Mum picked up the kettle and turned on the tap, 'I don't know, Julia. I think he might have been planning to go to England, but I don't know if he will go or not.'

Paul did go away, but not to Europe. And as a result, everything changed.

'Why?' Julia asked out loud now, as she turned the car into the hospital drive. 'Why?' She parked in the shade of a tree, turned off the engine and rested her head on the wheel; it was ridiculous, going over all this. It had happened more than twenty years ago. It was gone, just like Paul and Mum and Dad were gone. Paul had died two years after that last holiday, and Mum and Dad had been killed five years ago, hit by a car as they crossed the road to go to the corner shop. They'd run out of milk and that was all it took, a driver blinded by sunlight. That was what life was like, and wishing the past had been different was a waste of time. 'If only that hadn't happened so that something else hadn't happened so that something else . . .' An endless trail of cause and effect – how far back could you take it? Other people had bad things happen when they were kids but they didn't dwell on it for twenty years. They didn't feel like throwing up because of a little thing like a passport.

'Jesus Christ.' She opened her eyes and sat up. She had loads of stuff to do, important stuff like letting out the house: instead of getting in a state and coming here, she should have gone to see the agent. Well, she was here now so she would go and find Dorothy. And she would stop thinking about Paul and her parents, all that ancient history. But even as she thought this, the mantra went through her head: 'I'll never forgive you. I'll never forgive you.' Pushing the words aside, she got out of the car and gave a wry laugh: was she a hopeless case or what?

Inside, the hall was cool and empty. There'd been a time when the building was busy with nurses, patients, visitors, but these days Mountview only served outpatients and was primarily for research and training. The door to the old chapel was open and Julia wandered through. Two of the original stained-glass windows had survived the building's varied fortunes and the polished parquet floor near the doorway was patterned with flecks of coloured light. Otherwise the chapel was empty except for four wooden benches and, on the far wall, one of her own watercolours, 'Room with Woman and Birds'. The woman sat at the end of a table criss-crossed with louvred sunlight, and through the pattern of light and shade there darted quick yellow birds, small smudges of movement.

Looking at the painting now, Julia was aware of the stillness of the room and the woman, and the speed of the birds – which were in one place for a brief moment and then in another. It was there, somewhere, the something that was eluding her in her work now; it was there in the painting. What had she been thinking about when she was working on it, almost eight years ago? About time passing – about the woman, still and unchanging in the room for an afternoon, or a lifetime – and time, the coming and going of the birds, passing by.

'Ms Truelove,' one of the older receptionists stopped in the doorway, 'we haven't seen you for a while.'

As she turned, she caught sight of herself in the painting's glass: tall and thin in a creased linen dress, with red hair almost to her waist. When she first came here her hair was cut to the scalp; she'd done it herself with her mother's pinking shears in order to look as ugly as she felt. 'Hi there,' she said. 'Is Dorothy – Dr Jenkins – in her office?'

'Not when I last looked. But I expect you know where you'll find her.'

Julia went back down the steps, into the familiar perfume of flowers, the sensual, damp heat of foliage. And there, up ahead, was Dorothy, wearing the white hat and veil of a beekeeper. Caring for the bees had been her hobby for years but over time she'd become allergic to the stings and now had to wear the protective veil. She looked like a ghostly bride.

'Hi there!' Julia called.

Pushing back the veil, the woman put her head to one side and said, 'Now who do we have here?' It was the same greeting she'd used the first time they'd met all those years ago. Julia had sat hunched under a tree and a woman in a businesslike white shirt and grey trousers had walked across the lawn, looked down at her and said, 'Now who do we have here?' 'A nutcase,' Julia had replied. 'A fruitcake, a weirdo, a retard, a *slut* . . .' The woman had smiled, turned on her heel, and a few minutes later returned with a sketchbook and some pencils. 'We have to be seen to be doing something,' she confided, 'so while I sit here, admiring the garden, you can try drawing it.' Julia had been so taken aback that she'd complied, drawing a tree, and that was when it all started. People thought she was joking when she said she was an artist as the result of going crazy, but it was true.

'The bees all right?' she asked now.

'There's a nasty disease going around but, thankfully, we don't seem to have any signs of it. They're a tough old lot.' Dorothy smiled. 'Now tell me, what's this news of yours?'

Julia blinked into the sun. 'I'm going to Europe. I've got a grant from the Australia Council – a big one this time, for a year off and travel – and a British passport; it arrived this morning.' She swallowed. 'I'll spend most of the time in England. I'm having a couple of weeks in Mallorca, then a week in Paris before going to London.'

'Oh, Julia.' Dorothy beamed. 'You're doing so well, this is such exciting news.'

An hour later they walked out to the car. As Julia unlocked the door Dorothy shaded her eyes. 'I hope you don't think I'm being too inquisitive, but what about your anthropologist, Liam?'

Julia almost dropped the keys. 'As it happens, he's going to be travelling too: not in Europe but Africa. We might manage to meet up.' She went on quickly, 'My Aunt Molly, Mum's sister, is going through a genealogy craze at the moment. She's doing an evening course and is drawing up our family tree. I've promised her that while I'm in England I'll go to see where my father's parents lived.' Family roots: Dorothy would approve of that.

'She's your only relative, isn't she? Well, I think it's an excellent idea. Where did your grandparents live?'

She had to think. 'Brighton.'

'Oh, you'll enjoy Brighton. I went there once for a conference and it was enormous fun.' She kissed Julia's cheek. 'If there isn't too much going on, do send me a postcard; the Royal Pavilion is magnificent.'

As Julia switched on the engine a flock of lorikeets darted overhead, flashing rainbow colours; she watched them disappear into some trees, then reached for her sunglasses. She was pleased she'd come; it was good to see Dorothy and she felt a lot happier. There'd be plenty of time this afternoon to make enquiries about letting the house.

Twenty-seven

Brighton, July 1990

Three months later Julia sat in the sun on a bench outside the Royal Pavilion. On the lamppost next to the bench was a faded flyer, *Freedom for Mandela! Celebrate with the Socialist Workers*, while a few feet away a bag lady in a pink-sequinned dress fed the pigeons. 'Promise me you'll go to Brighton, for your mother's sake,' Aunt Molly had said. 'It breaks my heart to think Hazel never got to England. She very much wanted Kyril to see where his parents had lived.' So here Julia was, visiting the place where her father was conceived. It was a disconcerting thought.

She went back to concentrating on the feeding birds, a blur of blue-grey feathers: movement and non-movement, space and its absence. She'd been playing with these ideas since the fortnight she'd spent in Mallorca. She'd flown into Palma and then taken a taxi to Puerto Pollenca. And it was on the way there that she'd seen it: a dilapidated windmill, its white and red arms moving fast – movement which was made up of space and the absence of space. The *sensation* of movement: this was what she'd been looking for.

A couple of days later she paid another taxi driver to drive her half the length of the island, from Puerto Pollenca back to that particular windmill, but it wasn't moving any more. When she climbed out of the car and examined it up close, it was so battered and rusty that the driver, a plump man in his fifties, who was sweating despite the car's air-conditioning, refused to believe she could have seen this windmill moving at all. She saw a number of working windmills over the following days but never again captured exactly the same feeling. She'd come close to the sensation again when she joined the edges of a crowd gathered outside a village church for mass one evening. In the middle of the service a group of girls performed a traditional dance, and an almond-skinned teenager with heavy glasses and a long plait swung her black-sleeved arm down across her green swirling skirt. Down came the arm, and up: space, and not space.

Julia had experimented with these ideas in Mallorca, sketching furiously. Then she'd had a week in Paris (a wonderful week but she didn't want to think about that too much) before coming to England, where things had been fine at first. The Camden flat that had been found for her was made up of a well-lit studio with a bed-sit attached, and for the first month she'd worked there very happily. But since then – well, nothing. In the last couple of weeks all she'd produced was rubbish, and she was constantly coming up with excuses not to work: a gallery specialising in aboriginal art was having an opening; she had to spend the morning writing letters. She tried telling herself it was England, it simply didn't suit. But it wasn't England, it was her.

'Pathetic.' She said it aloud, shifting on the bench: to come around the world in order to achieve absolutely nothing. And over the last few days inertia had sprawled into tiredness and by mid-afternoon she was yawning her head off. Which was why she'd caught the train down to Brighton this morning: she could keep Aunt Molly happy and have a few days' rest, because it was obviously rest that she needed. A few days off and she'd be back to normal.

Looking up, she saw the bag lady had disappeared. Time to get the main tourist attraction over and done with.

'Aaahhhh!' Julia's head tilted back with the others. Overhead there was a palm tree, and in the palm tree – two glaring red eyes, hunched bronze wings – a dragon.

'The central chandelier, which the dragon holds in its claws, is thirty feet in length and weighs one ton.' The guide cleared her throat. 'If you look around the Banqueting Room's ceiling you will see fabulous beasts. These are Masonic symbols, as are the moon and planets on the canopy, where there can also be seen the Masonic All-Seeing Eye. The Pavilion was used as a military hospital during the First World War and we can only imagine what it must have been like for wounded soldiers to awake and find themselves regarding ceilings such as these. The stories at the time were that some of the soldiers, on first seeing the white-uniformed nurses, believed they were seeing angels . . .'

She exited via the gift shop, where she chose three postcards of the dragon chandelier. As she paid for them she yawned widely.

'Jet-lagged?' the cashier asked sympathetically.

After a night's sleep she felt better. The hotel breakfast was uninspiring, but at nine in the morning it was pleasant enough sitting at a table in the bay window, eating toast and cornflakes and looking out over the water. From here she could see there were two piers. She'd seen the closest yesterday but hadn't turned to look behind or she would have spotted its ghostly twin at the other end of the beach. The far pier appeared to be a ruin, but with its cluster of delicate buildings perched on the top of the metal framework it was definitely the more elegant of the two. It reminded her of an old but still beautiful woman.

Beyond the piers a ship hung suspended against the horizon. In her mind Julia pictured Europe in an atlas; if she dropped a ball from where she was on the south coast of England it would bounce down the coast of France, through Spain and then down to Africa. Where Liam was now, although he wasn't on the west coast but further south and in the middle of the continent. Liam, who she tried not to think about too much, although the truth was she was here because of him. 'Why don't you try to get to Europe at the same time?' he'd suggested when his research project had been approved. 'We could meet up.' They already had met up, for a week in Paris, where they'd spent their time visiting museums and galleries, and having sex.

Pushing the empty bowl away, she picked up her cup of tea. They didn't have firm plans about when they'd see each other again, but Liam was flying up to a conference in Rome in a couple of months and there was the chance he could come over to London, or she could go to Italy. 'It would be great,' he'd said, 'seeing Rome together. Let me know what you decide.' All right, she should have let him know by now, but it wasn't her fault she hadn't; the problem was she simply didn't know how to reply to his last letter, which had finished, *Love you, Liam.* How was she supposed to know what that meant? Was it 'love you' as in 'lots of love', 'much love' – in other words nothing more than an affectionate signing-off? Or was it 'love you' as in 'I am in love with you' – a declaration? In the year or so they'd been going out, the 'l' word had not been mentioned by either of them. They were busy, ambitious people, both with a number of relationships behind them, so this 'love you' was something of a nuisance in that it required her to think about her own wording.

'Is everything all right?' The bored waitress took the empty bowl.

'Thank you. By the way, the second pier; how long has it been like that?'

'The West Pier's been closed for years.'

'It must have been wonderful.'

The waitress shrugged. 'It's a wreck now. One day it'll get washed away.'

An hour later Julia set off along the esplanade overlooking the beach, skirting the beggars and winos who'd slept the night on wooden seats in the old-fashioned shelters. She passed the Aquarium and the Palace Pier, with its amusement arcades, and then took the lower path leading along the top of the pebbly beach. Halfway between the piers she stopped. This looked suitable: deckchairs and umbrellas for hire and not too many families in sight. She had a hat, sun cream and a towel – not that she was going for a swim in the chilly water; no, she'd just stay where she was, doing absolutely nothing.

Later in the morning her patch of beach was proving popular and the neighbouring kids had kicked their beach ball under her chair for the umpteenth time. She handed it back to a toddler, who scampered away. 'Say thank you to the nice lady!' his mother called. 'Won't!' He turned and glared. 'Won't!' It was time to move on; she'd go and explore the intact pier.

Flakes of greying paint stuck to her arms as she leaned over the railing, eating an ice cream. A few yards away a black teenager with dreadlocks was feeding the seagulls, throwing chips and laughing as they caught them in mid-air. Julia watched: the birds were far bigger and more aggressive-looking than their antipodean cousins. Catching her eye, the boy grinned happily. 'Wicked, eh? You want a go?'

Smiling, she shook her head. Further along, a grey-haired woman sat fishing, an old metal bucket next to her. It was too deep to see if there were any fish in the surging water below, but they'd be there all right, feeding around the base of the pier. Julia wondered what sort they'd be. The fish they'd caught off the jetty as kids had mainly been bream or flathead. Dad or Paul would ease the metal hook through the fish's mouth and then, if it was big enough for eating, would quickly hit it on the head with the rounded piece of wood called a priest. She'd asked Dad why it was called that one day and he'd rubbed his chin, making a rare joke. 'I suppose it's what sends them to fish heaven.' When Julia said to Mum later she thought it was cruel, hitting the fish like that, Mum explained that Dad always insisted on a fish being killed straight away, instead of simply putting it into a damp hessian sack like some people did, because he thought it was wrong for them to suffocate slowly. 'We had a mouse once,' Mum said, 'and I put out a trap, but Dad was up most of the night, checking in case it was injured. I had to throw the trap away. I don't think your father could even bear to see a snake suffer.'

Julia could picture her father now, cleaning a fish at the water's edge. He'd cut off the head with a sharp knife then slit open the belly and pull out the bloody insides, throwing them into the water for the gulls to fight over. Then he scraped off the scales, holding the tail in his left hand and making quick downward strokes with his blade. If you stood too close while he was doing this the scales would fly out and stick to your bare legs; when they dried they itched and shone silver in the sun, mermaid legs.

She looked back at the shore, to the sweep of hotels that made up the sea front. This was where her grandparents, Richard and Nina, had lived; they would have strolled along the esplanade and walked along this pier. As a child she'd never heard any family stories about Brighton, Cheltenham was the only place that got a mention . . . She shuddered. God, they'd been awful, those Sunday afternoon visits to Aunt Anne in the old Toowong house. Cucumber sandwiches weeping salt in the heat, heavy slabs of marble cake, and too-strong tea. Time slowed in Anne's front room, became the relentless ticking of the heavy wooden clock. The sun had to be kept out at all costs, thick red curtains drawn over the windows, and Anne sat there in the gloom surrounded by English women's magazines that had been sent sea-mail and were months out of date. Julia could still remember the feel of the cheap yellow paper and the grainy black and white photographs of the Queen and scenes from Ascot, women in ridiculous hats and elbow-length gloves. But it was Cheltenham that was Anne's staple. The world she'd painted was populated entirely with leftovers from the Raj: ancient colonels with gammy legs, their wives left delicate after years of tea-dances and bullying the servants. 'The Hamilton-Masons brought their ayah back with them,' Anne would nod. 'The children were so attached. She was sent back when they went to school, of course.'

Ayahs in India and aboriginal servants in North Queensland. Dad had been brought up by a series of aboriginal girls, not that he'd talked about it much. Julia had tried to quiz him a couple of times, and once he'd said something about being well looked after by them. But then he'd quickly added that you couldn't trust them, that was the problem. That was Anne's line, Julia knew: the blacks weren't to be trusted and could turn on you at any moment. She could hear Anne now: 'They were completely unreliable and often told lies.' Anne had died in her mid-seventies after developing Alzheimer's. In her last years she didn't recognise any of them and vigorously denied any suggestion she'd ever been married to a vicar. 'Me, a vicar's wife? My husband owned the biggest building firm in Brisbane!'

Anne had been monstrous: even as she thought it, Julia couldn't help smiling at the memory of the story Mum used to tell, about the first time Dad had taken her to meet his aunt. Mum had been overawed by the lace tablecloth and silver tea service, and then Anne asked her when she'd 'come out'. As Mum told the story, tears of laughter would fill her eyes. 'And I said I hadn't come out at all, I'd been born in Australia – it never crossed my mind she was talking about debs!' The thing was that for years Julia didn't understand what a 'deb' was. Mum must have told her but it didn't sink in and she'd thought it had something to do with girls named Deborah.

Julia laughed aloud now and the woman with the bucket looked up and gave a broken grin. 'Good here, isn't it?'

'Yes. It is.' The woman was still grinning expectantly, so Julia added, 'Having any luck?'

The woman tapped the side of her nose. 'No fish today, if that's what you mean, but that doesn't mean I'm not lucky; I'm enjoying myself and that's the important thing.' Chuckling to herself, she started reeling in her line. Watching her, Julia wondered what Dad would have been like if he had been brought up here. For that matter, what would she have been like? A completely different person, quite probably not an artist at all but one of the mums on the beach, with three children . . . But that was ridiculous. She stood up abruptly. If Dad had been brought up here he wouldn't have met Mum, and she herself wouldn't exist.

'Hey, love!'

She turned to see a woman calling from a booth plastered with photographs of celebrity customers. 'Like to have your palm read?'

'Sorry.' She held up her ice-cream cone. 'Sticky fingers.'

The woman didn't laugh. 'No problem, I've got wipes.'

Julia shook her head.

'Tea leaves?' the woman persevered. 'You'd be surprised what they can tell you. Or the cards?'

'No thanks.' It was turning out to be hotter than she'd expected; if she wasn't careful she'd burn.

'About love in particular. Are you sure there aren't any questions you'd like to ask about your love life?'

'Positive.' Putting on her sunglasses, Julia walked back to the shore.

She should have bought a map. There seemed to be any number of cafés yesterday, but today she'd evidently wandered from the main tourist path: the shops were tatty and downmarket and there wasn't a café or restaurant in sight. Coming to the entrance of an arcade she went in; it was cooler here and there'd be a greasy spoon, surely, where she could have a cup of tea and ask directions. Turning a corner she saw a pet shop, the window full of goldfish, and next to it a comic exchange. Then she found herself gazing at a sign advertising the services of yet another fortune-teller: *Tarot Readings, Palmistry, Tea Leaves, Crystal Therapy* . . .

'Come on then.' A woman's head appeared through the faded curtains hanging over the doorway. She had iron-grey curly hair and gypsy earrings.

'Oh no.' Julia stepped back. 'I was just looking. I'm not a' – she wasn't sure what the word would be: client? customer? patient? – 'I've been wandering around in search of a café. Is there one near?'

'There isn't, but I've got a pot of tea waiting.'

'No, really . . .' She hadn't walked that far but her feet were aching and the tiredness was setting in again.

'You're not interested in having your fortune told, I can see that. But my appointment hasn't turned up so you might as well come in for a cuppa and a biscuit.' The curtain opened wide. 'Come on, it'll be stewed.'

It was more of a cupboard than a room. There was a heavy smell of incense and the walls were covered with pictures and advertisements: *Findhorn Faith Healing, Aura Palpation* . . .

Her hostess nodded in the direction of a small table covered with a red and white checked cloth. 'Which part of Australia are you from?'

'Queensland.' Julia pulled out a wooden chair and squeezed into it. In the middle of the table a crystal ball sat on a wooden stand.

The ball was pushed aside and a teapot put in its place. 'The ball's for decorative purposes only. I bought it at a flea market years back because I liked the look of it but I knew I wouldn't be able to use it. I've tried with balls but I've never seen a thing. I did give it to a friend who had the gift but she brought it back – said a flaw distorted everything.' Opening a cupboard, the woman took out flowered cups and saucers. 'I've been to Australia but didn't get to Queensland. My brother emigrated forty years ago and lives in Darwin. Married an Aussie he met over there, a very nice woman. He kept on writing, saying I should join them. I did go for a holiday but can't say I'd want to live there: the people were friendly enough but I couldn't stand the heat and the flies. And the men wearing shorts and vests, no shoes most of them, and drinking lager straight from the can while the women were tied to the kitchen. Though from what my sister-in-law says, things are changing. Is this your first trip to England?'

'Yes, I've travelled quite a bit in Asia and I've been to the States, but Europe – I don't know, I kept putting it off.'

'Milk and sugar?'

'Just milk, thanks.' On the wall opposite a dog-eared chart showed the tarot cards. When Julia was at art college one of the lecturers had done a series of etchings based on the tarot and she could still remember some of the names: the Magician, the Papess, the Emperor, the Pope, the Lovers . . .

A teacup appeared in front of her. 'Don't worry about the stains. For the readings the tea has to be black and it's the devil to clean off. I'm Audrey, by the way, Audrey Proctor. I used to be Audrey Vice, which was the Anglicised version of Weiss, you see, but went back to my maiden name after I got divorced.' Sitting down, Audrey took the lid off a tin of chocolate biscuits and pushed it across the table.

'Thank you. I'm Julia Truelove.' She reached into the proffered tin.

'Are you now? Truelove's not a name you come across often. I've always thought it was a lovely name.'

'I was called "Trueliar" at primary school.' She hadn't thought about her nickname in years. Where did that pop up from?

Audrey started pouring the tea. 'And why was that?'

'There was a session on family history and I stood in front of the class and told the story of how my Great-Uncle Jeremy was eaten by a crocodile and how they knew they'd killed the right crocodile when they found his gold watch inside it. The kids all thought I'd stolen the idea from *Peter Pan*. Even the teacher wasn't convinced.' She could still see the disbelieving look on Miss MacPherson's face.

'Well, I can understand that.' Audrey chuckled. 'Now let me guess, Julia Truelove – you're an artist.'

She stopped mid-bite.

'Your hands.' Audrey nodded. 'You've got paint under your nails.'

Julia spread her fingers: aquamarine. From two days ago when she'd tried to do an ink wash. It hadn't worked.

'And if you'd said, "You're wrong, love, I was just doing finger painting with the kids," I could have said, "I meant inside you. Inside there is an artist."' Audrey nodded amiably.

Not a witch then, simply a con artist. But a likeable one. 'You're right, I'm a painter.'

'And you're in Brighton to paint?'

'No, I need a few days' break.' She sipped at the tea, which was hot and strong and very welcome. As she put the cup back in its saucer Audrey reached across the table and caught her palm.

'Don't worry, it's on the house.'

Julia fought to keep a straight face.

'I see a long journey over the sea.' Glancing up, Audrey winked. Then her tone became more serious. 'You're a determined person and will have a successful career – oh yes, I can see fame ahead. You've known pain and loss in your life but there's happiness and love as well.' She nodded. 'And a child. A daughter, but only one.'

They always said stuff like that; Julia drew back her hand.

Audrey didn't seem to notice. 'You don't have any other reason for coming to Brighton then? No family connections?'

'Well, my grandparents, my father's parents, did live here a long time ago.'

Audrey gave a satisfied nod, as if she'd somehow been expecting this. 'So you *are* from a Brighton family.'

'Not really. My grandfather came here from Cheltenham. He was killed during the First World War, before Kyril, my father, was born.'

'Kyril?'

'It's Russian. My grandmother was from Russia. Dad was teased as a kid because of his name; you don't come across too many Kyrils in Brisbane.'

'My brother went to Australia with some sort of group. The Big Brother Movement, something like that. Sounds sinister now, but as far as I know it wasn't.' Audrey shrugged. 'I don't know how he got involved, he was never much of a joiner. Who took your dad out there?'

'His father's sister, Anne. Her husband, Jeremy, was a vicar and they emigrated because of his interest in tropical plants.

Jeremy had a degree in botany from Cambridge and wrote books about the plants of North Queensland. But he died young.'

'Eaten by the croc.'

'That's right.'

'And your father's aunt stayed in Australia?'

'She did, but heaven knows why – she loathed everything about the place, the heat, the accent . . .'

'What was your grandfather's first name?'

'My grandfather? Richard.' Her attention was caught by a brochure pinned to the wall. *Past Life Retrieval: How Do Your Previous Lives Influence Your Present One?*

'Richard Truelove – well, if that doesn't take the biscuit.' Audrey laughed. 'I thought there must be some connection when you told me your name; there can't be that many Trueloves in the world, can there?'

'I'm sorry . . .'

Audrey was grinning. 'Your grandfather's name was Richard and your grandmother – no, don't tell me . . .' Rolling her eyes, she put her fingertips to her temples like a Victorian stage act before announcing triumphantly, 'Nina!'

Julia felt the hairs rise on her arms.

'I never forget a name.' Audrey was laughing. 'Dear me, no. In this business you never know when it might prove useful.'

It must be some sort of trick, she couldn't read minds. Julia made her voice as nonchalant as possible. 'How did you do that?'

Audrey waved a teaspoon at her, as if wagging a finger. 'Don't you mean "How did you *know* that?" That's the mistake people always make. I didn't *do* anything, apart from remembering. But I've always had a good memory, it said that in all my school reports. "Audrey has a good memory so it's a great pity she doesn't pay more attention in class."' She pulled a face. 'They were right there, I spent my time dreaming. I'd go home and Mum would ask what we'd done that day and I couldn't have told her for all the blessed tea in China.' She shook her head. 'Who would have thought it?' Her arm suddenly went up in the air. 'Pickled herrings for the countess!'

Julia measured the distance to the door. Nobody knew where she was; a photographer she'd known had fallen for a scam in

Bangkok, accepted an invitation from a stranger, and finished up being beaten and having his camera stolen.

'Ah yes.' Audrey was still congratulating herself. 'Now, how do I know your grandparents' names? Because my dad's Aunt Fay worked for your grandmother during the First World War, and then Dad's cousin Violet worked for her up to the Second.'

It wasn't possible. 'No.' Julia shook her head. 'No one could have worked for my grandmother after the First World War because she died . . .'

Audrey's eyes narrowed. 'And who told you that?'

Twenty-eight

Two hours later Julia stood peering up at a narrow-fronted three-storey house a couple of streets away from the beach, to the west of the abandoned pier. It stood on a corner and from the attic windows there'd be a clear view of the sea. Someone looking out this morning could have watched her lying in her deckchair, walking along the front. Her eyes dropped to the next floor, where the windows had lace curtains, and for a moment she started, thinking she was being watched.

'Your grandmother didn't die after the first war,' Audrey had said. 'Dear me, no. She went to France and then returned to Brighton before the Second World War started. I know because Violet worked as her housekeeper when she came back. And I often used to see her when she came to my Uncle Ern's stall in the market. Ern was Violet's youngest brother and his stall was as good as any delicatessen, better than most of the shops. I used to hang around as a kid, watching him measure things out of these big glass jars with cork stoppers: rice, semolina, noodles. The countess was his favourite customer. She wasn't really a countess, that was a joke between them, but when he saw her coming he'd call to his assistant, "Pickled herrings for the countess!" and everyone would turn around to look. I expect he thought it was good for business. He had a great head for business, Ern. He never married, mind.'

Julia's chest felt strangely tight. She pictured herrings in her mind, silver in a jar.

'She was quite a figure around town and there were all these stories about her I knew weren't true: that she was a Russian princess; that she'd lived in Paris and been a Chanel model. Though she certainly could have been that – she was very tall and beautiful. Some of the gossip was that there had been some sort of scandal in her past. It was rumoured she'd posed as a nude model and that a duel had been fought over her. As she got older she took to carrying a silver-topped cane and I always thought that looked so grand.'

Audrey thought for a moment. 'Her second husband was Monsieur de Senerpont – he was always "Monsieur" and she was always "Madame" because he was French. Or at least his father was; his mother was Russian, or half-Russian. He was a fair bit older than your grandmother, and he died – I don't know, in the late fifties it must have been.'

She frowned as she reached for another biscuit. 'I know exactly when it was, 1959. That was when I was starting out in this business. I had a secretarial job but I couldn't stand it, all that typing and the girls always at each other, they were a catty lot in that office. Anyway, I'd known since I was a kiddie that I had a gift, because of the premonitions, so I was trying this out after work and on the weekends. One day I saw your grandmother on the street and I walked up to her, bold as anything – I remember I was wearing a new pair of navy court shoes, they'd cost a whole week's salary and must have given me the confidence – and I reminded her who I was and asked if she'd like a reading of the cards. Well, she said she'd already had her cards read when she was a girl, but she'd ask around her friends. Good as her word she was and I did a number of posh afternoon teas as a result; in fact a couple of the elderly ladies became regulars. It was one of them, Mrs Laing, who told me that Monsieur de Senerpont had died and that Madame de Senerpont was terribly cut up about it. I sent her a card, saying how sorry I was. I'd seen him but never spoken to him. He looked the perfect gentleman, always with a silk cravat. He had two daughters from his first marriage and I always thought they were a bit snooty, but that might just have been because of their clothes and their French accents. Violet certainly had a lot of time for them and even more for your grandmother. I don't know if Violet knew she'd had a son but if she did she never mentioned it to me – but that was like her, of course, she wasn't one for spreading gossip. What Violet always did say was that Madame de Senerpont was a wonderful mother to her stepdaughters.'

'A wonderful mother . . .' The small room was horribly stuffy.

Audrey looked up and grinned. '"A stranger from far away will need to be put in touch with a lost relative." That's what the leaves said last week. I should have known when I saw you out there. Right then, I think you'd better talk to her, don't you?' Pulling up the edge of the checked cloth, she disappeared under the table.

'Talk to her? Oh God, no, I mean . . .' Julia avoided looking at the crystal ball. 'I couldn't. I'm sorry but I don't believe in any of that – you know, spirits or the afterlife.' She was feeling very strange. The incense had got to her throat and the small room was hot and claustrophobic. She really needed to get out and think about what all this could mean.

Audrey reappeared, her hair awry and clutching a telephone directory. 'Oh dear, haven't I made myself clear? Your grand-mother isn't dead. Or at least she wasn't a few weeks back – I saw her as I passed on the bus. It was a lovely sunny day and she was walking along the front. There was a younger man with her. It was ever so long since I'd seen her and I waved but she didn't see me. Or maybe she didn't recognise me – after all, she must be ninety or getting on for it. Either way, she didn't wave back.'

So here she was, staring up at the house where the woman who might be her grandmother lived. Although it could all be some bizarre coincidence: Madame de Senerpont might be an old Russian woman but that didn't mean she was the right old Russian woman. Her real grandmother might have died decades back; maybe she did die after the war. After all, why would Anne lie?

'You've got her height and bearing.' Audrey had sized her up before she left. 'I think you'll find you're very much like her.'

Despite the heat, Julia shivered. 'You're like her, like my mother. That's what's caused all this.' She'd been fourteen years old when Dad said this, lying in a hospital bed with a drip in her arm. He sat upright on the hard chair, staring rigidly at the bottom of the bed. In his hand he held a bunch of flowers, red roses from his garden. And then he'd sighed and said, 'Oh well, maybe it's for the best. There's sometimes a reason for these things even if we can't see it.'

She'd known what he meant, of course, that she would have made a terrible mother, like his mother had been.

As soon as she got out of the hospital she'd started cutting herself and a few months later they'd taken her to Mountview. Years afterwards, when they could talk about it a bit, she'd told Mum what Dad had said and Mum said no, she was sure he hadn't meant that at all. But Mum was always pleading Dad's case. 'I know he can be distant,' she'd say in what Julia came to think of as her this-is-why-we-must-forgive-your-father voice, 'but he had a loveless childhood. He thinks Anne was simply doing her best but I've always thought she was unnaturally cold and strict. I realise it was lucky for him that she was there – there weren't any other relatives and an orphanage would have been terrible back then – but she never let him forget that his mother hadn't wanted him. I think he's always felt that he was somehow to blame and that's a terrible thing to grow up with.' She frowned. 'If his mother were alive now do you know what I'd like to ask her? "Why Anne?" If she wasn't prepared to be a mother herself, why couldn't she at least have found someone better to take her child? Even if it wasn't a relative. With a different upbringing your dad would have found things, life, much easier. Oh well.' She shrugged. 'His mother was mad, of course, so that might explain things.'

Julia stared up at the house. What if Dad had found life 'easier', what then? For a start, Paul might still be alive. Her own life would be very different. All of this because of a choice made by a crazy woman over seventy years ago. Although from what Audrey said she wasn't crazy – so she didn't even have that as an excuse. Julia's fingers tightened on the strap of her bag: she needed time to think. She'd go back to the hotel and decide whether to come back tomorrow, or whether to simply forget all about it and return to London.

Twenty-nine

Just after nine the next morning she was back, about to ring the doorbell.

She'd been awake half the night; at two she woke from a bad dream, the usual one in which Paul was standing there in his army uniform, his arms open to greet her. It was always the same – 'Paul!' she'd cry, so excited, and then as she ran towards him she would see it wasn't Paul at all, but a young man with shorn hair she didn't recognise. 'You're not Paul!' she'd scream. 'I don't know who you are!' She'd woken up sweating and couldn't get back to sleep. At one point, around five o'clock, she'd got up and packed her bag, ready to head out on an early train. But then, at seven, she'd asked the desk to put a call through to Australia and had rung her Aunt Molly's number in Melbourne. Molly's husband, Jack, answered. 'She'll be so sorry to have missed you, love, but she's out tonight with the girls at bingo. What's the weather like over there, Julia? It's been bitter here the last week.'

The next number she tried was Dorothy's.

Dorothy was at home. She listened in silence and then said, 'It's all very extraordinary, Julia, stumbling across her like this. An amazing coincidence, if she really is your grandmother. As to what you should do next – well, is there a question you want to ask her? A question that's important to you, and that you feel you have the right to ask?'

'Yes, there is.' She held the receiver close.

'Well then. She's very old, Julia, and it's unlikely you'll get the chance to ask again. I believe there are some questions that it's wisest not to ask, but there are others that you *should* ask because if you don't they'll always be there, nagging in the background.'

Julia knew this was true.

And so she'd put on her green silk dress and a faint trace of lipstick and mascara. And here she was.

'You have a lot of anger in you, about your father and his family,' Audrey had said, pushing a box of Kleenex across the table. 'You mightn't be aware of it but it's discolouring your aura. You need to resolve this, Julia, especially as you're an artist. It could block your creativity,' she added darkly.

Shit. Julia pressed the doorbell.

Straining against the sound of sea and traffic she listened. There were footsteps; she held her breath as the door opened.

It wasn't an old woman. It was a man, in his early or mid-forties, with wavy, grey-streaked brown hair and a smile so open her resolve almost crumbled.

'Can I help you?' he said. But before she could begin to say anything he added, 'I've seen you before.'

He hadn't, she knew that much. 'No.' She shook her head. 'No, I don't think . . .'

'Yesterday afternoon. You were standing on the pavement, looking up at the house.' He leaned forward. 'I was tempted to twitch the nets.'

He was inviting her to laugh but she couldn't manage that. 'Yes,' she said, 'I was here.'

'I'm sorry if you're house-hunting but we're not on the market.'

Parts of the speech she'd prepared over breakfast came back. 'I'm looking for someone – an elderly Russian woman who was once married to a man named Richard Truelove. But it's possible she remarried . . .' Even as she said it she was hoisting her bag up her shoulder, ready to turn and leave because it was all so absurd. But he wasn't saying no; instead he was moving aside. 'Come in.' He looked away from her, the smile puzzled. 'You'd better come in.'

There was a silver-grey carpet with a red border in the hallway, and then they were in a large front room, larger than you'd expect from the outside of the house, with heavy antique

306

furniture, maidenhair ferns in ornate Chinese pots, framed photographs on the walls and a gilt-edged mirror over the fireplace. Julia's palms felt sticky and she wiped them against the silk of her dress before she could stop herself.

'Please, have a seat.' He pointed her towards a worn leather sofa and she sat uncomfortably on the edge.

'I'm sorry, I haven't asked your name.' He sank into an armchair, looking interested but wary.

'Julia.' She coughed. 'Julia Truelove.'

'Truelove.' The puzzlement deepened. '*Your* name is Truelove? Well, Julia Truelove, I'm Robert Harris.' He sat, waiting for her to speak.

On the mantelpiece stood a set of brightly coloured Russian dolls, a row of mothers and daughters staring quizzically down at her. She stared back: her name seemed to mean something to this man, but maybe he was just being polite. She took a breath. 'I'm from Australia and I'm looking for information about my grandmother, who was married to Richard Truelove. My father, Kyril Truelove, believed his mother had died shortly after he was born. However, I mentioned this family history to someone I happened to meet yesterday – I'm in Brighton on holiday – and she said a woman named Madame de Senerpont fitted my grandmother's description.' It was all coming out so clumsily. She swallowed. 'Her first name, my grandmother's first name, was Nina. She was Russian.'

The man was studying the carpet, not saying anything. She waited a moment and then shifted self-consciously on the sofa. 'Madame de Senerpont might not have anything to do with my grandmother at all. But it seemed worth a try.'

The man, Robert, looked up again. He gave a small smile, but even as he smiled he was shaking his head. 'It must be a coincidence,' he was saying, his voice soft, 'or a mix-up with names. I don't understand how . . .'

'Robert?'

An old woman stood in the doorway. She wore a sky-blue kimono decorated with pink flowers and her white hair was pulled back. Her face was still beautiful: she had cheekbones like wings and rice-paper skin. She was tall and leaned on a silver-topped cane.

She was staring at Julia.

Julia stared back.

'Sweetheart!' Robert turned round on his chair. 'I thought you were upstairs.' He waved a hand in the air for a moment, obviously unsure what to do, and then stood up and said very gently, 'We have a guest, all the way from Australia.'

And then things happened very quickly. The old woman stepped into the room, her face alight and her voice full of joy. 'Oh, Ruby, I knew you would come!' She started to move forward, and suddenly she was falling and Julia was jumping up, running across the room, moving to catch her in her arms.

Thirty

She was lying on the sofa with one of the big cushions under her head. On the armchair at the end of the sofa sat the woman with long red hair. The sky through the window behind her was such a deep blue that her hair seemed to burn, like the burning bush in the Bible. And there was a man's voice, although the words weren't distinguishable, just a murmur of sound. Nina felt herself smile.

Harry's sister didn't smile back, instead giving a frown and glancing at Nina's feet, which were still in their green slippers. They were Nina's old slippers and she wished Ruby hadn't seen them and that she was wearing the new slippers she'd bought the last time she and Vera went shopping. Why was she lying here like this? She took tablets for blood pressure – Robert insisted, although she didn't think it was necessary – and they sometimes made her dizzy; once she'd fainted. But all she'd done just now was catch her foot.

'Nina, this isn't Ruby.' Robert's face bent over her. 'This is Julia,' he was saying in an unnaturally loud voice. 'Julia's from Australia and she'd like to talk to you.'

Robert was worried, that was why he was speaking so loudly. But all she'd done was trip. Then it dawned on her: the red-haired woman was too young to be Ruby. Ruby would be the same age as she was. They must think her an old fool. No wonder Robert was acting like this. 'I'm sorry,' she said shakily, pushing herself up into a sitting position, 'but you reminded me of someone.'

'I don't understand.' The young woman was shaking her head, her cheeks flushed and her blue eyes bright. 'We thought you'd died after the war – the First World War.'

Who thought she'd died? She glanced at Robert, to see if he knew something, but he didn't meet her eye. The red-haired woman was now wiping her face with the back of her hand, like an unhappy child. At the moment none of this made any sense, but no doubt it would: Nina had learned long ago to be patient. 'I was very ill after the war,' she said carefully. 'But as you can see, I didn't die.'

The red-haired woman – Julie, was it, or Julia? – was shaking her head. 'Dad thought you were dead.'

Who was she talking about? Maybe someone who'd been a patient at the hospital? There had been Agatha, and a poor young man who wanted to shoot God. 'I'm sorry,' she said out loud, 'but I don't know who you mean.'

The woman was now wiping her nose with a tissue she'd taken from her bag. She began to say something but Robert stepped forward, his hands held out as if to quiet an unruly audience. 'I think', he was saying, 'that a cup of tea would be an idea right now. And then we can begin at the beginning . . .'

But there was something about the woman that seemed familiar. Her hair . . . 'What is it', Nina heard herself say, 'that you've come to see me about?'

The woman folded her hands in her lap and hung her head. Then she sat up very straight, like a soldier standing to attention. 'My father', she said quietly, 'was Kyril Truelove.'

The room was completely quiet and still, as if they had taken a step out of time. And in the stillness a red-haired child played on the sand. Seeing the child filled her with great longing.

Her throat was tight as she spoke. 'Kyril died as a baby. Anne, his aunt, was taking him to Australia but he died on the journey.'

She could still hear Anne's friend, Janet White, as she broke the news. 'I'm sorry, but I assumed you knew. Your son, Kyril, died of influenza on the ship, before they even reached Sydney.'

'What?' The young woman's voice rose. 'Dad died five years ago. He was hit by a car, he didn't die as a baby. Why are you saying that?'

The howling sound, like an animal in pain, couldn't be coming from her, for the red-haired child was laughing up at her for the first time, his arms outstretched. And she was running fast to swoop him up in her arms, kissing his face over and over even as he was taken from her.

She had never held her son in her arms, never taken him to her breast.

She had never known him as a man.

All those years he had been alive and she never knew. She had never walked with him along the sand or offered him a shell or told him a story. But with the pain there was also joy, for he had lived. He had grown into a man and had a family. 'He loved my mother very much,' Julia had said, 'and she loved him.'

Nina sat in front of the dressing table mirror now; an old woman whose face often caught her by surprise. Inside she felt just the same as she had when she was a girl. I must tell Mamma . . . she would think, or, What will Darya say?

Darya Fyodorovna had been right in all her predictions: she had lived a long life, with more than one husband and many houses. She had lived in this house for over twenty years. Her stepdaughter Vera was usually here – they had lived together since the death of Vera's husband – but Vera was away at the moment, visiting her sister Lizzie in Scotland, and so Robert, Vera's son, had been looking after her.

Now, Julia was staying. She had been here for a week and yesterday afternoon they had sat together in the bedroom and Julia had unexpectedly picked up the tortoiseshell hairbrush and brushed her hair for her. Nina had closed her eyes and it could have been Mamma: 'One hundred strokes, Ninochka, are you counting?' or Darya or Katya or Aunt Elena. She could still feel her aunt's fingers running across her cheek. 'I can assure you that Mr Truelove wouldn't expect, nor wish, for you to "fall in love" with him.' Opening her eyes she'd met Julia's in the mirror and they'd laughed awkwardly as her hair, brittle and crackling with electricity, floated around her head in a white cloud.

Tucked into the corner of the mirror was the small photograph of Harry she'd taken out of the metal box to show Julia. Reaching for it now she held it to the light. Harry sat on a camel and in the distance there was a pyramid. For over seventy years Nina had believed that all that was left of him were her memories and this photograph. But now there was the miracle of life as well. 'Kyril lived,' she whispered, the photograph trembling between her fingers. 'He grew up in Australia, just as you wanted, and now our granddaughter, Julia, is here.' Harry stared straight ahead into the camera, too distant in time, and too young, to acknowledge a grandchild.

It had been on a summer's day in 1933 that she'd seen Janet White in Oxford Street. She'd been tired from shopping and was staring into a milliner's window when for some reason she looked sideways, and through the crowd glimpsed a woman who looked familiar.

It was her, she was sure, Anne's friend from Kew Gardens all those years ago. 'Please!' She was crying out, stumbling over the pavement and oblivious to all the people around her. 'Please! You must remember me, I'm Anne's sister-in-law, Nina!'

Janet recognised her straight away, looking as though she'd seen a ghost. She started to move off but Nina clung to her sleeve. 'I'm desperate to contact Anne. About Kyril, just to hear how he is. I don't wish to interfere, you must believe that, but I need to know he's well.'

And then, standing there on the pavement, Janet had told her. She was very sorry, she said, her face pale, she'd assumed Nina knew. But Kyril had died of influenza fifteen years ago, before the ship even reached Sydney.

Maggie had come as soon as she heard. 'Oh, Nina,' she held her close, 'that must be why no one would tell you anything about him. They didn't want you to know. It was wrong of them, terribly wrong, to hide it all this time, but perhaps they were trying to be kind?'

It had never occurred to any of them that Janet might have lied – because who would lie about such a thing?

'Dad believed you'd died too,' Julia had said. 'Anne told him.'

She *had* almost died of influenza. Death had been very close, like coming to the end of a journey. She could clearly remember scanning the shoreline and seeing the palm tree and, standing on the dock, the woman with long red hair. The woman stretched out her arms in welcome, but as Nina went to step ashore, she'd tripped and a different pair of arms had caught her.

'It's a miracle.' The arms had held her tight. 'The doctor thought we were set to lose you for certain.'

The woman and the dock gradually disappeared until all that was left of the shore was a thin line in the distance. She'd held on to the line for as long as she could but then she blinked. The curtains were pulled open, the room flooded with light, and there was pressure at her lips.

'Come on, take a sip of tea, missy. I knew you had too much life in you to give up.'

A fortnight later she had left the hospital. Maggie and Frank came and took her back to London in a car. She'd lost so much weight her new clothes didn't fit and she'd had to borrow Frank's belt, watching as he used his penknife to make another hole. In the back seat of the car she and Maggie held hands. 'I must find where they've taken Kyril.' She squeezed the dry fingers, and felt Maggie nod beside her.

'But you must begin by getting well yourself.'

That was her purpose: to get well and to find her son.

At first she could barely walk across the room, but Maggie somehow organised lunches and suppers of boiled ham and haddock with toast, and soon she could manage the stairs unassisted. After a month Maggie went with her to Brighton, where they stayed at the Royal Albion. Nina contacted Fay Proctor, who came the next day and hugged her, saying, 'My poor lamb, my poor lamb.' She also called on Mrs Laing, whose husband had had a stroke on Christmas Eve. She kissed Nina on the cheek. 'You look amazingly well for someone who has had influenza. I always knew you were made of solid stuff – as is the major. I soon had him on his feet and we go for a walk along the front every day, no matter how inclement the weather.' Mrs Laing had developed a slight tremor and seemed to have forgotten Nina had left to have a baby.

Charles was also back in Brighton. He'd been gassed in France and although his lungs weren't badly damaged his eyes had been affected. However, he insisted on going with Nina to the warehouse to sort out her belongings. There were pieces of furniture, wrapped in felt and old sheets, and tea chests that had been carefully packed and labelled by Fay.

'My mother,' he levered open a tea chest marked *Main*

Bedroom, 'has moved to Surrey. On the whole she adores life in the country as it gives her something to complain about. I spoke to her on the telephone last night – she has the telephone but no gas or electricity – and the word she used most frequently was "primitive". "Life in the country is so *primitive*." She bought a pair of goats, intending to provide herself with milk and cheese, and now spends her time pursuing them around irate farmers' fields when they escape.'

'Does she get much milk?' Nina watched as he pushed up the lid.

'None at all. They both turned out to be billies, male. She's named them Bally and Hoo.' He smiled.

When they opened the box holding Richard's clothes, she held his smoking jacket to her face and breathed in his smell. Charles turned away, and for the first time she realised that at one time he and Richard must have been lovers. 'Richard and I loved each other,' she said, 'and we had an understanding.' He didn't say anything, so she went on. 'Kyril's father was Australian. He was killed at Ypres.'

Charles wiped his eyes and nodded. 'Thank you for telling me, Nina. I've been worrying you might be bitter about Richard, about him being reckless.' He leaned back against the crate. 'He was foolhardy in some ways, I don't know why.'

'I blamed myself that he went out that night.'

'You mustn't, I warned him often enough. Oh dear,' he said as she wiped her eyes, 'we make a fine pair, don't we? Come on, let's find a bite to eat.'

They had lunch in a nearby working men's café: thick onion soup, chunks of bread and cheese and tea the colour of strong coffee. Then they went back to the warehouse. She put her photographs of Mamma and Richard in the metal box, alongside Harry's letters. The box would go with her in a suitcase. Then they labelled the tea chests that were to be sent on to Nice.

Nina left for Nice herself a fortnight later, in the March of 1919. She was still thin, but Katya was shockingly gaunt and hollow-eyed, a fifth baby at her breast.

'We look like prisoners of war.' Katya gave a small smile.

Nina kissed her forehead. 'We will get fat again together.'

Katya looked after the baby while Nina took over running the house. Any spare time she had she spent in the wild garden, watching her growing nieces play. She always carried Richard and Harry's deaths, and the loss of Kyril, with her – these events shaped her every moment – and yet, over time, pleasure had a way of creeping up unnoticed so she would find herself smiling as a child skimmed a flat pebble across a pond or learned to skip a rope.

Curly-haired Irina sat in her lap, a dear weight, her breath so sweet with biscuits and milk that sometimes Nina couldn't resist closing her eyes and imagining it was Kyril she was holding. 'Aunt Nina,' the plump fingers played with the scarab bracelet or an earring, 'tell me about the farm where you and Maman grew up. Tell me about the painted garden.' And so these things lived on, spun into stories: luncheon under the lilac trees; the play of light on a garden wall; the brilliant flash of blue that was a kingfisher darting over the stream; skating parties on the pond, the bare trees hung with lanterns and Katya spinning fast as a top in a red skirt.

'Were there wolves?' the twins, Marina and Sofia, demanded. 'Did they chase your sledge?'

Papa and the men would go out on a winter night, she informed them, with lanterns and rifles, and at the crack of a shot echoing over ice the wolves would howl all around so that the farm dogs whimpered and slunk off to hide. All the men coveted a wolfskin coat and the skins would be left to cure in the barn.

In the afternoons, before their nap, she told them the folk tales she and Katya had learned from Darya. 'Tell us about the frog princess,' Irina would murmur sleepily. Or Marina would say, 'Tell us about Fenist the Bright Falcon.' And so she told them about Prince Ivan, who marries a frog not because he wants to – none of us wants to marry a frog – but because it is his destiny. And about the girl who falls in love with a golden falcon and, when he is stolen away by an evil queen, searches all the world for her lost love, wearing iron slippers and an iron hat and carrying a heavy iron staff.

'Every night,' Nina sat on the edge of the chair, 'the girl offers the queen – who has trapped Fenist with a sleeping spell – one of the three precious objects she has brought with her, so that she

315

should be allowed to watch the splendid falcon sleeping. But alas, no matter how loud she shouts or cries she can't wake him. On the third and last night she weeps in despair and the sleeping falcon feels the warm tears of the girl on his wing and wakes up. His eyes open and he recognises his true love. Then his wings open too, glowing gold in the starlight, and the girl watches in wonder as the wings become arms and they fold around her and hold her so the two of them are happy again and will be happy for ever more.'

'We would do that,' Sofia said matter-of-factly, exchanging a glance with her twin, 'search the world for our true love. If an evil queen stole him away.'

Running the house was tiring, but Nina still sat up late, writing letters to officials of the Church of England, requesting she be told the whereabouts of the Reverend Jeremy Gregory and his wife Anne. She sent the letters to addresses in England and also to faraway cities: Durban, Cape Town, Sydney, Adelaide, Auckland . . .

Katya would come through and lean over her shoulder, yawning: 'You'll find him, Nina, I know you will.'

In England, Maggie and Frank made their own enquiries. 'They've closed ranks,' Maggie said bitterly on one of her visits, 'and will tell us nothing. It's a complete disgrace; although no surprise in the light of the Bishops' Conference, where they announced contraception to be the work of the Devil. They are frightened of women. It's spiteful and medieval.'

And so life went on for almost four years till Nina met Nikol, a widower with two young daughters, still babies. It had been at a dinner party in Cannes, given by one of Ivan's business associates. She regretted having come and heard herself respond to some simple comment made by her dinner companion with a laugh that was inappropriate, a laugh that had too much in it – not madness, for she was no longer mad, but too much *knowing*. Her companion looked startled and she turned the laugh into a minor incident with a glass of champagne. When she looked up, however, she saw that the man across the table had understood. He'd understood the laugh, and the feint with the glass, and for a moment she felt less alone.

They met again at a ball a month later. At the end of the second waltz he danced her out on to a terrace, pulling her after him into the tangle of a half-wild garden.

The heavy smell of dying cherry blossom hung against a thick night sky. It had been almost six years since she'd been with Harry. Now a man pushed her against a wall, the bricks rough against her bare shoulders, his hand cupping her between the legs and his fingers sliding quickly inside.

As her knees gave way she gripped his coat hard and fell heavily against him, moaning like a cat.

Nikol had proposed a fortnight later as they trotted in a closed carriage along the promenade. 'It is obvious,' he said, 'that we should marry.'

Turning away from him, Nina looked out of the carriage window. Although it was sunny there was a breeze and waves and the seagulls squabbled noisily on the beach, flapping their wings and rising up at each other.

Just last night Katya had sat on the edge of her chair. 'Are you in love with him?' she had whispered. 'Or is it his money?'

Nina had almost laughed but then saw the concern on her sister's dear face. There were things that were impossible to put into words. 'He has known loss,' she said, 'and I can talk to him.' She hadn't wanted to say anything to Katya about passion. 'As far as I am concerned,' Katya would sometimes shrug, 'Ivan can have whatever woman he wants. I am no longer interested in sex with him; nor with anyone else. That side of my life has been a disappointment.'

Sex with Nikol was a chance for Nina both to lose herself and find herself at the same time. She'd felt nothing but emptiness and yearning for so long. Now physical passion took her to another place. Not a place where there was no pain or loss – such a place didn't exist outside death – but a place where there was, for a short time at least, an intensity which was so akin to these things that it overcame them.

She looked back at this man beside her. 'Listen,' she said. Against the sound of the sea and the horse's hooves she told him about Mamma and Papa and the hospital, and about Richard and Harry and her madness, and how she had lost her son.

'So,' he said when she finally finished, 'there have been two men in your life, a homosexual and a Catholic.' He folded his kid gloves across his lap. 'Now it is time for the Jew.'

'His father was of good French stock but his mother was a Jewess from Moscow and it is no secret his wife's family left Petersburg because of their links with the Decembrists. He's older than you by twenty years, and has a reputation; his wife only died eighteen months ago and he needs someone to look after his young children, but it is likely he will have affairs.' Ivan had lectured Nina in the morning room as if his own reputation were spotless and Katya not chewing her bottom lip. 'Your sister and I cannot believe this will lead to any happiness. I must insist that you accompany us to Mexico.'

Only the day before Katya had predicted they wouldn't be in Mexico long. 'Ivan's grand schemes all come to nothing,' she'd said. 'We'll be back within a year.'

Nina shook her head. 'I'm sorry, Ivan, for I will miss you all terribly. But I am free to choose my own path. I cannot come with you to Mexico. I am staying here and I am marrying Nikol.'

On 24 April 1923, a week after her twenty-fourth birthday, Nina had walked up the white steps of the church on Boulevard du Tzarevitch as Nina Truelove and back down as Madame de Senerpont.

For nine years they had lived in a grand house off the Promenade des Anglais. Although Lizzie and Vera, little more than babies, had a nursemaid, Nina bathed and dressed them herself. In summer they wore sundresses and straw hats and the three of them went for long walks along the sea front carrying buckets, their skirts hitched high, their legs itchy from sand and salt. 'A pebble!' Lizzie's eyes would open wide, Vera following behind on sturdy legs. 'Look, Maman, see what we have found!'

She took a photograph of Zinaida, the woman who'd borne them, from a drawer in Nikol's desk and put the heavy silver frame on the mantelpiece in the nursery. 'Make sure you don't forget her,' she'd say at the end of a quiet afternoon, in that lull between teatime and supper. 'Your mother loved you so very much and never wanted to leave you.'

Nikol told her that as Zinaida lay dying the priest had visited. 'She was in agony,' Nikol said, 'the cancer eating through her, and the priest told her she should be glad to share Christ's suffering – that she too had been chosen to carry the cross, and so demonstrate her faith, and for this she should give thanks. She was so weak by then she couldn't hold the baby but she still found the strength to sit up and spit in the priest's face.'

'Your mother,' Nina soothed the girls as she brushed the knots from their hair, 'was a very brave woman.' Lizzie raised her arms, a chubby ballerina, but Vera, the youngest, stamped her foot. 'We don't know that woman! You are our mother. You are Maman.'

Their love cut her to the bone.

The years passed quickly.

The girls had a series of English governesses, and Nikol's business did well. Some seasons they took a house in Cannes and threw dinner parties for Nikol's business associates and their wives. They also had a stone cottage in the Pyrenees, with a heavy key, ten inches long, and rafters that sent down a mist of dust when anyone walked in the rooms overhead. It was delightful in summer but evil in winter and stinking of wild cat.

Eventually, however, Nikol sensed another war coming. 'Look at my hands shaking!' he'd joke. 'They know.' The truth was he did know. He did a lot of business with the Germans and there were ugly rumours even then. 'They'll defeat us,' he said. 'It will be worse than last time.'

And so in 1932 they sold everything and made plans to go to England. 'We could live in London,' Nikol said. 'Are you sure you wish to go back to Brighton?'

'Yes,' she said. For there was always the chance that, when Kyril was old enough, he would come looking for her.

The house in Brighton was big, with a large garden, and Violet Proctor came to work for them. However, the shaking in Nikol's hands didn't stop. 'All of Europe', he predicted, 'will be in flames.'

Charles, who was based in a London bank now, gave them a copy of *The Brown Book of the Hitler Terror*. Nina read it first, in the evenings after Nikol had gone to bed. She screwed up her handkerchief and dug her nails into her palms: there was something monstrous growing in the heart of Europe, a creature that fed on cruelty. She tried to keep the book away from Nikol but he insisted and read it through in a day.

'What are we to do?' she asked him. 'How can we protect the girls?'

He sat with his head in his hands. 'We must fight.' He joined the Labour Party and, with Maggie and Frank's urging, the Fabian Society as well. 'We're all Socialists now,' he teased over the breakfast table. 'Even those who would be Anarchists. Who would have thought it?'

Meanwhile, Nina continued in her efforts to locate Kyril. She made appointments to talk to senior clergymen, waiting for hours on hard wooden chairs. More than one of them held her hand or fondled a knee; a bishop's secretary whispered in her ear that he'd like to make love to her. None of them helped her. She and Nikol went to Cheltenham, to ask Anne's neighbours if they had any news, but only one old man remembered the Trueloves, and he had no idea where Anne was now.

And so she heard nothing until the week before Vera's eleventh birthday, early in July 1933. Nikol was at a Fabian conference in London and she and Vera had come up to join him for lunch and choose a dress for Vera's party. They'd found the party dress, in blue and white lined tulle, and then, as they walked along Oxford Street, Vera went into a milliner's to buy hatpins.

That was when she saw Janet White, who told her Kyril was dead. And Anne had told Kyril that Nina had died so he wouldn't come looking for her.

Who would have thought that Anne was capable of hating that much?

Thirty-one

Standing in front of Julia's drawings at the top of the attic stairs, Nina leaned on her stick to get her breath. She had grown up with a painted garden, and now the walls of the last house she would live in were coming alive with pictures. They were wonderful; Julia was a wonderful artist. She said she worked slowly but that her paintings sold well and she had won prizes and awards. When she spoke about her work you could hear the ambition in her voice: she had so many hopes.

She was so much like Harry.

Steadying her breathing, Nina looked at the nearest drawing, which she had first seen two days ago. It had come as a shock then, and a slight thrill ran through her again as she saw the young woman catching the older one in her arms. The old woman appeared to be falling from the sky, her blue robe billowing and her hair streaming like flames. For a moment she felt herself sway and turned away to the next picture, which was of a man's head. He had wild eyes and gaunt features; the background was a wash of vivid blue so that it looked, curiously, as though he too were falling.

'Hi there.' Julia didn't look up from her work, which she said was going better here than it had done in London. She was leaning over an old kitchen table that had been stored up here for years. Robert had driven her to London to collect her belongings after it was decided she should stay, and had asked her if she required an easel. But she'd said no, not yet. The attic was a good room to work in she said, full of light.

Sinking into an old chair, Nina went back to studying the picture of the falling man. He looked like Christ. Not long ago, she and Robert had gone for a walk in the park to feed the ducks, just as they did when he was a boy. Robert was Vera's only child. He didn't have any children of his own but was a doctor, a paediatrician, and every Christmas the mantelpiece of his flat was crowded with cards from the children he'd helped. One man, whose daughter had died, had sent a card every year for fourteen years.

When they'd got to the pond Robert had opened a plastic bag and thrown crusts for the ducks. He threw some into the middle, watching the birds dash past each other. Then suddenly he'd asked her if she believed in God. When she answered no he said, 'Yet you believe in angels.'

'I have seen an angel,' Nina said, 'but I am an old woman now and in all that time I have never seen God.'

Robert looked straight ahead. 'Because of the work I do I know there is no God – at least not one that affects us at a personal level, at the level of human suffering. There's only chance or luck. And some people are luckier than others.'

Chance . . . luck. Nina turned her gaze away from the picture of Christ and looked at her granddaughter. 'I thought you were Ruby. That first morning,' she said. Julia knew this, of course: it was like passing her granddaughter a familiar nosegay. Her granddaughter who was, and yet was not, a stranger.

'Yes. It must have been a shock.'

'Harry said she was a violinist. And her mother was a pianist. His parents had a music shop.'

'Dad played the piano when he was young. I never heard him, but Mum said he played for her a couple of times when they were first married and she was surprised by how good he was. I don't know why he stopped. I'm not musical at all but Paul taught himself the guitar. He'd sit in his room playing.'

As she spoke, her body swayed, her fingers moving across the paper, hovering over the blue. She was smiling to herself as she did this, lost in shape and colour. 'Dad and Mum often went to concerts. Dad used to say it was Mum's idea but she told me she wasn't that interested and it was Dad who was really keen. Once he took Paul and me; I was only about nine or ten and it was classical music and I found it terribly boring. But when I looked up at Dad – it was very strange. He was wearing this expression

322

I'd never seen before and didn't look like Dad at all. He looked like a completely different person.'

A shadow passed over Julia's face and she pulled back her hair, suddenly looking tired. She seemed to tire very easily. Maybe she didn't eat enough, so many young women didn't these days, it was often in the newspapers. They should go down and have lunch . . . However, there was something about Julia's tiredness, the way it dropped over her face like a veil. It reminded Nina of someone, and she found herself trying to remember where she'd seen this before: the veil dropping and a woman's eyes closing from the corners.

But Julia was speaking quickly. 'He – Dad, I mean – thought it was the right thing to do, you know, that Paul should register for the draft. Not all twenty-year-old men were sent to Vietnam: those who were turning twenty had to register their date of birth and then certain dates were chosen by lottery. It was bizarre, grotesque really, when you think about it. Anne always told Dad his father had died a hero in the war, and when the Second World War came around and Dad was given a desk job, well I guess he felt he'd failed to live up to his father. It's ironic, now I know about Richard . . .'

She let her hair fall back again and stepped away from the table, into a pool of light. 'Paul could have left.' She rushed, as though daring herself to go on. 'He could have come to England and I don't know why he didn't. Dad thought the Vietnam War was justified but Paul didn't believe that. I didn't understand what was going on at the time, but now – well, I've never been able to understand, you know, *why*. There was an argument and Dad tore up Paul's passport but Paul could have got another one. Why didn't he? Did what Dad say really change Paul's mind, or . . .' Her voice was tight. 'Sometimes I can't help thinking, you know, that Paul stayed to spite Dad. That he died because he'd wanted to prove a point . . .'

The two women were in the kitchen, preparing lunch. Julia leaned on the kitchen table, holding the sepia photograph of her grandfather. Harry O'Connor, she said in her head. And then, Julia O'Connor. She shivered because it was so weird: she could have been a different person, this unknown Julia O'Connor. She wondered what Liam would say when she told him she'd found her family; she really should write, or even ring, he'd given her a number.

She moved the photograph into the light. This was the only thing Nina had to remind her what her lover had looked like. It was frightening, the way the faces of people you loved could fade from your mind; there were times when Paul's face was almost lost to her, although she had lots of photographs to go back to because Mum had been a keen photographer when they were kids. There were albums in which Paul smiled proudly as he held Julia on his knee when she was a baby; when she was older he swung her from his hands, her red plaits flying. Happy images, unlike the last ones, which showed him in military uniform, his hair shaved so he no longer looked like Paul. The very last photograph he had sent was a blurred Polaroid, in which he wore army shorts and stood in front of a signpost that read, *Saigon 15k. Hell 10k.* He looked older than his years, his face tense.

She closed her eyes. Paul had been so young; he wasn't to blame.

Maybe none of them were.

Putting the photograph of Harry back on the table, she picked up another. In this an older woman in a smart suit stood next to a middle-aged couple and a teenage boy. They were standing on the Brighton front, smiling into the sun. She recognised the boy as a young Robert.

'That's Katya's daughter, Irina,' Nina said, 'on a visit from Mexico, with Robert and Jimmy and Vera. Jimmy died just a few weeks later, from a heart attack. It was very unexpected and Vera was heartbroken – he was a good, kind man. They loved each other very much.' Her voice trembled slightly.

Julia looked at this woman who was her grandmother – what could she offer her? 'I remember once, I'd had a row with Dad and said something to Mum, and it's one of the few times I can remember her being really angry. She didn't shout or anything like that, she just said, very quietly, "Your father has never let me down. He has always been faithful to me." Faithfulness was a big thing for Mum because her own father had been a philanderer. She always said he was very affectionate and good company when he was around but they hadn't been able to rely on him for anything and her mother often had to take in washing to keep them fed. He'd disappear for months with other women and Mum and her sister Molly always suspected there were half-brothers and -sisters somewhere. He eventually disappeared and they never knew what had happened to him, whether he was dead or not. After her experiences with her father, Dad was just what Mum was looking for.'

Nina had turned away to the sink, her face hidden. Julia went on, 'Dad was frantic when Mum developed high blood pressure – I was amazed one morning when I went round and found him kneading dough on the kitchen table. It was an incredibly hot day and he was red in the face with flour all over the place, a terrible mess. He'd never cooked a meal in his life but was learning to bake bread so he could make it without salt for Mum. They also started walking more, to the local shops and places like that, rather than relying on the car . . .'

They'd both died as soon as the car hit them, that was what the coroner said.

Nina turned back, a glass in her hand. Putting the glass down she said quietly, 'I found another photograph. I will get it now.'

As her grandmother left the room, Julia rested her head on her arms. The rows with Dad had been terrible. After Paul's death Mum had shrunk into herself, whereas Dad was larger than ever and always ready to go into a fury. He became obsessed with the idea of Communists – they were taking over the unions, the universities, the government. At the time she had simply hated him but, thinking about it now, maybe he was trying to convince himself the threat was real and that Paul hadn't died for nothing. He'd aged so much after Paul's death, his hair went completely grey and his hands . . . His hands were awful, angry and red with eczema. They hadn't always been like that.

'Look at this, Julia.' She could see his hands now. She'd been playing in a corner of the garden when Dad called her over. He'd taken off his gloves and held out his hand; in the palm were a couple of tiny plants. They had purple flowers and small green seedcases. 'I haven't seen one of these in years,' he said. 'Not since I was a boy in Port Douglas.' He pulled a seedcase off and held it out. 'Eat this. It's all right, you'll like it.' The case had burst in her mouth, not strong-tasting but juicy. 'Now try this.' He peeled the bulb. It was a bit bitter, but she liked the taste. Looking up, she saw he was eating a bulb too. And then he said a word she'd never heard before; it sounded like a different language. She was going to ask him if the word he'd said was the name of the plant, but at that moment Mum called from the house and he brushed his hands off, his face almost ashamed. He shook his head at her as if to say what they'd done was secret. It had felt nice, sharing a secret, but there had also been an uneasy feeling, as though they were doing something wrong.

'I found this last night.' Nina sat down across the table.

'What is it?' Julia yawned.

'You will have to look carefully.'

The photograph was very faded. It looked like a picture from a circus, a squat woman in a Chinese jacket sitting on an elephant. 'Who is this?'

Her grandmother smiled gently. 'This is Darya Fyodorovna, at the circus. Darya was our housekeeper and a second mother to me. I thought I would never know what happened to her, but one day – it was after the second war – my cousin Tatyana sent this from Canada, with a letter describing how she'd met Darya's nephew by chance in Toronto, where he was a lecturer in engineering at the university. Darya's brother had worked on the Trans-Siberian Railway and after the revolution he fled with his family to Harbin, in Manchuria, where the old Russia lived on for some time. Tatyana wrote that Darya died peacefully in her sleep and that her nephew said she prayed for my mother and me and Katya each day. She insisted on wearing a Chinese jacket and became addicted to the cinema. If she enjoyed a movie, she would go to see it every night it was on.'

'What a wonderful story.' As she said it, Julia couldn't stop herself yawning again. 'I'm sorry.' She looked up to where her grandmother was studying her. 'I'm not usually like this but I just can't seem to stay awake these days. I've never felt like this before; it must be the English air.'

Nina reached across the table and took her hand, and Julia looked down to see the blue veins under her grandmother's skin and the blue wash under her own nails. It was nice, that Nina was holding her hand. She'd just like to lay her head down on the table and go to sleep.

Nina stroked the back of her hand as she spoke. 'I have always felt it was a small miracle, finding out what happened to Darya. Like you finding me, Julia, that too feels like a miracle.' Her voice came from far away. 'I hope you don't mind, but I have been thinking, seeing you like this. Julia – forgive me – but have you ever been pregnant?'

Julia had once been pregnant, which was how she knew she couldn't be pregnant now. It was so long ago she couldn't remember what it was like – well, not the pregnancy bit at least – apart from her period not starting, and feeling very, very frightened. She was fourteen years old.

Paul, her lovely brother, had died and her world had fallen apart. She loved him so much and it wasn't possible that he'd gone away and left her for ever. She couldn't bear to think about it – and so she stopped thinking altogether and her body simply took over. Her fingers were always slipping to the place between her thighs – in the toilet cubicles at school, against the locked laundry door at home, even in the back of her parents' car, her school jumper spread across her lap. She was always gripping, squeezing, in search of release. The nights were hot and merciless. Let's do it, she mouthed desperately against her pillow, pulling its heavy weight against her breasts. You're going to do it, you're going to do it now.

And then she did do it, in the back of a beat-up panel van complete with a sticker, *Don't laugh, it could be your daughter inside.*

'Wow,' the blond surfie boy said, like it was a miracle, 'your hair's red down there too.' After he lifted himself awkwardly off her and lit a joint she let her hand creep downwards and came again and again and again, oblivious to him watching and stopping only when she was exhausted and tearful, the enormous hunger and emptiness still unsatisfied. The boy passed her the joint and smiled benignly. 'Trying to set a record, are you?'

A few afternoons later the panel van was waiting for her outside the school gates, three blond boys crowded in the front seat. As she calmly climbed in the back, rather than joining the bus queue, the whisper of 'slut' went out; by the next morning it was common knowledge that she'd done it with all three. Which wasn't completely accurate. The prettiest of the trio, Davie, golden-skinned with emerald eyes, had apologised. 'I don't think I can,' he'd whispered. 'You know, get it up. Not with the others around.' His hands fiddled with the edge of a tartan blanket. 'You don't mind, do you?' She was a bit disappointed, but also a bit sore, so she smoked a joint with him instead and arranged to meet him a week later at the pictures, where they became friends.

Six weeks later she was sobbing on his shoulder because although the boys had used condoms they hadn't seemed very sure of what they were doing and now her period hadn't started. A week later, when it still hadn't begun, Davie introduced her to his sympathetic twenty-year-old sister who worked as a receptionist in a hairdressing salon in Indooroopilly. She gave Julia an address written on the back of an envelope. 'Don't tell anyone who gave you this,' she warned. 'It'll cost two hundred dollars.'

Julia had seventy-five dollars in her bank account and took twenty-five from her mother's purse. Davie asked the other boys for fifty each. When they asked why he wasn't paying anything he explained he was going to go with her, to see she was OK.

The woman who met them at the door was grandmotherly, with a reassuring smile. Julia found herself staring at her hands: everyone knew that if the abortionist didn't have clean hands you'd get blood poisoning. She couldn't see if the woman's hands were clean or not.

'Come in.' She gripped Julia's shoulder. Davie was close behind, but the woman said, 'You take yourself off for a walk, laddy. Come back in about three hours.' To Julia she said, 'You have got the money, haven't you, love?'

This was death and she deserved it.

'Look at the light,' the voice told her.

The pain was a fierce white light, cutting her in two.

It was done; she was no longer pregnant. Julia lay on the narrow bed and cried. The granny briskly told her to pull herself together: 'I haven't lost one yet,' she said, 'and I've been doing this for twenty years. Now get yourself dressed and make sure you wear the sanitary towel. And then come through to the kitchen for a cup of tea and a couple of Panadeine.' As Julia sat on the cold metal chair, shakily putting on her underwear, the woman deftly pulled the bloodied sheet off the plastic-covered mattress. 'There,' she bundled it up, 'I'll just pop it in the bleach.'

When Davie came back Julia managed to greet him with a nod, her teeth chattering against the edge of the teacup.

'All she needs is rest,' the woman said, 'then she'll be right as rain.'

He held her hand, clammy with sweat, and they slowly walked the hundred yards to the bus stop, Davie helping her up the steps to the front seat. Within five minutes the seat cover was sticky with blood, and they got off at the next stop. The blood wouldn't stop, there was so much of it: running down her legs, soaking through her skirt. And there was something else besides the blood, a heavy weight in her pants.

'Christ,' Davie sobbed, 'I'm going to throw up!' He ran to call an ambulance and watched for it from a milk bar across the street.

At the Royal Brisbane she was told that the surgeon, a man with a grey moustache and rough hands, had saved her life. He came to check on her a couple of times and informed her she was lucky she hadn't died. It was clear from the way he said it that he thought she'd brought this on herself and deserved everything she got. Behind him a group of medical students smirked and whispered. After the surgeon moved on, one of the students flicked through her notes. 'Fourteen,' he called to the others, and they sniggered.

The nurses, the young ones at any rate, were kinder. 'Look at it like this,' one of them said matter-of-factly. 'You'll never get fat on the pill. Or get an IUD stuck inside you.'

Because she'd never have to worry about using contraceptives again.

'Ninety-nine per cent,' the matron announced, 'that's your chances of *not* getting pregnant. Don't expect to have children, because you won't. You might find a man who doesn't mind – but most of them do want a family.'

It didn't seem such a very big deal at the time, the infertility part of it, not at fourteen.

She was in hospital for three weeks. Davie and his sister rang.

'I'm so sorry,' the sister said, 'but I've been to her twice and it was fine.'

Davie told her everyone thought he was the father. 'They think I got you up the duff,' he said. 'You have to laugh. You know, girls can be really weird: I've had three of them come on to me in the past week because of this. You'd think they'd run a mile.'

Mum came twice every day, walking the length of the ward with her eyes fixed straight ahead. When she got to Julia she pulled the pink curtains around the bed and cried, her eyes and nose red. 'You're angry with us, aren't you? That's why you've done this to yourself. Because you blame us for things – for Paul.'

Then Dad came by himself one evening and said that she was like his mother and that maybe it was all for the best. 'There's sometimes a reason for these things . . .'

He'd brought a bunch of roses he'd picked from the garden, and he sat there holding them. When he left he was still holding them. A little while later a bemused nurse came in and handed them to her. 'Your dad says he forgot to give you these. And there's a note.' The note read, *Love from Dad*.

Julia sat in Nina's bathroom and stared at the plastic vial she'd bought in the chemist shop.

'Nina, I can't be pregnant,' she heard herself say. 'Ninety-nine per cent, they said. I can't be.'

'We can always hope for one chance, Julia, just one.'

Thirty-two

She hadn't used her diaphragm. When she'd got to art college, and started having sex again, she always used something. Not because of the one per cent chance, but because if she didn't, the men she slept with became nervous, and she soon discovered that having to launch into a detailed explanation of what had happened to her was off-putting for both parties.

'I can't do it', a budding young sculptor scrambled back into his jeans, 'now you've told me.'

What did he think was up there? she thought bitterly as she kicked his T-shirt at his head. Dead baby?

Putting in the diaphragm, or using a condom, became automatic. But one afternoon in Paris she forgot. She leaned back into the sun spilling over the bed, feeling the nakedness of the man behind her, nuzzling her neck, stroking her nipples. Liam. His erection was hard against her spine; his fingers found her clitoris. She cried out; then she straddled his body, pushing him deep inside as waves of pleasure went across his face. And she forgot.

A one per cent chance. What they'd meant was never, ever. What they'd meant was that she was sterile, barren, and would never have a child.

'You can't be a mother and an artist, ladies, not a serious one,' one of the woman lecturers at the college had tipsily informed them when they'd gone to the pub for an end-of-term drink. 'If you're a woman and you have a child it sends out the message you're not committed to your art. Simple as that. A man can do it: ninety per cent of the male artists I know have fathered kids all over the bloody shop, spreading the seed of their pathetic genius. For them it's all right – more than all right, it goes with the territory. Most women don't seem to realise it, but that's what Bohemia is all about. Don't kid yourselves it's about artistic freedom or sharing great philosophical truths. It's about having as many women as possible. It's about having it all: sixteen-year-old models and starry-eyed art students who are just gagging for it, and a wifey, who was probably once an artist herself, staying at home doing the cooking and looking after the kids. But it isn't the same for a woman. She has to choose, art or kids, it's as simple as that. It stinks, but that's the way it is.'

It wasn't entirely true, but it was true enough. There were a few women Julia knew who'd done it, had children and kept painting, but not many, and they had a partner who worked and helped pay for child care. You couldn't do it alone.

Which was the assumption she had to work with because Liam had never signed up for a child. She was thirty-five but he was only twenty-eight. He'd just finished his PhD in anthropology, and this research trip was to be the first of many. He had so much energy, so many plans. In their time together they'd never discussed a joint future. For all she knew he could be in bed with someone else at this very moment.

No, if she decided to keep the baby, she'd have to be prepared to look after it by herself. She owned her flat in Brisbane, bought with the proceeds of the sale of her parents' house. There was money in the bank from them too, but she'd need all that and more, and although she made enough to live on she couldn't afford a full-time nanny. No, she'd have to do something else as well – teach. She'd have to be prepared to no longer be a full-time artist. Which was as good as not being an artist at all.

'Damn, damn, damn.' She pounded her fists on the floor because she was working again and was almost there . . .

'Julia.' Nina was standing in the doorway.

From this angle her grandmother was ancient, wattles of skin hanging from under her chin. She was wearing a pink blouse, which made her hair look a dirty grey, and was leaning heavily on her silver-topped cane. She could have a heart attack coming up here.

'You haven't had any supper. And, Julia, I have spoken to

Robert on the telephone; you see, in my parents' house there was an iron safe, it was in the morning room . . .'

But Julia couldn't listen; she needed to get out. Grabbing her leather bag, she hurried down the stairs and out of the house.

Julia closed the front door behind her then instinctively headed in the direction of the sea.

She half-walked, half-ran.

I cannot keep this baby, she told herself over and over. Despite the almost miraculous nature of this pregnancy. Despite the deep yearning to feel the silkiness of baby skin, breathe in the smell of warm baby hair.

Coming to the crossing she stopped, suddenly aware of music and people: not the usual number of strollers and tourists taking in the evening air, but a lot of people, many of them in fancy dress.

'Hallelujah!' a young man dressed as a nun roller-skated past, attracting whistles and cheers. He curtsied, lifting his skirts to reveal black fishnets and a red garter, then skated on. A serious-faced young woman held up a placard reading 'Gay Pride'.

'I just can't do it.' Julia manoeuvred her way past the revellers to the railings. On the beach below figures held coloured paper lanterns on poles, weaving graceful patterns in the air. A scattered audience clapped and called in delight, and a small girl laughed as she broke free from her mother's hand, slipping on the pebbles and jumping high as if to catch fireflies.

'Damn!' She pushed away from the rails and made her way to the Palace Pier. Out on the water there were a couple of small boats with lights and for a moment she thought one had a figurehead, then realised it was a woman in a swimsuit, leaning out over the bow. The woman's laughter carried over the water.

'What will I do?' Julia asked desperately into the breeze. 'What am I going to do?'

And then there came a voice.

'Julia!' the voice called. 'Julia Truelove!'

Julia looked wildly up into the sky. But the voice wasn't coming from there.

'Over here,' the voice called again, 'behind you!'

It was Audrey, her head poking out of a booth.

Julia walked over, her feet slipping on salt and grit.

'I sometimes do a shift here when my friend, Sal, is busy elsewhere. But not if the weather's really bad. A night like this is always good business, of course, all the boys and girls wanting to know about true love. Now, what's been happening with you?'

'I found my grandmother.' Julia's hair whipped her face like angry snakes. 'I've been meaning to come and tell you.'

Audrey gave a little tug at her headscarf.

Julia took a breath. 'And I'm pregnant.'

'I tried to tell you that,' Audrey said, 'when I looked at your palm. I always know; there's something about a pregnant woman though I couldn't say what it is. I remember when I was ten years old, my aunt knocked on the front door and I looked out of the window and saw she was holding a baby so I called down, "You've got a baby, Aunty Jo!" Well, she almost fell over. It wasn't a baby at all, it was her handbag, but she'd just been to the doctor who'd told her she was pregnant and now she was coming to announce the good news to my ma. She'd been trying for years, though I wasn't privy to that, of course.'

Julia's throat was tight. 'You said I've have a daughter.' The words fell like copper coins on the wooden boards.

'I believe I did.' Audrey peered closer. 'What's up? Don't you want this baby?'

'Yes! But . . .'

'But what?'

'I'm an artist.'

Audrey hooted. 'Aren't we all!'

A wave of irritation went through her. 'I need time to work!'

Audrey raised her eyebrows. 'If a woman doesn't want a baby, she's barmy to have one, that's what I say. Talk about a rod for your own back; on top of which, it's only storing grief for the future, bringing up a child that knows it's not wanted. But if you do want one, well, you have to make compromises. And let's be honest, you're not getting any younger. Now, what's the father's name? If you don't mind my asking.'

'Liam.' Her lips were dry.

'Well, won't Liam be doing his share? Most young men today seem to be able to help with a baby, my sons-in-law do. It was different in my day, of course – my dear husband never lifted a

334

ruddy finger, but he was lazy. I broke my arm once, slipped on the ice lugging the coal bucket in, and he never so much as made me a cup of tea.'

'I don't know if a baby is what Liam wants . . .'

'Don't you really?' Audrey's eyes were slits. 'Does he love you?'

In her mind she saw the writing on the letter, *Love you, Liam*. Feeling slightly giddy, she said 'Yes, he does.'

'And do you love him?'

Just because you loved someone, that didn't mean they were always going to go away. She needed to move on, take a risk. 'Yes,' she said. The pier vibrated.

'Well then,' Audrey appeared satisfied. 'These things usually have a way of working themselves out, if people are sensible and try to do their best. I said happiness and love, didn't I? Though we should do a proper reading of the cards, don't you think? It'll be a fiver, mind.'

Julia's hand went automatically into her bag and drew out her purse. 'Here,' she held on tight to the five-pound note, because of the breeze, as she passed it over.

Audrey took it and moved back into the dim booth, 'Come in.'

Julia stepped forward, then stopped. 'Ninety-nine per cent,' the matron had said, her voice a stone. 'That's your chance of not getting pregnant.' Under her feet the timbers sang.

'No!' She shook her head. 'Keep the money, I don't want my future told. We make our own fates.'

'As much as we're able, allowing for mad politicians and acts of God.' Audrey chuckled. 'But don't go round telling the punters that.'

'I'm going to keep the baby,' Julia said, realising she'd known this all along.

'Good on you,' Audrey tucked the money into a pocket.

'And I'm going to keep painting. I'm going to make it.'

'Anyone with two eyes could see that.'

A group of young men, one in a silver evening gown, was headed in their direction and Audrey eyed them with professional interest. 'So glad I could have been of help, dear, but I'm just the one who passes on the messages. Let me know how everything turns out, won't you?' She winked.

'I will!'

And with that, Julia turned and strode back towards the shore, red hair streaming in the breeze, the future bobbing inside her as a row of Catherine wheels spun into being along the distant beach, golden sparks firing into the night sky. A seagull swooped low overhead. Julie waved up at it, laughing. The gull flapped clumsily against the breeze, then turned and flew gracefully on, leaving her to follow more slowly behind. She'd go back now and tell her grandmother her decision, and tomorrow she'd try to contact Liam.

And then?

She didn't know exactly what would happen then; nobody did. But that didn't matter because what she did know was that it was all hers: the wild card, the amazing coincidence, the miracle. The one per cent chance.

Thirty-three

'How did you know?' Julia had whispered. 'How could you tell I'm pregnant?'

She had been close to knowing in the attic, but then Julia had started talking about Kyril and Paul. Later, in the kitchen, she'd watched her granddaughter yawning and tried to remember where she had seen this tiredness before. She thought of Mamma's face as she slept on the sofa in the morning room and then as she lay in her coffin, weeping ice tears. She thought of Maggie at the top of the pagoda, her lips blue and her eyes wide.

Whose face was it? The young woman's eyelids had dropped straight down, and then she'd opened them again, with effort. They had been sitting close to one another and Nina had reached out to stroke a cheek.

And then it had come to her. Vera.

Vera, sitting on a chair in the sunlight, in a room with polished floors. 'It's happened,' she whispered. 'At last. I'm going to have a baby. We wanted you to be the first to know.'

Her stepdaughter Vera, when she was pregnant with Robert.

The bedroom curtains were open now and she saw an arc of light streak across the sky, and then another and another: red, blue, gold. Fireworks from the front. Nina knew how the colours would be reflected by the water but didn't stand up to watch, instead turning to the small metal box which was sitting beside her on the bed.

Unlocking it was like unlocking a life.

There was a photograph at the top, of Mamma and Aunt Elena in the conservatory, the trunk of the palm tree behind them. They sat close together, unaware of death or war. And so young: Mamma was only thirty-eight when she died. 'She'd had miscarriages,' Katya told Nina when she went to live in Nice, 'between my birth and yours. Darya told me. It was dangerous for her to have a child.'

Under the photographs there were wraps of tissue paper enfolding small pink shells; a baby tooth; a seagull feather; silk flowers from Vera and Lizzie's first balls; hand-drawn birthday cards covered with childish hearts and kisses. In a piece of golden Cellophane two locks of hair curled inside each other; she knew which was which because Vera's was always slightly darker.

Inside a small envelope was an Egyptian scarab, which she'd bought after losing the bracelet Harry had given her. She'd dropped it on the beach in Nice, taking the girls for a walk. It had slipped from her wrist. She'd noticed it was gone and they'd walked the length of the beach again, searching for it. 'We'll find it for you, Maman, don't cry!' But they hadn't found it, and under their straw hats their faces had been so tragic she'd wiped away her own tears and taken them to an English tea shop, where they ate bowls of vanilla ice cream and forgot the incident completely. Or so she'd thought. It was only a few months ago that Vera said, 'I can remember you crying once when we were in Nice. We'd gone to the beach and you lost a piece of jewellery – a diamond earring, wasn't it? I often used to daydream about finding it for you, or about someone else finding it – a very desperate, poor student, walking along the beach and seeing the diamond sparkling. I used to imagine how excited they'd be and how it would change their life.'

In another wrap of tissue was a delicate ivory comb. Did that belong to one of the girls? But even as she thought it, she remembered how she'd come across the comb on the bedroom floor of Nikol's small Paris apartment. He was often in Paris on business and had had the apartment for many years. She sometimes stayed there with him, but not often. On one of her stays she'd dropped a hairpin and had got down on her hands and knees on the carpet, feeling with her fingers under the edge of the bed, where she had discovered the comb. She'd knelt there, turning it over in her hand, strands of blonde hair drifting across her palm. 'He has a reputation.' Ivan's words came into her mind. 'It is likely he will have affairs. Your sister and I cannot believe this will lead to any happiness.'

She'd closed her hand tight around the comb, the teeth cutting into her fingers, waiting for the anger and the tears. But there'd been none. They were happy, she and Nikol. How did this comb change that? It might have been there quite innocently, or it might not. But even if Nikol did have affairs, he was discreet about them – unlike Ivan – and had never given her any cause to feel cast aside or not valued. The comb suggested the possibility of a separate life in Paris, but didn't she too have her own inner life, separate from him? It was impossible to know another person completely.

Sitting on the edge of the bed now, over half a century later, she gently folded the comb back into its paper. The next layer in the box was made up of documents and letters. There were letters from Richard and the letters she'd exchanged with Harry. She had last read these many years ago, but it had been like reading someone else's correspondence. The writers were so young, so full of hope and pain.

She put the bundles aside, instead opening an envelope with Mexican stamps. This held the crudely printed certificate which had made its way to Katya in Mexico, a year after Papa's death in 1926. *Our father is now officially dead*, Katya had written. *He put a pitchfork through his foot and died of blood poisoning in his own hospital.*

In Nice, in the years following the revolution, Nina and Katya had sometimes had to lift their skirts and cross the street to avoid being abused or, on one occasion she remembered, spat at. There was so much jealousy: some families escaping with great wealth while others had nothing. The prettiest of the Russian girls went to Paris to work as mannequins in the big fashion houses, while those who were not so pretty, well . . . Meanwhile, noblemen and generals found work as street cleaners and waiters. Some did attempt to set up their own businesses but these usually failed.

'The Russians are no good at business.' Nikol would shrug. 'They don't have the head for it. It's a good thing my father was French.'

Whether or not they had money, the émigrés were united in bitterness and suspicion. 'So-and-so is a spy,' would be the rumour one week, and then, 'So-and-so is an informer.' It was widely believed that Papa was allowed to stay on at the farm because he was a Party member. Nina and Katya couldn't imagine their father joining anything; no doubt the peasants tolerated him because the clinic had helped many of them, while the Bolsheviks needed his knowledge about modern farming.

She refolded the thick sheet of paper. If Papa hadn't died when he did, he wouldn't have survived Stalin. Because freedom, when it came to Russia, just like everywhere else, was considered to be too dangerous and was ruthlessly rooted out. Years ago she had tried to discover what happened to Mrs Kulmana and Leila, but could find out nothing about them at all. It was as if neither of them had ever existed.

She pushed the certificate back into its envelope, then found what she was looking for: the address of the London bank where Mamma's jewels were kept. 'We'll know where they are if we ever need them,' Richard had said. Nikol referred to them as 'the family treasure'. She'd given the diamonds to Lizzie, and the pearls to Vera, on their twenty-first birthdays, both of which were celebrated during the second war. 'I stole these when I was fourteen,' she joked, 'so you might travel the world.' Three years after the war, Lizzie had done just that, before returning to marry and settle in Edinburgh. Vera had used her share to buy a flat in London.

'Julia should have the emeralds,' Robert had agreed when they had spoken this afternoon. 'Whether she decides to go ahead with the pregnancy or not, she's at a point in her life when she could use some money.'

Julia, who even now was running towards the sea.

Once, long ago, Nina had sat under a kitchen table. There was a cherrystone between the cedar floorboards, and the smell of beeswax. Under a cupboard was a tray of knives, while overhead a voice predicted, 'A journey, yes, but not as long as yours.'

'I don't expect we'll be in Mexico for much more than a year,' Katya had said staunchly. 'As usual, Ivan's grand schemes will come to nothing. It won't be long before we're back together.'

They had never seen each other again.

Had that been in the cards?

Had Darya foreseen that Nina would lose her sister? That the future she might have had with Harry would never happen?

Did she know that Nina would have a son and never once hold him in her arms?

There was no answer.

Nina's eyes swam as her hands moved blindly in the box until they came to a square of silk. It was threadbare in places and faded but once the blue must have been as deep as the blue Julia had used around the Christ's head. This was the last thing Katya had sent before her death, many years ago. She'd written to say she'd found it in a street market and that the Indian woman who sold it to her had said it was very old. *This tree is like our family, its branches spread across the world.*

The silk trembled as Nina spread it across her lap. The tree's embroidered branches reached up into the sky, and on each branch there perched plump rainbows of brightly coloured birds. A family of birds that had migrated around the globe.

Except they weren't birds. Pushing her glasses further up her nose, Nina peered closer. How could she have never noticed before? Each rainbow had two wings, yes, but also a halo . . .

'Angels!'

Through her tears she couldn't help but laugh at the bright angels, sitting in a tree whose branches reached up to heaven while its roots, a complicated pattern of threads, sank deep into the earth below: their purpose being to hold tight, whatever calamities occurred on the surface above.

Acknowledgements
and Sources

I am indebted to the many people who have helped me with this book, beginning with my mother, Audrey, whose earliest memory is of seeing a Zeppelin over London during the First World War. Her memories and accounts of my grandmother's stories about the war are woven through this novel from the very first page. My late friend, Cynthia Stallman Pacitti, told me wonderful tales about Russia over the kitchen table and got me started. Andrea Badenoch, Julia Darling, Kitty Fitzgerald, Rabbi Jennifer Krause, Debbie Taylor, Margaret Wilkinson and Rabbi Roderick Young all provided enormously helpful comments during various stages of the manuscript. Marianna Taymanova and Professor Pavel Dolukhanov generously responded to a request from a complete stranger. Helen Jones provided information about Brighton's history; Paula Ruddall answered questions about Kew Gardens and plants; Chris Sumner explained some aspects of architecture. Toni Pride and John Weaver kept me company via e-mail from Australia during the final push. Philip Plowden was first reader and, as always, provided support and encouragement throughout.

Many thanks to my incomparable and very patient agents: Broo Doherty shone a torch when I couldn't see and I would have been lost many times over without her; meanwhile Jane Gregory waited when others wouldn't have. My editor, Kirsty Dunseath, has worked wonders.

Library staff at the University of Queensland pointed me in the right direction at the beginning of my research, particularly in the area of newspaper reading, and historians at the Royal Pavilion in Brighton kindly answered my frequent and often odd questions about the Pavilion and Brighton during the First World

War. I read widely for this book – a deeply enjoyable and satisfying task – but would particularly like to acknowledge the following authors and works: Samuel Hynes, *A War Imagined*; Ronald Pearsall, *Edwardian Life and Leisure*; the Reverend Andrew Clark, *Echoes of the Great War*; Norman Stone and Michael Glenny, *The Other Russia: the Experience of Exile*; Roy Porter (ed.), *The Faber Book of Madness*; Clifford Musgrave, *Life in Brighton From the Earliest Times to the Present*; John Roberts, Colin (C. J.) Fisher and Roy Gibson, *A Guide to Traditional Aboriginal Rainforest Plant Use*; C. J. Fisher and Bella Ross-Kelly, *Aspects and Images of Kuku Yalanji Life at Mossman Gorge. North Queensland, The Holiday Land*, a pamphlet published in the 1920s by the Queensland Government Tourist Bureau, provided the inspiration for the fictional *By Way of Reefs and Palms* in Chapter Eighteen, while the operation in Chapter Four is based on descriptions in a work not for the faint-hearted, *Pyogenic Infective Diseases of the Brain and Spinal Cord: Meningitis, Abscess of Brain, Infective Sinus Thrombosis* by William Macewan (Glasgow, James Maclehose, 1983).